THE
SHAKTRA

ALSO BY CHRISTOPHER PIKE
PUBLISHED BY TOR BOOKS

The Cold One
Sati
The Season of Passage
The Blind Mirror
The Listeners
Alosha

THE
SHAKTRA

Christopher Pike

TOR®

A TOM DOHERTY ASSOCIATES BOOK
NEW YORK

THE SHAKTRA

This book is printed on acid-free paper.

A Tor Book
Published by Tom Doherty Associates, LLC
175 Fifth Avenue
New York, NY 10010

www.tor.com

Tor® is a registered trademark of Tom Doherty Associates, LLC.

ISBN 0-765-31099-6
EAN 978-0-765-31099-6

First Edition: October 2005

Printed in the United States of America

0 9 8 7 6 5 4 3 2 1

For Jason

THE
SHAKTRA

CHAPTER

1

When thirteen-year-old Ali Warner answered the knock on her door, a policeman was standing on her porch. She was not surprised. Officer Mike Garten had stopped by two weeks earlier to ask about the disappearance of Karl Tanner. Although it was partially a lie, she had told him she had no idea where her classmate was. Apparently her answers had not satisfied the cop. He was back and he was not smiling.

"Ali Warner, you remember me, don't you?" he asked. He was on the young side for a policeman, in his mid-twenties, and his dark mustache looked so out of place on his pale face that she thought it might wash off in the rain. Tall, too thin for his neat uniform, he nevertheless carried a gun and a badge—two items she could not ignore, even if she wanted to.

"Of course, Officer Garten," she said. "What can I do for you?"

Garten tried to peer past her. "Is your father home?"

"No."

"Will he be home soon?"

"No."

"I have a few questions I wanted to ask about Karl Tanner. You know we still haven't located him?"

"That's a shame. What do you want to ask?"

He took a step forward. "Mind if I come in?"

She did not move out of his way. "Sorry, my father doesn't let me have strangers in the house while he's gone." She could not let the policeman inside because she feared he might see the leprechaun sitting at her kitchen table, and hear the troll that was pacing her basement. Just before answering the door, she had told Paddy and Farble to be quiet, something neither was very good at.

Garten appeared annoyed, but quickly hid it. He took out a pen and notepad. "When I was here before, you said the last time you saw Karl was Tuesday, June fifth. You said he came over to your house in the evening to talk. Is that correct?"

"Yes."

"May I ask what you two talked about?"

"Stuff."

"What kind of stuff?"

"Music. TV shows. The weather."

"He didn't say anything about going away?"

"No."

"You're sure?"

"Yes."

Garten was unconvinced. "Because that same night, according to his parents, he began to pull out his backpacking equipment. They said he did so minutes after getting home from your house."

"He didn't say a word to me about going camping," Ali lied.

"Had you been up on the mountain that day? And the day before that?"

Ali hesitated. Several people in town knew she had tried to stop the loggers from cutting down the trees. It was possible Garten had spoken to some of them.

"I often hike in the woods," she said evasively. "I can't remember if I went those days or not."

"You didn't see anything in the woods that you might have shared with Karl? Something that might have inspired him to go hiking?"

Nothing except a few trolls, she thought. "No," she said.

Garten sighed and put away his notepad. "You're not being straight with me. I've already spoken to your friends, Steve Fender and Cindy Franken. They both admitted that they went hiking with you in the woods a month ago—*on* June sixth and seventh."

"Really?" Ali began to feel uneasy. She had a lot on her mind, important things to do. She did not have time to get arrested, although she doubted there was a jail on Earth that could hold her. She added, "Did they say Karl was with us?"

"No. But I think he was. I think the three of you are hiding something."

"I haven't a clue what you're talking about," Ali said.

The cop remained stern. "I warn you that I have shared my suspicions with Karl's parents. They're pressuring local law enforcement—and the district attorney's office—to take legal action against you three."

He was exaggerating, Ali could tell. *He* was being pressured by Karl's parents, and since the Tanners were the richest family in town, he was probably going out of his way to impress them. Tiny-town deputy was trying to get himself promoted to tiny-town sheriff. Ali let a faint smile show on her lips, but hardened her voice.

"I seriously doubt that," she said. "Why would the district attorney be interested in us? You're just fishing. You don't have a shred of proof that we did anything wrong—with Karl, or anyone else for that matter."

There was a power in her voice that caught him by surprise, a strength of will that came from deep inside, and he took a step back. But right then a loud sound, of breaking glass, came from her kitchen. The cop frowned and once more tried to peer past her.

"What was that?" he demanded.

"A friend."

"I thought you said you were alone?"

"I never said that." She started to close the door. "Now, if you'll excuse me, I have things to do."

"Ali . . ."

"Thanks for stopping by, Officer Garten," she said as she closed the door on his face. She hated to be rude but knew it was dangerous to keep talking to him. He was not dumb. The more she spoke, the more inconsistencies he would notice in her story. Best to keep it simple and vague, as she had done. She did not step away from the door until she heard him climb off her porch. A minute later his patrol car started, and he drove off. Only then did she turn toward the kitchen.

She found Paddy bent over the floor, trying to clean up the glass. He had broken a coffee mug that belonged to her father, but apparently he knew nothing about brooms and dustpans. He was trying to gather the shattered pieces together with his hands and an old newspaper. Glancing up as she entered the kitchen, the gold streaks in his big green eyes dimmed. He probably thought she was going to yell at him. They had known each other only a month, and he was incredibly sensitive to even a frown from her.

Of course, as queen of the fairies, he saw her as someone worthy of worship. He hastily straightened as she approached—nevertheless, she still towered above him. He couldn't have been three feet tall.

"Didn't mean to break it, Missy. Just fell from Paddy's hands," he said.

"It's fine, I drop things all the time."

"So sorry." He asked nervously, "Did the constable hear me?"

"He heard you, but he didn't see you. That's all that matters." Opening the closet door, she reached for the broom and dustpan. "Here, let me clean it up."

He shook his heavy green head, or rather, his green *face*. Paddy had dark curly hair; although thick stranded, and completely uncombable, it looked almost normal. But his face, especially when he was not wearing five coats of makeup, was hard to mistake for a human face, although she had done just that when they had first met. Ali supposed her initial blindness had come from the fact that—prior to that memorable day—she had only met humans in her lifetime. . . .

At least when it came to creatures who talked.

Paddy's untouched skin was not only green, it was *coarse*, as if it had been woven from the bark of trees and the salt of the earth. Yet there was a tenderness in his eyes, a desire to please, that she found endearing. For example, at present, he could not bear the thought of her bending down to clean up *his* mess.

"No, Missy, you should not be tending to the floors," he said, trying to take the broom from her hand. She held it out of reach.

"Remember, I'm not a queen in this world, and I don't want you treating me like one. I'm a thirteen-year-old girl, nothing more, nothing less. Now sit and relax. When I have cleaned up this mess, I'll cook you something. What would you like?"

Her mention of food did wonders for his mood. Rubbing his palms together with relish, he hiked himself into a chair. "Could I have four hard-boiled eggs like you made me last week? Some toast and tea, and maybe a side of bacon and a few sausages? And butter if you have it, lots of butter, and sugar for the tea."

Ali smiled. "Anything else?"

He considered, then his face lit up. "Perhaps some cookies, Missy?"

"I don't know if I have any. I think you ate them all."

"No problem then, Paddy will make due. No need for Missy to bake more."

Ali laughed. "If that isn't a hint! Sure, I'll bake you some if you want."

"No need to bother for Paddy." He added, "But if you do, then those raisin ones, made out of oatmeal, are very nice with tea. And if you are baking some, then it is better to make lots, so Missy doesn't have to bake more at a later time."

"Sound leprechaun advice," she said, nodding.

Before Ali started cooking, she let Farble out of the basement, and the troll came up and sat on the kitchen floor—since he was too tall, and heavy, to sit at the table. The arrival of the troll dampened Paddy's mood, but the leprechaun was good at blocking out the parts of his mind that made him uncomfortable—a quality that made him an excellent liar.

Farble consumed a tremendous amount of food. He was destroying her bank account. Her babysitting savings were limited. She did not know how much longer she could go on feeding him without borrowing money from her father's account, something she was reluctant to do. Yet she feared to cut back on his portions. He was a troll, he was always hungry. Food was the center of his universe. Who knew what he might eat if she did not keep him happy? Many times Paddy had warned her of the dangers of having a hungry troll in the house.

However, in one way Farble was easier to feed than Paddy. She just had to toss him raw steaks several times a day, and let him drink out of the sink, and he was content. He would eat hamburger as well, uncooked, two pounds at a time, although he did not appear to like chicken or turkey. Paddy said—with a hint of fear in his voice—that it was because trolls craved red meat.

Unfortunately, she had only one steak left to give Farble, and no hamburger, and the troll ate the beef so quickly, with such relish, and then stared at her with such longing, that it stirred her worries. A month before she had decided to keep the two elementals in the human realm so that she might study them and thereby learn more about the elemental kingdom, and because she had made promises to help them. But in the last week, the reality of keeping them fed and hidden and—worst of all—*happy*, had begun to wear on her.

They were not pets. They had feelings, hopes, desires—perhaps none of which could be fulfilled in a human world. Why, Paddy couldn't even get a date for a Saturday night with a female dwarf from an insane asylum! She sensed his loneliness, and Farble's as well. Both looked up to her, they revered her, but try as she might, she could not be close friends with them.

They were elementals, they belonged with other elementals.

It was true but it was a hard truth.

They were difficult, and *weird*, but she loved them.

Ali had a sudden thought about Farble and his unique appetites, and turned to the ten-foot-tall troll. As usual, he had a smudge of green spit dripping from his wide toothy mouth, and his huge yellow eyes were bright and glowing. He looked less like a lovable teddy bear than a moving statue.

Farble had a square head that somehow appeared unfinished, and his hide was gray, and hard to the touch. He had hair but it was scant, and it could be as stiff as wire, particularly if he forgot to bathe, which he was prone to do unless she reminded him.

When they had first met, in battle, he had scared the heck out of her, but now she could not stare at him without smiling. Farble's many strange and oversized parts should have added up to a monster, but there was an innocence to his gaze that broke her heart.

"Farble, do you like eggs?" she asked.

"Eggs?" he said to himself, thinking—a slow process.

She held one up. "These are chicken eggs. Lots of people like them."

"Chickens?" he said, doubtful.

"They taste different than chickens. I like them better. Here, try one." She handed it over. "You have to break it carefully and . . ."

He put the whole thing in his mouth, the white shell crunching under his moldy teeth. Paddy watched in disgust as Farble slowly smiled. She assumed it was a smile, although most small children would have run screaming from the expression.

"Eggs. More," Farble said.

"I've eleven here," she said. "I promised Paddy four. But you can have the rest. Would seven be enough?"

Not bothering to stand, he held out both his four-fingered palms, and she gave him two at a time. She could have been tossing M&M's to a chocolate freak. The eggs were gone in a minute and he still looked hungry. Paddy broke in.

"Don't be giving away me breakfast, Missy," he said. "Can't fill a rock like him. Best to give him a drink of water and send him back to the basement."

Farble cast Paddy a dull look, that might have been a frown, and Ali worried that the troll was thinking that if he could just eat the leprechaun, and shut him up once and for all, he could return to the basement content. The two barely tolerated each other, probably because in their world they were natural enemies.

"Green food," Farble mumbled.

"You don't want to be eating anything that's green," Ali interrupted. "I'll go to the store as soon as I'm done here, and buy plenty of steaks, juicy *red* steaks. You won't go to sleep hungry, Farble, I promise."

Farble grunted, which she hoped meant that he was willing to wait.

Because all trolls were allergic to sunlight, Farble preferred to sleep away most of the day. The troll's supper was often the leprechaun's breakfast. It was only when it was dark or extremely cloudy that Farble went outside—and only in her company—to stretch in the woods behind her house, or else wash in a stream a mile farther up the mountain. If Farble did not bathe several times a day, he quickly began to smell.

Paddy, on the other hand, when his face was plastered with cheap makeup, and he was wearing clothes that did not identify him as a creature out of a folktale, could go to a movie or even a mall by himself. He knew how to ride a bus and carry exact change. He was smart when it came to money. There were few things he liked more than the sound of coins in his pocket.

Unfortunately, he had a bad habit of stealing. What made it worse was that he was good at it, with his quick eyes and hands. The other day he had brought home a CD player, along with an Irish folk tune CD, and had been dismayed when she demanded that he take it back—*carefully*.

Heaven help them if the leprechaun was ever arrested, she thought. Officer Garten would probably be the one to catch him. Then the policeman's questions would get *real* interesting.

After Paddy had finished the bulk of his breakfast, and Farble had drunk a few gallons of sink water, Ali sat down and told them they needed to have a serious talk. They both stared at her with worried expressions, and she wondered how to start.

She decided it would be best to come straight to the point.

"What do you think about going back to the elemental realm?" she asked.

They looked at her as if they had been slapped.

"You want to send us away, Missy?" Paddy asked.

"No. I mean, you know, you're not from around here. I was just thinking maybe you both wanted to go home." She paused. "Does that sound like a good idea?"

Farble shook his head. So did Paddy.

"I've not got me pot of gold yet, Missy," the leprechaun said. "You told me you would help me find it. Paddy cannot go back without it."

Ali nodded. "True, I told you I would help you get your gold. But it was wrong of me to make such a promise. The reality is, you're going to have more success finding gold in the elemental world than here."

Paddy was unconvinced. He spoke in a wounded tone. "If Missy would use her fairy powers to help Paddy, he would have all the gold he needed in a single day. Then he would not mind being sent away."

"I'm not sending either of you away," she said. "We're discussing the idea. And I can't use my fairy powers to get you gold."

"Why not?" Paddy asked.

"Because . . . that would be unethical."

"What does that mean?"

"Ethics . . . they're something most leprechauns probably don't worry about. Look, this last month has been great. We've had a lot of fun together. But this world is not your world, it's not your home." She paused. "Don't you want to go home?"

Again, they both shook their heads. This time Farble spoke.

"Love Geea," he mumbled.

Geea. The name she was known by in the elemental kingdom. None of them knew her as Alosha, except for Nemi.

Alosha was her secret fairy name—a name, she had discovered, that possessed a power all its own. But who, or *what*, Nemi was continued to be a mystery. She had spoken to him only twice: once he had appeared as a tree, another time as a crystal-clear pond. Both times the communication had been telepathic. Although invisible to her eyes, his love had been unmistakable, and she trusted him more deeply than she could explain to herself. She missed him as well . . .

Ali felt a lump in her throat. "I love you both, I do. But it's because I love you that I think you should consider returning to your world."

"When does Missy want us out?" Paddy asked.

"I'm not kicking you out. Stop saying that."

Paddy lowered his head. "Paddy just wants to know when he should pack."

Ali felt her eyes burn; she had to wipe away a tear. She spoke as gently as she could, but the words still sounded harsh in her own ears. "I'm thinking of going back up the mountain soon."

"How soon?" Paddy whispered.

"Maybe tomorrow." Ali hesitated. "Maybe tonight."

Farble sighed but did not speak. Standing, he walked to the basement door and disappeared downstairs. For his part, Paddy did not finish his last egg, just went to the kitchen sink and brushed off his plate. Like the troll, he didn't speak, did not even look at her, but quietly stepped out the back door and walked into the woods. All the while Ali felt not so much like the queen of the fairies in human form, but like a monster who only thought about herself. It was not true, of course, but she had learned long ago that the truth did not always help.

CHAPTER

2

To soothe her guilty conscience, Ali went to buy them food. During the walk to the market, she debated if she would be able to pack enough meat and hard-boiled eggs so that they would have a fresh supply when they entered the elemental kingdom. Her own needs had to be considered as well . . .

For she planned to go with them.

To find her mother. To rescue her from Karl Tanner—Drugle.

"You'll never find her!"

Those had been the last words Karl had shouted, that magical night on top of the mountain, and the way he had said it right then, it was as if he had been taunting her. *Ali, my dear foolish queen, look all you want in this world, in every town and building, behind every tree and under every rock, and you will not find her.*

His arrogance had been clear and, upon reflection, his reason had been obvious. Karl was positive she would not find her mother because her mother was no longer in this world. He had taken her out of this world and into the elemental kingdom. It was the only thing that made sense. Ali could not *feel* her near— and she could feel a great deal simply by reaching out with her mind. She could not feel her mother anywhere. Yet she had been sure Karl had not lied to her when he had said her mother was alive. Karl had been too frightened to lie; she had been about to kill him.

"Maybe I should have," she said aloud, as she walked.

No, that would not have been wise, not if he had her mother tied up somewhere. Yet Ali regretted, more each day, that she had allowed him to go free. It was just that at the time she had felt she had no choice. The Yanti had been about to open; the elemental army was invading. She'd had her hands full, to say the least. Still, she feared she had let him go for the worst of all reasons: *her* own arrogance. At that critical moment, standing atop the mountain, with what she imagined was unlimited power in her hands, she had felt Karl was nothing; just Drugle the Fool, a cowardly and corrupt adviser from her elemental court; a bug in the mud, certainly not a decent adversary, hardly worthy of her scorn. She had figured, the minute she got home, she would use her powers and find her mother, and then they would all live happily ever after. . . .

Until she had gotten home and had reached out with her magical mind and found . . .

Nothing. Neither her mother nor Karl.

He could not be around, not even in the state, she would sense it.

He must be in the elemental kingdom as well, Ali thought.

Or else . . . what? Shielded somehow? From her? Was that possible?

"Anything is possible when nothing is clear," she told herself.

The biggest grocery store in town was on Breakwater's largest street, which was called, fittingly, Main Street. The street was also the address of the city's only barbershop: Harry's Haircuts. Ali was walking by the shop when she saw Harry Idaho passed out in the chair near the door. His mouth was wide open, he was snoring loudly. Had Harry been eighty years old and a habitual napper, she wouldn't have been surprised. But Harry was forty and fit—she had never seen him lying down on the job before. What made the sight even more peculiar was that there was a customer in the shop, near the back, an old guy with long white hair and a white beard. He was sitting patiently, staring at himself in the mirror, and appeared to be waiting for Harry to wake up. Had the old man not been dressed entirely in white—which gave him a vague resemblance to a wizard—Ali would have continued on her way without stopping. But her curiosity was piqued. She stuck her head inside.

"How long has Harry been asleep?" she called over, hoping her question would wake Harry up. His position was far from flattering; he had drooled on his shirt. He was out cold and did not even stir with her remark.

"He was asleep when I got here," the old man replied, glancing over. She noted his pale blue eyes, how old and young they looked at the same time.

Ali stepped inside. She was tempted to shake Harry, but kept thinking he would wake up any second. "Never seen him passed out like this before," she said.

"You've known him a long time?" the old man asked in a soft voice.

"Long as I can remember." Ali stepped closer to the old man. "You from around here?" she asked.

"Just passing through."

"I love your hair and beard. I hope you don't cut too much off."

The old man played with his hair for a moment. "It's more trouble than it's worth. People tell me it makes me look like Santa Claus."

He was way too skinny to be a Santa Claus, she thought. Indeed, his arms were so bony they hardly had room for skin. His face was austere, starved—if he ate more than once a day she would have been surprised. His long-sleeved white shirt was oversized and it hung from his narrow shoulders like a short robe. He did not look sick, but he did not look well, either. Mostly, he looked like no one she had ever seen before in her life. Obviously, she had never seen him before.

He appeared to study her, as she did him.

"Where are you from originally?" she asked.

"I don't think you would know the town. The name . . . it's just a place." He paused. "What's your name, may I ask?"

"Alison Warner. Everyone just calls me Ali."

"I'm Shane Bumpston." He offered his left hand; it was wrapped in a white glove. "Pleased to meet you, Ali."

"Same here." They shook, and his hard grip squeezed the blood from her fingers. She nodded to his gloves. "Those look cool."

"I don't wear them to keep warm or cool. No, I hurt my hands some time ago, burned them actually. Now I have to wear these to keep away infections."

"Sorry to hear that. Do they hurt?"

"Yes, they often do." He paused. "You wouldn't happen to be a friend of Ted Wilson, would you?"

She nodded. "I go to school with his daughter. You know him?"

"We talk now and then. That was a bad accident he had up there on the mountain. I'm so glad he's up and walking around. When I saw him the other day, he looked fit as a fiddle." The man added, "It was like nothing had happened to him."

"That's great," she said. The reason Ted Wilson had recovered so quickly, and completely, was because she had healed him after turning back the elemental army on top of Pete's Peak. But no one—other than Steve and Cindy—was supposed to know that. Ted himself did not remember what she had done. At least, that's what she had thought. The old man's next remark caught her by surprise.

"Ted told me how you helped him. He said you were a remarkable young lady."

Ted had been in a coma when she had zapped him. "What did he say exactly?"

"He said there was more to you than met the eye."

Ali frowned. "How do you know him? Since you're not from around here."

"I know a great many people all over the world." He added, "Now I know you."

"What Ted said about me—it's flattering and all that—but I don't know what he's talking about. I'm no healer."

Shane Bumpston stared at her with his strange blue eyes. The color was so faint around the pupils it was as if they had been removed, bleached overnight, and then put back in place. "Are you sure about that, Ali?" he asked.

She felt the *need* to meet his gaze. Indeed, she felt a surge of power run the length of her spine, and was surprised he did not turn away as she focused on him. Most people would have; they would have been forced to. But this man did not even blink. It was as if he challenged her with his eyes.

"I have no idea what you're talking about," she said coldly.

In response he tugged on a string around his neck, and pulled out a gold medallion that had been hidden under his shirt. The emblem was a small inverted triangle, and it had an odd jagged line through the center of it. The piece was the same size as her Yanti—the triangle matched the shape of one aspect of the

Yanti—but it was still something that could have been bought in a jewelry store. Nevertheless, she found it a coincidence that he wore it. She backed up a step as he stroked the medallion.

"I've had this for some time. What do you think of it?" he asked.

She hesitated. "It's pretty."

He glanced up. "May I see yours?"

A chill shook her. "My what?"

"I see the string. You must be wearing . . . something. *Please*, Ali, let me see it."

His voice was oddly persuasive. She found her hand reaching for the Yanti, and had to will it back down. "Why should I show you anything of mine? I don't know you."

He grinned; he had a mouth of perfectly white teeth. "Are you sure about that? I think we've met before. Yes, now that I consider it, I'm positive we met a long time ago. Don't you remember?"

"No," she said flatly. "When? Where?"

"It wasn't here, in this city. It was somewhere else."

Ali glanced toward the door. It was twenty feet away and it looked like a mile. Harry continued to sleep as if he had been injected with a drug. Shane Bumpston—she doubted that was his real name—never took his eyes off her face.

"It would help if you were more specific," she said.

"Let me see it," he repeated.

"Let me see your wallet, your ID."

"Why?"

"I want to see who you really are."

His grin widened. "You see me, don't you?"

The question was odd; she felt the layers hidden inside it. He was asking more than the obvious. Again, she felt him challenge her, as well as mock her. He not only looked like a wizard, it was as if he were trying to cast a spell over her. On the other hand, she did not feel he was trying too hard. He was just playing with her.

"You see me, don't you?"

Did she? Suddenly, Ali had the urge to turn around. To look in the mirror.

She started to move. The man jerked. "What are you doing?" he demanded.

"Show me your ID, Mr. Shane Bumpston," she insisted.

He let go of his medallion, leaned forward in the chair. All of a sudden, he did not look so old and kind, and for the first time she felt a stab of fear. The sensation was alien to her. Since returning from the mountain she had assumed nothing on Earth could harm her. But her stab of fear swelled into a spike as she stared deeper into the man's eyes.

There was *much* more to him than met the eye.

"I know you have *it,*" he whispered, and with that he stood.

Ali's left hand went to the Yanti under her shirt, and she raised her right palm to erect a force field if necessary, which she was quite good at. Yet *what* was she trying to repel? She needed to look in the mirror, she just knew it, but she feared to take her eyes off the old crow. Nevertheless, she tried a quick peek, but the instant she turned her head there came a sharp flash of light. It could have been lightning; it was white, alive with a blistering charge. It stunned her so badly she dropped to the floor, banged her head on a row of drawers beneath the mirror that ran the length of Harry's shop. The blow to her skull, or else the flash itself, blurred her vision. The room was momentarily filled with red, yet there was no blood in her eyes. But she did not black out, she was pretty sure she did not.

When her eyes cleared, though, the old man was gone.

"God," she whispered, slowly getting to her feet, taking a seat in the chair he had just vacated. It was warmer than it should have been; the brown leather felt as if it had been stretched out in the sun in a harsh desert. Plus there was a smell of ozone in the air and something else she could not identify, a faint odor of decay. Her heart was pounding, and she was afraid to let go of the Yanti. Perhaps it had saved her life. He had known about it, that's for sure. He had known about *her*.

Ali sat for a few minutes, trying to catch her breath.

She did not realize that the snoring had stopped.

Harry called to her. "What're you doing here, Ali? You know you don't like me cutting your hair."

"I stopped by to say hi, you were snoring." She added, "Did you fall asleep in your chair?"

Harry shook his head. "Must have."

"Did you see anyone?"

"What do you mean?"

"There was a man here with long white hair and a long beard. Did you see him?"

"Someone came in the shop, I remember. But I couldn't say what he looked like."

"Why not?"

Harry frowned. "I must have fallen asleep the second he got here. That's odd, don't you think?"

Still shaken, Ali could only nod.

CHAPTER

3

At the store, walking the meat aisle, Ali ran into Steve Fender. Well, *ran into* might have been pushing it—he had obviously come to the market to find her. She had spoken to him earlier in the day and had told him she needed to pick up a few groceries.

He might have *run* to the store, however, a physical act Steve was not known to indulge in very often. He was struggling to catch his breath. Like her, Steve was thirteen years old, on the cusp of high school, but unlike her he was plump and out of shape. He had a bit of troll in him—food was his first priority in life. Yet he had more refined tastes than Farble. Steve was discerning when it came to coffee and pastries and he seldom had one without the other. Paddy and Steve did not particularly get along, but when the leprechaun craved a great beverage, he always turned to Steve.

"I'm glad you're here," Steve said. "I finally did it."

"Did what?" she asked.

"Broke into Karl's computer."

Ali felt hopeful. The night she had returned from the mountain, a month ago, with her human friends and elemental buddies in tow, she had immediately gone to the hospital to heal Ted Wilson, then had returned home to reassure her father that she was okay. But when all the excitement had died down, and she had laid in bed and tried to find Karl and her mother in her mind, and failed, she realized she might need a backup plan. Clearly magic was not going to solve all her problems.

Yet she had known she had to act fast, before Karl was reported missing. That same night she had snuck over to his house and climbed into his bedroom through an open window, and had searched his desk and drawers for . . . what? Any clue of what he might have been up to since he had kidnapped her mother. Unfortunately, she had found nothing useful and in the end, partly out of desperation, she had swiped his computer, knowing Steve was a genius when it came to hacking into computer systems. But Karl's files had been protected by an encrypted password—like there was another teenager on the West Coast who would bother with such a thing. That password had stumped Steve until, apparently, this morning.

Karl's parents had noticed their son's computer was missing. They had told Officer Garten about it, and the last time he had confronted her, *he* had told Ali. It was possible the lot of them believed she had swiped the computer, although Ali was confident no one had seen her enter and exit Karl's room.

"Find anything interesting?" she asked.

Steve caught her eye. "Several interesting things."

She glanced around. "Let's not talk here. How's your house?"

"Empty. I've already called Cindy to meet us there."

Reaching out, Ali gave him a hug, although she imagined he would have preferred a kiss. Steve had had a crush on her since he had discovered girls were not the same as boys. "You're a master," she whispered in his ear.

He beamed. "A high compliment coming from someone like you. Or should I say, a *queen* like you."

Ali forced a smile, while feeling pain in her heart. She loved being queen of the fairies, being special, having power, but she hated it as well because it separated her from those she loved. It made it difficult for her to hang out with her friends, to just be silly, to just be Ali Warner. Those who knew who she was could not look at her without staring; those who did not could never really know her at all. Her father fell into the latter category. Since she had returned from the mountain—with her hair as bright red as a flame—she had spent as much time with him as usual, fixing his meals, begging him to sleep more, washing his clothes, and yet she had sensed *him* sensing that she had changed in some inexplicable way. For sure, she was no longer his little girl.

How would she and her mother get along when they finally met again? Ali did not know; she feared even to find out. They had been apart for more than a year, and so much had changed in that time. From the hints her mother had dropped, Ali could only assume her mother had known she was a fairy. But Ali wasn't a hundred percent sure about that, and if her mother *didn't* know . . . well, then, they would have a terrible time communicating, particularly if she saw that her daughter's method of putting out the garbage was simply to incinerate it with her eyes. She had done that *once*, for fun.

Worse, Ali could not see herself far in the future, older, and married with her own children . . . Because the truth was, she could not imagine it. She couldn't even see herself in the present with a boyfriend . . . Because she could not see herself as a *girl*-friend . . . Because she was not a girl . . . Not really.

"Watch your tongue," she said to Steve. "We're in a public place."

"Cindy's probably on her way. Can you leave now?"

She hesitated. "Sure."

They headed for the door. Images of the old guy in the barbershop continued to haunt her. She had no idea who he might have been. Nemi? She had always pictured him as a kindly wizard. Definitely, the two times they had spoken, she had been overwhelmed by his love. But the guy in the barbershop had given off scary vibes . . .

Ali debated whether he had knocked her unconscious or simply vanished before her eyes. The question was important because it led to another question. Was he from this world or the elemental world?

"Still struggling to feed Farble and Paddy?" Steve asked, when they were outside.

Ali nodded. "It's a full-time job."

"Why do you keep them at your house? Isn't the Baker place still empty?"

"When my dad's out of town, I prefer to keep them close. You know the two don't get along."

"Is Farble still trying to eat Paddy?"

"He paws him occasionally, but it's not that. I feel bad for them. I think they're lonely." She paused. "I spoke to them about going back to the elemental world. They got upset."

Steve stopped in midstride. "You're sending them back?"

"Yes."

Steve was astounded. "Do you know *how* to send them back?"

"I have some ideas."

"That's vague." He paused. "Have you figured out how to use the Yanti?"

The question caused Ali to pause. It was odd because Steve knew she had used the Yanti a month ago to send the elemental army back to their realm. But since then she had barely spoken

31

to her friends about it, partly because she felt uncomfortable talking about it, partly because she had nothing to report. After a month of fiddling with it, she had only a vague idea of how the Yanti worked, and absolutely no idea of where it had come from.

"Not exactly," she replied.

"Then how will you return them to the elemental world?"

"Let's talk about it at your house," she said.

Steve gave her a look, and for a moment she wondered how he saw her. Was she beautiful in his eyes? Like a queen? All she knew for sure was that she was taller than him by two inches, and that ever since she had used the Yanti that one time, her long hair was as bright red as her eyes were green. Steve had once written a poem about her eyes, had called them lost emeralds, which she supposed was a compliment. In the same piece he had described her oval face as a hallway mirror, and her button nose as a small period at the end of a long and moving sentence. Obviously he was into metaphors. But when it had come to her mouth, he had just said that it was wild and alive. Fair enough; she hoped it was as alive as the rest of her.

Steve had lost weight since their adventure up on Pete's Peak, not enough to transform him into a track star, but enough to reveal that his round face was not merely pleasant, but handsome. He had blue eyes—they usually looked as if they were laughing—and he wore his straight blond hair close to his scalp, almost in a buzz.

When they reached Steve's house, Cindy was waiting on the porch. Her best friend had also changed since their big adventure. Before, Cindy had been what some might have called talkative, but whom most would have referred to as an airhead. It was still a fact that Cindy liked to talk, but nowadays it seemed as if she considered the impact of her remarks before she spoke.

Up on the mountain, Cindy had almost had her throat cut by Karl, and Ali suspected that the near brush with death had changed her friend in more ways than Cindy let on.

Cindy was shorter than Ali, but her blond hair was long and curly. Like Steve, she had a quick laugh and plenty of friends, and her dark blue eyes lit up when she was having fun, making her appear dizzy. Yet Ali had noticed that since coming back from their trip, Cindy was not nearly as sociable. She stayed home a lot more, and read, or else came over to hang out with Ali. It was as if the things she had seen on top of the mountain had shaken her view of the universe.

The truth was, none of them were the same, and that was probably both good and bad. Good because it was always good to know what was real, and bad because reality itself was not necessarily a friend to them . . . or anyone else. The universe was not cruel, Ali thought, it was just indifferent.

Steve let them into his house, and fifteen minutes later they were sitting at his kitchen table, drinking strong coffee and eating bearclaws. The latter were from a bakery in town that Steve visited at least three times a week. All their pastries were excellent.

"I suppose you're both wondering what I found on Karl's computer," Steve said finally, between mouthfuls.

"Dying to know," Cindy said. "Stop eating and start talking."

"Just a second," Ali said. "There's something I have to tell you. Officer Garten swung by my house this morning and asked about Karl. I gave him the usual runaround, but he said both of you had admitted that you had gone hiking during the same days Karl disappeared—June sixth and seventh. Is that true?"

"We had no choice," Cindy said. "Our parents knew we went hiking, and Garten talked to them as well."

"We couldn't just act stupid," Steve added. "That worked for you because your father was out of town during most of our trip."

Ali nodded. "I'm not here to yell at you guys. I just would have preferred to know is all."

"He came over just before he went to your place," Cindy said. "Then my parents started grilling me about Karl. I didn't have a chance to warn you."

"Same here," Steve said. "My mom only left half an hour ago, just before I ran down to the market to get you."

Ali frowned. "Garten might end up being a bigger problem than I thought."

"Any idea how to make him back down?" Cindy asked.

Steve chuckled. "Show him Karl's body."

"Not a bad idea," Ali muttered.

Steve snorted. "I was joking!"

Ali stared at him. "I'm not. Karl kidnapped my mother. When I see him again, I'm not sure what I'm going to do. But you can be sure, whatever it is, he's not going to hurt any of us again."

Her remark weighed heavily on the room. Finally Cindy spoke to Steve.

"Tell us what was on his computer," she said.

"Don't you want to know how I broke into it?" he asked.

"Nope," Ali and Cindy said at the same time.

Steve sipped his coffee. "At first glance his files looked pretty ordinary. He had folders for homework assignments. He had downloaded a lot of information on different sports teams. He had tons of notes on what it would take to run his father's businesses—in the event his father was not around."

"Do you think he was planning to kill him?" Cindy asked.

"I don't know. But for a kid, he sure was prepared for the old man to keel over. Anyway, things got interesting when I dug into copies of his e-mails. He probably thought he had erased them all. There were signs he had tried to destroy them. But if you know where to look, you can often find what is called a ghost record. That's a copy that doesn't show up on a simple search, but which the hard drive has not actually copied over. It was in the ghost records that I found he had been e-mailing a person named Shak666."

"Who is that?" Ali asked, very alert.

Shak . . . Shaktra?

From what she understood from talking to Lord Vak—who was no less than the king of the elves—it was the Shaktra that was driving the elementals to attack humanity.

"I'm not sure," Steve said, reaching for a paper. "Whoever it was, they always signed their e-mails with the letter 'S'. The e-mails are all brief. I'm sure that's on purpose. It makes it hard to know what they're saying." Clearing his throat, Steve began to read from his notes. "KarlKan says: 'Have taken care of business and made delivery as you ordered. Let me know of your progress.' Shak666 replies: 'Progress continues, no need to ask. Keep attention on Subject.' A month later KarlKan writes: 'Subject is boring. Will die in ignorance.' Shak666 replies: 'Subject is dangerous. Do not underestimate.' Six months later, KarlKan writes: 'Request permission to destroy Subject.' Shak666 replied: 'Do not harm Subject! Important!' Finally, about a month ago, KarlKan wrote: 'Subject is awaking. Visiting wrong place at wrong time. Permission to destroy?' Shak666 replied: 'Accompany to Doorway, if Subject allows. Do not harm until Power is secure.' "

They sat a moment in silence. Then Ali asked, "Is that all?"

"That's all I was able to retrieve," Steve said. "But I'm sure they exchanged more e-mails. Those ones must have been permanently erased."

Ali held out a hand. "Let me see." Steve handed over the copies of the e-mails. Ali studied them a minute. "The words 'subject,' 'power,' and 'doorway' are capitalized."

"I think the Subject must be you," Steve said.

Ali nodded. "The Power might be the Yanti. The Doorway might refer to it as well."

"I agree," Steve said. "I'm sure Karl planned to kill you the moment he had it in his hands."

"Did you get an IPN number on Shak666?" Ali asked.

Steve nodded. "I was able to trace it to a corporation, not a person. It belongs to Omega Overtures."

Cindy was puzzled. "Are they the ones who make the video games?"

"Exactly," Steve said, showing excitement. "And get this— their headquarters are located in Toule. You must have heard of the place, it's a small town on the other side of Pete's Peak. That can't be a coincidence. The president of the company is named Sheri Smith."

"A woman," Cindy said. "But she signed her e-mails with only one 'S'."

"She might have thought it was enough," Ali said, still thinking of the spellings of "Shak" and "Shaktra."

Cindy nodded. "When we were up on the mountain, right after we found out who Karl really was, he said he didn't kill you for all these complex reasons. Now we can see he was just doing what he was told."

"It sure sounds like this Shak666 has him on a tight leash," Steve said.

"When was the e-mail sent that refers to a delivery?" Ali asked Steve.

"A little over a year ago."

Cindy gasped. "Could it have been your mom, Ali?"

She shook her head weakly. "I don't know."

"That reference—if it is to your mother—is not bad news,"

Steve said. "It means they have her, and that they've made accommodations for her."

"You mean they found a prison for her?" Cindy said.

Steve shrugged. "What matters is that she is still alive. Right, Ali?"

Ali nodded, spoke in a soft voice. "You've done great work, Steve. I'm grateful."

"Don't be. I love your mother, the whole town does. Now we just have to find her and bring her back home."

"What do you suggest?" Cindy said.

"It's obvious," Steve said. "We have to go to Toule and check out this company, and their president."

"Easier said than done," Cindy said.

"It won't be too hard with the queen of the fairies on our team," Steve said, a note of pride in his voice. But Ali shook her head.

"I do not feel my mother is in Toule," she said. "I do not feel her anywhere."

"But you said Karl was telling the truth when he said she was alive?" Cindy said.

"She can be alive and not be on the Earth." Ali added, "I think he has her captive in the elemental realm."

Steve saw where she was heading, looked worried. "So when you return Paddy and Farble to their homes, you plan on accompanying them?" he asked.

"Paddy and Farble are leaving?" Cindy asked, surprised.

"Yes," Ali said, answering them both.

Another long silence. Cindy broke it. "I'm not sure if I'm ready to go on that kind of trip," she said.

"I'm not asking you to," Ali said.

"Wait a second," Steve said. "We're all in this together. You're not going anywhere without us. If you feel you have to enter the elemental kingdom, then we're going with you. But I think it's a mistake. No disrespect to your intuition, but this lead on Omega Overtures is real. Karl was writing to someone at that company and they were telling him what to do."

"The lead is strong," Ali agreed. "Your work on Karl's computer wasn't wasted. Let's go to Toule this afternoon. Let's check out the bus schedules. I think there's one that leaves at two o'-clock." Ali paused. "But you have to understand, Toule is one thing, and the elemental kingdom is something else altogether."

"What do you mean?" Cindy asked.

Ali sighed. "I know I have to go there, and not just to find my mother. We made Lord Vak back down on top of Pete's Peak. That was great. But he hasn't changed his mind about invading the Earth. The elementals are still coming. I can't let that happen. But I can't stop it from happening by sitting here and waiting for them to make the next move. I have to go on the offensive."

"What will you do in their world?" Steve asked.

"I'll figure that out when I get there."

"But you say you don't even know how to make the Yanti work," Steve said.

"She got it to work before," Cindy said.

"I might not need the Yanti to get to the elementals," Ali said. "The seven doors we encountered when we were in the cave—each of them leads to a different kingdom."

"How do you know that?" Steve asked.

Ali stared at him. "By logic. The third door was yellow, and it was open. When we went through it, we stayed here, we did not enter another dimension. It was that door that led us to the top of the mountain."

"I hope your *logical* argument has more to it than that," Steve said.

"It does, but the major part of it, neither of you remember, and it's not something I've discussed with you. You see, the first time we reached the seven doors, we did not take the third one, the yellow door. We took the first one, the red door."

They stared at her like she had lost her mind.

"What *first* time?" Steve finally asked. "We only went there once."

"Twice," Ali said.

"Ali," Cindy said. "Are you feeling okay?"

"I tried to explain these things when we were on top of the mountain, Cindy. I even tried to explain it to Karl. None of you, including Paddy and Farble, remember the *first* time, but it did happen. There's a reason you don't. The first time we reached the seven doors, I insisted we take the red one. None of you wanted to, especially Paddy, but I bullied you guys into it, and in the end you followed me. But the tunnel eventually dead-ended in a deep chasm, and suddenly we heard an army of dwarves approaching from behind us." She paused. "Using a rope, I managed to crawl across the black hole, but the rest of you didn't make it."

"What do you mean, we didn't make it?" Cindy asked.

"You died," Ali replied.

Steve snorted. "We didn't die! None of this happened!"

"It did happen—in another timeline. You see, the dark fairies live on the other side of the red door. Other creatures might live there as well, I don't know, but the place is like hell. There's fire and smoke and pain and . . . it's just too awful to describe. But trust me when I say I've been there, deep in that realm. It was there I passed the last of the tests that allowed me to realize that I'm the queen of the fairies. It was there I met the queen of the *dark* fairies, a creature named Radrine. She tortured me, tried to get the secrets of the Yanti out of me, but I managed to escape and return to the seven doors. But before that I realized something amazing: *Beyond the red door, time flowed backwards.* The whole time I was there, my watch went in reverse. So did your watch, Cindy."

"I don't remember any of this," Cindy said.

"Because I came back and stopped you guys—no, I stopped *myself,* from going through the red door! It's complicated, I know, and I don't pretend to understand how or why time flows backwards there. It might have something to do with the fact that it's like hell. The beings that live there are all going backwards—in evolution. That's a theory of mine, but it doesn't matter, it might be wrong. What does matter is that the different colored doors lead into different dimensions."

"You're asking us to swallow a hell of a lot right now," Steve said.

"No pun intended," Cindy added.

"You've both seen the dark fairies in action. You've both heard Paddy describe how no one likes them. Let me ask you something: If what Paddy says is true, then why did Lord Vak use the Yanti to bring them into our world?"

Steve frowned. "I don't know."

Cindy was puzzled. "I had wondered about that. I didn't know why Vak would have anything to do with them. It seemed . . . out of character for him."

Ali nodded. "The answer is that he did not bring the dark fairies here. They came here on their own, through the red door. They did not use the Yanti to come here. That's another reason why I know the doors lead to other realms. That is why I'm sure I can use one of them—the fourth one, the green door—to enter the elemental kingdom."

"How do you know the fourth door is the right one?" Cindy asked.

"I just know," Ali said.

"Do you *remember* this?" Steve asked. The question was not a casual one. Both of Ali's friends were intensely curious about what she recalled of her life as a fairy. The truth was, she recalled a ton of nothing—a million pieces of a puzzle that was light-years away from being fitted together. Many of her memories were hard to separate from her normal dreams, although she wondered if she spent most of the night dreaming about her past life as a queen. The biggest problem was that she had no one to turn to who could check the accuracy of her memories.

If only I could talk to Nemi!

"I think so," she said quietly.

"You're not sure?" Steve said.

Ali shook her head. "I cannot wait around to be sure of anything."

Steve went on. "Like you said, the red door and the yellow door were open. The rest were locked tight. How do you plan on opening the green door?"

"I have ideas," she said. "But I don't want to talk about them, not now, and I'm sorry I have to give that type of answer. I trust you guys with my life, but I have a feeling that it would be a mistake to talk about certain things."

"Why can't we go with you?" Steve asked. "Don't tell me it's too dangerous."

"You would slow me down. When I go, and it will be soon, I have to go at night. Farble cannot travel in the daytime, not without a lot of hassle. I want to hike all the way from where we started—the last time—to the cave in one night."

"That's physically impossible," Steve said.

"Not for Farble, he's strong. Not for Paddy, he doesn't tire easily. And to be frank, since I regained some of my old powers I can run up that mountain if I have to."

"We can still go. It will just take longer is all," Steve said.

"I don't want to have to worry about you. It'll divide my attention."

Steve looked offended. "We helped you pretty good the last time."

"The last time we were not planning on entering another dimension," Ali said.

"I think she's right," Cindy said to Steve. "I don't say that because I'm a coward—even though we all know I am. We can help Ali more by figuring out what's going on in Toule."

"I agree," Ali said. "I'll go with you this afternoon, at least for a few hours."

Steve took a moment to grasp what she was saying. "Are you thinking of going up the mountain *tonight?*"

"It's possible," Ali said. "It depends what we find in Toule. Let's talk about that. I've never heard of Omega Overtures. You guys act like it's famous."

"If you play video games it is," Steve said. "Their products have great visuals and complex plots. The stories always deal with the end of the world. Their biggest seller is Omega Overlord. Cindy's played it with me. It starts after a major nuclear war, a century from now. It's all about the remnants of humanity struggling for survival."

"The game is totally addicting," Cindy said.

"Sounds lovely," Ali said. "I remember something else about Toule. Wasn't it the site of a major catastrophe twenty years ago?"

"Thirteen years ago," Steve said. "An electric power plant blew up, killed over a hundred people, pretty much burned the city to the ground."

"What caused the explosion?" Ali asked.

"When I saw Karl was writing to someone in Toule, I looked up the town online and read about it. To this day, the reason for the explosion remains a mystery."

"How large a company is Omega Overtures?" Ali asked.

"They have three hundred employees," Steve said. "But don't let that fool you. Like other successful software companies, they make a lot of money on a few products. The markup on those games is high, and Omega has the four best sellers in the country this year. They're raking in billions."

"You're exaggerating," Cindy said.

"Nope," Steve said.

"But any company that size . . ." Ali began.

Steve was insistent. "I've studied their profit-and-loss statements. That company is medium-sized and it's worth five billion dollars. It's almost as if . . ." He didn't finish.

"They have magic?" Ali suggested.

Steve nodded. "They know how to package and sell the end of the world." He stopped and stared at her for a moment, then reached over and touched her head. When he withdrew his hand, there was blood on it. "What's this?" he demanded.

Ali forced a smile. "I fell and hit my head. It's nothing."

Yeah, she had hit it in the barbershop when the wizard had blasted her.

It was odd, she thought, how the old man's eyes had not been entirely human.

"I know you have it."

CHAPTER

4

The headache hit as she was walking home from the market with the meat she had bought for Farble. Since Steve had interrupted her original shopping expedition, she'd had to go back to the store. The pressure started between her eyes, spread across her forehead, moved around the side, and then to the spot where her neck and skull joined. The headaches came often these days, and they were painful, lasting two or three hours. This one had nothing to do with her struggle with the wizard in the barbershop.

The headaches had started a week after she had returned from the top of the mountain. Although she was not positive what caused them, she suspected they were a result of her fairy power running through her human body. Her nervous system was used to ten volts—now it was living with a thousand.

At first she had thought wearing the Yanti was causing the headaches, but taking it off did not help. She had the Yanti on now, under her red sweatshirt. Steve and Cindy liked to look at it, but she was always reluctant to let them hold it. Actually, she never let them touch it without her hand on it. She was not sure what she was afraid of. They wouldn't steal it, of course. Perhaps she feared that it might overload them somehow.

No, the Yanti could not be blamed for her pain. She simply had too much fairy juice in her head, and there was no off switch. She was a walking atomic reactor. The power felt like a magnetic field, an invisible dome that surrounded her on all sides. But she never felt *possessed* by the power, or anything silly like that. At the same time, she did not feel she had complete control over it. She was not entirely sure what she could and could not do.

Yet she had a measure of control over the elements. There appeared to be six of them—not the usual four or five the ancients spoke of. Earth, water, fire, air, space, *and* time. She knew exactly what she could do with the earth. She was the wrong girl to get in a rock fight with. A boulder weighing two hundred pounds was like a pebble to her—she could throw it a hundred yards. Water was also easy. There wasn't a river current or an ocean wave that could move her an inch. In the last month she had learned the art of boiling a whole bathtub in a matter of seconds. She could also make it freeze. She just had to will it to happen, focus, and it happened.

Fire could not burn her. And she could take even a small flame, say from a match, in her magnetic grasp and expand it a hundred fold. The ability frightened her. She was not sure what limits there were to it.

When it came to air, she could cause a mighty wind to arise within seconds. And because words were carried on the air, she could tell when someone was lying or telling the truth, no matter how crafty they were.

Yet she could not cause the wind to lift her body into the air.

Here she was supposed to be queen of the fairies and she could not fly.

Space? How could anyone control that? It was not a thing, nor was time for that matter, and she certainly had no grasp over the latter. But she believed there was more to space than met the eye. It was invisible, it could not be touched or tasted or smelled. But occasionally she heard music, faintly, deep inside—flutes and bells, stringed instruments, and exquisite soulful horns— and she wondered if she was hearing the music of inner space. Whatever, it was a blessing. When the music came, even if she had a raging headache, or was anxious about her mother, everything was suddenly all right. At such times she would lie in bed with her eyes closed, drift on the currents of the supernatural melodies, and forget all her problems. She could listen to them forever. . . .

Too bad she couldn't hear the music while carrying ten pounds of beef.

Somehow Ali made it home. Farble was still in the basement, looking sad, but he cheered up when he saw the steaks she had bought. He patted her back and gave her a hug, and she left him to enjoy his meal. But there was no sign of Paddy, and that worried her.

There was something else that helped when it came to her headaches: stardust, or at least her version of the stuff. When they had hiked up the mountain, Paddy had brought up the topic and it had gotten her thinking. Along with Cindy, she had drilled Paddy about it.

"What can you do with fairy stardust?"

"Many things, Missy. Fly for one."

"Have you ever flown using the stuff?"

"Leprechauns can't fly. Only fairies fly, and only if they have enough stardust."

"How does it run out? On fairies, I mean."

"Don't know, it just does. Disappears quick when they are up in the air."

"Where does it come from?"

"Fairies."

"No. Where do they get it?"

"Don't know, never asked them."

"Is it made from gold?"

"Maybe. Maybe not."

Paddy had not wanted to say, for whatever reason, but she had known it was related to gold, and when she had returned home, she had begun to experiment with pieces of her mother's jewelry. Her knowledge of chemistry was dismal. On the other hand, what she was attempting to do was more of an alchemic process than a scientific one. At first she did not know where to begin, but sitting with the gold over time, the inspiration came.

She realized she had to dissolve it first, before anything else, and was pleasantly surprised to discover a dozen different techniques of doing so on the Internet. The method she chose required hydrochloric acid and nitric acid, along with baking soda and ammonia. Fortunately, she was able to order the supplies right off the Internet. It was amazing the stuff that could be purchased on the Web, and a little frightening. Except for having to do the operation outside because of the obnoxious fumes the chemicals gave off, the entire process was no harder than baking a cake.

Two days after starting her experiments, she had a beaker full of dissolved gold.

She felt inspired to expose it to sunlight, and she left it outside for close to a week, but nothing happened, other than some of the solution evaporated. The missing step hit her out of the blue. The gold solution could not just sit in the sun, the light had to first be *channeled* through her hands. She recalled vague images of herself sitting outside in the elemental realm—under a *green* sun—making the stardust. She also remembered that when she swallowed the stuff—as a fairy—she got stronger.

That's why she wanted to make it in the first place. . . .

The first time she tried to gather the sunlight to flow through her hands, she felt foolish. Sunlight was akin to fire, but it was not an element per se. She almost felt as if she needed to ask someone's permission before she tried it. But in the end she just did it, and was delighted when the sunlight responded to her magnetic field. Using her hands as a giant lens and concentrating hard on the sun, she actually saw the light waves bend and focus on her gold solution. Within seconds the glass began to bubble furiously. When all the liquid had vanished, she was left with a fluffy white powder that looked strangely familiar.

Yet she did not swallow it. Instinctively, she knew there was another step to perform. The stardust had to be exposed to concentrated starlight, the same way she had exposed it to concentrated sunlight. *Duh!* That was where the name came from! That very night, under the clear band of the Milky Way, she zapped it with her hands and watched as the white powder turned a light shade of blue. When she put a few grams in her mouth, and let it dissolve, she felt her power increase manifold. It was only after she ingested the stardust that she was able to gain such breathtaking control of the elements.

The stardust helped with her headaches but it did not get rid of them. Because she had a limited supply of gold, she had only a few ounces of the magical dust, and she hated to squander it simply to dull her pain. She feared she might need lots of it if and when she squared off against her enemies in the elemental kingdom.

She did not feel guilty destroying her mother's jewelry.

Her mom would have been the first person to tell her to go ahead.

Yet this headache was particularly severe when she got home, and she ended up swallowing a few grams of the stardust, along with two Tylenol. After a brief nap, she felt somewhat better.

She was sitting on the edge of her bed when Cindy called to say that the bus for Toule was at one o'clock, and that she had better hurry over to the station. Ali told her she would be there.

In the middle of getting dressed, Ali called and tried to talk to Ted Wilson about the old man at the barbershop, but his wife said he was out of town. Seemed he was looking for a new job.

It was only as she was leaving the house that she realized she should speak to the head of Omega Overtures alone, without Steve and Cindy present. The e-mails Steve had found bothered her. Clearly the woman behind the company had secrets she was keeping.

But could she be the Shaktra? It seemed highly unlikely. That creature *had* to be in the elemental kingdom, where it was causing endless grief.

On the other hand, was she so sure of her facts?

Lord Vak might have asked her that question . . .

"Geea, what is wrong with you? The Shaktra came from the human kingdom!"

Ali ran back in the house and grabbed her entire supply of stardust—just in case.

CHAPTER

5

To Steve, Ali was not so much a queen as a princess—although, unfortunately, he never felt he deserved to play the part of the prince. Not that he saw himself in the role of the frog, either, it was just that his feelings for her were not something that he could talk about. Especially to her.

It didn't matter. He knew *she* knew how he felt, and that was enough. He loved her and she loved him. Their love simply sprang from different regions of the heart.

Sitting in the middle section of the bus, beside Cindy, on the road to Toule, Steve watched as Ali appeared to nap on the backseat, her long strands of red hair touching the floor. Her eyes were closed but he did not think she was *truly* asleep. He did wonder if she was in pain, though. He had never seen her lie down in the middle of the day before.

Cindy said she had caught Ali taking a number of naps in the last month. And here Ali said she could dash all the way up the mountain without stopping. To Steve, since they had returned from their big adventure on Pete's Peak, Ali appeared far more powerful and far more delicate. It was almost as if her fairy powers were burning her up.

"She'll be all right," Cindy said, noticing his gaze.

"Do you think?" Steve replied quietly, not wanting Ali to overhear them.

Cindy set aside her magazine, glanced at Ali. "She just gets headaches is all."

"She told you that?" Ali had never said anything about it to him.

"No. But I've seen her buying Tylenol. I don't think it's a big deal."

"I hope you're right. She doesn't look in any shape to run up a mountain."

"I think she's anxious to go while her father's gone."

"How long is he gone for?"

"A week."

Steve considered. "There might be another reason. Did you know it's a full moon tonight?"

"Do you think she needs a full moon to use the Yanti?"

"Who knows? She never talks about it. The whole subject is a mystery to me. That's why I was trying to get her to talk about it at the house. Did you notice how she changed the subject?"

"Sure. But I don't think she was trying to be rude."

"She went from the Yanti to those colored doors."

Cindy frowned. "That was weird. She said we went there twice. That we *died* the first time. Do you believe that?"

"Of course not. Then again, maybe I should. Ali changed when we were in that cave. She changed big time."

"I remember. It was like she was glowing."

"She still glows," Steve said.

Cindy nodded. "I think she has the power all the time now. Not just when it's an emergency."

"But you're not sure?"

"No."

51

Steve nodded. "That's what gets me—there's so much she doesn't want to talk about. I don't understand why. Doesn't she trust us?"

"She could be afraid we'll fall into the hands of the bad guys and they'll torture the truth out of us."

"That brings up another point. Who are the bad guys? First it was the elementals because they were trying to invade our world. But then, after she sent them back to their realm, she dropped hints that it was not their fault." Steve added, "She used that word once, the 'Shaktra,' but then she never explained what it was."

"I don't think she knows what it is," Cindy said.

"Then how does she know about it?"

"She's remembering parts of her life as a fairy. She's told me that much."

"But she doesn't give you any details?"

"Not really," Cindy said.

"Has she told you anything about the Yanti?" Steve asked.

"Hints. When she first found it on the mountaintop, she knew exactly what to do with it to send the elementals packing. Since then I think she's been experimenting with it, but not getting very far. She did tell me that she had no idea where it came from. In fact, she gave me the impression that she didn't even know where it came from when she was a fairy."

"That's odd," Steve said.

Cindy studied Ali. "The poor girl, she really does have the weight of the world on her shoulders."

"What do you think about her going into the elemental kingdom alone?"

"She won't be alone. She'll have Farble and Paddy with her."

Steve waved his hand. "They could turn against her in a heartbeat."

Cindy shook her head. "They love her, or at least they respect her. But I told you at the house how I felt. It's one trip where I don't think we can help her."

"I don't like it," Steve muttered.

"You don't like it because you feel guilty for not going. So do I. But she's right, we would just slow her down."

"I disagree. Say she's able to open the fourth door. What if she's killed the second she gets over there? We wouldn't even know. She would just be . . . gone."

"I don't think Ali's that easy to kill nowadays," Cindy said.

"She has power but she's still human. If she gets shot in the heart with an arrow, or stabbed in the back with a knife, she'll die, just like you and me."

"Don't talk that way," Cindy said.

Steve shook his head. "I'm not ready to let her go off on her own."

"Do you think you can stop her?"

The question shut him up. He went back to staring out the window, while Cindy returned to her magazine. The scenery was lovely—with great views of Pete's Peak, its snow-covered summit brilliant in the summer sun—but the trip was nevertheless long and tedious. It seemed to Steve as if the bus stopped every time it saw a bench. He could not wait until he was sixteen and had a driver's license.

Ali finally sat up and waved for them to join her in the back. They were quick to oblige, and asked how she was feeling. Fine, she said, although her eyes looked tired.

"I heard you two talking about me," Ali said.

"You were supposed to be sleeping," Cindy said.

"Did you hear what we said?" Steve asked.

"You can doubt me, I don't mind. Half of what I say must sound crazy."

"*Half?*" Cindy said.

Ali smiled. It was such a simple thing: teeth, lips, and a mouth working together. But to Steve Ali's grin was more magical than the Yanti and the entire elemental kingdom put together. Ali did not simply smile—she *radiated*.

"I guess it's pretty freaky to imagine another timeline," Ali said.

"How did we die in that . . . time?" Steve asked, not sure if he wanted to know. Ali lost her smile and stared at him.

"Bravely," she said.

Steve felt a chill. "Well, if we die in this timeline, go back there and save us again. Okay?"

"Sure." Ali changed the subject. "When we get to Omega Overtures, I want to go in first—by myself."

That did not go over well.

"The only reason we're taking this stupid bus ride is to help you out," Cindy said.

"We're not going to stand out in the parking lot," Steve said.

Ali raised her hand. "I just want to check out the scene, then you can join me."

"You're worried the person who sent those e-mails is the Shaktra?" Cindy asked.

Ali looked surprised, wary. "I never spoke to you about that."

"You spoke to Lord Vak about it, and I was there, remember?" Cindy said.

"We know you're worried about it, whatever it is," Steve said.

Ali was evasive. "I doubt it's at Omega Overtures. I'm just being cautious."

"If the Shaktra is there, it's odd it would use its name in an e-mail," Steve said.

The observation struck Ali. "It is odd," she agreed.

"What are you looking for at the company?" Cindy asked her.

"Anything unusual. I plan to go in as a big fan of Omega Overlord, try to weasel my way in to see someone in publicity. To do that, I need you guys to tell me everything you know about the game."

"Do you have a fairy power that allows you to force your will on someone?" Steve asked.

"That doesn't sound like a power I would want," she replied, not answering his question. "And it's not necessary. I just need to get my foot in the door, that's all. I'm pretty sure I'll sense if something is wrong there."

For the next thirty minutes Ali drilled them about the game, and by the time they reached Toule, she probably could have played it and won. Steve was not sure if it was because of her recent change or not, but it seemed to him that Ali had developed a virtually perfect memory.

The bus let them off downtown. For a city that had been leveled by an explosion, they saw no overt signs of calamity. Of course, that had been thirteen years ago, almost fourteen. Why, Steve thought, they had been busy being born right then.

Yet there *were* signs, if one looked close. The buildings were mostly new. None had the flair of structures that had been hammered together at the turn of the last century. Also, the town had many trees, but none were that tall, or etched with the deep lines of a proud history. Toule was pretty, surrounded by thick forest, as was Breakwater, and it was considerably larger than their own hometown.

Yet the city lacked a center; more, it seemed to lack soul. There was a main street, no town square, and the former looked as if it had been erected hastily, maybe to put a quick bandage on the agony the city had gone through when the waves of fire had swept its streets.

However, on the north side of town, closest to the mountain

and sheltered by the trees, was a modern structure that could only have been the home of a successful business. Omega Overtures headquarters was an awesome mosaic of glass cubes. It was as if each section had been fused together without regard to gravity, falling trees, or, for that matter, cost. Steve doubted there was an office with a lousy view in the whole building.

Omega's logo—fitted in ruby red on the side of the structure, in exotic contrast to the darkly tinted windows—was a bundle of three hypnotic wavy lines. He recognized the logo from the side of the game boxes.

Ali stared at the building for a long time without speaking. Cindy and Steve could only watch and wait. Finally Ali lowered her gaze, put a hand to her head.

"You okay?" Steve asked.

"I'm fine," she said.

"Is Darth Vader in there or what?" Cindy asked.

"There's something weird . . ." Ali frowned. "Not what I expected."

"That's helpful," Steve muttered.

Ali glanced at him. This time her smile was forced. It did not shine, it just made him more uneasy. He could not help feeling a pinch at the thought of her high up on the mountain at night, with only a leprechaun and a troll for company. Worse, he could not imagine having the courage to walk through a door—whatever its color—without any idea where it led. That was part of the reason he admired her. She reminded him of all his shortcomings, and desires, with the same look. When she spoke next, it was almost as if she read his mind.

"You're not my slave, you know," she said. "You don't have to do what I say."

"We're afraid not to," he said.

Ali scanned the area, pointed. "If you want, you can hang out in that park until I return. I don't think I'll be long."

"I want ice cream," Cindy said.

"Get whatever you want." Ali began to walk away. "Wish me luck."

"Always," Steve whispered, although he did not think she heard him.

CHAPTER

6

Ali had felt as if she was being watched when she had studied the building. The odd thing was, two weeks earlier, she had felt the identical sensation, as if the same pair of eyes had stared at her both times. Back then, in the middle of the night, she'd had a disturbing dream. She was standing in an icy chamber, with five glass coffins set on top of a row of low black boulders. The clear box on her left drew her attention, for a beautiful woman with long red hair lay sleeping in it. But as she approached, the case began to fill with bubbling red liquid. It might have been steaming blood, or worse, acid. As the red goo spread over the woman, she began to dissolve, like a wax doll in a boiling pot. In seconds there was nothing left but the sick liquid, with bits of hair and bone. It began to spill onto the floor and splash her legs, and she let out a scream. . . .

And that's when she had awakened, feeling a terrible sense of loss.

Then she had heard a sound outside.

Someone . . . a woman . . . whispering.

Putting on her robe over her pajamas, she had climbed out of bed and went out on the front porch, where she had searched up and down the block.

Only there had been no one there. The whispering had stopped.

"Must have imagined it," she muttered to herself.

Yet she had felt as if she was being watched.

Even when she had gone back inside, the feeling had persisted.

Now she felt the same sensation, but it was lessening, as if whoever was watching her was slowly turning their gaze in another direction. Halfway to Omega's headquarters, Ali lost the sense of being watched altogether.

Inside the building's lobby, she found a receptionist and a blind man. The latter sat on a sofa near the front door, holding a long white cane. He was close to thirty, with dark wavy hair and sunglasses so thick she could not catch a glimpse of his eyes. He was extremely thin, incredibly pale—so white he could have been born on the moon.

The receptionist was on the phone, preoccupied, but the man turned his head in Ali's direction as she came through the door. It was a curious sensation to feel his stare, and know that there was nothing behind it. But it did not remind her of the cold feeling of being watched she had experienced minutes ago. The man stared a few inches off to her left. It was obvious that he was completely blind.

"Are you the messenger boy?" he asked.

"No. I'm just . . . a girl."

"Oh."

She noticed his ID badge. "Do you work for Omega?" she asked.

"Yes."

"I'm a big fan of your games."

The man was interested. "Which game is your favorite?"

"Overlord. My friends and I play it all the time."

The man gave her a gentle smile. "I'm so glad. I helped design it. If you'll permit me to brag a little, I'll go so far as to admit that I came up with the idea for it."

"Really? Are you a programmer or something?"

"I can program computers, but technically I'm called a systems analyst. I oversee a group of fifty programmers. Most of us worked on Overlord together." He added, "It took us three years to design that game."

"I'm not surprised. The game has great visuals and the plot is so complex." She realized she was repeating Steve word for word. Stepping near the blind man, she said, "I'm doing a report for a summer school English class on your games. I came here to see if I could talk to someone who worked on Overlord. Would it be okay if I asked you a few questions?"

"Sure. But when the messenger comes, I'll have to take the package he's bringing to a few of my people in the back. It's promotional material we're working on for a new game—the sequel to Overlord." The blind man added, "You might want to mention that in your paper."

"What's it called?"

"Armageddon."

Ali rubbed her hands together in anticipation. "Sounds wicked, I can't wait. So it carries on the theme of the end of the world, and machines taking over, and all that?"

"It's a little more complicated than that. As you know from playing Overlord, the machines alone don't really take over. It's the hybrid of them, and humans—the cyborgs—that gain ultimate control. But in Armageddon we take it a step further. We introduce a third element."

"What is it?" Ali asked.

The man smiled again. His lips were thin, a little dry, and he had the whitest teeth. "That's a secret, I'm sorry. My boss would have my head if I talked about it."

"Who's your boss?"

"Sheri Smith. She's an amazing woman. She started this company only seven years ago and built it into an industry leader. If I was in your shoes, I'd try to interview her for your paper. She's very quotable. Would you believe she's younger than me?"

"How old are you?" Ali asked.

He chuckled. "How old do I look?"

"Thirty."

He nodded. "Thirty-two. You?"

"Thirteen."

"You sound older."

"I try," Ali said.

"What's your name by the way?"

"Lisa Morgan. Yours?"

He held out his hand. "Mike Havor. Pleased to meet you, Lisa."

She shook his hand, he had a light grip. "Pleased to meet you."

"Are you from around here?"

"I'm from Bale." That was twenty miles south of Toule.

"I live here in town so I don't have to drive to work." He smiled at his own joke. "Actually, I'm able to walk to work. I live down the block."

"May I ask a blunt question?"

He nodded. "You want to know how a blind person is able to work with a team of programmers designing a video game?"

"I would imagine it would be hard."

"I wasn't born blind. I lost my sight in an accident when I was young. So I know what stuff looks like, and I know what I want the games to look like. But I admit I need constant input on how the game is coming to life. I don't rely on just one person. I listen to a dozen people, then form a mental image. Ms. Smith helps me the most. We work together closely. Maybe you can use that fact in your paper. You see, Ms. Smith doesn't come from a computer background, but a literary one. She's published several children's books under various pen names."

Ali made a mental note to check out those books. "Isn't it strange for someone to start a computer company and not be versed in computers?" she asked.

"It's not as strange as you would think. Programmers can be hired and told what to do. It's vision that's crucial, and Ms. Smith has that in spades. I told you I came up with the concept for Overlord, but she was the one to see its potential. Before we met, I tried shopping it all over the country and got nowhere. I owe her a lot."

"Is she in today?"

"She's in a series of meetings. I've been trying to talk to her myself all day. But if you hang around, you might get five minutes with her. I can't promise you anything, but I can put in a word for you."

"That's awfully nice of you, Mr. Havor."

"Mike, please."

"I notice you never call your boss Sheri."

He chuckled. "Well, she is the boss, and she is a little less informal than most of us around here. Not to say she's unpleasant, you understand, she's always very polite. But she hates to waste time. If you do get to meet with her, ask your questions quickly. That way you'll get the most out of her."

"I'll keep that in mind," Ali said.

A minute later the messenger boy arrived with the package Mike was waiting for. Mike signed for it and started for the back, but he asked Ali if she wanted to have a look at the promotional materials and she said sure. So without really trying, she took one step deeper into the company.

As they were walking down a long hallway—Mike expertly waving his cane in front of him—they passed a painting of a beautiful woman with long blond hair and green eyes. The name at the bottom of the painting read: SHERI SMITH. Mike was right, she looked younger than he did, not more than thirty, perhaps a lot less. And the woman's green eyes were so bright, Ali felt as if she were staring into a mirror.

Outside, in the park, Cindy licked a chocolate ice cream cone while Steve worked on a thick vanilla shake. The dessert—from a small shop on the main street—was better than any Steve had tasted before. Apparently they made their own ice cream fresh every morning. If there had been a similar shop in Breakwater, he thought, he would weigh two hundred pounds.

Despite the fantastic sugar fix, the two of them felt frustrated. They wanted to help Ali save the world, and they knew they could not help her because the world was too big and they were too human. When it came right down to it, he thought, they were no better than cheerleaders. Steve expressed his thoughts aloud to Cindy.

"True," Cindy agreed. "There ain't nothing a mere mortal can do to stop Lord Vak from bringing that freaky army back here again."

"How do you think he's going to do it without the Yanti?" Steve asked.

"I don't know, but Ali sure thinks he can. And watching those two arguing on top of the mountain, I'd have to say that's one elf king who's used to getting his own way. I told you before, he could have taken the Yanti from Ali if he'd wanted to. Her magic was not working so good on him."

"I've never understood that. Why didn't he take it?"

"He must have thought it didn't matter."

Steve got an idea. "Is it possible he wanted her to have it?"

"Who knows? But one thing's for sure, he was not your warm-and-fuzzy kind of elf."

A young girl came over to them, and reached for Cindy's ice cream cone. She was small, maybe six years old, had short red hair and dull violet eyes. Her eyes were so flat, Steve was not sure if she was able to see out of them. Her expression was utterly blank, as well. Steve suspected she was mentally retarded, or worse. Yet her hair, although poorly kept, was as bright and shiny as Ali's. Steve could not help noticing it was *exactly* the same color, and had *exactly* the same luster. It looked like a living flame.

The girl wore white pants and a torn yellow shirt. There were dark smudges on her right cheek and between her eyebrows. Her fingers—as they reached for Cindy's cone—were dirty. She looked like an orphan.

"Want . . . want . . ." she said, the words badly slurred.

Cindy glanced at Steve. "What should I do?"

"Say no."

"Steve! You see how she is."

"Give it to her then, as long as you don't want it back."

Cindy looked around. "I wonder if she has a guardian or something."

"Want . . . want . . . want . . ."

"She looks like she needs one," he said.

Cindy handed over the cone, spoke kindly. "You can have it if you want, sweetie. But try not to spill it on your clothes. . . ."

Too late. The second the girl took the cone, she opened her mouth wide, tried to bite off the entire top, and a clump of the ice cream plopped onto her pants near her knee. The girl did not even notice; she kept digging into the cone. Within a minute her face was smeared with chocolate. They were not even sure if she was enjoying herself. She didn't smile, that's for sure. Maybe she did not know how.

"I think she's hungry," Steve said.

"She looks famished. Do you think we should find a cop, turn her over to him?"

"That's an idea. What do you think of her hair?"

"It looks like Ali's."

"Think that's a coincidence?"

Cindy paused. "What do you mean?"

Steve was not given a chance to reply. A middle-aged Latina woman suddenly appeared, carrying a grocery bag, and from the look on her face she appeared relieved to see the young girl.

"Nira, where did you get off to? You had me scared to death!" the woman cried, bending over to take the cone from the girl, wiping her face with a piece of tissue paper. The woman was dressed plainly in a long brown dress, had a thick accent, and more than a hint of gray in her hair.

"Sorry, we gave it to her," Cindy said.

"She was begging for it," Steve added.

The woman glanced at them, smiled. She had a broad face, and looked as if she'd had a hard life. For some reason, Steve immediately got the impression she'd come from a tiny village where people labored from sunup to sundown. She was big boned, and had heavy calluses on both hands. Yet, unlike the girl, her face was expressive. Clearly she was not dumb, although she had managed to lose the little girl for a time.

65

The woman nodded her head at their remarks. "You were just being friendly, which is more than I can say for most of the folks around here. What are your names?"

"I'm Cindy and this is Steve," Cindy replied.

"I'm Rose. Nice to meet you both." She did not offer her hand.

"Nice to meet you. Do you take care of this child?" Cindy asked.

"She is my responsibility. But she got away from me in the store. I don't know how. She was there one second, gone the next." Holding on to Nira's hand, Rose took a weary breath and gestured to their bench. "Mind if I sit down?"

"Go right ahead," Cindy said, moving closer to Steve as Rose sat down. It seemed Cindy could not take her eyes off the girl. "Her name's Nira?"

"Nira Smith. Her mother's president of that big company you see up there on the hill. She's a busy woman, smart—an important person in the community. She hired me a year ago to take care of Nira, and that's what I do." Rose added, "I'm from Colombia."

"Do you have family here?" Steve asked.

Rose lifted Nira onto her lap, continued to wipe at her face with the tissues, while Nira struggled to get her ice cream back. "*Want . . . Want . . . Want . . .*" It was not to be. The woman threw what was left of the cone in a nearby garbage can.

"Nira's my family now," Rose replied.

Steve hesitated. "What's wrong with her?"

"She's autistic."

"Was she born that way?" Cindy asked.

"Her mother says no. But Nira got vaccinations when she was a year old and she had an allergic reaction. . . ." Rose shrugged. "The shots might have done it, who knows? She's been this way since I met her."

66

"Does she recognize you?" Cindy asked.

The woman smiled at the girl, touched her right ear. "She *knows* me. We're best friends, aren't we? Yeah, you're my girl, the best girl in the whole world." She glanced at them, tried to explain. "There's lots of love inside her. She can't express it but I feel it."

"She has beautiful hair," Steve said. "Does it come from her mother?"

"Her mother is blond, but their eyes are similar. Why do you ask?"

"Just wondering," Steve said.

"Thanks so much for finding her. I'm so embarrassed. She's never gotten away from me before. For a minute there, I was in a total panic. I was imagining having to call Ms. Smith and tell her that I had lost her daughter." Rose shuddered. "That would have been terrible."

"How did you meet Nira's mother?" Steve asked.

"In Colombia, through friends. She was there, shopping. They have the best emeralds in Colombia, and they go so well with Ms. Smith's eyes. She has a beautiful collection of them."

"They sound lovely. Do you miss home?" Cindy asked.

"This is my home now," she said, partially repeating her earlier remark. As they spoke, the woman continued to stroke Nira's hair, which seemed to make the girl forget about the ice cream cone. Nira just stared off into the distance, her face as empty as a prison wall.

It occurred to Steve he might be able to find out more about Omega Overtures from Rose than Ali could fumbling around inside the company's headquarters. Anything to quit being a cheerleader . . .

"Ms. Smith's company makes computer games, doesn't it?" he asked.

"Yes. They're very successful."

"I've played a few, they're great," Steve went on. "I've always been impressed that their company grew so quickly. Ms. Smith must be a genius."

Rose hesitated. "She's more a businesswoman, rather than a creative type. She works long hours and she makes everyone around her work hard. Understand, I'm not saying that's a bad thing. To be in her position you have to know how to get the most out of your people." Rose lowered her voice, leaned closer. "But—between you and me—I wish she took more time for her daughter."

"Toule is sort of out of the way," Steve said. "I'm surprised she decided to locate her company here. Why didn't she set up shop in Silicon Valley? Or in a big city like L.A. or San Francisco? Or Portland or Seattle?"

"It's a pretty town. Anyone would want to live here. Where are you two from?"

"Bale," Steve said. Ali had told them not to speak of Breakwater. She had also told them not to give out their real names to anyone in town, although Cindy had already broken that rule.

Steve was about to ask more about Ms. Smith when something horrible happened fifty feet in front of them. A blond teenage boy—he was a year or two older than them—was casually walking across the street, in the crosswalk, with headphones on, a skateboard in his hands, when a red SUV came around the block and raced toward him. Even with the music in his ears, the guy heard the vehicle and looked up. That was it—he didn't have time to react, or if he did, the sight of the onrushing monster froze him in place.

The SUV hit him smack on, doing at least forty-five miles an hour. The force of the impact tossed the guy into the air for a second, then he hit the windshield and flew even higher. Before he landed, the vehicle was already accelerating, tearing down the main street.

The rest of the day Steve kept remembering the noise the guy's body made when he finally crashed onto the asphalt—a sick mushy sound, as if half his bones had shattered on impact, and then *sliced* into his muscles. Steve doubted that anybody could take such a hit and survive. They all jumped to their feet.

Rose screamed. "That's Freddy! Freddy Degear!"

"Oh no! You know him?" Cindy cried.

Obviously, Rose knew him well. She had let go of Nira, and put a trembling hand to her mouth. "He's the son of our next-door neighbor. This is horrible." She drew in a breath. "Is he alive?"

A pool of blood had begun to form around Freddy, but he was moving, making noises. Steve did not run to his side. Already a policeman knelt beside the guy, and other help was on the way.

"He's alive. I'm sure an ambulance will be here soon," Steve said to Rose.

Rose trembled. "Oh God. I have to tell his mother."

"I have a cell phone you can use," Cindy offered, reaching for her back pocket, clearly upset by the accident.

Rose shook her head. "I can't tell her this on the phone! Freddy's her only son! I have to see her!" Rose paused, glanced down at Nira, then up at the sky. It was almost as if in the midst of her misery, she was praying to be told what to do next. Cindy, who had yet to regain her color, took a step toward the woman.

"We could watch Nira for a few minutes, if it would help," she said.

Rose hesitated. "I don't know. Poor Freddy. What should I do?"

"You have to tell his mother what's happened," Steve said.

Rose came to a sudden decision, nodded her head. "All right then, I'll go, I have to go. Just keep Nira beside you at all times. I won't be gone long, I promise."

Cindy nodded. "We'll keep an eye on her. Take as much time as you need."

Rose hesitated once more, just for a second, then hurried off down the street.

An ambulance arrived a few minutes later. By then a sizable crowd had gathered around the fallen boy, and it was difficult to tell if he was still moving. Steve could see the blood all over the ground, and people got it on their shoes—that did not look good.

"It was like that SUV hit him on purpose," Steve said.

"It didn't look like an accident," Cindy agreed, sitting with her back to the scene of the accident, trying to shield Nira from the gruesome sight. For her part the girl appeared unaware that anything out of the ordinary had happened. Nira played with Cindy's blond curls, which seemed to relax her.

The ambulance loaded up Freddy and turned on its siren and raced off. From talking to people in the crowd, Steve discovered the hospital was only two blocks away.

As the sound of the ambulance's sirens faded, the gathering began to disperse. However, two policemen remained and roped off the area, and took pictures of the puddle of blood from a dozen different angles. Eventually they asked around for witnesses. Steve and Cindy were, of course, prime material. They had been standing only a few feet away. But Steve was reluctant to get involved. He said as much to Cindy.

"But we have to tell the police what we saw," Cindy said.

Steve nodded in the direction of Omega's headquarters.

"I see Ali coming, let's ask her," he said.

───────

Walking back to her friends, Ali had heard the ambulance but had no idea what had happened. Yet that was not entirely true. Just before she had said goodbye to Mike Havor, she had felt a wave of dizziness, and had known from experience that there was a good chance that someone in the immediate environment had just been hurt. The empathic response was just another one of her fairy gifts, and it was a hard one to live with because it was a hard world and people were always getting hurt.

Then she had seen the dark puddle of blood in the middle of the crosswalk, her friends waiting nearby, and policemen scouring the area. Steve gestured for her to talk to them away from the cops, on the other side of the small park. For some reason Cindy was holding on to a little girl with a listless face and bright red hair. None of them spoke until they were some distance from what had clearly been an ugly accident.

"You won't believe what we just saw," Steve began. He told her the whole story about Freddy and the SUV, before Cindy backed up in time and explained how they had managed to inherit Nira.

"Does this Rose expect you guys to stay here?" Ali asked.

"Yes," Cindy said, but she gave Steve a quick glance.

"I think she'll go to the hospital first, with the guy's mom, to see how he's doing," Steve said. "That's what I would do."

"We could go there and meet her," Cindy suggested, and there was an odd note in her voice.

"If Rose comes back here looking for Nira and you're gone, she'll report you as kidnappers," Ali said.

"We still think we should go to the hospital," Steve said.

"Why?" she said.

Steve and Cindy exchanged looks.

"We were wondering, you know, if you could help the guy," Cindy said.

"The way you helped Ted Wilson," Steve added.

Ali frowned. "He was just taken in. I doubt I could get close enough to help him. I certainly couldn't get him alone."

"The SUV smashed him real bad," Cindy said, wiping away a tear. "He was a nice-looking guy. I was just thinking it would be a pity, with you so close and everything, if we didn't at least try to help him."

Ali turned to Steve. "You say he was run down on purpose?"

"It looked that way." He added, "If we go to the hospital now, you might be able to act like you're his sister. They might let you in to see him."

"It sounds like his mom is going to be there," Ali said.

"We could beat her there," Steve said.

"Don't you want to try to heal him, Ali?" Cindy asked, pain in her voice.

"Sure I want to help him. But I cannot afford to call attention to myself, not when I'm just about to go back up the mountain." Ali glanced toward the blood, added, "Odd that guy should get run down the minute we show up."

"I thought the same thing," Steve said.

Cindy was not buying it. "It had nothing to do with us!"

Ali studied Nira, the little girl's red hair and the mark between her eyebrows. At first the mark looked like dirt to Ali, but when she knelt in front of the child and examined it closer, she saw that it was more a scar or a tattoo. Gray in color, with flaky red edges, it bore the distinct impression of a human thumb print.

Ali stared deep into Nira's eyes. The girl's blank expression did not change.

Yet Ali felt something in those eyes. Something vast and inexplicable, and it made her shiver. Looking at the girl's face was like reaching the edge of a cliff that overlooked an ocean without waves. She probably was autistic, but what did the word really mean? A soul without a personality attached? Ali sensed that Nira was cut off from the world, for whatever reason, but that there was still a world of life inside her.

"Rose hardly knows you guys. Why did she leave Nira with you?" Ali asked.

"She was in a panic. She could see we were good people," Cindy said.

"*We* were the ones who offered to watch her," Steve said, adding, "Seriously, Ali, if you're going to try to help the guy, we have to go now."

Still, Ali had her doubts. "Rose works for Ms. Smith?"

"Yes," Steve said. "She seems like a nice lady."

"So Nira is Ms. Smith's daughter?" Ali asked.

"That's what we were told," Steve said.

"Is there a Mr. Smith?" Ali asked.

"We don't know their whole family situation!" Cindy cried impatiently.

Ali ignored her for a moment. "Did Rose give you a phone number where you could call her?" she asked.

"No," Steve said. "But if you'd like, I can stay here until Rose returns."

"Someone should stay here," Ali agreed.

Cindy acted exasperated. "That guy could be dying this very second! Are we going to the hospital or not?"

Ali continued to study Nira. Their hair could have been cut from the same cloth.

"Let's go to the hospital," Ali said.

As they walked down the main street, leaving Steve behind, Nira reached up and took Ali's hand. She took it and would not let go.

———

They were too late. There was a small crowd gathered in the lobby of the clinic and they quickly heard that the teenager who had been hit by the SUV was dead. Ali was surprised to see Cindy burst out in tears, but felt too distracted to comfort her. The death of Freddy continued to strike her as an extraordinary coincidence, although for the life of her she could not imagine how he could be connected to them.

Even if he was dead, she still wanted to see him.

She told Cindy as much, and her friend stared at her like she was a ghoul.

"Leave him alone," Cindy whispered, obviously drawing a line between healing and resurrection.

"You brought me here," Ali said. She tried to give the little girl back to Cindy. "Here, take Nira, and look around for Rose."

But Nira would not let go of her hand, and she was surprisingly strong. Ali was not sure what to do. Autism or not, she did not want to expose the girl to a dead body, particularly a bloody one. On the other hand, she was not even sure if she could get to Freddy. Steve's idea of acting like Freddy's sister was good in theory, as long as there was no family around, but in practice it might get her arrested. Again, she hated to take unnecessary risks with Pete's Peak looming in her immediate future.

Ali knelt in front of Nira, in a corner of the lobby, spoke in a firm voice. "Nira, I have to go. You have to let me go. Cindy will take care of you until Rose comes back."

In response Nira reached out and put her hand on Ali's chest. *Exactly* where Ali had the Yanti hidden beneath her shirt.

Again, Ali felt a vastness, as if the little girl was not an empty shell, but a window into a place where there were no boundaries. Yet not a flicker of light shone in Nira's dull eyes. She could have been the one who was dead.

The Yanti suddenly felt *hot*. As it had when she had healed Ted Wilson.

Another coincidence. Ali wondered what it meant.

But how could they heal Freddy? He was already dead. . . .

Ali stood. "I'll take Nira with me," she said.

"You're not taking her into the morgue!" Cindy snapped.

Ali hesitated, not sure if she was trying to further her investigation of Omega and Ms. Smith, or if she was just indulging in careless behavior. She spoke to Cindy, "I'll try to keep her from seeing anything gross."

Cindy shook her head, angry now. Ali ignored her.

Hand in hand, Ali and Nira walked deeper into the hospital's ER.

They never did run into Freddy's family—which in itself was odd, Ali thought—but they bumped into plenty of nurses and doctors, and when Ali said that she was there to say goodbye to her brother, she was led to an isolated cubicle, whose windows had been curtained off. Freddy was inside, she was told by an elderly nurse, who withdrew out of sight.

Ali tried to keep Nira outside, yet the little girl refused to give up her hand. Ali could have broken the grip by force, of course, but it was as if Nira was trying to tell her that she liked her. Under Ali's shirt, the Yanti continued to throb with waves of heat. It had never been so hot before. . . .

Together, they stepped inside the tiny room.

A weak corner lamp was the only source of light. As a result, there were more shadows than details, which Ali found particularly distressing with a dead body lying in the center of the room. He was covered, largely, but his blond hair stuck out of the top of a green sheet that was stained red, and the sight of it depressed Ali. As did the idea that their arrival in town might have caused the guy's death. She had to fight to remind herself that she had not been driving the SUV, and that there was still a good chance it had been nothing but a horrible accident.

Hoping Nira could not see up on the bed, Ali stepped to Freddy's side and, with her free hand, gently pulled back the sheet. The nurses had done their best to wipe away the blood, but the right side of his face was badly swollen, and a sad blue color. His eyes were closed, thankfully. He did not look at peace but he was not suffering anymore, either—and for that she was grateful.

It was as Ali had anticipated. She did not recognize him.

Nira had finally let go of her hand, but she was trying to climb up on the bed.

"Stop, you have to leave him alone," Ali scolded, trying to get her back on the floor. But once more the girl was tough, and she was beside Freddy, and staring at his wounded face, before Ali could get a grip on her.

Yet Nira did no more than stare. She did not reach for Freddy's hand, nor did she try to touch his bloody hair. Ali assumed the girl did not understand what she was looking at, and decided it was probably for the best.

But the Yanti under Ali's shirt, resting on the skin above her heart, went from being hot to unbearably hot. Letting out a cry, Ali took a step back and reached under her shirt and pulled out the Yanti. The heat was like a flame. She did not even try to pull it over her head. Breaking the silk cord it was strung on, she tossed it onto the edge of the bed, near Freddy's left arm. Even after she had let it go, she could feel the waves of heat radiating from it. Had Freddy been frozen, and not dead, they could have fixed him in a hurry.

The Yanti was a seven-sided gold band, with a gold triangle inside, which in turn had a tiny diamond in the center of it. The entire band was only two inches across. But the most remarkable thing about it was that the three pieces—the band, the triangle, and the diamond—had only space between them. Yet they were each held in place, in perfect symmetry, by an invisible force that could not be crossed. Many times she had tried to slip a needle between the pieces and had been blocked. Once, she had taken a hammer and nail from the garage and pounded away, and even that had been unable to pierce the field that cemented the medallion. She did not remember much about the Yanti from her life as a fairy, but she did recall that more than a few high fairies believed it to be indestructible.

Nira reached over and picked up the Yanti.

"Don't! You'll burn yourself!" Ali cried, lunging forward.

The strange girl stared at her. The heat did nothing to her flesh.

Ali froze. "Who are you?" she gasped.

As if in response, Nira placed the Yanti on her forehead, her heart, and then on the top of her head, in quick succession before she reached over and grabbed Freddy's left hand. It might have been rigor mortis setting in, but his spine slowly arched as his head tilted back and his eyelids popped open. The pupils were rolled back; the whites of his eyes were pink, and they were staring at nothing, and always would be. . . .

Because the guy was dead . . .

Yet he was not acting like it. He should not have been acting at all! It was as if a force had entered his body, a watery snake, and it was crawling through him. As his head went back his jaw dropped and his mouth opened and a lungful of air escaped his crushed chest. Ali prayed it was nothing more than an extremely tardy death rattle, but as his final breath came out of his body, she heard a word, and it echoed in the room like a moan in the coffin of a soul who had been placed too soon in the grave.

"Shakkkkkkkk . . . traaaaaa . . ."

Ali put her hands over her ears, closed her eyes, and if she didn't scream she should have. The ugliness of the word, the *name*, the horror of its source, made her want to vomit. But she gathered herself quickly, for she realized the heat radiating from the Yanti had stopped. Indeed, the room felt cold, as if the previous air had been sucked right out of it, through a crack in reality. Opening her eyes, she snatched the Yanti from Nira, who let go of Freddy's hand. Once again, he lay still, although his eyes were still open. Moving closer, Ali reached out to shut them. It was then, under his blond hair and drying blood, that she saw the same thumbprint that Nira had between her eyebrows.

Outside, in the sun, in the park where Cindy and Steve had been waiting earlier, Ali sat on a bench with her friends and debated what she should do next. The debate was both inside and out. Rose had not returned yet. The next bus to Breakwater left in fifteen minutes. Ali needed to catch it if she were to get home in time to pack for her trip up the mountain. Earlier, after saying goodbye to Mike Havor and Omega, she had decided to go that night. But now she had to wonder what was more important . . .

Nira. The girl had a power over the Yanti Ali did not possess.

The Yanti . . . Ali had it in her pocket now.

Yet Nira was autistic. She could not speak. Cindy had bought her an ice cream cone—apparently it was her second of the day—and the girl had smeared half of it on her face. Ali worried she could examine Nira for days and learn nothing new. Yet she supposed talking to her nanny might teach her a thing or two. Where was Rose anyway? Ali still found it hard to understand why the woman had run off and left Nira with them. None of them had seen Rose at the hospital. Ali found the behavior suspicious, and said as much to the others.

"You didn't meet her, she's great with Nira," Cindy said.

"As far as I can tell, she's lost her twice in the same afternoon," Ali said.

"I'm sure she'll be back soon," Steve said. "When you think about it, she's only been gone half an hour."

"It feels longer than that," Ali said.

Steve checked his watch. "Thirty-five minutes since Rose left, that's all."

Ali gestured to Nira. "There's something weird about this girl, beside her mental handicap. I don't want you to hang out with her if I leave."

"That's silly," Cindy snapped. "She's harmless."

"*If* you leave?" Steve asked. "I thought that was a done deal."

"I'm having second thoughts," Ali muttered.

"Why? What did you learn at Omega?" Steve asked.

"As you know, the president of Omega is named Sheri Smith. From talking to one of her main employees, she sounds like the kind of person who can move mountains. She's tough, smart, and pushes her people to exhaustion."

"That doesn't make her a threat to the human race," Steve said.

"True," Ali agreed. "But I saw a picture of her, and it was weird; she has the same eyes as Mom and me. And here she has this daughter—that no one is bothering to keep track of—who has the same hair as us."

"What are you saying?" Steve asked.

Ali hesitated. "I don't know, but this little girl seems to recognize the Yanti."

The others gasped. "How do you know that?" Cindy demanded.

"I don't think she can recognize her own mother," Steve said.

Ali held up her hand. "I'm telling you the truth. She has some connection to the Yanti. She might even have some control over it. That's why I don't want you guys to hang out with her if I leave. To me, she's a wild card."

"Are you saying they are fairies, too?" Steve asked.

"I'm not sure what they are," Ali said.

"What exactly did you find out at the company?" Steve asked.

Ali gave them a quick rundown on her meeting with Mike Havor.

Neither Steve nor Cindy acted that impressed.

"He sounds like a nice guy," Steve said.

Ali hesitated. "He was very appealing. But . . ."

"But what?" Steve asked.

"Nothing," Ali said.

Cindy had Nira on her mind. "We cannot leave here until Rose comes back."

"*I* have to leave here in a few minutes," Ali said.

"*If* you go," Steve said.

Ali nodded. "If I go."

"I don't think you should," Steve said. "Like I said before, the e-mails to Karl were real. If you suspect this woman, Ms. Smith, is the Shaktra, I don't see how you can justify leaving. You have to dig deeper into them, into the company, into this town. To me, this whole place is a mystery. I mean, how many towns get burned to the ground?"

Ali glanced at her watch, fretted. "I'm torn, I don't know what to do."

"Stay," Steve said.

"Tell us what Nira did with the Yanti to make you suspect her," Cindy said.

Ali regretted bringing up the girl's strangeness. She saw now that it made them more curious about Nira. And she was aware that they felt frustrated that they could not help her more. If she left tonight, she feared they would return to Toule tomorrow and try to follow up on an investigation she probably should never have started. At least she had not told them about the wizard in the barbershop. If she had, they would no doubt race over to have Harry cut their hair. . . .

The wizard added to her conflict. The same questions plagued her. Where was he from? When he vanished, did he pop back into the elemental kingdom? Was that a Yanti around his neck? Did he show it to her to mock her?

Another question: If he was from here—Earth—was that enough reason for her to listen to Steve and postpone her trip up the mountain? Certain facts made her doubt his humanity. Besides his weird-looking eyes, he had been afraid to let her see him in the mirror.

Ali shook her head in response to Cindy's question.

"The family's weird," Ali said. "They have a nanny who loses little girls, the girl herself can't talk, and Ms. Smith sounds like a slave driver. I need you guys to promise me you'll stay away from here until we can examine the situation together." She added, "Trust me, I'm not trying to cut you out of the action."

"But you are trying to protect us," Steve said. "You're always trying to do that. That does not help you or us. Cindy is right—we cannot leave until Rose returns. We have already made friends with her, and she is a great source of information about Ms. Smith—who might be the Shaktra if I read you right."

"She's not the Shaktra!" Ali snapped. "That creature is in the elemental kingdom! My mother is there, too! That is why I have to go!"

An uncomfortable silence settled between them. Finally Cindy spoke.

"Ali, you're worried about the Shaktra and Lord Vak, and you're anxious the elementals are going to return. But it's your mother that haunts you. If you're sure she's not in this world, then you must go into the other world. We support you in that decision. That's why you have to get on the next bus. But Steve's right, you can't keep treating us like children, even though we are children. You have to let us take some of the risks, and trust our judgment sometimes."

Ali heard the truth in her friend's words, knew in that instant that she was going to try to enter the elemental kingdom—*that* night. When all was said and done, she could not stop thinking about her mother.

Yet Ali did not answer Cindy right away. She studied Nira, who was still obsessed with her ice cream cone. "Why would they leave her here?" she whispered.

"Who is *they?*" Steve asked.

Ali looked over. "I hear you guys. You have to hear me. Nira is more than she appears. So is this Omega company. The man I spoke to there, Mike Havor, he told me that all their games are focused on the end of the world."

"That is why they're called Omega Overtures," Steve said. "The end of the world sells."

"But now the end might be at hand . . ."

"Ali . . ." Steve began.

"I don't like this town," Ali interrupted, standing. "Okay, I agree, you have to get Nira back to Rose, but the minute you do, catch the next bus back to Breakwater. You might get there in time to help me pack."

"We won't get there in time and you know it," Cindy said. "The next bus isn't for three hours. You will be long gone by the time we get home."

Ali nodded. "You're probably right."

"How are you going to get up to the trailhead?" Steve asked.

"With Farble and Paddy? You can't take a cab like we did last time."

"I'm going to drive my father's truck. Not the one he hauls freight in, the smaller one. Farble can sit in the back."

"When did you learn to drive?" Cindy asked.

"I've been taking the truck out late at night, trying to get the hang of it."

"That is so cool! Why didn't you take me with you?" Cindy asked.

"Because at first I kept running into stuff," Ali said.

"How are you now?" Steve asked.

Ali shrugged. "I wouldn't trust me to drive you cross-country, but I'm okay."

"You still don't have a license," Steve said.

Ali checked her watch again. "Right now that's the least of my worries. Look, call me on my cell when you're on your way home. That will put my mind at ease. Promise not to come back here when I'm gone. That's not too much to ask."

Steve stood and hugged her. "You do what you have to do and we'll do what we have to do."

Cindy hugged her as well. "Quit worrying about us. Just find your mother and come back to us."

Ali was near tears. She felt their love and their doubts, as well. Cindy and Steve had accepted that she was powerful, that she probably was queen of the fairies. But they had not accepted her as their leader. Ali could understand that, it was not right that she control their every move.

But it was not right that she should get them killed, either.

"Try to be wise," she said, as she kissed them goodbye.

Turning toward the bus, Ali glanced back at Nira. The girl had finished with her ice cream and was once more staring at her. Nira was mentally impaired—she couldn't take care of herself in the most basic ways. Nevertheless, for the third time that day, Ali felt the power of her gaze, and got the strangest impression that Nira knew something the rest of them did not.

Something that was *yet* to happen . . .

Was it possible? Nira's brain was mush, but it seemed as if records floated around inside her skull, or simply in the air near her head, of events that were yet to happen. Of course, Ali herself had gotten glimpses of the future from time to time, of things that eventually did occur, but this was far different. Here the subject matter was life and death, and as Ali stared at Nira, she couldn't shake the conviction that her last words to her friends had been totally in vain.

In the days to come, *none* of them was going to act wisely.

And one of them was not going to live long enough to talk about it.

"Not true," Ali swore, turning away from Nira and walking toward her bus.

CHAPTER

7

How does one pack to enter another dimension? When Ali returned from Toule, she sat down to make a list of what she absolutely had to bring, and discovered, to her dismay, that she had no idea what she needed. For the last month she had questioned Paddy about where he came from, but for the most part he had answered her by saying that leprechauns went about and minded their own business. Even when it came to describing the physicality of the realm, Paddy had been vague.

"It's hot in some places, Missy, cold in others. Lots of trees there. Some mountains, some desert, a little of everything."

Then he had stared at her, as if to say, You're a fairy, you should know.

One thing she had made that was going to help was a backpack for Farble, which was large enough to hold three hundred pounds. She had sewn it together using a variety of bags and belts she had purchased at an army surplus store. Farble had already tried it on—he seemed to like it. Indeed, he acted like it made him more human—or fairylike—and less trollish. To Ali, it appeared as if all trolls had lousy self-images.

Another trip to the grocery store was a necessity, and this time she had to tap into her father's account to afford her supplies. Fortunately, they all knew her at the store and did not ask any questions. As always, Farble's needs were costly. She ended up buying a hundred pounds of steak, and the box-boy was so concerned about the weight of her bags he insisted on driving her home. To save time, she let him but she did not let him past the front porch. Paddy had returned and he was in a bad mood, and Farble was in the bathroom trying to trim his eyebrows with a hacksaw. The troll wanted his sunglasses to fit better.

At the store she had bought plenty of stuff for Paddy and herself: beef jerky, cans of nuts and tuna fish, chocolate bars, trail mix, cereal, and batteries for her flashlights. But Paddy looked so sad as he watched her packing that she felt she had to say something to soften the blow of his leaving her house. So she sat him down and told him that she was going to accompany him and Farble into the elemental realm. To her surprise, he did not look too happy at the news.

"Missy should stay in her own world," Paddy said.

"Why is that?"

Perhaps to taunt her, he paraphrased her earlier remarks. "That world is not your world, it's not your home." He added, "There are dangers there, Missy."

"Such as?"

He shook his head. "You do not know the place."

"Don't you want my company?"

"Paddy is only concerned that Missy might get hurt."

She saw he was being sincere. "I have to go, Paddy. My mother is there."

He hesitated. "Does Missy know that, or does Missy wish that to be true?"

Ali stiffened. "I know what I know."

Paddy lowered his head. "Missy is a high fairy."

Softening her tone, she pulled out a wad of cash and handed it to him. "Before we leave, go to the liquor store and buy yourself six bottles of whiskey. You know where it is. Be sure to make up your face before you go. Don't skip any green spots. If you have any money left, you can get some tobacco for your pipe. Does that sound good to you?"

He brightened. "Does Missy mind how large the bottles are?"

"Missy does not. Buy what you can carry. But for heaven's sake, don't get in an argument with the guy at the store, like you did last time. And if he asks for photo ID, tell him you don't have any and come back here and I'll take you to another store."

Paddy pocketed the cash, then stared at her a moment, uncertain what to say next. "Paddy knows Missy is a friend," he said quietly.

Ali leaned over and hugged him. "Missy knows Paddy is a great leprechaun."

Paddy was gone over half an hour, which made Ali nervous, but by the time he returned she was done packing. Farble did not seem to mind having a hundred pounds of meat stuffed in his pack. Her only fear was that he would eat it while they hiked. She explained to him that the food had to last, but the troll just nodded and stared at the steak. Ali suspected that troll brains lacked long term–planning ability.

It had been raining earlier, then sunny; now the clouds had returned and covered Breakwater in a sober gray light. The dim was actually an advantage. Farble's skin only hurt when exposed to direct sunlight. The clouds gave them an extra two hours. They did not have to wait for dark to set out.

However, as she loaded up her father's truck, she buried Farble under a bedsheet and ordered him to remain still until they were high on the mountain. But she let Paddy sit up front beside her. As they pulled out of the garage, he already had a bottle of whiskey open and was drinking heavily.

"Does Missy know how to drive this thing?" he asked.

"Sure." The word was no sooner out of her mouth when she backed into their trash can and spewed garbage onto the street. She dared not stop to pick it up. She added, "I just need a little practice is all."

"I saw Missy out practicing many times."

"You did not!"

"Aye. Late at night, swerving all over the road."

"You think you could do better?"

"Aye. Paddy should drive."

"You know nothing about driving!"

"Paddy knows. Took the truck out a few times when Missy was gone."

Ali was stunned. "You did not!"

"Aye. Let Paddy drive."

She shook her head. "Your feet won't reach the pedals."

Paddy glanced down at her legs. Even with the seat pushed all the way forward, her feet barely reached the gas and brake. "We could drive together," he said.

"Hardly," she replied.

Her skills improved the farther they went up the mountain. She kept their speed down, her eyes locked on the dark road. They didn't pass another vehicle, which was a good thing. The truck strained under Farble's weight—the sunken rear made them look as if they were towing a granite statue. The troll fell asleep under the sheet and his snores sent the material billowing into the air. Farble's weight forced her to keep her foot on the gas. The fuel gauge sunk rapidly.

Ali had not been far up the mountain since their big adventure. As they wound through the trees, they passed the spot where she had first hid her bike and tried to hike across the forest to the logging site. It was on that particular hike that she had run into Farble and his friends—before they *were* friends—and had almost been buried alive. Driving farther, they also passed the logging site itself, which had yet to reopen since Ted Wilson's *accident*. The local loggers still got spooked when Ted described the creature that had attacked him, which by no coincidence sounded a lot like Farble, although Ali was pretty sure it had been one of Farble's pals who had done the dirty work.

After thirty minutes, the road ended and they were in the same spot they had been when they had started their last journey—except last time Karl had been acting like their leader, while all the time he had been planning to steal the Yanti and kill them. Parking, Ali climbed out and woke up Farble and sucked in a deep breath of fresh air. Previously, their initial goal had been a spot called Overhang, a rocky formation twelve miles distant. But if everything went as she hoped, they would reach Overhang with the night only half over. They had better! The cave that held the seven doors was at least another ten miles beyond Overhang. The total distances didn't sound that impressive to the uninitiated but the trail also included a two-mile rise in elevation and Ali was never going to forget how thin the air got on top of the mountain.

Before they hit the trail, Ali stopped to phone Steve. He answered on the first ring and assured her that they were on the bus on their way back to Breakwater.

"Rose picked up Nira?" she asked.

"We didn't kidnap her, if that's what you mean," he said.

"Did Rose explain why she was not at the hospital?"

"As a matter of fact she did. Before they could even leave for the hospital, a friend called Freddy's mother and told her that her son was dead. The poor woman fainted right away, and Rose had to stay with her until another ambulance came." Steve added, "Rose might be working for a monster, but you have to understand what a sweet woman she is. She really does take good care of Nira."

"I'll be happy to have my opinion about her changed." Ali added, "Remember what I said about not going back there. Not everything is as it seems in Toule."

"I hear you. Where are you now?"

"About to start up the trail. If you want, I can call you before we enter the cave. You know after that my cell phone won't work."

"Sure. Call me then." Steve hesitated. "Best of luck, Ali."

"Thanks," she said.

Next she called her father, who was halfway to Miami with a load of freight. He sounded good. They talked a few minutes and she assured him that she was staying at Cindy's house. It bothered her to lie to him, but she felt none of it would matter if she brought his wife home to him.

His wife! As she said goodbye to her father, it hit her that she was finally on the road to saving her mother. Searching for Karl's whereabouts for the last four weeks had worn on her nerves. Now she was taking charge of the situation and it felt great. She chided herself that she had taken so long to make up her mind what to do.

They fastened on their respective backpacks—she forced Paddy to wear one as well, to carry his whiskey bottles—and set off at a stride so quick it was closer to a jog than a walk. The first part of the journey was through a tunnel of thick-branched pines and ferns that completely cut off the sky. Ali reached for her flashlight, only to discover that once her eyes had adapted to the gloom, she could see fine. She was relieved. She could save the batteries for when they entered the cave.

Paddy drank as they hiked, and finished an entire bottle, and started on a second, and sang loudly, and badly, but she did not care as long as he kept moving. His short legs belied his stout heart. He was able to match her step for step, and she could only pray his endurance kept up. Farble, of course, loped easily along; it seemed as if he hardly took a deep breath.

Ali could not help but reflect on their last hike through these woods, when Steve and Cindy had struggled from the beginning. She had been smart to leave them behind, but she had been an idiot to bring them with her to Toule. Steve had acknowledged he had heard her when she had told him to stay away from there.

But he had not said he *would* stay away from the town.

The branch-tunnel ended and they came to the open woods, and Ali pushed them hard. A huge moon had risen—its bewitching light shone through the silent trees like the ghostly rays given off by a haunted castle. Ali sensed a mysterious waiting in the forest, as if it remembered the previous month and the opening of the Yanti, and was preparing for another brush with magic. Or perhaps the woods were just happy to see her, as she was to see them. She felt more at home in the forest than she did in her own house.

Four hours of hiking brought them to the spot where they had camped last time and been attacked by the dark fairies. Already they were high up on the mountain, and Breakwater was but a toy village beside a silver sea. On their right, the moon had risen above the eastern ridge, and although it was a day short of being full—contrary to what Cindy had told Steve on the bus—in the clear thin air it looked as bright as a searchlight. She felt as if she could see as easily with the moon as with the sun.

The old campsite still bore the scars of the dark fairies' attack. There were plenty of fallen trees and burnt bark, and the odor of ash remained. Yet as she reached out with her mind, she did not sense any of the creatures in the area, and it made her wonder. Why had they returned behind the red door? Were they afraid to attack without the support of Lord Vak's army? Were they afraid of her? She stopped to reflect on Radrine's exact words to her.

"You are mistaken, the end will not come in days. The war will be long and bloody. Humanity has physical weapons, true, but lacks magical powers. Both sides are equally matched. But in the end we want the dwarves and elves to be destroyed, as much as we want humanity wiped out. Did you not know? The whole world can glow with radioactive dust and we will be happy. Because it is then we will move fully into the third dimension, and take over, and make all who have survived our slaves."

The dark fairies were spoilers, cowards. They only liked to attack when they were sure of winning. They were waiting for the Shaktra to once more push the elementals into the human kingdom. However, it was possible they might emerge from their painful realm, from time to time, before the war started and cause mischief. For that reason, it was her intention to lock the red door before she went in search of her mother.

How she planned to accomplish these amazing feats remained to be seen.

Near the old campsite, down in the ravine, they took water from the Mercer River, before resuming their hike. The farther they went up the mountain, the stronger she felt. Soon she was running, with Farble beside her, and the thin air felt fine in her lungs and the moonlight lit her red hair. But her enthusiasm took its toll on Paddy. When she paused to get her bearings, she saw that the leprechaun had fallen behind, and they had to wait while he staggered up beside them. Of course, he was well into his second bottle, and he had lit his pipe and was blowing smoke rings. She tried to explain that such things did not make for good hiking, but he just waved his hand.

"Paddy can out-hike you both any day of the week," he said.

"If you don't keep up, Farble's going to have to carry you."

The leprechaun looked disgusted. "He might eat me!"

"Stop drinking, stop smoking, stop singing. We have lots of ground to cover."

Paddy was hurt. "Missy doesn't like me songs?"

"Missy doesn't want the whole world to know we're coming."

However, when they started off again, Ali stayed behind with Paddy, while Farble went ahead. Once more she tried to question the leprechaun about what they could expect to find in the elemental kingdom.

"I need to know what we'll see when we first come out on the other side."

Paddy acted confused. "A mountain."

"A mountain like we have on this side?"

"Aye. The same but different."

"Where does this mountain reside in the elemental kingdom? Is it where the fairies live? Is it where the elves live? The dwarves?"

"It is in the south, Missy, not far from the sea."

"Who lives there?"

"Not sure, Missy. Lord Vak claimed it when he marched his army to the mountain. The dwarves did, too. But now they have gone back to their own places. Maybe another has claimed it by now."

"You mention south, and you mention the sea. How far is the mountain from the sea? Is it closer than *our* mountain is to *our* sea?"

"Aye. It is not such a pretty mountain. It has no trees."

"No trees?" The remark surprised her. And here she had thought the elemental kingdom was completely green. "Why are there no trees?"

"The mountain is in the south, near the desert."

"Who lives in the desert?"

Paddy looked away. "No one."

"Paddy?"

"No people, Missy. Paddy promises. No reason to go there."

"But is there something dangerous in the desert?"

"No!"

"Paddy?"

He took forever to answer. "Scabs."

"Scabs? What are scabs?"

"Scabs are scabs. They are dangerous. No reason to go into the desert."

"Fine. We will not go into the desert. What lies directly north of the mountain?"

"Land, rocks, some trees, a wide river."

"Who lives there?"

Paddy paused. "I do, and other leprechauns."

Ali had to smile. "Is it a nice place?"

Paddy shrugged. "It is what it is. It is not as beautiful as Karolee."

The word sent a wave of warmth through Ali. "What is that?"

Paddy looked up at her. "Missy must know."

Ali spoke the words as if in a dream. "It's where the fairies live. And the center of their kingdom is named Uleestar." She discovered she was shaking. "Is that correct?"

"Aye. But Paddy has never been to Uleestar, only heard of it."

"But you've been to Karolee?"

"Aye. From time to time."

"What is it like?"

"Full of trees, running water, flowers, and fairies."

"How do fairies and leprechauns get along?"

"There are fairies and there are fairies. Some like leprechauns, some do not."

"But fairies allow leprechauns to cross their borders?"

"Aye. They did, Missy, not so much now."

"Why?"

"Things change. Another war comes, leprechauns get pushed aside."

"Would you say the fairies guard their borders well?"

"They guard Uleestar. It is strong."

"How long would it take us to hike from the mountain to Uleestar?"

"Paddy does not know. Never been there."

"Guess."

"Missy?"

"I want you to give me your best guess."

Paddy looked miserable. "Five days?"

Ali nodded. "Who lives to the east of Karolee?"

"Lord Vak and his elves."

"And south of him is Lord Balar and the dwarves?"

"Aye. Dwarves are in the mountains, in their caves."

"Where do the trolls come from?"

"The far east."

"Are there mountains there?"

"Many mountains, Missy."

Ali remembered a dream she'd had before they went up the mountain the first time. In it there had been huge white mountains in the sky, like floating icebergs, and a vast dark shadow on the western horizon. She asked Paddy about what she had seen.

"You mean the kloudar, aye. They are up in the sky."

"Do they float all over the place?"

"They float around Anglar."

"What is Anglar?"

"The moon."

Ali was stunned. "You mean they orbit the moon?"

He was uncertain. "Paddy sees them near Anglar."

"Does anyone live on the kloudar?"

"Dragons visit."

Ali had to laugh. "There are dragons there?"

"Aye. Missy must know. Dragons visit the kloudar."

"So these dragons, they fly?"

"Aye. The kloudar are high up."

"Do fairies fly up to the kloudar?"

"Aye, the high fairies."

"Does anyone else live on the kloudar?"

The leprechaun hesitated. "Paddy should not say."

"Why not?"

"Paddy does not want to say."

"Why don't you want to say?"

"It is . . . my pa told Paddy . . . it is . . . too sacred to say."

"Sacred?"

"Aye."

"Do you even know what that word means?"

He just stared at her, didn't speak.

Ali tried another tack. "What about in the west? What's there?"

"The sea."

"Is there something out in the sea? A place you know about?"

Paddy was suddenly agitated. "No."

"Paddy?"

"Nothing there, Missy."

"Is the Shaktra there? Is that where it came from?"

Paddy stopped walking and lowered his gaze. "We do no. the word."

"How could it come out of the sea? What's out there? Is there an island?"

Paddy nodded reluctantly. "The Isle of Greesh."

"Who controls the Isle of Greesh?"

Paddy hung his head. "The fairies did."

"*Did?* What happened? Did it fall?"

"Aye. It fell . . . It . . . We do not speak of it."

Ali persisted. "It fell to the Shaktra? Is that what happened?"

"It just came." Paddy glanced up, and in his huge green-and-gold eyes there might have been tears. "No one knows where it came from."

She asked what *it* was, but could get no more out of him.

It took them another hour to reach Overhang. The name fit the spot; the rock ledge protruded from the side of the mountain like the edge of a giant, half-buried plate. Ordinarily, she would have considered it an ideal place to take shelter, but she planned to stop only long enough for them to eat and gather their strength for the final push. From her watch, she estimated they had only three hours of night left.

Nevertheless, she left the others in search of a nearby pond where she had spoken to Nemi previously. It was probably silly to think he would talk to her there again. Nemi had made it clear that neither a tree nor a pond were that important when he wished to talk. But still she hoped to reach out and grab his attention. She had so many questions in her head, and so few answers.

The pond took only a few minutes to find. It looked smaller than before, probably because some of the water had evaporated since June had changed into July. But it was as clear as she re-ll, and on its surface the moon could have been ...ne from the depths of the earth. Sitting on her ... edge, she stared at the watery sky and prayed

...our help," she said. "I'm not sure where my ...om is. I'm not sure who the old man is, or Nira, or Rose, or Ms. Smith. I don't even know how to work the Yanti, not any more than when I found it. I'm tired of thinking that I'm the only one who can save the world when I'm not sure I can save myself. I keep getting these headaches—they're getting worse. I give Steve and Cindy orders, and decide what Farble and Paddy are supposed to do, and all the time I think I'm supposed to be this great fairy queen, and I don't even feel like a great person. I don't feel like a normal girl anymore, either. It's like each time I look in the mirror, I want it to break and find you on the other side. I need to feel you near, Nemi." She lowered her head. "I need to feel your love . . . just to keep going."

He did not respond, no one did, and she felt foolish.

Yet as she stood to go, an unexpected warmth touched her chest.

It was faint, she might have imagined it. But it brought a tear to her eye.

This tear, it was not sad, nor salty, and it reminded her of him.

"Nemi," she whispered.

If it was not his hand on her heart, then at least she remembered her love for him. *That* might have been enough, for she suddenly felt stronger, more sure of the course she had chosen. She bowed to the pond as she left, and this time she did not feel foolish.

CHAPTER

8

They reached the cave two hours later, high on the bare slopes, which put them ahead of schedule. The only problem was that the entrance was piled high with boulders. Ali did not have to study the huge rocks long to figure out what had happened. Many of the boulders were scarred with black lines, as if they had been torched by powerful lasers. The dark fairies had been busy with their fire stones—Radrine had deliberately cut off this entrance into her realm, and Ali had to wonder if the evil queen had blocked the other end of the cave as well.

"Looks like we should go home, Missy," Paddy said hopefully.

She cast him a hard look. "Go sit on a rock and keep quiet."

The leprechaun, seeing her foul mood, scurried off. Ali was angry with herself for not having anticipated the blocked cave. Her focus had been on the doors, how to open them. Yet it was not as if the barrier was unassailable. Given time, with Farble's help, she was sure they could dig her way inside. But the clock was not on their side. One hour to dawn, and it would not be easy on Farble if the troll had to stand out in the sun. Sure, she had brought an umbrella and sunblock, like last time, and there were clouds over the sea. But they might take two hours to blow inland. In the meantime, Farble could get burned.

The area was different for other reasons. There was still plenty of snow on top of the peak, but around the cave it was all rock and gravel. The latter was dark, like volcanic sand, and the moonlight gave it an otherworldly feel. For that matter, the top of the peak looked like a crystal cathedral erected on an alien moon. She had not talked about it, but the summit was her backup plan if she failed to open the green door. If the door would not budge, she was going to try to use the Yanti tomorrow night when the full moon was straight overhead. It had worked before . . .

Yet she feared her alternative plan. It was dependent on time and place.

Aware of the full moon, Lord Vak might be waiting for her on the other side.

Better to go through the green door, she thought, do the unexpected.

Ali turned to Farble. "We're going to move these rocks out of the way, and we're going to do it fast. The sun will be up in an hour. Move your rocks to the right, I'll move mine to the left. Try not to crush Paddy."

Farble nodded. "Help Geea."

They set to work, and at first they made excellent progress. To Ali, the boulders were just big rocks, and she casually tossed them aside, while Farble, who was supposed to be partially made out of stone, worked without tiring.

Unfortunately, she had underestimated the blockage. The boulders did not cease when they finally dug beneath the cave ceiling. Radrine had not simply brought down the roof. Her slaves must have stolen boulders from other parts of the mountain, and jammed them into the entrance.

Light appeared in the east. They worked faster.

The heavy clouds over the sea had moved closer, but not close enough.

It was amazing how quickly the light grew.

Finally, Ali gestured for Farble to stop. "How do you feel?" she asked, panting.

"Hungry," Farble said.

Ali ignored him; he was always hungry. She could see him turning more frequently to the east. The sky near the horizon was already turning red. Farble was well aware of the situation. Paddy called from behind them.

"We should go back down to the trees, Missy," he said.

"We're not going back," Ali swore, reaching for her backpack. The last time she had fought Radrine, she had taken the evil queen's fire stones and she had brought them along on this trip—just in case. The thought of using the dark fairies' tools annoyed her, yet they did give her a channel through which she could pour a tremendous amount of her energy. Blasting the side of the mountain was not her idea of a deft approach. Anyone inside the cave would know she was coming. Yet she refused to let Farble burn.

Gesturing for the others to stand back, she focused the crystal globes toward the blocked entrance. Her breath was her battery, her will, the on switch. Power ran up her spine and the globes exploded in red light as a thin beam shot away from her. A dozen boulders instantly shattered, and their dust rained down all around them. Firing ten blasts in a row, she only stopped when she could no longer see what was in front of her. Luckily, a breeze came up right then, and the dust cleared, and she saw that the opening to the cave had been badly damaged, but that at least there were no longer any boulders in the way. Farble looked relieved, Paddy, disappointed.

"Nice cave," Farble mumbled.

"Probably full of dark fairies," Paddy said.

Ali smiled. "It's not the *dark* fairies you have to worry about."

She gave her father, and Steve, another call before she entered the cave. Steve continued to act evasive when she told him to stay away from Toule. She feared he had some silly plan up his sleeve . . .

Together, Paddy, Farble, and Ali went inside the cave.

Paddy carried a flashlight, as did she. As before, they had not hiked far when the walls and ceiling narrowed. Farble had to lean over to keep from hitting his head. The rough square shape was as she recalled, as was the material of the walls—a hard smooth black lava. The floor was also familiar; the grainy black sand clung to Ali's shoes like magnetic dirt.

The cave went neither up nor down, but the temperature increased the further they went inside, and soon Ali removed her jacket. Since she had gained her fairy powers, hot and cold did not affect her much. However, using the fire stones might have taken energy out of her. Hurrying through the long cave, she realized she had a headache. Two grams of stardust and some water helped, but what she needed to do was lie down and rest.

After an hour the cave suddenly swelled in size, and they came to three metal doors, one set beside the other, arranged in a semicircle. She had seen them before. The metal was dark, dirty; all three doors were rectangles and had no markings, although each had a domed curve at the top. Each had a black handle as well, but there was no place to insert a key. All three were closed, and it was only the middle one that swung open when she tugged on it. Just before they went through, Ali gestured to the other two doors.

"Do either of you know where these doors lead?" she asked.

Farble and Paddy shook their heads.

They continued on. The cave began to angle upward, and for the first time Ali felt the effect of the altitude, as did Paddy. The steep slope demanded more effort. The two of them began to pant loudly, and the leprechaun signaled a few times that he had to stop. Ali did not begrudge him the rest. Since they were inside and out of the sun, she was not bound by any particular timetable. Yet that did not feel entirely true. A part of her gnawed at her to hurry.

While they were resting, the ground lurched slightly. An earthquake? Or was the mountain, which had once been a volcano, becoming active again? It was a sobering thought. If Pete's Peak blew, the entire area would be buried in ash. Breakwater would be completely destroyed, along with Toule.

Ali wondered if the minor earthquake had anything to do with the elementals.

After another hour of hard hiking, the walls of the cave transformed into a small cavern, and they reached their first major goal, the seven doors. They were similar to the previous three, made of metal. But there was one significant change: Each door was a different color. Starting on the left, there was a red door, followed by an orange one, a yellow one, a green one, a blue one, a violet one, and on the far right there was a white door.

As before, it was the fifth door, the blue one, that intrigued her the most.

She did not know why. She was here to open the fourth door, the green one.

And to lock the first door, the red one. She noticed that—like the third door, the yellow one—the red door lay slightly ajar. She knew about both doors. The yellow one led to the top of the mountain, the red one, to hell.

She tried the other doors. They were all locked.

She even tried knocking on the green door. No one answered.

Paddy and Farble stared at her with big wondering eyes.

She gestured. "Sit and rest. I need to be alone for a few minutes," she said.

Setting her flashlight on the floor of the cavern, Ali moved in front of the red door, closed it, took out the Yanti, held it between her hands, and quietly repeated three times, "Alosha . . . Alosha . . . Alosha."

The Yanti warmed, she felt an expansion of her field. The red door in front of her, the walls of the cavern, and even the other doors—she suddenly felt connected to them. The last time that had happened, on top of the mountain, she had known that everything in her immediate environment was under her command. This time, she ordered the red door to lock and stay locked.

But it did not obey her. It remained unlocked.

She repeated the process. The feeling of expansion returned.

The door remained unlocked.

Ali moved in front of the green door. Holding the Yanti in her right hand, she put her left palm on the center of the door. Once more she repeated her secret name three times, and the sense of heat and expansion grew even greater. Loudly, and mentally, she ordered the door to open. Her confidence was high, she felt as if her fairy power was at maximum strength. . . .

The green door remained locked.

Ali switched the Yanti into her left hand, repeated the process. Nothing happened. She did not know what she was doing.

Ali sat down beside her flashlight to think. Paddy called over. "Does Missy want to go home now?" he asked.

"Oh brother," she muttered.

She closed her eyes, to think, but might have dozed for a moment. No surprise, she had skipped the entire night's rest. A few sleepy minutes seemed to go by, and she feared she might doze again.

Then a sound caught her attention.

It appeared to come from far off; a disturbing noise of whirling air and beating wings. It was coming from the other side of the red door!

Ali was on her feet in a second. She called to the others, who might have been sleeping. "Dark fairies are coming!"

Paddy and Farble jumped up, ready to do battle. Ali gestured for them to remain silent, motioned them away from the red door. Taking out the fire stones, she crept near the first door and opened it ever so slightly. For a moment there was only pitch black, but then a red glow began to grow in the depths and she saw a concentrated cloud, filled with batlike shadows, buzzing and hissing like a plague of locusts, moving swiftly toward her.

Ali felt no moral imperative to let the dark fairies take the first shot. Surrounding herself with a force field that was capable of repelling any of the elements, even empty space, she opened wide the red door and raised the fire stones close to her chest and let loose with a blast that more than rivaled the shots she had aimed at the boulders. The laser beam exploded down the length of the cave like a mass fired from an atomic cannon. She hit the swarm dead center, and there came a hideous screech of pain, followed by a dozen return blasts. But the dark fairies had nowhere near her juice. Their red beams bounced harmlessly off her field. Letting loose another dozen shots, she was not sure how many she was killing but, from the cries, she knew it must be a lot.

It was almost too easy, yet the destruction of her enemies brought her no pleasure. Her empathetic nature had no off switch. Evil was opposed to good, but pain was pain—their screams echoed in her heart as much as her head. She kept shooting but wished they would quit coming.

Didn't they know who she was?

Then a cruel voice spoke at her back; it hissed like a reptile.

A creature that knew her perhaps better than she knew herself.

"Time to stop, Geea," Radrine said.

The queen of the dark fairies was a cross between a human, a lizard, and a bat. Coated with black scales, she had claws instead of fingers, and a long dark tongue that slithered in a nauseating motion as she stared at Ali. Her wings were rotting leather hides. The pulsating light of her eyes—buried deep in an egg-shaped skull—glowed a wicked red. Yet Ali saw that the queen had not fully recovered from the injury Ali had given her at their last encounter. Scarred veins and purple blood pulsed beneath her clear skull. Her brains were visible, and they were a horror— a dish of maggots steadily crawling on a lump of meat. However, like before, Radrine wore no ornaments, no gold or silver crown, only her deadly intelligence.

Yet she carried weapons, two exceptionally large, red fire stones, which she had pointed at Farble and Paddy. Radrine's tactic was now obvious. She had sent her minions to attack from the other side of the red door merely to distract her and, like a fool, Ali had fallen for the simple trick.

Ali regretted the pounding she had given to the entrance. It had probably alerted Radrine. The evil queen must have flown out the far end of the cave, near the top of the mountain, under the cover of the clouds, or perhaps *in* them, and circled around to catch her unaware. Not that any of it mattered now.

Radrine stood close behind the leprechaun and the troll.

Ali could not get off a shot, not without hitting one of them.

Radrine smiled again. "Put down your fire stones. Or should I say *my* stones? You stole them, you know, although I must admit that I am flattered you have taken such good care of them." The queen nodded. "On the ground, please."

Ali ignored her. Her force field—shimmering a faint blue in the cavern gloom—surrounded her still, but did not extend to Farble and Paddy. Slowly, raising her right palm—the fire stones were in her left—she mentally stretched it out. But Radrine was not so easily fooled; she came up at Farble's neck.

"I think not!" Radrine snapped.

Ali drew her field back, but did not drop it. Behind her, on the other side of the red door, she heard a gang of dark fairies gathering, hissing like a bowl of snakes. It was not a pleasant feeling, to be assailed on both sides. But she refused to show Radrine any fear.

"You have a reason for being here?" Ali asked.

Radrine grinned. "I have come to congratulate you. Everyone is still talking about how you defeated Lord Vak on the mountaintop. Sent his army packing, I understand."

"There was no fight. We merely talked."

Radrine nodded. "Still, Lord Vak is not easy to talk to. And you took the Yanti from him. I see it there, hanging from your delicate neck. How lovely. May I have a look at it, please?"

"Really, Radrine, you have grown so tiresome. I would just as soon hang it on the neck of a dragon than hand it over to you."

Radrine lost her smile. "But I do think you will hand it over to me, yes, I honestly do. And I think you will tell me about the mystical code you placed on it." She added, "If you don't, I will kill your two friends."

"Kill them. They are no friends of mine. I hardly know them." Ali added, "But when you are through killing them, I will kill you."

Paddy was anxious. "Missy, you said you were our friend. You said you would protect us and that you—"

"Stop," Ali snapped.

"But Missy, I don't want to—"

"Paddy! Shut up!"

The leprechaun stopped, lowered his head, as if preparing to die. Farble stood frozen, his eyes fixed on her face. He would not speak, not at a time like this, but Ali felt him pleading for her to save them.

"They trust you, Geea," Radrine taunted.

Ali took a step toward them, while behind her the dark fairies hissed with joy. "I'm not going to give you the Yanti," she said. "That will never happen, in this world or the next. But if you leave now, I'll let you and your servants live. That is my offer. Take it or die."

Radrine touched the back of Farble's neck with her fire stones; the troll flinched. "You lie, Geea. You forget how well I know you. How long I watched you rule Karolee from your beautiful palace at Uleestar. So wise, but so sensitive. The latter made you weak, I think. You are too sensitive to stand here and watch this troll and leprechaun be tortured to death. Yes, tortured. What a gruesome word. But you see, I would hate for them to leave this world and not hate you. And they will hate you, because as I peel off their skin, they will know that you could stop their agony, just by handing over a piece of jewelry."

"What will you do when they're dead?" Ali asked. "You'll have no one to stand behind."

Radrine smiled once more. "Oh, I don't think it will come to that."

The evil queen let her fire stones grow brighter, and a tiny line of red light poured out of them onto the top of Farble's back. There was dark smoke; Ali heard hair burning, smelled charred flesh. The troll shook and howled in pain. Without thinking, he dashed toward Ali, but immediately ran into her force field, which knocked him flat. He tried to sit, to escape the agony, but Radrine crouched behind him—still using him as a shield—and returned to burning off his skin.

Radrine was right; Ali could not stand it.

But she was nowhere near ready to surrender.

Raising her right palm, Ali momentarily dropped the field from around her body and rammed it into the floor. The volcanic sand exploded in a black wave, and the swell surged toward the others like a breaker thrown off by a deep space meteor crashing into a primordial sea.

The wave hit them hard, buried them in a gravel blanket, but Radrine's reflexes were equal to Ali's. Just before the sand hit, the evil queen fired two shots. The first one was a gem, or a curse, depending on whose side you were on. Because the bulk of her energy was bent toward the floor, Ali's body was exposed. Still, her field took something out of the blast. The shot hit her hand, burning her badly, but it did not take off the hand, or any fingers.

"Move!" she shouted to Farble and Paddy.

It was advice *she* had to follow. Radrine's second shot—which was clearly off balance—hit the ceiling above Ali. But because it was not filtered through Ali's field, it packed far more punch. The red beam tore a chunk out of the ceiling. Suddenly rocks were falling as the wave of sand hit the far side of the cavern and rebounded. Ali's fire stones were knocked out of her hand as she dove to the left.

The chamber was a bubble of dusty confusion. The flashlights got buried with everything else, and in the almost pitch dark, Ali wiped at her eyes and saw Paddy crawling toward the right wall, while Farble tried to limp back down the cave. In the middle was Radrine, her back to the far wall, apparently stunned.

Fortunately, one of the boulders the evil queen's blast had brought down had wedged itself against the red door, closing it fast. For the moment at least, Radrine was on her own. Ali went to grab her.

Radrine stood up suddenly, reached for her stones. Ali raised her palm, ready to deflect whatever was coming. But her right hand was in agony, and strangely, partially numb, and no power flowed through it. She was stunned. Were her hands that important when it came to using her abilities? All along, she supposed, almost unconsciously, she had been using them when she had performed magic. Radrine's first shot had probably been highly calculated. Ali was right-handed. Mentally, she tried switching her energy to her left palm but she felt she had no control. And all the while Radrine took aim with her stones . . .

Ali leapt to the right, toward the red door, just as Radrine let loose a blast. The red beam missed, barely. Ali felt the cloth on her left sleeve catch fire. There was no time to worry about it. Flowing through a graceful roll, Ali grabbed one of the rocks Radrine had broken from the ceiling and stood and threw it at the evil queen. There was still so much dust, Ali was not sure if Radrine saw it coming. Certainly, she did not try to move out of the way as it hurled toward her chest.

The rock hit her dead center, threw her back, forced her to drop her fire stones. The back of Radrine's flimsy skull hit the far wall, and she slumped down as Ali strode forward. But the queen was resilient, and not stupid. She knew she was facing a foe she could not beat, not without help. Staggering up, she managed to unwind her black wings, and glare in Ali's direction.

"This is only the beginning," she swore.

Ali paused, feeling her own weakness. "The next time I see you, I will kill you," she promised.

"Destroy her if you can!" Radrine shouted to her hissing minions, who clambered against the boulder that jammed shut the red door. Then the evil queen batted her hideous wings and flew away, swooping low over a panicked Farble, back down the cave, toward the entrance Ali had so unwisely blown open.

There was no time to celebrate. The boulder would not hold the door, and with her wounded hand, Ali doubted she could erect a force field strong enough to protect her friends from the swarm of dark fairies. Farble was wounded—he was moaning—and Paddy looked like he was in shock. She had to get them out of the cavern. They needed time to regroup.

Choking on the dusty air, Ali managed to grab her friends and pull them through the *yellow* door, the only other door that was open. She did not have a clear goal in mind, but she did recall a series of six tunnels farther up the cave. They had been round-shaped, with three on each side. Because each had sloped slightly downward—when they were hustling to climb *out* of the cave—they had not stopped to inspect the tunnels. But now Ali thought they might be a perfect place to disappear into. If she remembered correctly, they were not far away.

Paddy and Farble were too stunned to talk. Ali ordered them to keep moving. The pain in her hand was devastating. She had saved only one flashlight from the cavern, but it was enough to show that Radrine had melted virtually all the flesh off her palm. Through the dripping blood, Ali could actually see her raw muscles and veins. She knew if she did not bandage it soon, or better yet, heal it, she was going to be in serious trouble.

After a half hour of jogging, Ali heard demented shrieks at their backs.

Very faintly, she could see a herd of shifting red dots.

She had saved a flashlight but had lost her fire stones.

"Missy!" Paddy cried.

"Don't be afraid," Ali said, although she felt very afraid.

Fortunately, right then, they came to the caves, and Ali chose the second one on the left, for no other reason than it felt right. Into the pitch black, into a place they knew nothing about, they fled.

CHAPTER

9

That same morning, Steve and Cindy arrived in Toule by bus, and headed to the town's public library. That afternoon they planned to have lunch with Nira and Rose. To thank them for watching Nira, Rose had invited them to Sheri Smith's house. Of course, when Steve had last spoken to Ali, before she had entered the cave, he had not mentioned any of these facts. There came a time in life, Steve thought, when a man had to act like a man, even if he was still a kid. This, he was confident, was one of those times.

The time was ten-fifteen in the morning. They had three hours to kill before lunch. Because both of them were curious how Toule had been destroyed in the power plant explosion thirteen years earlier, they wanted to spend as much of that time as possible in the local library doing research. But one of the first things they learned when they began to go through the back articles related to the tragedy, was that the word "destroyed" was a slight exaggeration.

Toule had a population of 4,332. Only 114 had died in the explosion, although another 250 had been injured, many of those badly burned. "Only" seemed a pitiful word to apply to such devastation, but it was a fact that the town had survived the explosion, although most of the main street and over three hundred homes had burned to the ground. For Steve, it was a lot different to scan through the library's microfilm—which was largely made up of articles taken from the local paper, *Toule Talk*—than to search the Internet for national stories on the tragedy. For one thing, two local reporters had been there the night the power plant had gone up in flames. Indeed, both had been slightly injured in the blast, and they wrote with a passion that brought the night home in a way that was very personal—and painful.

Briefly, the facts of the matter were that while the town was in the middle of celebrating the local high school's victory at the state basketball championship game two weeks earlier, the power plant had blown up. That was it—thirteen years later no one had a clue why it had happened. The rest was statistics, although there was a slight discrepancy in the number dead. Most of the articles they read said 114 had died—a few said 115.

"Does the number matter?" Cindy asked, sitting across from Steve. Given the size of the town, the library was more than respectable. They had to assume the local citizens were ardent readers, although they pretty much had the place to themselves. The librarian on duty was a Ms. Sarah Treacher, who looked like a kindly old woman until she opened her mouth. She had already snapped at them for mishandling the microfilm—she called it microfiche—yet she continued to be helpful, in a scowling sort of way. Their excuse for being there was far from creative: They were supposedly doing a paper on the big blast for a summer school class. As if they had summer school back in Breakwater.

"Probably not, but I think we should ask the old witch about it," Steve said.

Cindy nodded toward the front desk. "Not so loud, the old witch might hear and turn you into a troll."

"Better a troll than a leprechaun," Steve said.

"You would rather be Farble than Paddy? Farble is dumb, he stinks."

"There is bliss in ignorance, and Farble can eat over twenty pounds at one sitting."

"I think Paddy is cute," Cindy said.

"All females are attracted to dwarf men. It is a scientific fact."

"But Paddy hates dwarves."

Steve suddenly chuckled. "You know what I just thought?"

"What?"

"How weird this conversation is."

Cindy smiled. "Ain't that the truth."

Steve gestured to the stacks of microfilm. "Anyway, Ms. Treacher said she was there that night. We should talk to her about the discrepancy in the number. She might be more helpful than all these articles put together."

"What would help me is if I knew what we were looking for."

"An excellent point. When we were riding here on the bus, I had the brilliant idea that we would pore through all these records and come across early warning signs of an elemental invasion. Well, maybe I wasn't being that lame, but I thought we might at least find something that related to Ali's problem."

"It isn't Ali's problem, it's all our problem," Cindy said.

"Slip of the tongue. Anyway, what we're looking for in the explosion is anything that cannot be logically explained. And we have that; it's staring us right in the face. No one has a clue why the plant exploded. But I don't know what to do with that. To solve a mystery you need at least a few clues."

"Nothing struck you as odd? Besides the question over the number of dead?"

Steve considered. "There is one thing that might be a clue. This plant generated electrical energy by burning gas. Most of the plants in the U.S. do the same. It's cheaper than using nuclear power. Until solar or wind technology get more sophisticated, it will continue to be the way electrical plants are fueled."

"So?" Cindy asked.

"So this was the only electrical plant in the state that did not import its gas. It got it from right here, pumped it directly out of the ground."

"Would that explain why it blew up?"

"No. I bring it up only because it's unusual. I mean, in Texas it's not, but the West Coast doesn't have many large natural gas reserves."

"Where are you going with this?" Cindy asked.

"Beats me. The underground reserves did not explode. Toule was lucky. If that had happened, they would have had Hiroshima on their hands. Everyone in town would have died."

Cindy was thinking. "But say the explosion was intentional, and someone set the plant to blow. Is it possible they were hoping the underground reserves would ignite?"

"Sure. It would explain why of all the plants in the country, this was the one that blew up. The people behind it might have been after the biggest bang that money could buy."

"*If* there were people behind it," Cindy said.

Steve nodded. "That's our problem. We don't even know if a crime has been committed. No, I take that back. Our problem is that none of this appears to relate to elves, fairies, dwarves, trolls, and leprechauns. For some reason, I seriously doubt that Lord Vak plotted to blow up this city."

"What about the Shaktra?"

Steve shrugged. "Yeah, what about it? What is it? Who is it?"

The questions only emphasized how feeble their research efforts were.

They went over to talk to Ms. Treacher, and to return the microfilm. She snapped it from Steve's hands. He could only assume she did not like the way he held the metal containers. Her face was not merely old; her wrinkles were arranged like hard lines of opinion. Yet her gray eyes had a twinkle in them, they seemed to shine when she was being particularly nasty. She was a grouch, he thought, but she knew it and thought it was funny. She was probably too old to care one way or the other.

"Well, did you two figure out why it blew up?" she asked.

"Not yet," Steve said. "But we're confused how many people died in the blast. Some articles say a hundred and fourteen, others, a hundred and fifteen. Did someone die later or what?"

"A dozen people died later, mostly from burns, but they're included in the total. What you're asking about is Lucy Pillar. She was a high school student. She was listed as missing right after the explosion, but the police couldn't locate her body. However, in the end, they recovered enough remains to make an identification."

"Did that happen to anyone else?" Cindy asked.

"Lots of people were blown to bits. There were body parts everywhere."

"Did they have DNA testing back then?" Steve asked.

"It was primitive. They didn't try to use it on Lucy. After a few days, they knew for sure it was her."

"Did you know her?" Cindy asked.

"Yes."

"What was she like?" Cindy asked.

Ms. Treacher scowled. "Why do you want to know?"

Cindy shrugged. "I was just curious is all."

The question seemed to shake Ms. Treacher. She softened her tone. "Lucy was a lovely girl, before the accident."

The way she said "accident," Steve knew she was not referring to the explosion. He asked if that was the case and the librarian nodded reluctantly.

"A year before the power plant blew, Lucy was in a car accident. Her boyfriend at the time—Hector Wells, he was on the basketball team—was driving. He was drunk, and he crashed into a tree and was thrown from the car. But Lucy had her seat belt on. She got trapped inside, and the car exploded, and she was burned over most of her body." Ms. Treacher's voice was sad. "I'll never forget those days. I was a teacher at the high school then—I saw Lucy every day. She was a cheerleader, happy as a lark. Smart as a whip, too. We had her IQ tested and the psychologist went away shaking his head. She had a photographic memory. She could write, sing, play the flute. Then, just like that, it was all over for her . . . or it should have been. God forgive me, but I used to pray that she had died that night. She should have died, every doctor I spoke to said so. She was left with only twenty percent of her skin. The next year, she was in and out of the hospital constantly, having skin graft operations. If she hadn't died when the plant exploded, she would have had surgeries for another five years. That's no life for a young woman. That's no life for anyone."

"Are Lucy's parents still alive?" Steve asked.

"Her mother is. Her father died the same night as Lucy, in the explosion."

"Where does her mother live?"

"I don't know. She moved away some years ago."

"How about Hector?" Cindy asked.

"He was hurt in the blast, but he recovered." The librarian added, "He's a local contractor, he lives here in town."

"Do you think we could interview him for our paper?" Cindy asked.

"Doubt he would talk to you." She did not add, "you two snot-assed kids," but it was there in her voice. At the same time, it was obvious she liked sharing the local gossip. They hardly had to prod her to keep talking. She was probably bored.

"Do you know Nira Smith?" Steve asked.

"Everyone in town knows Nira. Poor child, her mind is not right. Why do you ask?"

"We took care of her yesterday for a few hours." Steve added, "We're going to have lunch with her and Rose this afternoon."

"Rose?"

"Her nanny. She takes care of Nira for Ms. Smith," Cindy said.

"I don't know her. I only knew Patricia Hassel. She watched Nira for years."

"When did she quit?" Steve asked.

"She didn't quit. She was killed last year, in a car accident." Ms. Treacher added, "It was a shame, she was a lovely woman."

"You have your share of car accidents around here," Cindy said. "We saw Freddy Degear killed yesterday, right in front of us."

"I heard about that. That was the name of the boy?"

"Yes. Didn't you know him?" Steve asked.

"No. I don't think he was from around here."

"Really? We were told he was," Cindy said.

"I never said I knew everyone in town. But what is it with all these fool questions? Are you trying to build a conspiracy theory around the plant explosion? Trying to blame poor Lucy because she was already burned? I tell you, that girl was a saint. Never had a mean word to say about anyone."

"Even after she got burned?" Cindy asked.

"That remark isn't fair. Of course, she changed after that.

119

Who wouldn't? But I never heard her place a word of blame on Hector." Ms. Treacher added, "Hector hasn't had much luck in his love life. Patricia was also his girlfriend."

Steve felt an odd sensation in his gut, and wondered if he was catching a glimpse of what Ali felt when her intuition was on fire. Contrary to what Ms. Treacher had just said, he did not see any major conspiracy in what the librarian was telling them. But he did feel that a heck of a lot of these people seemed to know each other, and intimately. Maybe it was just because of the town's size . . .

"So Hector must know Nira?" Steve asked. "If Patricia was her nanny?"

"The three of them were always together. Used to see them around town all the time."

"Does Hector still see Nira?" Steve asked.

"How would I know what he does with his time? And what does that have to do with that silly paper you're writing? What is it called anyway?"

" 'The Ghosts of Toule,' " Steve said.

Ms. Treacher quieted. "We have too many ghosts around here. Only a few rest easy. Have you been to our cemetery?"

"No," Cindy said.

"Don't go. It's a terrible thing to see so many headstones all in the same place with the same year on them."

"Ms. Treacher, why do you think the plant blew up?" Steve asked.

"It exploded because they built it badly, there's no mystery behind it. It was just that the timing could not have been worse, what with the celebration we were having and all."

"Why were you guys celebrating in front of the plant?" Cindy asked.

"Everything in Toule was in front of the plant. It was huge."

"May I ask one more fool question before we go?" Steve asked.

"I don't know, I'm getting tired of both of you."

"Talking to people around town, we hear a lot about Ms. Sheri Smith, and Omega Overtures, but nothing about Mr. Smith."

"There is no Mr. Smith," Ms. Treacher said.

"Then who is Nira's father?" Steve asked.

"No one knows," the old woman said.

CHAPTER
10

They were twenty minutes deep into the round cave, running hard, when Ali saw an orange light up ahead. It looked like the glow of a torch, but she could not be sure. It might have been more dark fairies and their nefarious weapons. She told the others to halt, to rest, that she would go forward alone.

"Don't leave us, Missy," Paddy said, breathing hard.

Farble moaned. He felt the same way.

She listened behind them—in the cave.

"I do not hear the dark fairies at our backs. We might have lost them, at least for now. But there's someone in front of us, I have to check it out. You'll be safe here, I think. But if you hear or see dark fairies approaching, call out and I'll come."

"Was Missy going to let that dark fairy kill us?" Paddy asked, shaken. She wanted to pat him on his big green skull, reassure him, but she had only one good hand to hold the light. She shook her head.

"No one is going to kill either of you," she said.

Turning her flashlight on low, keeping it aimed at the floor, Ali crept forward. The air in the cave had changed dramatically.

It was fresher, cooler, there was a scent to it she had never experienced before. Wild flowers mixed with cow dung? She could not be sure. There was also an odor of sulfur. Certainly, it did not smell like Pete's Peak. From what she knew of the internal geography of the mountain, she doubted they could be anywhere near the outside.

The orange glow was coming from a single burning torch. Moving forward, Ali turned off her light, walked softly, trying to maintain the element of surprise. Her injured hand was a furnace; the burn could have been inside her brain. She could only bear it by reminding herself that she had no choice. Just as bad, she continued to feel a total energy block in the palm, and worried she would not be able to direct enough power to defeat a swarm of dark fairies. She needed a break soon or they would all die, and they had yet to enter the elemental kingdom.

She caught sight of a dark teenage boy. He wore a brown skin around his narrow waist—it could have been an antelope hide—had powerful shoulders, long thin legs. His hair was black, shoulder length, uncombed, and he had the most fascinating face she had ever seen on a boy her age. There was strength there, a wild savagery, but an intellect as well. His black eyes were round and luminous; he had the most intense stare.

Yet he was not looking at her, he did not know she was there. His gaze was fixed on a small brass-colored altar that had been set up on the muddy black floor. There was a metal plate covered with a dark pile of ash, a candle and incense holders, as well as tiny dishes of rice and water. The torch was above and behind the boy, fixed on the wall. For the first time Ali noticed how different the cave walls were; no longer smooth frozen lava, but rough stone, unchiseled, cool to the touch.

The boy seemed to be chanting before the altar.

Ali did not recognize the language. She hated to interrupt.

"Hi," she said.

The boy jumped up, grabbed a sword, lifted it high, peered in her direction. She was not sure he could see her. He was standing close to the torch, and she had to remind herself that her senses were much more acute than a normal human being. She could even hear and see better than Farble and Paddy. Ali stepped toward the boy, into the glow cast by the torch. He did not lower his sword, but spoke in a strange language.

"Wewe ni nani?" he said.

"I'm sorry, I don't understand," she said.

He paused, frowned. "You're an American. What are you doing here?"

He had a distinct English accent, and there was a seriousness to his tone.

"I might ask you the same question," she said. "Who are you?"

"My name is Ra Omlee."

She held her injured hand close to her shirt, feeling the blood soaking through the material. The pain had her breathing heavily, even when she was standing still, but she did not want him to see she was injured.

"I'm Ali Warner. How did you get here?" she said.

"I climbed up here this morning. This is my uncle's cave. No one comes here without his permission." He added, "All climbers are warned not to come to this part of the mountain."

"Who is your uncle? I don't know him."

"Everyone knows my uncle. He is Tar Omlee. Chimvi of the Kutus." Ra glanced down at the pile of ash. "He was our greatest chimvi."

Ali understood the ashes were the man's cremated remains. Other than that, there was little else she understood.

"What is a chimvi?" she asked.

Ra struggled to find the word. "Shaman."

"You use the word 'shaman,' and you look like someone from the African plains. How did you come to be here?" she asked.

"I told you, I climbed the mountain this morning."

As far as she knew, it was still morning outside.

"Are you spending time in Breakwater?" she asked.

He lowered his sword slightly, did not set it aside, came closer. She saw a hint of blue in his dark eyes, and realized that his skin was more brown than black.

"I do not know this Breakwater," he replied.

"How can you *not* know it?" she asked.

He shook his head. "Answer *my* questions. How did you come to be here?"

"I climbed the mountain last night."

He snorted. "In the dark? We are six thousand meters up. No one can do that."

Six thousand meters was over eighteen thousand feet.

Pete's Peak was tall but not that tall.

"I'm not alone." She glanced behind her. "I have friends with me."

He was suspicious. "Why do they hide back there?"

"I told them to stay there. Until I could see who was here."

"And they do what you say?"

"Yes. Why shouldn't they?"

Ra gestured. "You are a young girl."

"Really? You are a young boy." She added, "I'm almost fourteen."

"I'm almost fifteen," he said proudly.

"You don't look it. You don't look any older than myself."

"That's because you're an American, and all Americans do is eat and grow fat."

"I'm no fatter than you."

He looked her over. "You do not look thirteen. I think you are lying."

Ali stopped. The conversation was not exactly going in an intelligent direction.

"That language you spoke, when you first saw me. What was it?" she asked.

"Swahili."

Ali frowned. "Where are you from?"

He stared at her. "Here."

Ali almost froze. "Where is here?"

"You silly American. You do not know where you are?"

"I thought I did," she muttered, frowning. "This is not Breakwater?"

"I told you twice, I do not know that name."

"Then tell me where we are!" she ordered, and she put some power behind it.

He seemed to feel her power; he was suddenly wary. "You are in Tanzania, in a sacred cave on the slopes of Kilimanjaro."

Ali sagged against the wall. "That's impossible," she gasped.

"What is impossible?"

Her pain was making it difficult for her to think clearly. "I cannot be here."

"That is what I am saying. I have come here to honor my uncle. You are disturbing me. Leave now, with your friends. You can reach camp five before the sun sets. You will be safe there."

She shook her head. "I cannot leave here. I have things to do." She nodded to the ash. "You say this is your uncle's cave. How much do you know about it?"

He appeared to know something, for he hesitated. "I have told you, this place is sacred. It is for machimvis . . . shamans, not young girls."

Ali was amused. "You call yourself a shaman?"

126

He was offended. "I'm an apprentice. One day I will be a chimvi—a famous shaman." He added, "I have power."

"I am glad you have power. I have power, too. But now is not the time to talk about it. Did your uncle ever describe to you that this cave leads to other places?"

Ra got angry. "Have you been exploring this cave? That is forbidden! Even I have not been allowed to walk into its depths. Not until I am sixteen. That is the law."

"I don't care about your law. I *am* from the depths of this cave. I'm not from around here. Neither are my friends." She paused. "Would you like to meet them?"

"I want them to leave, with you, that is what I want."

Ali would have called out to Farble and Paddy, but was afraid her voice might carry. Ignoring his last remark, she started back the way she had come. "I'll return in a few minutes. When I do, when you see my friends, do not get scared," she said.

"I never get scared," he said.

"I used to say that," Ali muttered as she walked away.

She found Paddy and Farble where she had left them, cowering in the pitch black. Without explaining, she told them to follow her. They were too shaken to argue, and two minutes later Ra was staring at them in amazement. To his credit, he did not try to attack anyone with his sword. But he continued to hold on to it.

"Huu ni muujiza!" he whispered in awe.

"I know how you feel," Ali said. "Ra, this is Farble and Paddy. Farble is a troll, and Paddy is a leprechaun—in case you were wondering. Guys, this is Ra, he is a chimvi from Tanzania." She added, "You don't have to shake hands if you don't want to. But you might want to put down your sword, Ra. We mean you no harm."

"Hili haliwezi kuwa linatendeka," he mumbled.

"English, please," she said.

"My uncle spoke of such things," he said quietly. "I was . . . not convinced."

Ali teased. "You thought maybe he was lying?"

Ra stared at her, lowered his sword slightly. "Who are you?"

"I told you, I'm Ali Warner, a skinny American. Look, this mountain is more than it appears. Have you heard of America's Pete's Peak?"

"No."

"It's in the Pacific Northwest . . . of the United States. A little while ago we were there. And if you hike deeper into this cave, you'll end up there as well. But it sounds like your uncle knew that about this cave." She nodded to the ashes. "May I ask how he died?"

Ra shook his head. "You would not believe me if I told you."

Ali glanced at her elemental friends. "Are you sure about that?"

Ra reconsidered. "I found him here. His chest had been . . . burned away."

"When did you find him?"

"A week ago. I brought him back to our village to be honored, and now I have brought his ashes here, where they are to stay."

"Do you know what killed him?" Ali asked.

Ra was slow to answer. "Demons."

"Your uncle spoke to you about demons?"

"Yes."

"Have you ever seen any?"

"No."

Slowly Ali took her hand away from her shirt, showed him her raw palm.

"A demon did this to me," she said.

Ra paled. "My uncle was burned that same way!"

Ali nodded toward the rear of the cave. "My friends and I are here because we're running from a bunch of demons. They have weapons that are able to shoot bolts of fire—like laser beams." She paused. "You know what lasers are, don't you?"

"I have seen your *Star Trek*," he replied.

Ali was delighted with his reference. When she thought about it, his command of English was excellent. She suspected he had grown up on a diet heavy with American TV and video games. At the same time, he gave the impression that he was from a simple tribe. It was a puzzle.

"Those are phasers, actually, but it is the same difference. These demons are real. We came here, into your uncle's cave, to hide from them. But I have to go back to where they are, and probably confront them."

Ra finally set down his sword and examined her palm. He had courage; the sight would have made most kids their age faint. For that matter, looking at it made her dizzy. But Ra did not flinch as he studied the exposed muscles.

"You need medical attention," he said. "A hospital. There is one in Arusha that is good. This wound will get infected soon." He added, "I will help you down the mountain. My uncle's ashes can wait."

Ali shook her head. "I don't have time for a hospital. These demons I spoke of—they come from another realm, and I have to close the door to it."

His earlier insolence returned. "How can *you* close such a magical door?"

"Laddie, watch your lip. Missy is queen of all the fairies," Paddy said.

Ra jumped back. "It speaks!"

"Aye. I can wiggle me ears, too, if you like. Now help Missy with her hand and treat her with the respect she deserves."

Farble grunted and nodded his head. "Geea," he said.

Ra was confused. "Who is Geea?"

"I have a few names," Ali said. "Look, I would love to go to a hospital and have a doctor treat this, but I don't have time. Do you have any bandages?"

Ra nodded, stepped to a pile of clothes beneath the torch. Ali saw that he had pants, boots, and a jacket. He probably had only put on the antelope hide to perform his uncle's burial ceremony, but she thought he looked kind of cute in the skin.

Ra returned with a first aid kit, opened it for her to see. There were rolls of gauze, white tape, rubbing alcohol, scissors, and antibiotic cream. There were also several crudely rolled cigarettes.

"What are those?" she asked.

"Opium. You should smoke some."

"I don't do drugs."

"You are not *doing* drugs when you use them to stop pain." He added, with a note of respect, "Your pain must be great."

She forced a smile. "I've felt better. But I cannot take any opium now. I need all my wits to get past the dark fairies."

"They are fairies?" He was confused. "You are a fairy?"

"I am a fairy, that is true, but I am also a girl." She added, "I'm not a dark fairy."

He stiffened. "Do you say they are demons just because they are dark?"

"No! They are demons because they are demons!" Sitting down on the floor, she rested her flashlight on a nearby rock so she could tend her hand in the white beam. "Give me some of that bandage."

Ra knelt in front of her. "I will tend your wound. Let me get my water, clean it as best I can." He added, "You have lost a lot of skin. You need an operation."

Ali closed her eyes, nodded weakly. "Maybe later I can have one."

Ra fetched his canteen and set about cleaning the edges of her burn, but was hesitant to tackle the areas where she had no skin at all. She understood; she wanted to cover the bloody mess as quick as possible. Sitting gave her a chance to catch her breath, but it just made her pain more noticeable. The opium cigarettes tempted her, but she knew she had to get her power up and running. Without magical protection, the dark fairies would slice them to pieces.

Time pressed on her more than the others could have guessed. No doubt Radrine planned to return to the red door by circling around to the top entrance of the cave. That would take time—the route was at least a dozen miles, probably more—but the queen could fly. Unlike last time, Ali had failed to damage Radrine's wings. Ali just wished she had been able to kill her when she had been standing in front of her. She remembered the vow she had spoken in the cavern in front of the seven doors. The next time would be the last time for that monster.

Yet Ali did not want to confront Radrine until she had healed some.

While Ra worked on her, she swallowed about a third of her stardust.

If it helped, she did not notice. All she felt was pain.

Ra splashed a little rubbing alcohol on her palm and she almost jumped out of her body. "Ahhhh!" she cried.

"Sorry," he said.

Ali sucked in a breath. "It's all right."

"You're not really a fairy, are you?"

"It is hard to explain."

"You don't have any wings."

She opened her eyes, smiled at him. "How do you know I don't have wings?"

For the first time, he smiled back. "You have courage, at least . . . Ali."

"So do you, Ra."

Ali closed her eyes again, let Ra do his work, and found herself thinking about Nira. She had thought about the girl most of the way up the mountain—her eyes especially, the spell they cast, the feeling of vastness behind them. When they had been alone together, with Freddy's corpse, the Yanti had gotten so hot and then the body had moved, spoke that one word, "*Shaktra.*" It had said "Shaktra" just when she had asked Nira who she was.

Had Nira been trying to tell her she was the Shaktra?

Somehow that did not feel right. Nira intimidated her, but did not repel her, as she assumed the Shaktra would. No, Ali sensed, the Shaktra was tied up with the answer to that question, but was not the answer itself.

The heat of the Yanti had not harmed Nira. Why? Seconds before the corpse had moved, Nira had grabbed the Yanti and Freddy's hand. No, Ali strained to remember, first Nira had picked up the Yanti, placed it on her forehead, her heart, and then the top of her head. Ali felt her heart pound as she recalled the sequence. It felt familiar! She had done it herself! As a fairy! The name alone, Alosha, was not necessarily enough to activate the Yanti, not for certain jobs.

Ali opened her eyes and sat up.

She was suddenly sure she knew how to open the fourth door.

"Hurry up," she said to Ra, as he rolled the bandage around her outstretched hand. "I have to go back."

He was concerned. "Where?"

"Back to the place I was before I came here," she said.

Ra was against the plan. He could see Farble and Paddy were

132

real, and that she was probably telling the truth about the cave connecting to another place, but nevertheless he tried to persuade her to go down the mountain to a hospital. For an apprentice shaman he was practical. She stood when he finished with her hand, waved off his concerns.

"There are things I have to do that can't wait," she said. "But I want to thank you for your help. You've been great."

"What are you going to do if you run into the demons again?"

"I can take care of myself," she said.

Ra glanced at her hand. "Listen, I should go with you. Besides my sword, I have a bow and arrow. I am an excellent shot."

"I believe you, Ra. But with these dark fairies, I don't think a bow and arrow is going to do much good."

Ra was proud. "I killed a lion with one shot. I was ten at the time."

Paddy was impressed. "Missy might need another hand, when her hand is sore and all."

Ali came close to Ra, sizing him up, glanced again at his climbing clothes. "How close to the top of Kilimanjaro are we?"

"We're almost at the top," he said.

"And you climbed up here all by yourself?"

"I climbed up here pulling my uncle on a sled." He added, "I'm stronger than most people my age."

"Why is that?"

"I don't know. But I do know I can help you, and that you are injured and need help. Take me with you."

"You don't understand. We're not just trying to return to our part of the world. If that were true, I would accept your offer and climb down the mountain with you and take a jet home. I'm trying to return my friends to *their* world. In another part of this cave there are magical doors, and one, I believe—if I can open it—will take me into their world."

Ra was puzzled. "You have not opened it before?"

"It's a long story, I don't have time to go into it now. Suffice to say, if you come with us, your chances of dying are pretty good."

Ra remained stubborn. "I'm not afraid of dying."

"I used to think that. Until I ran into the dark fairies."

Ra shook his head. "You say I do not understand you. *You* do not understand me. These creatures killed my uncle. It was my uncle who raised me. I have to take vengeance on them."

"My goal is to get through this magical door. I will avoid the dark fairies if I can. Even if you come with me, it doesn't mean you will have vengeance." She added, "And that is not a reason to do anything."

Ra looked at his uncle's ashes. "That is easy for you to say."

Ali sighed. "None of this is easy for me. Honestly, I would like your help. There is something about you—I don't know what it is. But I sense that you do have your own power. But if you come, and you die, then how will I feel?"

"The decision to risk my life is mine, not yours." Ra studied Farble and Paddy. "This could be the adventure of a lifetime. If you leave without me, how can I hike back down to my village and go on with my simple life? It will feel so empty. Listen, I want to help you, I long for revenge, but I also want to see what you are going to see." He added with feeling, "I *need* to see everything."

Ali understood his reasons. Had the roles been reversed, she would have wanted to go. Plus she was not sure what kind of force field she could project. Paddy could be right—she might need Ra's bow and arrow, after all. She stared him in the eye.

"All right, you can come," she said. "But you have to know up front that I am in charge of this expedition. You can offer me your opinion, you can argue with me. But in the end, I decide what we do next. Understand?"

"It is not our custom that a female should give the orders to a male."

"I don't care about your customs. I only care about succeeding in my mission. Do you understand?"

Ra hesitated. "Yes."

"Good. Get out of that skin, get your hiking clothes on, and let's get out of here."

Ra was ready to leave within fifteen minutes. But he did take the time to pack up his altar and his uncle's ashes, and hide them in a crack in the cave. He extinguished his torch, but brought out a flashlight and Ali was happy for the backup. But she told him to keep it off for the time being.

They hiked deeper into the cave, with Ali leading the way, Paddy next, then Ra and Farble. Surprisingly, the troll and Ra hit it off right away. Ra spoke to him like he was a person and Farble nodded agreeably. Paddy, too, appeared comfortable with Ra, much more than he had ever been with Steve and Cindy.

Ali didn't know what to make of it.

Because they were not racing, it took them forty minutes to reach the main cave. There was no sign of the dark fairies. Ali could not hear a sound in either direction. But she worried that Radrine might have set a trap for her. Ali pointed to the right, toward the cavern.

"We don't speak from here on, unless I say so," she said.

It took another hour to reach the seven doors, but Ali stopped short of the spot, killed the flashlight, and went forward alone. Even in the pitch black, she was surprised to discover she could see the walls, the floor; not well, but enough to get by. Her right hand continued to throb with pain, but the bandage helped. Yet she did not feel her force field flowing through her hand, and that was bad.

Ali peered around the edge of the yellow door, into the cavern.

Three dark fairies stood guard in front of the red door.

It was still open. No surprise.

Ali almost fainted. So was the green door!

Radrine must have gone through it!

Why? To warn the Shaktra that she was coming?

Ali cursed silently. She had given Radrine too much time to circle around.

She crept back to the others, spoke to them in the dark, explained the situation.

"We have to take all three out at once," she said. "Fortunately, there are rocks all over the floor. What we're going to do is creep down to the yellow door, then burst through, and turn on our flashlights and blind them. Then, Farble, you and I'll grab a big rock and throw it at them. In fact, Farble, you take out the dark fairy on your right." She paused. "You know what your right is?"

The troll nodded in the dark, but then shook his head.

"Never mind, just hit one of the dark fairies and Ra and I will get the others. Ra, can you fit an arrow now, in the dark?"

"I already have," he said.

"Good. Have your flashlight ready, too. Hold it in your mouth if you have to. Remember, the element of surprise is everything. We need to kill them before they can use their fire stones."

"Those are like phasers?" Ra asked.

"Every bit as bad," Ali said.

"What should I do, Missy?" Paddy asked.

"Just be yourself."

Hopefully prepared, they crept down the cave toward the yellow door. The three dark fairies were acting like they had been given easy duty. They appeared to be joking with one another— it came across as a flock of ravens cackling over a rotting rabbit. Ali could hear them from far away.

When Ali's team reached the edge of the door, she did not

give anyone on either side a chance to think. Turning on her flashlight, she leapt into the cavern and pointed the beam at the dark fairies, before reaching down and picking up a fair-sized rock with her right hand. Yes, despite the fact that it was killing her, she used it because she had the flashlight in her left hand and she trusted her right arm—even with limp fingers attached to it—to deliver a fastball better than her left.

The dark fairies were raising their fire stones when Ali hit the one on the left in the face. The blow was perfectly thrown—the fairy's evil expression turned to benign pulp. Simultaneously, she saw the fairy in the center go down with an arrow through his throat. But Farble missed with his throw and the fairy on the right was given time to take aim at Ali. She was the only one the creature had eyes for. Ali saw the fire stone glow, prepared to leap to the side.

Then a second arrow struck it in the chest and it fell dead.

Purple blood soaked the filthy floor and it stank.

Stunned, Ali turned to Ra. "How did you reload so fast?" she asked.

Holding his wooden bow, he shrugged. "A shaman's secret."

Searching the area, Ali found the fire stones that she had carried up the mountain, undamaged beneath some rubble. It was clear Radrine had not had time to scour the floor when she had returned or else she would not have left them behind. That made Ali even more confident that Radrine had been in a hurry to enter the green door ahead of her. But why had she left the door unlocked?

Was Radrine deliberately baiting her to follow?

One thing was for sure, Ali did not want to leave the red door open. Asking the others to stand at a discreet distance, she took out the Yanti, held it in her right hand, put her left palm on the red door, chanted the word "Alosha" softly, placed the Yanti on her forehead, her heart, and then on top of her head—while all the time, inside, she silently commanded the red door to lock. Finally, when she was done, she opened her eyes.

The door was still open.

"Having trouble, Missy?" Paddy called behind her.

"Hush," she said.

"She's still learning to be a fairy," Paddy explained to Ra.

Again, Ali tried to remember *exactly* how Nira had handled the Yanti when she had caused the corpse to stir. It took her a few moments, but then she had it. Nira, with her tiny right hand, had purposely placed the tips of her fingers on the inside triangle when she had put the Yanti to her forehead. Then she had moved her fingers to the seven-sided exterior when she had held the Yanti over her heart. Finally, at the top of the head, Nira had held the Yanti with one finger, the middle finger, over the Yanti's central diamond.

Ali repeated the process, with Nira's addition. The rapid movement of the fingers took skill and, with her injured palm, she messed up the first few times. But on the sixth try she got it right, and the red door closed.

Finally, the door to hell was shut.

Ali gestured for the others to join her in front of the green door. Beyond it, all she could see was another dark cave. "When we go through, should I lock the door behind us?" she asked.

"Can you open it from the other side if you do?" Ra asked.

"Beats me," Ali replied.

The four of them stared at each other in the dark.

"Leave it open then," Ra said finally.

She teased. "Afraid I won't be coming back with you?"

Ra shrugged. "Who knows?"

Ali considered, then nodded. "We will leave it open, for now."

Together, the four of them stepped through the green door.

CHAPTER

11

Before visiting Rose and Nira for lunch, Steve and Cindy tried to talk to Hector Wells—infamous boyfriend of the late Lucy Pillar and Patricia Hassel. They found his address in the phone book, went to his house, knocked, but there was no answer. Cindy acted relieved.

"He's not going to spill his guts to us about his past because we babysat Nira for a few hours," she told Steve, as they climbed off the porch. "And he's not going to care that we're writing a paper for school on the plant explosion."

Hector's house was tiny but elegant; it showed signs a contractor lived inside. The brickwork on the walls and porch was flawless, and the doubled-paned windows were expensive. The cedar shingles used to form the roof were old world—they even smelled good—and the landscaping showed exquisite care.

"We'll need an angle to get him to talk," Steve agreed, glancing at his watch. "We better get up to Rose's."

"The house belongs to Sheri Smith," Cindy corrected him, as they hurried down the block toward the company headquarters. Rose had told them that the house was located directly behind Omega, in the trees. Cindy added, "Wonder if she'll be there?"

"I'd like to meet her," Steve said.

"What if she's the one who sent the e-mails to Karl?"

"So much the better."

Cindy stopped him. "You don't mean that. We're going against Ali's advice just being here. She told us Ms. Smith might be dangerous."

Steve nodded. "If she's the one who had Karl kidnap Ali's mother, she's going to be dangerous."

"Then why are we doing this? What's your plan?"

"I don't have one. We're just here to gather information for Ali."

Cindy considered. "I think I'm here for Nira."

"I've noticed that you like that little girl. Feel sorry for her?"

"It's not that. For some reason, I feel close to her. Like I want to protect her."

"From whom?" Steve asked.

"It's just a feeling is all. But her autism throws me. You saw how much more animated she was around Ali?"

Steve nodded. "Maybe the Yanti helped the girl."

"Ali said Nira had power over the Yanti."

"Yeah, but she did not explain why she said that." Steve added, "I like Nira, too. When she stares at me, I don't feel she's dumb."

Actually, when she stared at him, *he* felt happy.

"Didn't you say autism and retardation were two separate things?"

"Some autistic people can be geniuses. But they're not able to express themselves. Their minds don't connect with their bodies. They're all bottled up inside."

"Ali was fascinated by that scar between her eyebrows."

Steve nodded. "It doesn't look natural."

The day was warm and sunny; they were both sweating by the

time they climbed the long winding driveway to the Smith residence. It was largely uphill, through a pretty stretch of woods. Steve was not surprised to see that the home mimicked the architecture of the main headquarters. The place was all glass and cubes, wonderful for views, but hell on the furnace in the winter. He found the ultramodern look sterile, at odds with the green trees, and wondered what type of person would want to live in such a home.

Rose met them at the door, wearing a simple black dress and looking more relaxed than the day before. She explained that they had the house to themselves—except for Nira. The cook and the cleaning staff had already left for the day.

"Marge made a wonderful lunch before she left," Rose said, leading them deeper into the house, tugging at her elbow-length black gloves along the way. Steve found the white furniture as bland as the exterior. The dining room was a savior, however. There was a nice wooden table that overlooked downtown Toule, and there were plants in the corners. Rose had them sit, said they could have anything they wanted to drink. Cindy asked for a Coke, Steve, coffee. Rose chuckled as she walked toward the nearby kitchen.

"A man after my own heart. I drink six cups a day, all of it from Colombia," she said. "Makes me think of home."

"Do you ever go back?" Steve asked through the kitchen door as she fiddled with the coffeepot. Rose glanced over.

"Who would look after Nira?" she asked, surprised.

"But you must take time off?" Cindy said.

Rose shook her head. "I told you yesterday, Nira is my life now."

"Is she going to be joining us for lunch?" Steve asked.

"No," Rose said. "She's in her room."

"We were wondering if we could take her out for ice cream later?" Cindy asked.

"I don't think that would be a good idea." Rose didn't elaborate.

"Does her mother play with her in the evenings?" Cindy asked.

Rose returned with the Coke and coffee. Steve sipped his drink—a bit weak, too much cream, but smooth.

"Ms. Smith is not the playful sort," Rose said. "She spends time with Nira each evening, and they will read together and watch TV. But Ms. Smith usually brings home a lot of work."

"Does Nira understand what she reads? What she watches?" Steve asked.

"She has favorite books and TV programs. But it's impossible to say how much she grasps."

"How did she get that weird scar on her forehead?" Cindy asked.

Rose shook her head. "She had it when we met."

Lunch was Indian: tandoori chicken, vegetable samosas, basmati rice, pappadums. Steve was in seventh heaven. Breakwater, naturally, given its size, did not have an Indian restaurant, and neither of his parents liked Indian food. The only time he got close to such delicacies was when Cindy's mom made it, or Ali tried her hand at it, which was usually a disaster. Her fairy powers aside, Ali was a dreadful cook. She knew how to keep her dad happy, but all he ate was meat and potatoes.

For a time Steve blotted out the many town mysteries and just ate.

He was on his third helping of chicken when Cindy brought up the electric plant explosion. Rose's face brightened. "I've read about that, and talked to Ms. Smith about it. She was there, you know, that night. She saw the whole thing."

"I didn't know Ms. Smith was from here?" Steve said.

"She was born and raised in Toule. That's why she put Omega here. She wanted to give something back to the community. She employs a hundred locals." Rose paused. "I'm surprised you didn't know?"

Rose had not mentioned any of those facts yesterday.

She had acted like she had no idea why Sheri Smith had built Omega in Toule.

Steve mumbled, his mouth full. "We don't know that much about your local history."

Rose offered him another samosa. "Finish it, or I'll have to eat it later."

Steve accepted the samosa, cut it up, and mixed it in with his rice. "Was Ms. Smith injured that night?" he asked.

"No. It was something of a miracle she wasn't, at least the way she told it. To celebrate the basketball team's big victory, they had a short parade down the main street, then a party with food and speeches and drinking in front of the power plant. Ms. Smith was alone with her boyfriend in the plant when it exploded. I don't know what they were doing, I didn't ask. But when it blew, a wave of fire roared over her head. But she was not harmed."

"What about her boyfriend? Was he hurt?" Cindy asked.

Rose hesitated. "No."

"Amazing," Steve said, surprised to get so much information out of Rose, who did not seem like the type to gossip. "I thought everyone in the immediate area was burned to death."

Rose shook her head. "That woman doesn't have a mark on her." She added, "You can meet her if you'd like, ask her about that night. I told her about you two, how you took care of Nira while I was with Freddy's mother. She said she would like to thank you in person. She told me to ask if you would like to have lunch with her tomorrow. Like I said, she is a very busy woman, and almost never home. She must really want to meet you." Rose paused. "Would you like that?"

Steve glanced at Cindy, who ever so slightly nodded her head.

"That would be wonderful," he said.

When they were through eating, Rose told them to go say hi to Nira in her room. It seemed the girl spent a lot of time there, alone. Steve and Cindy were surprised when they entered the place; it was painfully sparse. There was a bed, a tiny desk, a chest of drawers, a closet of neatly hung clothes—that was it. There was not one book, no TV, not a single decoration on the walls. The room did not even have a decent view. Its sole window stared at a thick pine trunk. It could have been a nun's cell.

Nira glanced up as they peeked inside her room, but if she smiled it was too faint to detect. Yet she stopped what she was doing—playing with her fingers on the center of her bed—and stepped over and took Cindy's hand and led her into the room. The slight gesture of affection warmed Cindy's face. Maybe she was just happy the girl remembered her. Yet Nira's eyes kept straying to the door in anticipation, and there was no doubt that she was looking for Ali. Who wasn't, Steve thought.

Nira and Cindy sat on the bed together, and the little girl took Cindy's palm and began to draw circles on it, around and around, in the center. Cindy told Steve she had very warm hands.

"They feel like they just came out of the oven," she said.

"Repetitive behavior is common among the autistic," he said.

He might have spoken too soon, or maybe he shouldn't have spoken at all. Nira suddenly reached out and took his hand, and stared at his palm a long time, almost as if she were trying to divine his fortune. Then she looked up at him without blinking, and her strange eyes seemed to darken, and she slowly closed his hand and shook her head. He did not know why, but her fingers were the opposite of what Cindy had described. They were like ice, and he felt a chill run through the length of his body, and it did not go away, even when she let go of him.

CHAPTER

12

There was no Emerald City for her to see, not yet, but the soft green sun in the sparkling clear verdant sky was a treasure. Not because of its beauty, which was great, but because of the centuries of forgotten memories it invoked inside. Ali did feel at home the instant she exited the mountain cave and beheld the sun, yet she also felt fear. Home would not be exactly as she remembered, she knew. It was the reason she had left home in the first place, to be born as a human being. These days, there was much to fear in the elemental kingdom.

Still, coming out of the dark cave and into the light, she was happy.

The green sun was almost straight up, as the yellow sun would have been above Breakwater. She had entered another dimension but it did not look as if she had to reset her watch. She was pleased to see that the green light did not bother Farble.

The light of the sun surprised her in another way. Because of its soft radiance, it did not color everything green. The sand that surrounded their mountain was still yellow. The slopes of the bare peak were brown. Indeed, there wasn't single tree, not even a bush or a blade of grass, on the entire mountain. She asked Paddy if it had always been that way.

"Aye. As long as Paddy can remember." He added, worried, "But Paddy does not remember desert so close to the river, and so close to Tutor." He pointed to a two-mile stretch of sand that lay between the base of the mountain and a vast river. "The sand has spread," he said.

Tutor must be the name of the mountain, she thought, and she asked the name of the river, which Paddy called Elnar—not *the* Elnar. The "the" seemed unnecessary with such pretty names. As far as she could tell, the river flowed east to west, into the sea, which stretched forever to their left, and started not far from the western base of the mountain. Yet looking east, in the distance, she saw that Elnar was really made up of two rivers, one that came straight from the north, and one that flowed out of the east. They joined about ten miles inland. She pointed to the rushing water coming out of the north, and Paddy told her it was called, Lestre, after the Lustra.

"What are the Lustra?" she asked, although she believed she already knew.

"It is what the high fairies call themselves," Paddy said.

"Lestre runs through the fairy kingdom?" she asked.

"Through the heart of it, and all around Uleestar." Paddy added, "It is Lestre that makes Uleestar difficult to attack."

Ali nodded, having vague memories of a magical green island surrounded on all sides by a vast flowing river. "I hope it's still safe," she said.

"It was fine when I left, Missy," Paddy said.

The green ocean was enchanting. Never before had Ali seen such crystal-clear water. They were a mile up on Tutor—not nearly as high as they had been on Pete's Peak—and still she could see the floor of the sea as far out as two miles. With her fairy eyesight she could see different-colored fish and gigantic blue and gray shapes moving in the depths. Clearly the elemental sea was brimming with far more life than Earth's.

Far out at sea she saw an island.

"What about in the west? What's there?"

"The Isle of Greesh."

"Who controls the Isle of Greesh?"

"It fell . . . It . . . We do not speak of it."

"It fell to the Shaktra? Is that what happened?"

"It just came . . . No one knows where it came from."

Ali asked Paddy what they called their ocean.

"The ocean," he said.

She gave him a look. "Why do you guys all speak English, anyway?"

Paddy shrugged. "Why do you speak it?"

He had a point there, she thought. Who was mirroring whom? Paddy had told her before that much of what was in the human kingdom was also in the elemental kingdom, only in a changed form. The relationship was not direct—there were differences—but he had once said that a large toxic spill on Earth could damage their realm. That was another reason the elementals were angry at mankind, because of all the pollution people were making.

South of Tutor was all sand, and the desert appeared to stretch far into the east, along the edge of Elnar. But on the north side of the great river was normal brown earth, and not too far north she saw a low stretch of hills that was cut in half with the southward plunge of Lestre. The softly sculpted hills, along with the river Elnar, appeared as natural barriers between the desert and the lands of the leprechauns and the elves. Paddy agreed with her observation.

"None of us come this far south unless we have to," he told Ali.

"When Lord Vak was assembling his forces to invade Earth, did he drive his army up here?" she asked.

"Aye. We came over the bridge you see crossing Elnar, then hiked up here, along a path."

The stone bridge he referred to was an imposing feat of engineering, for Elnar was three hundred yards across—three football fields set length to length. It was when Elnar joined with Lestre that the river swelled dramatically. But the sight of the bridge caused her to reflect on what type of tools the elementals possessed. For all she knew, the bridge had been built by magic alone. She questioned Paddy but he had no idea who had made it, only that it was very old.

"It was there when Paddy was a boy, and his pa was a boy," he said.

The path Paddy had spoken of wound back and forth up the mountain, without actually circling it. It was broad, made up of well-worn marble stones, and Ali could easily see an army marching up it to the top of Tutor. She assumed that was where Lord Vak had positioned his force, just before he had opened the Yanti and materialized on Earth. It scared her to think how bitter their retreat from Tutor must have been, after she had sent them back. The last thing Lord Vak had promised her was that the next time they met, he was going to show no mercy. She had to either join him or die. . . .

Yet Ali did not feel that was the choice that had to be made.

The Shaktra was their common enemy.

She did not see any road between the base of Tutor and the bridge.

"It was there a month ago," Paddy said when she questioned him. "The sand must have covered it. I told you, the desert has grown."

"How could it have grown so quickly?" she asked.

Paddy shuddered. "The scabs."

"What exactly are the scabs?"

"Best not to talk about them."

"What if we run into them? I need to know if they're dangerous."

"Very dangerous, Missy," Paddy said in his most unhelpful manner.

"Not good enough. I need to know ahead of time how to handle them."

"Use your fairy powers."

"To do what?" she asked.

Paddy shrugged. "Kill them."

"Is there any way to detect them before they attack?"

"We won't see them until they come out of the ground."

"Can they fly? Do they have weapons? Is their bite poisonous? Are there lots of them?"

"Yes," Paddy said, nodding. "All those things."

"Oh brother," she groaned.

Ali turned to Ra, who stood in silent awe. She understood the glow in his eyes. Since exiting the cave, she had almost forgotten about the pain in her hand. Farble, for his part, also seemed happy to be back. But he kept clawing at his backpack, trying to sneak steaks when he thought she was not looking. She suspected that he had already finished off half his food. It did not matter, the meat would have spoiled anyway. She had to assume there was food to be had, at least when they got beyond the hills.

"I bet when you woke up this morning, you didn't think you'd end up in a place like this," she said to Ra.

He turned to her. "I have you to thank."

"Don't be silly. You have earned your keep already. But now that you've seen this place, you might want to head back. There's no predicting what we're going to run into on the road."

"Do you know where you're going?"

"North, into a land called Karolee, where the fairies live. There's an island there called Uleestar, where I think I can get some answers."

"What kind of answers are you looking for?" Ra asked.

Ali shook her head. "It's a long story, I don't have time to tell it all now. Just know that my mother has been kidnapped, and that I'm pretty sure she's being held hostage in this dimension."

"Did the fairies kidnap her?"

"It's complicated," she said, thinking of Karl Tanner, Drugle, who used to serve on her high court, before joining forces with the dark fairies and the Shaktra.

Ra was sympathetic. "I would be honored to help you find your mother."

His comment touched her. She pointed to the two miles of sand that separated Tutor from Elnar and the stone bridge. "Paddy says creatures called scabs live in that sand, and that we need to avoid them at all costs. We'll climb down and cross as fast as we can. But I think you had better be ready with your bow and arrow at all times."

"Understood," Ra said.

She grinned. "I think you're getting used to taking orders from a girl."

"As you like to say in America, don't push it."

Ali patted Farble on the back. "You all right?"

He nodded. "Hungry."

"Hungry? I just saw you eating!"

The troll bowed his head, embarrassed. "Not hungry."

They climbed onto the stony road, started down the mountain. Although the path wound vigorously—in an obvious attempt to take the sting out of the decline—Ali still found the way steep. It reminded her how tough elementals were compared to humans, and how badly it might go for humanity if they ever invaded Earth. Despite mankind's high-tech weapons, the elves, the dwarves, and their partners were a determined foe. When she had spoken to Lord Vak, he had acted like they had no choice but to take over the Earth.

The climate was warm and humid; there were odors in the air that reminded her of candy stores and flower shops rolled together. The air was richer in oxygen—each breath seemed to satisfy the lungs more. The descent was jarring to the bottom of her feet, but she felt herself carried along by the dual forces of gravity and a wonderful sense of adventure. What Ra had said in Africa was true. This journey was the chance of a lifetime. She just hoped that at the end of it she would find her mother.

Halfway down the road, she felt the ground move, a minor tremor. Indeed, it was identical to the quake she had felt in the cave in Pete's Peak. It made her wonder if Tutor had the potential of transforming itself into an active volcano.

They took three miles to descend one mile, to reach the flat sandy plain. The latter started suddenly, the road just disappeared. Ali asked Paddy about wind and sandstorms. The leprechaun looked worried and shook his head.

"The scabs spread the desert," he repeated.

"So they've always been here?"

His answered surprised her. "They came a few years ago."

"Where did they come from?"

"Some say the sea, Missy."

"That makes no sense. They come out of the sea and they spread desert?"

Paddy eyed the sand nervously. He made Ali feel as if the three miles to the water and bridge was a hundred miles. "Some say they were *made*, Missy," he said.

Ali paused. "On the Isle of Greesh?"

Paddy nodded. "Must keep them off our heads. Important."

"What do they do if they get on your head?"

The leprechaun shuddered. "Eat your brains."

Ali turned to Ra. "What do you think?" she asked.

Holding his bow ready, Ra peered in the direction of the bridge. "This sand might not be deep. If we stay on the road, it's possible we might avoid these creatures."

"What road? I can't see any road," she said.

"It must be there, buried beneath the sand. It should run straight across, between here and the bridge."

Ali took out the fire stones, balanced them in her left palm. If she could've erected a force field around them, they wouldn't have had to face such danger. Radrine's shot had cost them dearly. As it was, she was not sure how much power she could generate in the stones. Her initial excitement was cooling, she felt exhausted. It had been ages since she had slept.

Yet Ali drew herself up, tried to look confident in front of her friends.

"We'll run across the sand," she said. "We'll stay close together, keep our eyes open. Anyone see anything, they shout out. Ready?"

Paddy and Farble hemmed and hawed at the edge of the sand. Farble must have known about the scabs, too. The troll kept trying to grab her hand. She had to explain that she had to keep her hands free to use the fire stones. In the end, she decided to put them between her and Ra. The move pacified the elementals only slightly.

"Now, on the count of three, we go," Ali said.

"The troll can't count up to three," Paddy muttered.

"He'll get the idea. One . . . Two . . . Three!" she shouted.

They ran, or more accurately, they *tried* to. The sand was extremely fine, plenty deep. It slipped beneath their feet like coarse liquid. They could have been attempting to sprint through mud, and in fact pushing too hard caused them to slip more. Ali discovered a medium pace was best, but even that was exhausting. The sand seemed alive, hungry; it did not want them to leave before it was sated. She felt as if she were trying to climb a wall, and falling off a cliff, at the same time.

They were halfway to the river when the scabs attacked.

The first one came out of the sand on her right, thirty feet away. At first she was not impressed. It looked like a lump of jellyfish with a burnt top. Then its lower portion began to spin quickly—the tentacle part—while the top inflated with air, vigorously sucking it in, making a farting sound, growing in size until it was as large as a basketball. Ali could not figure out how the bottom could spin while the top remained still.

She was not an engineer, but she knew that such a combination of moves would require spokes and an axis—things nature did not make. Then she remembered Paddy's remark. The scabs had probably been *designed* and bred on the Isle of Greesh. They were not natural at all.

The spinning tentacles gave the creature a hovercraft capability. Slowly, the thing began to lift off the sand, spreading dust all around. The latter was a problem. The single creature stirred up enough sand to sting their eyes as it began to move toward them.

Ali told Ra to shoot it.

Ra let fly an arrow.

The *slow*-moving scab suddenly jerked to the side.

The arrow missed. Once more the scab started in their direction, but not all of its lower portion spun. It still dangled long tentacles. These were covered with red suction cups that oozed a slimy green fluid.

Behind them, two more scabs poked out of the sand and began to inflate.

Ali turned to Paddy. "Can we outrun these things?"

For a leprechaun, he was awfully white. "Don't think so, Missy."

They tried anyway. The scab seemed to respond to their running. It accelerated toward them. Ali felt they had to stop and face it. As choking dust spread around them, the creature made a diving swoop over their heads. Its purpose was obvious: to drop down on top of their skulls, to get its tentacles into their mouths and nostrils and ears. But it missed on its initial pass, and Ali took aim with her fire stones. Off to her left, she could see the two other scabs rising off the ground, while another three stuck their gross bodies out of the sand.

Ali fired. She was happy just to get off a shot, but the beam was feeble. It hit the scab; the creature seemed to recoil, to lose elevation. Unfortunately, it did not fall, it did not die. Ali went to shoot at it again when Ra called out.

"Behind you!" he cried.

Ali whirled, discovered a scab she didn't even know about swooping toward her head. She barely managed to get off a shot. It was almost straight above her, three feet from her hair. It was possible the creature's underbelly was sensitive. Her blast was as weak as her first, but the scab convulsed in midair—a gory pink balloon touched by a match—and it dropped to the ground, just missing her.

"Can you hit any of them?" she cried to Ra.

"Trying!" he shouted back. She saw him miss again, just as she turned to face two more swooping scabs. Yet these guys seemed to have taken note of their comrade's fall. They did not try for her, but for Farble and Paddy. The troll and leprechaun did the worst thing possible. They panicked and ran from her side, toward the bridge. As a result, she had to shoot at the scabs from behind, and at a greater distance. She had to hit each one three times before they went down. But by then there were over *twenty* scabs crawling out of the sand.

"Stop!" she yelled at Farble and Paddy, and there was power in her voice. They froze in midstride. Ali and Ra hastened to them, and put their hands over their eyes as a miniature dust storm rose around them. The scabs must have had intelligence, or else profound instincts. Ali had killed three, and they were clearly not used to that. Now it appeared they wanted to act as a group. With cunning they surrounded them in a broad circle, then—as more of their partners emerged from the sand and rose up, spinning dust and farting the air they swallowed—they began to tighten their circle. Ali counted thirty. It might as well have been three hundred. Farble whimpered and Paddy started to weep.

"Missy!" he cried.

"Don't be afraid!" she said.

Farble moaned. "Geea . . . Geea."

"It will be all right!" she snapped.

The scabs' circle went from sixty feet across to thirty, while another ten of the creatures joined the fray. The scabs angled their bottoms in their direction, hitting them with more wind, more dust. Their odor was nauseating: moldy meat soaked in boiling vinegar. They chirped as they closed, making an odd clicking sound, probably gloating over how tasty the four bipeds looked. Ali could not imagine what it would feel like to have one drop on her head and begin to eat her brains.

"What do we do?" Ra asked, his back to her.

Ali focused her gaze hard on her side of the enveloping circle. The scabs seemed to feel her, they slowed their approach, yet they did not back off. Even at full power, she realized, she was not going to be able to shoot all of them.

"There's a Bic lighter in my backpack, in the top on the right," she said. "Hand it to me."

She felt Ra fumble in her pack. "You don't want to smoke that opium now, do you?" he asked.

She almost smiled, spoke softly instead. "A month ago I passed the test of fire, the test of air. I might be able to combine the two elements and treat these creatures to a barbecue."

Ra put the lighter in her left hand. Dropping the fire stones, she transferred it to her *right* hand, took a step away from her partners, closer to the scabs. The dust was a bank of yellow fog. The ghosts that hovered in it were images from a witch's dreams. The circling scabs had created a scary cauldron, she thought, a soup kettle that they planned to feed from. What they didn't know was that she was about to reach outside the kettle and throw a huge log on the fire.

Ali raised the lighter to her lips, struck the flame, focused her will, and blew.

The flame magnified itself a hundredfold. It swept the area in front of her. Six scabs immediately caught fire. Their top shells ignited like newspaper, while their lower halves cracked and sparked like bowls of Jell-O soaked in gasoline. Another six scabs fled her attack, but she blew again, before they could get out of range, and the roaring flames scorched both their spinning and dangling tentacles as they caught fire. And the air they had sucked inside must have somehow changed itself into gas because suddenly the scabs began to explode like ponderous zeppelins caught in the crosshairs of a World War I machine gun.

Turning on her heels, Ali blew fire all around. She was a volcano attached to a carrousel. She felt like a ballerina, a dragon, and most of all, like the queen of the fairies. Power had returned to her right arm—she believed she could throw thunderbolts. The scabs snorted in disgust as they popped and fell to the ground, burning in the sand, and she shouted with joy. She wanted to burn them, she hated them so much. She was not even sure why.

Drawing in another deep breath, enough air to feed forty lungs, she blew . . . and a geyser erupted from her lips. It could have been a dream; she did not feel herself, or else she felt much *more* than herself. She was a match, her red hair was a flame, the center of her brain was a smoldering coal. The scabs tried to run, to fly, but she kept breathing fire on them, and they kept dying, horribly, balls of seared jelly bursting from the inside.

She did not know how long this went on . . .

Ra suddenly grabbed her, though, stopped her, knocked the lighter away.

"Ali! Your hand!" he cried.

Her right hand, the injured one, was bleeding again. The red had already soaked her bandages, and was dripping onto the sand. She had not even noticed, but when she did, her body shuddered, and it was not her palm that seemed to go numb and throb with pain, it was her whole arm. Once again, she had let the power carry her away, and now the power deserted her. The scabs were burning but she was not in a whole lot better shape. A wave of dizziness swept over her. She had to lean on Ra to keep from falling.

"Help me to the bridge," she whispered.

Ra *carried* her to the bridge. She didn't know how, what with his bow and arrow, sword, and backpack. He had not been boasting—he was unusually strong. Ali felt a deep weariness slip over her mind, but managed to keep her eyes open long enough to see that no scabs were following. Paddy marched proudly by Ra's side, and kept telling her to relax, that she was in good hands.

They reached the bridge and Ra kept walking, carrying her

out until they were far over the water. There he set her down against a stone pillar, one of many, that supported the bridge against the powerful green current. Ali saw that the top of the bridge was made up of smooth gray rock tiles, that had been cemented together with dark plaster, but that underneath the tiles were aged tree trunks of incredible length and thickness. Indeed, the wood looked so old, so strong, it might have been petrified stone. Paddy was right, the bridge over Elnar was ancient.

Ali rested her aching head on the pillar. "Did you pick up the lighter?" she asked.

"Yes," Ra said.

"Did you get the fire stones? I dropped them."

"Got them, Missy," Paddy said.

"Try to relax, Ali. I have to attend to your hand." Ra searched through his pack. "I've never seen bleeding start up like that again."

Ali closed her eyes, tried to relax. "It's the power, it has a mind of its own. This human body can hardly contain it."

"You better learn to contain it," Ra said. "That was an impressive show, but it almost killed you."

Ali felt herself smile. "Do you believe I'm a fairy now?"

"I believe that you are a young woman who is pushing her limits."

"You know, you speak very good English for a shaman savage. How is that?"

"Are you trying to insult me?"

"Of course," she mumbled, her weariness deepening. The pain in her hand and arm was ghastly, but it was such a relief to be safe, she didn't care. And it was nice to have Ra caring for her. They had just met but she trusted him, she was not sure why.

"I watch a lot of American TV," Ra said.

She continued to rest with her eyes closed. "Ah-ha, I knew it. You envy us fat Americans."

"I did not say that. You are fat and stupid. But you have good programs."

"I enjoy me *Mr. Ed*," Paddy remarked, but he sounded far away.

Ali was not sure how long she lay there. She felt Ra removing her soaked bandage and cleaning her wound, before rolling on a fresh layer of gauze. After that, she was not sure what happened. She might have dozed. Her pain did not vanish but it receded into the distance. But she was still aware of the sweet breeze on her face, and the sound of water running beneath her. Elnar, she knew, was as deep as it was fast, and she could almost remember swimming in it as a fairy. . . .

She heard a horrible scream and sat up and opened her eyes.

Ra and Farble were gathered around Paddy.

It was Paddy who had screamed.

There was a scab attached to his left arm.

They were trying to get it off. It was not coming off.

Ali jumped up. "What happened?" she cried.

"We were resting, but I had my eyes open," Ra explained. "I told them I would stand guard. But I was looking at the water, I must have stared too long, and a scab must have come onto the bridge. No, it must have come from *under* the bridge. I would have seen it otherwise. I thought we were safe on the bridge!" He added, miserable, "This is my fault."

Ali knelt in front of Paddy, studied the creature, which looked even more like a jellyfish since it wasn't spinning in the air. It was smaller now that it had deflated—as large as a softball instead of a basketball. The top of the scab's body lay on the back of his arm, while the tentacles were wrapped around the inside. The dozens of tiny suction cups on the tentacles were stinging him—he was obviously in great pain. Tears ran down his face as he looked at her.

"Help me, Missy!" he cried.

"Do you know *how* we can help you?" she asked.

Paddy shook his head. "They say they never come off."

Ali glanced at Ra. "Did you try pulling it off?"

"We were just doing that," Ra said. "It's hard to get a grip on."

Farble nodded, anxious, patted the leprechaun on the head. "Paddy," he murmured. It was the first time he had ever said the leprechaun's name.

"Stand back, let me try," Ali said.

"But your hand—" Ra began.

"I don't care about my hand!" Ordering the others to hold Paddy still—not an easy task, he had begun to struggle—Ali tried grabbing the scab's top, but its tenuous surface slipped between her fingers. She had no more luck trying to pull off individual tentacles; they were coated with an oily residue. Besides stinging her own fingers, the stuff made them impossible to hold on to.

Ali looked around for her fire stones. "We're going to have to burn it off," she said. Paddy shook in terror at the suggestion.

"Don't burn me, Missy!"

Ali sought to calm him. "I'm not going to hurt you. I can control the amount of energy I send through the stones. This will just be like a little laser surgery back on Earth."

Paddy could not stop staring at the scab. "I feel it eating me skin!"

Ali suspected the creature was beginning to eat him. And she could not help but notice that it was moving up his arm, toward his shoulder, probably seeking out the head.

Resting the stones in her left palm, she focused on sending a fine beam of energy onto the surface of the scab. And she was successful, or so it seemed—a pencil-thin red laser reached out and struck the top coat of the scab. Unfortunately, the burn caused the creature to squeeze Paddy's arm so tight with its tentacles that Ali thought the limb might burst. Paddy's pain went off the deep end. He screamed bloody murder. Ra and Farble had to fight to hold him down.

"Kill it!" Ra shouted.

Ali nodded and increased the level of energy, but again it backfired. The scab just gripped tighter, while it injected more stinging venom into Paddy's arm, turning the skin on his hand a black-green color. At the same time, the burning drove it more quickly up his arm, toward his head. Once it got off his arm, Ali knew, he was done for.

"Keep it up!" Ra shouted at her as she paused. Shaking her head, Ali sat back on her knees.

"The more I burn it, the more poison it injects into his system," she said.

"You have to keep trying," Ra said.

"It will kill him before it will let go," she said.

Ra went to snap at her, but then looked down at Paddy's face, his sweaty agony, and slowly nodded his head. "You have to take his arm off," he said quietly.

Ali nodded. "I was thinking that."

"Better do it quick," Ra warned.

Ali got up on her knees, moved into position above Paddy. The creature was already well past his elbow—she would have to take the arm off near the top. That would cause him to bleed, of course, but she was confident she could muster enough healing energy to keep him alive. Anything would be better than letting the scab eat his brains.

So she told herself. But as she placed the fire stones near his joint, the leprechaun stopped thrashing and stared at her with pleading eyes. "No, Missy," he said.

"It's the only way to stop it," she said.

Paddy shook his head weakly, spoke in a strangled whisper. All the time, his eyes never left hers. "I couldn't find me gold, Missy. Came back empty-handed. Now I can't lose me arm. Lea . . . she would not have me. No one would."

Ali's eyes burned. "But I can't let it eat your brain."

"Kill me, Missy."

"What? No!"

"Yes." He gripped her hand with his free hand. "You have to do it. Paddy cannot live with one arm, and Paddy cannot take this pain. Stop it, Missy, please stop it."

"Paddy . . ."

He wept. "Do it for poor Paddy!"

Ali had never known such anguish, and it was hers to bear alone. The other two could only look at her and watch as the scab slowly moved higher. Yet Ra was shaking his head—he still wanted her to take the arm—and Farble was trembling, gently rubbing Paddy's hair. Ali felt she had not entered the elemental kingdom, after all, but had taken a wrong turn and dragged them down into hell with her.

Then, in a moment, she knew what she had to do.

Ali let go of Paddy, set down the fire stones, and began to unwrap her bandage. Ra looked puzzled for a moment, then anxious. "What do you think you are doing?" he demanded.

"I'm going to stop it," she said.

"How?"

"I'm going to let it drink my blood."

"What?"

"It can have my arm," she said.

Ra was aghast. "That's crazy! You'll die!"

She stared at him. "When it's on me, then I'll cut off my arm, with the stones, and I'll live."

"Ali . . ."

"I can survive the trauma." She added, "I can heal myself."

Ra reached over and tried to stop her. "You can't operate on yourself! You can't heal yourself when you're bleeding to death! Why, you can't even heal your burnt hand!"

He was strong but she was stronger. She shook him off.

"It's the only way," she said.

Ra suddenly stood. "I will not let you do this."

Ali looked up at him, sad. "You won't be able to stop me."

Ra blinked, rubbed his eyes. "*Why* are you doing this?"

"Because I brought them to this place. I'm responsible for them."

"That's not true!" Ra said.

"It is true." She tore off the last of the fresh bandage, looked down at Paddy, who appeared to be going into shock. She added, "I'm responsible because I'm their queen."

Ra saw she was determined. The strength seemed to go out of his legs, and he sat down beside her as she placed the palm of her injured hand in front of the scab's path. As she suspected, it was immediately drawn to her exposed flesh, her blood. She watched as a tentacle reached up and gripped her pinkie, and another coiled around her wrist.

Perhaps it preferred human meat to leprechaun . . .

Within a minute the creature had moved onto her lower arm, and let go of Paddy.

She felt poison in her veins. The stinging sensation was worse than her burn.

Ali sat back on her knees, lifted the fire stones, glanced at Ra.

"If I pass out, tear some cloth, put a tourniquet on my elbow," she said.

Ra looked as if he would be sick. "Then what?" he asked bitterly.

"Then slap me in the face, wake me up, and let me finish the job."

Ali raised the fire stones and tried to concentrate on a spot six inches beneath her elbow. She felt the venom go deeper into her blood, as the stones began to warm. But Ra reached over and knocked the stones from her hand.

"Wait!" he pleaded.

"Ra!" she complained, feeling a wave of nausea as the scab crawled up an inch. "I have no choice!"

"Listen. I watch tons of American programs. That's where I learned to speak such good English. My favorite is your Discovery Channel. I watch it all the time—I've learned amazing things from it. There was this one program, it was on saltwater fish, how most of them can only survive in a narrow range of ocean depth. Most of the fish you see when you snorkel—take them down two hundred feet and the pressure will kill them." He gripped the arm that carried the scab. "Do you know what I'm saying?" he asked.

She had to struggle to understand. "You mean that, even if these creatures originally came from the sea, they might be sensitive to pressure?"

Ra nodded. "They look like jellyfish. They might be as vulnerable as jellyfish."

The bridge was supported by multiple pillars, but had no true railing. She glanced over the edge into the churning river. The water was green and blue and alive. A current like that could carry her out a mile in a matter of minutes, and there she would find plenty of deep water.

Deep enough to drown in. She felt far from strong. Ra seemed to read her mind.

"You said it yourself, Ali, you're more than human. You can swim way down, two hundred feet if you have to." Ra added, "When it falls off, and you return to the surface, I can swim out and rescue you."

Ali snorted. "Rescue me? You're from the middle of Tanzania. I like to watch Discovery Channel, too. Tanzania's bone dry. I bet you don't even know how to swim."

Ra hesitated. "I sometimes splash in a friend's pond."

Stumbling to her feet, Ali shook her head. "You cross the bridge with Farble and Paddy. Hike toward the beach, wait for me there. But do not go in the water. It will just give me one more thing to worry about."

Ra stood and patted her on the shoulder. "Swim deep, my friend. Kill it."

Ali nodded. "One of us is going to die."

There was no reason to wait, plenty of reasons not to.

Ali turned and jumped off the bridge. Over a hundred-foot drop.

She hit the water hard, went down deep, then the current gripped her body—an overpowering hand that she didn't try to struggle against. Kicking toward the surface, she was disappointed to see that the impact had not loosened the scab. It had moved further up her arm.

The river was fresh water, moving fast, but she did not realize until it went past the borders of the beach that the ocean itself was not salty. Despite her dire predicament, the fact amazed her. The entire sea was like one huge lake!

The collision of the river and the sea kicked up a ministorm. The river had miles of momentum, the ocean had waves. She felt as if she were caught in white-water rapids, and had to fight for breath. But she had faith Elnar would shove her into deeper water.

The scab appeared to blame her for the rough ride and stung her repeatedly. It was as if the monster was aware of her plan; she felt a huge evil behind its petty mind. The creature had definitely been programmed, not by nature, but by a twisted psyche. As it clawed up her arm, she sensed it was hungry to consume her brain because it wanted to grow its own brain. It was not merely a starving parasite—it was a vampire, a demon, it sought to possess its victim.

Around her, the water finally began to calm, and she looked back and saw she was far from the sandy shore. Beneath her the water was more green than blue, clear but deep, full of promise. Sucking in several quick breaths, Ali lowered her head and reared her feet into the air. Then she was kicking and pulling herself down, using all four limbs, even the one with the scab on it, fighting the natural buoyancy of the water, and her own aching lungs, and tired muscles. Her last words to Ra had been a vow. She was not returning to the surface until one of them was dead.

Down she went, through swarms of colored fish, until the clear liquid turned as dark as a midnight lagoon, and still she did not stop. The pressure grew until it felt as if a mountain of water danced on top of her skull. She had to pop her ears continually. But she knew the scab did not like it. As if in a blind fury, it stung her repeatedly, tried to grip her arm tighter. But it was hanging on for dear life. She had no doubt—the creature was in pain.

So was she. It was just a question of who could take more.

The distant surface vanished. The water turned pitch black. She could not see a thing, and still, she continued down. At least she thought she was going down. All sense of direction was lost. Her blood pounded in her head, lava swelled in her bursting lungs. She was dying, she could feel it, almost accepted it, but she wanted to die alone, not with this thing attached to her. God, how she hated it!

Then, she must have won, the scab fell off. It was just gone.

Ali stopped swimming, floated, not sure which way to go, while the furnace in her chest screamed for her to do something. But it was her hope, as she drifted, that she was moving back toward the surface.

Then she saw it, a faint green glow. It was above her, but more off to her right—and she kicked toward it furiously. Now the pressure swept over her in reverse. The air in her inner ears did not know how to take it, nor did her lungs, which pleaded with her to open her mouth and get rid of the stale fumes they were holding and give them something fresh to drink. This time, the millions of colored fish, as she swept past them, seemed to sparkle with their own light. And she recognized them, not from Hawaii, when she had gone with her parents, but from another life. Her trip into the abyss had changed her. As she hit the surface, sucked in a dozen blessed breaths, she felt like she had been reborn.

She took a leisurely swim back to the beach, through the delicious green surf, just north of the current caused by Elnar striking the sea. When she came out of the water, her friends were waiting for her on the sand, and her heart broke to see Paddy up and smiling, and he hugged her, and called her Missy, and she hugged him back, and cried, and Farble and Ra were there, and happy, and even without resting, or talking much, they started on their way again. North, up the white beach, then over the sculpted brown hills, and into the lands of the leprechauns and the fairies.

CHAPTER

13

Once more, they stood on Hector Wells's front porch and knocked on his door. Only this time they knew he was at home—they had seen him drive up twenty minutes earlier—and they felt they were armed with enough information that he would want to talk to them.

Yet Steve knew, even if they were lucky, that they would have a hard time with Hector. They had asked around town, and everyone had a favorable impression of the contractor, both personally and professionally. In a sense they were coming to him for help. They were there to trade information. But because they were never going to tell him about Ali and their search for the Shaktra, the sharing would be somewhat fake. Hector, if he was as sharp as people said, would probably gather that much.

Hector answered quickly. Dressed in dirty blue jeans and a sweaty red T-shirt, he looked like a contractor who had just put in a full day on the job. His wide shoulders had muscle, his hair was thick, dirty blond, and he had serious blue eyes. He did not appear to smile much. Yet there was an integrity to him—Steve could sense it—and he regarded them with casual politeness. He probably thought they were selling something.

Steve introduced himself and Cindy and told Hector they wanted to talk to him about Nira and Patricia. Hector frowned at the mention of his old girlfriend's name, and Steve wondered if it had been a mistake to bring up Patricia at the start. Yet the promise of information on her was probably their only ticket through his door.

"Did you know Patricia?" Hector asked.

"We know a bit about her," Steve said vaguely. "And we know Nira and her new nanny. We had lunch with them at their house this afternoon."

They were off to a bad start.

"What does any of this have to do with me?" Hector asked.

Cindy spoke up. "We found out some things today that might have a bearing on Patricia's death, and the boy who died in this town yesterday."

Hector showed interest, but remained wary. "Heard something about that."

"Did you know Freddy Degear?" Steve asked.

"No."

Steve and Cindy exchanged a look. They had asked around, and it seemed no one, except Rose, had heard of Freddy before. It was that fact, among others, which made them feel confident approaching Hector with their wild conspiracy theories—because there was a good chance they weren't so wild. Yet they had to play their cards right, and not reveal them all at once.

"We would like to talk to you about how he died," Steve said. "And about Nira, how she's being treated these days. We understand you don't see her much anymore?"

"Who told you that?"

"Ms. Treacher, at the library," Cindy said.

"Forgive me, but I'm not sure where you guys are coming from."

"It would be easier if we could come inside and explain ourselves," Steve said.

"Please," Cindy added.

Hector considered for a moment, but Steve could see that the man had too much small-town politeness to simply shut the door on their faces. At the same time, they had sparked his curiosity. And how dangerous could two kids be? Finally, he relaxed, held the door wide open.

"You guys thirsty?" he asked.

"Always," Steve said.

The interior was as simple and elegant as the outside. Unlike the Smith residence, Hector loved wood. He had mahogany floors, maple shelves, cedar cabinets. The overall effect was warm. It was clear he lived alone, but he was a tidy bachelor. He brought them bottled Cokes, had them sit on the couch, and plopped down on an easy chair across from them holding a bottle of Evian.

It was a critical moment, Steve knew. They had dangled secret information in front of him, but they still had to get plenty out of him before they handed over the goods.

Once seated, Steve appeared to change the subject. He brought up the electrical plant explosion of thirteen years ago, and said the mystery around it had always fascinated him. He did not frame the remark in a personal way, and Hector was not threatened by his question. Hector spoke of the tragic night in an offhand way, as if he had done so dozens of times before.

"That would have been a crazy night even if the electrical plant hadn't blown," he said. "The town was celebrating our team winning the state championship in basketball, but it was two weeks after the game. During those two weeks there had been nothing but arguments about how we were going to celebrate. Some people wanted to have a parade, others wanted a party. And no one at City Hall wanted to pay for anything. In the end we had a half-assed parade and plates of cold cuts."

"What position did you play?" Steve asked.

"Guard. I had won most valuable player in the final, so I was the one who held the trophy up for all the photographers. I did it during the parade, hated it. I didn't see myself as a jock back then. I only played the game because I liked it, but I had no plans to play in college."

"Did the plant blow at the start of the party?" Steve asked.

"In the middle. After listening to all the speeches, and having some food, I snuck off to be alone with Lucy, my girlfriend. For some reason, the gate leading to the plant was open, and we went inside to walk around. But we didn't touch anything, or break into the turbine area." Hector added, "Later, I had to tell the cops that a thousand times."

"Why?" Steve asked.

"Because Lucy and I were inside the plant when it exploded."

"How did you survive?" Steve asked.

"The plant blew at the other end of the facility—closer to where the gas burned that heated the water and drove the turbines. Lucy and I were shielded by the control room and a storage area. Or I should say, *I* was shielded. That's not to say I didn't feel the impact. When the plant blew, the ceiling ruptured above me and the walls collapsed. There was fire and smoke everywhere. I was lucky to get out alive."

"But Lucy didn't?" Cindy asked.

"Just before it blew, she said she had to go to the bathroom, and went looking for one." Hector added, "That was the last I saw of her."

"That must have been rough on you," Steve said.

Hector took a swig of his Evian. "That whole year had been rough."

"Nira's new nanny, Rose, told us about Sheri Smith, how she was also in the plant when it exploded," Cindy said. "Did you see her when you and Lucy were there?"

Whoa . . . Cindy had pounced too hard. Steve saw it.

The sudden shift in the conversation caught Hector completely off guard.

"Huh?" he muttered.

Steve tried to smooth things over. "It was just something we heard."

Hector shook his head. "I know who Ms. Smith is. She was nowhere near there. What kind of question is that?"

"We're talking about the woman who founded Omega Overtures?" Cindy said.

"Yeah. I told you, I know her. She didn't go to school with us."

"But Rose told us that she went to school with you guys," Cindy said.

"This is a small town, we have a small school. I knew everybody when I was going there. I certainly would have remembered someone like Ms. Smith."

"What's she like?" Steve asked, trying to regroup from Hector's revelation.

"You haven't met her?"

"We're supposed to have lunch with her and Nira tomorrow," Cindy said.

"She's pretty, smart, but I found her controlling. I wished Patricia had never gone to work for her."

"Why?" Steve asked.

"She was always ordering her around. She made her work unreasonable hours. Patricia thought she was a terrible mother. I saw more of Nira than Smith ever did." He added, "I miss that kid."

"She's sweet," Cindy said.

Hector nodded. "She does have a sweetness to her. Most people around town don't see that. They just think she is a mental case. But I felt it whenever I was with her. So did Patricia. That's why she stayed so long on the job, and put up with that woman's demands."

"If Ms. Smith is not from around here, where is she from?" Steve asked.

"No idea." Hector turned away, looked out the window, and it was as if he paled slightly. He added quietly, "I try to stay away from that woman."

"Why is that?" Steve asked. There had been a sudden note of fear in the man's voice. But Hector shrugged off the question.

"You haven't told me what any of this has to do with Patricia's death," he said.

Wariness had returned to Hector's face. No doubt he was beginning to wonder why two kids were grilling him about such a variety of subjects. Steve had to ask himself the same question. They were jumping all over the place because their ideas about Toule and its mysteries were undeveloped. They could not sit down with Hector and connect all the dots. All they had was a brown bag stuffed with wild clues, strips of paper with names on them that kept overlapping with other names. When Steve mentally reviewed the facts, he got a headache. There was no set logic to them.

Rose worked for Sheri Smith, taking care of Nira.
Patricia used to work for Sheri Smith, taking care of Nira.
Hector used to date Patricia.
Hector used to see Nira.
Hector used to date Lucy.
Lucy and Sheri Smith had been in the plant together when it blew. According to Rose, but not according to Hector.

173

Hector's two girlfriends had died in Toule.

Freddy Degear had died in Toule, but only Rose knew him.

Freddy Degear was the reason they had gotten to know Nira.

Yeah, Steve thought, it was all interesting, but how did it add up?

"We'll get to that in a second," Cindy said, unaware of how annoyed Hector was getting. "But we need to ask you a couple of questions about Lucy, and what happened to her the year before the electrical plant blew. We understand she was in a car accident, and that she got badly burned?"

"Who told you that?" Hector demanded.

Cindy lowered her voice. "Ms. Treacher."

Hector shook his head, he had reached his limit. "It's your turn to talk. You tell me what you know about Patricia's death and I'll decide what to tell you about Lucy."

They had reached an impasse. Steve decided it was time for a little honesty.

"We went to your local library," Steve said. "We were there this morning, but we went back again after we had lunch with Rose and Nira. A lot of stuff was bothering us about Rose, that we'll get into in a minute, and we wanted to check it out. But from talking to people around town, we knew about your connection to Patricia and Lucy and Nira. That inspired us to look up all the old articles on Patricia's death, and we saw that she had been hit with a black SUV." Steve added, "Some witnesses said it was a Ford Expedition."

"So?" Hector said.

"We were there when Freddy Degear got run over yesterday," Steve said. "He was hit by a black Ford Expedition."

Hector sat up, interested. "Have you told the police this?"

"Not yet," Steve said.

"Why not?"

"Because we're still confused about Rose, Nira's nanny," Cindy said. "It's one of the reasons we came to see you. We thought you could tell us more about her."

"I've never even met the woman," Hector said.

Steve saw their problem. They kept swinging from Rose to Patricia to Lucy. He apologized and asked Hector if they could focus on Rose for a second. Hector nodded, reluctantly. He was beginning to look like he wished he had never invited them inside.

"At first we liked Rose," Steve explained. "It seemed like she really loved Nira, and took good care of her. But when we went for lunch this afternoon, she wouldn't let Nira join us. She kept her in her room the whole time. And this room was like a jail cell. It has no toys in it, no TV, nothing on the walls. Rose wouldn't even let us take Nira out for ice cream."

"All this sounds like the mother's fault," Hector interrupted.

"Maybe," Steve said. "But as we left the house, Cindy and I felt uneasy about Rose, and we started thinking about something Ms. Treacher had told us. She said she'd never heard of Freddy Degear—the guy who had just died—when Rose had told us that Freddy was a neighbor of hers. So Cindy and I checked it out. We went to all the houses in that area, and we couldn't find anyone who knew Freddy Degear. And you never heard of him. That's because he's not from Toule."

Steve had recaptured Hector's interest. "Why would the woman lie?" he asked.

"I don't know," Steve said. "But talking to you right now, we discover Rose told us another lie. She said Ms. Smith went to school with you guys. You say she didn't."

"I have my old yearbook. You can see it if you want. You won't find her inside."

"You don't have to show us, we believe you," Steve said.

"Rose said Ms. Smith was in the plant when it blew up," Cindy added.

Hector snorted. "Lucy and I were the only ones inside that plant."

"Another lie on her part," Steve said.

Hector struggled to keep up. "It sounds to me like Sheri Smith is behind the lies. That I can believe. Smith lied to Patricia all the time. It was second nature to her."

Steve shook his head. "I might buy that if Rose had not lied to us about Freddy just *a few seconds* after he got ran over. Think about it: The poor guy is lying there in the street bleeding to death and she's acting like he's an old buddy of hers."

"That's cold," Hector agreed.

"I said the same thing," Cindy said.

"And this is the woman who is taking care of Nira?" Hector asked.

"She's her only nanny," Steve said.

"So you're saying Rose had something to do with this guy's death?" Hector asked.

"Yes," Steve said.

"And Patricia's death?" Hector asked.

"It's possible," Steve said.

"It was definitely the same vehicle each time?" Hector said.

"Near as we can tell," Steve said.

"And think, Rose benefited from the fact that Patricia died," Cindy said.

"How so?" Hector asked.

"She got her job," Steve said.

Steve could see the wheels finally turning inside Hector's head.

"Do you know why Ms. Smith hired her?" Hector asked.

"Not exactly," Steve said. "But Rose says she's from Colombia, that she came to this country only a year ago, to take over Patricia's job. But she doesn't act like someone from there. She has a strong accent, but she never inserts Spanish words into her speech. And the way she talks, the rhythm of her sentences, it's like she was raised here."

"You think she's faking the accent?" Hector asked.

"It feels like it," Steve said.

"She keeps inviting us back to her house, which is kind of creepy in itself," Cindy said.

"Why do you keep going back?" Hector asked, the question of the hour.

"We were witnesses to Freddy's death. We feel responsible to find out why he died," Steve said, telling a half-truth, which was another mistake. Hector was perceptive. He didn't buy it at all.

"I know it's fun to play detective," Hector said, "but you have to give the police your description of the SUV. You can't sit on it. And you have to explain to the cops the connection the SUV has to Patricia's death. If this Rose, or Ms. Smith, has anything to do with either death, they'll figure it out."

"We promise to talk to the cops," Steve said. "But we need more information."

"About what?"

"Lucy," Cindy said.

Hector was annoyed. "There's nothing to say about her. She died in the blast."

"We're asking about the car accident," Cindy said.

"Ms. Treacher told you about that?"

"Yes," Steve said. "But don't blame her, we squeezed the information out of her."

"I doubt it, that old woman loves to gossip." Hector added, "Lucy has nothing to do with what you're discussing."

"Probably," Steve agreed. "But there's a lot of coincidences going on here. You have to admit it. We're just trying to sort it all out."

"Why?" Hector persisted.

"We told you why," Steve said.

Hector stared at him, shook his head. "You haven't told me the half of it, but I guess I'll have to let that go for now. There's no mystery to what happened with Lucy. That day I was at a friend's house, and we were playing computer games. The Internet was just getting going back then. We used to play this game, Ultimatum, online with people from back east. The graphics were crude by today's standards and so was the story. But it was the new thing, and we were addicted to it."

"Did Lucy play with you?" Steve asked.

"Just my buddies and me. We liked to drink beer when we played, and I had a few too many. After we were done, I went to pick up Lucy. We had to go to a wedding, south of here somewhere. It was on the way there when I veered off the road and crashed into a tree. I was stupid, I didn't have my seat belt on. But it saved me that time. I was thrown from the car, Lucy was not. The car caught fire and she got burned." He added, "It's as simple as that."

"But why did you veer off the road?" Steve asked.

"I told you, I was drunk." Hector added, "Don't drink and drive."

"You didn't see anything that caused you to veer?" Steve asked.

Hector hesitated. "To tell you the truth, I remember very little about that night. I told the cops that, when they arrested me. The trauma must have caused me to block it out."

"Did you go to jail?" Cindy asked.

"For six months. It was nothing compared to what Lucy went through."

"But you guys got back together," Cindy said. "You were with her a year later."

"Sort of. I mean, we tried. *I* wanted to try, but she had lost so much skin in the fire. It was amazing she was alive. She had to keep having operations. She practically lived at the hospital. The scarring was severe. She couldn't stand to have people see her. She used to wear a rubber mask when she went outside. She thought she was hideous."

There was an uncomfortable pause. "Was she?" Cindy asked quietly.

"What can I say? She wasn't the same Lucy I had known. The accident hadn't just taken her face, it stole her spirit. By the night of the big blast, she was only a shell of what she used to be. I almost wish . . ." Hector didn't finish.

"What?" Steve asked, although he knew the answer.

"That she had never been given that year," he said.

"Because she died anyway?" Steve said.

Hector nodded. "Twice the fire came for her. The second time it got her."

CHAPTER

14

The hills went up and down, no rise too high, no valley too low. There was a path, and soon grass, a few trees, and quiet streams. The way was not difficult. Except for the green sun in the sky, and her odd collection of traveling companions, Ali could have been hiking in her own world. The trees, although varied for a single area, were little different than at home. The clean water in the occasional brook was a delight to drink. It tasted a bit like honey.

Yet it was best not to pretend. Her relief over having escaped the scabs was tempered with caution. The creature had gotten to Paddy because she had relaxed her guard. It was not a mistake she would repeat.

They came across neither fairies nor leprechauns, and Paddy was puzzled.

"Should have seen some of me own folk by now," he said.

"Could they have moved further north, into Karolee?" she asked.

"Maybe," he said, but he was doubtful.

"Do leprechauns have cities like elves and dwarves and fairies?"

"No, Missy. Leprechauns go their own way, in private. No one sees much of them."

"But did you live in a cave? In a tree?" she asked.

He was offended. "I had me own place. It was not much, but it was clean."

She tried to explain that she had not been trying to purposely insult him, and he seemed to drop the matter quick enough. Yet she never did get a clear idea how they lived. Two things were obvious, though: Leprechauns did not build big structures and they did not farm. They were hiking through the heart of leprechaun land—Plantar, he called it—and it was as if the land had never been occupied.

Although the landscape was similar to home, there were differences. On the whole the trees were taller, and some appeared ancient with massive rippling branches, leaves as large as wooden plates, and thick trunks that could have swallowed a house. There was a dignity to the old trees, as if they had seen many battles, many times of peace, and lost neither their silence nor their beauty. There were so many types: maples, oaks, elms, and pines—all could be found huddled together. And while the maple leaves showed signs of autumn, orange and red, the oaks were still green. As a result the woods were richly colored.

The grass itself was taller, the blades more round than flat. Ali saw a type of daisy with a purple center and yellow petals. Then there were other flowers that had no earthly parallels. One was a single tall blue petal that arched its spine like a swan on a lake. There were lots of them all over the place, and they gave off a wonderful fragrance. The farther they walked, the stronger the scents in the air grew, and the odors both enlivened her and lulled her into a waking dream.

It seemed fitting to her that a fairy should stumble into a fairy tale.

As they hiked, however, they began to see disturbing signs. Approximately every half mile they came across a roughly circular area about two hundred feet wide where the trees had been *pulverized*. It was as if asteroids had fallen from the sky and crushed the trees, only there were no piles of rocks around, although deep indentations surrounded the splintered wood. She did not know what to make of it, and was worried when Paddy looked dismayed.

"Never seen this before, Missy," he said.

"All this damage occurred in the last month?" she asked.

"Aye."

Ali searched the skies. There was an unusual cluster of clouds in the north—they had a bluish tinge—but she saw nothing threatening.

"Could this damage have driven the leprechauns away?" she asked.

"Aye. Anyone would run from this."

Ali turned to Ra. "What do you think?" she said.

"You mentioned this Shaktra creature, and the possibility of a war. This area feels like a battle just swept over it."

"But there are no bodies," Ali protested.

"As long as you're not a tree," Ra said.

Yet she knew what he meant. The area felt like it had been . . . brutalized.

They continued on their way, with Ali and Ra leading the way and Paddy and Farble directly behind them, walking closer together than they had since they had met. When they had hiked through the cave in Tutor, Ra had tried to question her about how she had come to be a fairy, and she had evaded most of his questions. Now it struck her that she knew almost nothing about *him*. She tried asking about his life in Tanzania, and he looked over at her and smiled.

"It's boring," he said.

"Don't say that, you don't mean it."

He shrugged. "I live in a small town near the base of Kilimanjaro called Fiera. My people, the Kutu, grow a lot of corn and soybeans. We live off the grains and feed them to our livestock, our cattle, which we mostly trade. But Fiera is unique to that region of Africa because it also survives by taking care of tourists that come to see the mountain. Many of the men in the village act as guides for those who want to climb the peak. I've done it myself a few times—helped you fat Americans up to the top."

Ali chuckled. "I'm sure more Europeans hike Kilimanjaro than Americans."

"True. But they're fat, too."

"But do you go to school?"

Ra nodded. "I did go to school, up until I started working with my uncle. Our school was lucky to have a satellite dish, and a big-screen TV. That allowed us to study programs broadcasted from all over the world. We also have an excellent teacher from Britain—Ms. Danridge."

"I bet you were her favorite pupil."

"Why do you say that?"

Ali teased. "She's the one who gave you that great James Bond accent."

He smiled briefly, nodded. "Ms. Danridge taught me a great deal of the world." He added, "Unfortunately, in my village, people only go to class until they are twelve."

"Must be nice," Ali muttered.

"It's a crime. No one can learn enough to get into a decent college with only six years of schooling. When I began training with my uncle to be a chimvi—a shaman—he insisted that I keep reading books and studying math and science. He had high hopes for me to escape the area and maybe go to England and attend Cambridge or Oxford."

"He sounds like he was a wonderful man," she said.

"He was the best."

She hesitated. "I assume he raised you because both your parents are dead?"

Ra nodded. "They died when I was young."

"How? If you don't mind me asking."

"My mother died giving birth to me. My father was killed by a lion."

"The same lion you killed?"

"No. My father died when I was three. But my uncle—as part of my training—insisted that I kill a lion to avenge my father's soul."

"Did you kill the lion in the wild?"

"Of course."

"Were you alone?"

Ra nodded. "Yes. Alone in the dark."

"The lions I've seen at the zoo are huge. How did you have the guts to approach one?"

"I knew my arrow was going to kill it."

"How did you know?"

Ra hesitated. "My uncle taught me certain things, secret things. Just know that my archery skills are not just dependent on practice and physical ability."

Ali considered, trying to get a sense for what he was saying. "Are you able to charge your arrows somehow? So that they go where you wish?"

He paused, seemingly struck by her insight, then nodded. "My uncle taught me many wonderful things."

"You miss him, don't you?"

"Yes."

"Tell me what else he taught you. Don't be shy, I won't tell a soul."

Ra smiled. "They all say that."

"Who is they?"

"The girls in my village."

Ali laughed. "I bet you have lots of girlfriends!"

He blushed. "That is not true."

"You must have at least one. What's her name?"

Ra shook his head. "I am too young for women."

Ali laughed harder. "Women? I'm talking about *girls*. You mean to tell me you're not dating anyone? I don't believe it."

He looked at her. "It is true, I don't date. No one in our village does."

Ali quieted, sensing that he was speaking the truth. "So tell me more about what it takes to be a chimvi."

Ra was silent for a moment. "When I first started to train under my uncle, he told me that the secret of becoming a chimvi was to be fearless. He said that all weakness in life, all suffering, came from fear alone."

"What about the type of suffering that comes from others?"

Ra shook his head. "I asked him that. He said that a person's internal fears caused such catastrophes to come to him. But he said if a person was completely at peace, as firm as a rock inside, then nothing bad would ever happen to him."

"Do you believe that?"

"I do." Ra added, "But I have a long way to go to find complete peace."

Ali nodded. "I hear that." She added, "Will anyone be missing you right now at home?"

"Not for a few days. I told them I was going to stay on the mountain for a while."

"And after that?"

Ra just smiled. "Don't worry about it." He added, "What about you?"

"What about me?"

"Anyone going to miss you?" he asked.

"Not really. There's just my father, and he's away right now, on business."

"How did you become a fairy?" Ra asked.

"I did not *become* a fairy, I was always a fairy. I just didn't know it is all."

"Then how did you learn you were a fairy?"

Ali pointed to Farble. "First off, I was walking in the woods, minding my own business, when I was attacked by a couple of his pals. That was my first exposure to elementals. No, wait, I take that back. I met Paddy in town before I ran into the trolls. But I didn't know he was a leprechaun."

"What did you think he was?"

"A dwarf. I mean, he had on tons of makeup. He looked like some weird short guy to me."

"Did he just walk up to you on the street?"

"Yeah. He was trying to sell me something. Something he had stolen."

"Your town sounds much more interesting than mine."

"It wasn't that interesting until the elementals showed up."

"So when you met your troll friends and Paddy you learned you were a fairy?"

"Not exactly. A tree told me that I was a fairy."

Ra frowned. "A tree?"

"It was a talking tree. Well, actually, the tree was unimportant. It was more like this person I used to know—when I was living here—came to me in the form of a tree and told me all kinds of stuff about myself. He was the one who said I had to climb the mountain and stop the elementals from invading the Earth."

"Could you see this person?"

"No. Just the tree." She added, "He came as a pond later on."

"A pond?"

"Yes. A small clear pond."

"And you could hear his voice?"

"No. Actually, it was only in my head. It was like telepathy."

"But if you couldn't see him, how did you know you could trust him?"

Ali smiled. "Because of his love. I could feel it whenever he came. His love was . . . is . . . so wonderful."

"Does he have a name?"

She hesitated. "I probably shouldn't say his name out loud."

Ra teased her. "Like you, I'm great at keeping secrets."

Ali suddenly leaned over and whispered Nemi's name in his ear.

She didn't know why, she just trusted him. Trusted him with her life.

They had hiked for another hour when Ali heard sounds up ahead, and glimpsed through the trees a half dozen people approaching. Quickly, she got her friends off the path, behind some bushes, and waited for the strangers to come closer. From what she could see, they looked like normal people—a bit thin perhaps, with bright red hair that shone beneath the green sun, deeply tanned skin, and wearing green clothes.

But Paddy said that they were fairies.

Ali had to smile. "They look like humans. Even more so than elves." The elves she had seen, at least, had pointed ears.

"Humans look like fairies, Missy," Paddy corrected her.

The group came closer. They had their heads down, as if they were heavy, and their expressions were blank, and she asked Paddy about it. But he seemed reluctant to comment.

"We should let them go their own way," he said.

"No way. If they're fairies, I want to talk to them." She went to get up, to wave to them. Paddy grabbed her arm.

"No, Missy! Don't speak to these ones!" He added in a dark whisper, "They've been *marked*."

"Marked? What does that mean?"

The leprechaun shook his head. "Paddy only saw it a few times, before he left for your world. But a few fairies and elves—they have a mark on their heads. These ones—they have no minds."

Ali thought of Freddy Degear and Nira Smith—always Nira.

"Does the mark look like a thumbprint?" she asked.

"Aye. Like it was burned into their skin." Paddy continued to try to pull her back behind the bushes. "Let them pass, Missy. Don't mind them."

Ali shook him off. "Where does the mark come from? Tell me, I need to know."

He cowered. "Paddy does not know."

She knelt in front of him, made him look her in the eye. "Does the Shaktra do this to people?"

"Paddy doesn't . . ."

"Does it touch them and then control their minds?" she insisted.

He shook his head. "Paddy has only heard stories."

"Tell me about these stories."

"That when they're marked, *it* can see through them!"

Ali glanced at the troupe of fairies. "They move like they're drunk. They don't look dangerous."

Paddy was anxious. "They can be dangerous if it . . . awakens them."

Ali stood, turned to Ra. "Do you think we can handle them?"

He nodded. "We need to talk to someone around here."

Leaving Paddy and Farble behind, Ali and Ra stepped onto

the path in front of the fairies. None looked up, slowed down, or made a sound. Their green eyes were marbles fished from the mud. Ali had seen snakes with more emotion on their faces. Feeling cold despair, she tried to block their way, but they went around her. They had the exact same marks on their foreheads as Freddy and Nira.

Yet Ali could see that they had been beautiful at one time. Their robes were not entirely green, but mixed with lines of white and yellow, colors that seemed to shift as the sun moved in the sky. Their red hair was still bright, braided with silver and gold thread in long strands that reached past their waists. Each wore bracelets and anklets made of red and blue flowers, and their ears—although more human than elfish—were longer and *thinner*. It seemed the green sunlight passed through the soft skin without hesitation, and took the shadows from their eyes.

Yet the marks on their foreheads destroyed it all . . .

They were walking shadows. They were living nightmares.

Ali turned to Ra as the troupe started to walk away.

"Look what direction they're headed!" she cried.

Ra, his sword in his hand, nodded. "If they keep going they'll hit the desert."

"The scabs will get them you mean!"

Putting away his weapon, Ra touched her arm. "This was going on long before we got here. You can't change it in a day."

Ali shook her head, took a step toward the gang's lone straggler, a tall girl with a narrow face who couldn't have been much older than herself. "Get Paddy. Drag him out here if you have to. I cannot let this go on," she said.

The girl resisted Ali, but her effort was feeble and not sustained. Ali managed to sit her on the trunk of a fallen tree, and Ra reappeared with Paddy and Farble. The whole time the girl kept her eyes down, and did not respond to Ali's questions. Ali went so far as to strike her—the girl's head swung like a branch in the breeze. Ali turned to Paddy.

"They are all heading south. That cannot be by chance. I assume the Shaktra sends them to the desert to be eaten by the scabs. Is that true?"

Paddy hesitated. "Aye, Missy."

"Is there more to it than that?" she persisted.

Paddy pointed to the girl. "She will change into a scalii."

"What's a scalii?" Ali asked.

"It's when a scab lands on someone and eats their brains. They turn into a scalii."

Ali was stunned. "They don't die?"

Paddy was grim. "They wish they could die."

Ali had to force herself to ask her next question. "What do scaliis do?"

Paddy shuddered. "Eat other people. Anyone they can get their hands on."

The girl tried to stand, Ali forced her back down. "We can't let her go," she said.

"How are you going to stop her?" Ra asked.

"I don't know. But I have to stop all of them. Or . . ."

"Or what?" Ra asked. "Head back to the desert? Try to burn up all the scabs? There could be millions of them for all you know. There probably are."

Ali turned to Paddy. "What do you mean that the Shaktra can see through them?"

"What Paddy heard," the leprechaun muttered.

"More the reason to leave her behind," Ra said.

"What is your problem?" Ali snapped. "Is this what it means to be a chimvi? To be cold and heartless?"

Ra hesitated. "Sometimes, if the situation demands it."

"I'm going to save this girl. No matter what it takes."

Ra nodded. "I agree, you have to try. But she might not be under a simple spell. It's possible the damage is permanent. The Shaktra might have burned her brains out."

Shaking her head, Ali drew out her Yanti. "Leave me alone with her."

With the others gone, Ali was still not free to concentrate. The girl kept trying to leave, and Ali had to grip her wrist tightly. That left her fewer fingers to manipulate the Yanti. Nevertheless, she managed to repeat the cycle she had learned from Nira, while simultaneously focusing on releasing the girl from her mental bondage. Unfortunately, as she brought her power to bear, the girl began to shake as if she were having a convulsion and blood dripped from her nose. Ali's own hand began to bleed as well, and she had to stop.

With her uninjured hand, Ali stroked the girl's hair. "Can you tell me your name at least?" she asked.

The girl did not respond, did not even look at her. Ali signaled for Ra to return. She explained what had happened when she used the Yanti on the girl.

"I want to take her with us," Ali added.

"Bad idea," he replied.

Ali glared at him. "*Who's* in charge here?"

Ra shook his head. "You may be in charge but it's still a bad idea, and it's my responsibility to tell you so. This woman has only one thought in her head, that's to go south. We're going north. She'll wear us out, fighting her."

"How can you just leave her to such a horrible death?"

Ra shrugged. "You're leaving the others who just walked by to a horrible death. Why? Because you know you can't manage them all. You can't manage this one." Ra added, "The best you can do is tie her to a tree, off the path, where she won't be spotted."

"She would be helpless. A wild animal could walk by and eat her."

"I don't like it, but at least it gives her a chance. Then, on our way back, maybe you'll know more what can be done for her. By then, you might be able to reverse it." Ra added, "Paddy shares my opinion."

Ali snorted. "So now we're going to the leprechaun for advice?"

"Paddy's smarter than he looks. And this is his world, after all."

Ali felt frustrated. What Ra was saying made sense, but to simply abandon the girl felt so cold. And what about the others who had just passed by? She did not have enough rope to bind them all. Yet, if she let them be, the scabs would have their brains for dinner before the sun went down.

Standing, she handed the girl over to Ra. "There's rope in my backpack. I left it behind the bushes. Tie her to a tree around there, make sure she's sitting down, that the spot is comfortable, and that she can't break free."

"Where are you going?" Ra asked.

Ali nodded toward the way they had come. "I'm going to disable the others."

Ra called after her. "A lot of times, being a leader means knowing when *not* to do something."

Ali snapped back. "Just take care of the girl!"

The marked fairies moved slowly. It took her only a few minutes to catch up with them. For a time she walked beside them, trying to talk to them, but it was hopeless. She could force one to stop, but the others would continue on without pause.

She discovered she was trembling. She could not bear to step on an insect, and now she was being asked to break the poor fairies' legs. Of course, no one was really asking her, it was the situation.

Best to get it over with quick, she thought.

Picking up a grapefruit-sized stone, she threw it at the leader's calf. Threw it hard—the bone made a distinct popping sound as it snapped, and the guy went down, and the others walked around him. Then the guy started crawling, using his arms for traction, and Ali felt as if she might vomit.

She picked up another stone, went to throw it at another fairy, but her trembling practically changed into a convulsion. She started shaking all over and couldn't stop. The pain in her right hand soared, and the rock fell from her left hand as tears burned her eyes. Ra's words returned to haunt her.

"A lot of times, being a leader means knowing when not *to do something."*

"But he's wrong, if I do nothing they'll suffer more," she told herself.

The truth was . . . she did not know if that was true. To leave a dozen fairies in the wild with a mass of broken limbs was an intolerable idea. To allow them to be changed into scaliis was equally unbearable. The paradox hit Ali hard, as she imagined it must hit all leaders at one time or another. She could not do the right thing because the situation was too horrible for any choice to be right.

In the end, she saw she did not have the stomach to injure any more of the fairies, and she lowered her head and turned away. However, she made a vow to herself: to return to this area as soon as possible, when she knew more about the Shaktra's curse, and help as many of the marked fairies as possible.

When she caught up with her friends, she did not even go over to see how the girl was doing. Ra assured her she was as comfortable as he could make her, and they started hiking north again.

The path curved slightly to the west, and for a time they saw the ocean again. The beach was no longer flat sand, but steep rocks and cliffs, and they were forced to stay on the path, which eventually led them further inland. Close to sunset, they began to give serious thought as to where they should camp, but as the sky started to darken, they found themselves at the end of a long narrow gully. Here there were no trees, few bushes, and long shadows. Ali did not like the look of the area, yet the path ran through it.

"Have you been here before?" Ali asked Paddy.

"Aye. Pa took me here a long time ago." The leprechaun sniffed the air. "Had a sweeter odor then."

Ali understood. Although she could see no carcasses, the gully smelled of spoiled meat. Worse, it looked like a perfect place to get ambushed in. She shared her concerns with Ra.

"We could try circling around," he said, studying the top edges of the gully. The rock and gravel were loose, the walls steep. Once inside, it would be difficult to get out.

"We don't know the land," Ali said. "We could get lost."

"We can backtrack, camp near that stream we passed a half hour ago," Ra said.

The gully was silent, protected from even the faint noise of the evening breeze, but she sensed a watchfulness inside, a haunted hunger. "I would prefer to camp on the other side of this place. Have it behind us," Ali said.

Ra nodded. "There is a creepy vibe here."

Ali smiled. "You said 'vibe.' That's cute."

"I know all kinds of *cute* American words."

Another decision to be made. Ali felt exhausted by how quickly they kept piling up on her. The day had been forever, the dangers unimaginable, and now her right hand throbbed again. Trying to stretch out her field, and see around the boulders and through the shadows, she found her subtle psychic energies drained. She saw nothing, but worried if they were attacked in the gully—by scaliis or dark fairies—she wouldn't have the strength to defend her friends.

Yet the urge to go forward was on her. She told the others as much.

"Let's get through it as fast as we can," she said. "Stay alert, and no talking."

There was a major flaw in her plan, and if she had considered it longer, she might have chosen differently. The gully curved as they hiked through it, both to the right and the left, and as a result, she could not see the end of it. Paddy's memory was of no help. She did not know if the ravine was one mile long, or ten. The latter was a scary thought. She absolutely did not want to camp in the gully. The farther they walked, and the darker it got, the stronger the foul odor grew. She could not be sure—so deep in the ravine—but she feared the sun had already set.

They were two miles into the gully when the attack came.

Never in her dreams could Ali have imagined she could have been caught so off-guard. When the scaliis raised their grotesque heads from behind the rocky crevasses—and there were dozens of heads—she had to ask herself why they had not shown up on her mental radar. She was tired and injured, true, but those were not excuses. The only explanation was that these creatures were psychically *shielded*, probably by the Shaktra itself. Whatever, they were surrounded on all sides!

"Scaliis!" Paddy cried, grabbing ahold of her leg. Gently, Ali made him release her and turned to Ra. Paddy went from hugging her to holding on to Farble, who had begun to groan pitifully.

"Any ideas?" she asked.

Ra drew out his bow and arrows. "There's fewer of them up ahead. Let's fight our way through. There's no point in going back." He added, "How much power do you have left?"

She shook her head. "Not enough. Make every arrow count."

Ra nodded. "These creatures should be easier to hit."

A hopeful remark. As the scaliis came scurrying into the gully, Ali noticed several disturbing physical characteristics. They did not move like the zombie-fairies they had met on the path. Their strides were rapid and purposeful, and their feet were stringy masses of gelatin—similar to pink tentacles—and they were able to navigate the incline without falling, almost like spiders. Their red hands appeared hard and sharp, like crab claws that could cut stone; and they were naked, their bodies were of all sizes and shapes. Ali realized she was staring at scaliis that had been made from fairies and leprechauns, as well as elves and dwarves. Indeed, she thought, she was looking at the worst nightmare the Shaktra could have unleashed on the elemental kingdom. The Shaktra had changed friends and foes alike into monsters.

The worst horror was their heads. The scaliis had only one eye; it floated where the mouth should be, dark and bulbous, a fish lens taken out of an ocean depth that had never seen a sun. Above it, where the eyes should have been, was a single wide mouth, devoid of lips, mounted with rows of razor-sharp teeth, and oozing red and blue fluid. The creatures' claws kept clicking; their mouths drooled as the scalii platoon drew closer.

As Ali took out her fire stones, Ra asked if he should open fire. Before answering, Ali spoke to Paddy. "Where are they most vulnerable?" she asked.

Although terrified, he managed to speak. "They have no brains left in their heads, Missy. Just eyes and teeth."

She nodded to Ra. "Aim for their chests. Their hearts are probably still intact."

Ali did not know exactly how many arrows Ra had brought,

but when he started shooting, she saw he was as effective as an expert rifleman. He did not pause between shots to aim and he did not miss. Each arrow struck a scalii chest and, soundlessly, the creatures would sit down and remain still. Not a single one cried out in pain, and Ali wondered if they were happy to die, to have the pain stop.

Yet she felt pain in her right hand as she raised the fire stones and took aim. Power moved through her arm, and she felt her psychic field expand to perhaps five times the size of her body, but both sensations were erratic, weak. Her first few fiery bolts took down a handful of scaliis, but the penalty was a nauseating wave of dizziness. She almost fell over. On top of everything else she could not stand still and shoot. She had to keep Farble and Paddy going forward, because Ra was right, there were fewer creatures in front of them.

"We're going to get out of this!" she shouted.

For a time, it looked like that might be the case. The scaliis had no weapons. They did not even bother to pick up and throw rocks at them. Pushing aside her dizziness, Ali managed to keep firing, while Ra was taking down a foe every ten seconds. The scaliis understood they were losing big numbers. Right in front of Ali, the creatures' ranks began to split, to spread up the walls of the gully, seemingly trying to get out of their way. Ali took the opportunity to press the others to greater speed.

"Let's make a run for it!" she yelled.

They broke through the front, and for a moment they were no longer surrounded. The way before them was clear, and the walls of the gully began to lower, to flatten, as if the wretched area might soon come to an end. But behind them the platoon of scaliis was changing into a division. The creatures swelled like a herd of red ants. They did not pick up their speed, but they did not slow their approach, either. Ra and Ali kept shooting at them, but if they killed a dozen a minute, it made no difference—there were three dozen to take their place.

Finally, Ali gestured for the others to stop.

"I have to try the flame," she gasped.

Ra shook his head. "That almost killed you last time."

Ali searched in her backpack for her lighter. "We have no choice. Stop shooting and take Farble and Paddy and make a run for it. I'm going to make a stand here."

"We're not going to leave you," Ra said.

"That's an order!" she snapped, finally finding the lighter. "And I told you before we came here that I would be giving the orders! Now get out of here while you still can!"

It was Paddy who stepped forward right then. The leprechaun's wide face dripped yellow sweat and his green eyes were swollen with fright. Yet he reached out and patted her arm. "None of us is going to leave you, Missy," he said.

Ali stared at him, touched, then looked at the approaching mass of scaliis, which could not have been more than fifty yards away. Bidding her friends to take shelter behind a nearby boulder, she went down on her knees and held up the Bic lighter and strained to focus on the tiny flame. Yet she felt weak and her lungs ached. It hurt to breathe, and she knew she was not going to be able to tap into the power that had overcome her when the scabs had attacked. At best she might frighten off the scaliis for a few minutes. But since they did not have brains, they would probably come right back.

Ali went to blow, then stopped, frowned.

A slithering black shape suddenly appeared atop the right side of the gully. It was massive, a thick worm over a hundred feet long. She assumed it was an ally of the scaliis, but they did not look happy to see it. The huge snake emitted a low roar rather than a hiss and then it was moving fast, sliding down the loose walls of the endless gully, right into the midst of the scaliis. Its size was its weapon. The scaliis tried jumping on it, cutting into it with their claws, spreading out their tentacles, but the creature flopped vigorously, from side to side, showing breathtaking agility, and its sheer mass crushed dozens.

Yet the scaliis did not run, and by now there were hundreds of them, swarming over the creature, and Ali was uncertain who was going to win the contest. Nevertheless, the sight of the snake coming to their aid—she could only assume it was trying to help—gave an unexpected boost to her power. Once more raising the lighter's tiny flame, she felt a current rush through her arm, and she blew as hard as she could. Fire roared forth—a flame that did not burn the snake, but one which swept over it, and pushed back the bulk of the attacking scaliis.

The reprieve was all the huge snake required. Crushing the remaining scaliis that clung to its scaly hide, it threw off the monsters and slithered toward them, pausing a few feet in front of Ali and raising its smooth black head. She was not sure if it was a snake or a lizard, or even a giant worm. But its huge red eyes, she could see, were deep and clear, and it spoke to her in a heavy, low, but still powerful voice.

"Come with me if you wish to live," it said.

Ali took a step back, intimidated by its size. The others looked ready to run.

"Who are you? Why are you helping us?" she asked.

"Drash." He added, "Drash helps because he wants to help."

Paddy grabbed her good hand, anxious. "Do not listen to it, Missy! This is a koul. It's very dangerous."

"Then why is it defending us from the scaliis?" she asked.

"It wants to be the one to eat us!" Paddy cried.

Ali turned back to Drash. "Where are you going to take us?"

"A place, not far from here." Tossing its huge head in the direction of the smoking scaliis, it said, "You must decide quick."

"Will you harm us in any way?" Ali asked.

"Drash will not harm," he replied.

"How will you take us to this place?"

"Drash will take you on his back."

"Don't do it, Missy!" Paddy pleaded.

Ali sensed no lie in the words of the koul. Indeed, she could not help noticing that the creature was bleeding slightly from where the scaliis had chewed on its sides, and that its blood looked remarkably human. If it was just after a quick meal, she thought, it could have gone elsewhere and had an easier time. Also, the horde of scaliis was dazed and battered, but it appeared to be regrouping. If she said no to Drash, and the koul left, they would be in the same predicament they had been in five minutes ago, which was not very encouraging.

"We will trust you to take us out of here," Ali said. "But I must warn you, I am a powerful fairy. Try to harm us, and you will feel the bite of that power."

The koul nodded his gigantic head. "Drash can see what you are. Drash will not harm you or your friends."

The koul's hide was made up of smooth scales. There was a rubbery feel to them, as well as a slight oily texture, although they were not the least bit sticky. As they climbed onto his back, he smelled *fresh*, like new car upholstery, and there were protruding folds of skin that they could hold on to. It was not difficult to make themselves comfortable.

Except when it came to Farble. Apparently trolls were more afraid of kouls than leprechauns were. Ali had to get off Drash and slowly coax Farble into sitting beside her. She had to hold the troll's hand.

Ali positioned herself right behind Drash's head, and cautioned the koul not to let any of them slip off. The remark seemed to amuse Drash, for the creature smiled quietly.

"Drash has done this before," he said, and with that he slithered out of the gully, moving as effortlessly as a snake through sand, and left the scaliis behind.

CHAPTER

15

They ended up on top of a steep rocky hill, in a large cave that opened onto a stony ledge that commanded a view for many miles around. Ali figured no one could reach the spot—except for another koul—and for that reason she let herself relax. South, she could see the mountain where they had entered the elemental kingdom, Tutor, as well as the twin rivers, Elnar and Lestre. The latter ran north of them as well, and the sound of its running water reached their high cliff and filled Ali with odd longings. For some reason she felt the river was a key to her exploration of this world, although it was running south, and she was trying to go north.

"You mean the kloudar, aye. They are up in the sky."

The real shock lay to the north, in the sky.

The clouds had cleared in that direction and for the first time she laid eyes—human eyes—on the floating kloudar. There was also a deep blue elemental moon, which a vague memory told her remained permanently full. It was fixed where the Pole Star was in the Earth's sky, and Ali remembered that Paddy had called it Anglar.

The kloudar circled Anglar like a ring around Saturn, only

this ring was not made up of tiny particles of dust but huge blue-white icebergs that appeared immune to gravity. The kloudar were eighty percent encased in ice, and their color was probably due to the reflected light of the moon.

Ali did not understand the movement of the kloudar. Clearly they floated over a portion of this realm, but when they went behind the moon, did they go into outer space? She tried getting an answer out of Paddy, but since he had a poor conception of space and orbits, she was left uncertain. Yet, like the river Lestre, Ali felt the kloudar were going to be an important aspect of her exploration of the elemental kingdom.

At first Drash left them alone to eat and regather their strength. Ra risked a fire with her permission—they didn't want to be spotted—and they heated cans of soup, broke out the nuts and beef jerky, and Ra made them a pot of rice. Farble still had raw beef left, and contented himself by devouring the last of his supplies, and drinking a few gallons of water that trickled from a spring near the opening of the cave. Paddy loved the can of Spam Ali had bought at the market.

Not eating a lot of any one thing, but chewing her food thoroughly, Ali slowly felt strength return to her limbs. Yet her right hand continued to pain her, even when Ra put on a fresh bandage; there was no helping it.

Finally, Ali turned to Drash, and invited the koul to come closer to their fire, which he seemed happy to do. She offered him food, but he shook his head, and she imagined the amount she was offering was pitiful by his standards. Farble was big— weighed half a ton—but Drash was fifty times that. Ali loved staring into his shimmering red eyes. They were triangular in shape, burning pyramids in the night, and they gave off almost as much light as their fire. Again, she did not sense evil in him, but she did feel his pain. Was it because of the wounds he had received when he had fought the scaliis? She asked and he said no, the scaliis had only scratched him.

"I asked you earlier why you came to our aid," she said to Drash. "And you said it was because you wanted to. Why was that?"

He studied her a moment. "Drash does not care for the scaliis, he feels they are a perversion of nature. And Drash could see you were a fairy, although you are a type of fairy Drash has never seen before." He added, almost with a shrug, "For years, before this war, it was normal that dragons and fairies helped each other."

"Dragons?" Ali muttered, excited. She turned to Paddy. "Is he a dragon?"

"Aye, Missy, kouls turn into dragons. Then they are more dangerous than ever."

Drash said nothing to defend himself.

"So you are a baby dragon?" Ali asked Drash.

"Drash is not a baby, he is not an adult. Drash is a koul," he replied.

"He is on the verge of becoming a dragon," Paddy explained. "But not all kouls make it that far. It is said that they have to take three tests, and that most fail."

"I know about tests," Ali said, thinking aloud, perhaps somewhat carelessly. "I had to take seven to regain my fairy powers."

"How did you lose them to begin with?" Drash asked.

"She's not really a normal fairy," Paddy began. "She was born—"

"Shh," Ali snapped. But the damage, if there was any damage, had already been done. Drash stared at her with wonder.

"You are not the one, are you?" he asked.

"Probably not," Ali said. "Tell me more about these tests you must take."

Drash ignored her question, studied her up and down. "You are a fairy and you are not a fairy." He considered. "Where are you from?"

Ali hesitated. "Not this world."

Drash was suddenly very serious. "Are you from the yellow world?"

She assumed that meant Earth. "What if I am?" she asked.

Drash stared at Ra. "You appear somewhat elfish, but you are dark-skinned. You must be from the yellow world."

Ra glanced at Ali, then nodded. "I'm not from around here, either," Ra said.

Drash turned back to Ali. "Are you the one?"

"I'm sorry, I'm not sure who the one is," Ali said.

"My father told me about the queen of the fairies who decided to be born in the yellow world. The one who was trying to stop the war." Drash paused. "Are you that one?"

The koul had saved their lives. Ali felt she owed him the truth. "Yes," she said.

Drash shook briefly with wonder, then spoke in his usual deep voice. "You are Geea?" he asked.

Ali nodded. "That is one of my names. Tell me about your father. Is he a friend of the fairies?"

The pain she had earlier sensed in him came to the surface. "My father is Kashar, king of the dragons, and for as long as there have been tales to tell and remember, he has been a staunch ally of the fairies. Many times over the long years he visited the high fairies at Uleestar. But recently he has allied himself with the Shaktra, and set the other dragons to killing fairies, elves, dwarves, and leprechauns." Drash lowered his head in shame, and added, "Drash tried to talk to him, but he would not listen."

"Why wouldn't he listen to you?" Ali asked.

"Drash is merely a koul." But the way he said it, Ali sensed he was trying to say much more.

"Have you ever seen the Shaktra?" Ali asked.

"No. My father has, but he refused to describe it."

"But why would your father betray his old alliances with the fairies to support such a monster?"

"Because the Shaktra promised him the one thing dragons long for above all else. It told him that it would show him how to remain on the kloudar, even when they pass onto the other side of Anglar." Drash added, "That way all the dragons would be able to enter the blue universe, like the ice maidens, and leave the bounds of this world behind."

Ali noted that Drash referred to the blue realm as a "universe," whereas he saw the elemental kingdom as a mere world. She could only assume there were different levels to the worlds, and that the elemental one was above Earth, and that the blue one was above the elemental one. It was like the dragons were trying to evolve—perhaps everything was—and the Shaktra was promising a shortcut. From all she had seen so far, Ali doubted it was going to deliver on its promise. She said as much to Drash and he agreed.

"Drash thinks his father has been bewitched," Drash said.

"How so?" Ali asked.

Drash was silent a long moment. "Drash has heard a rumor that the Shaktra is able to give the dragons a *taste* of the blue universe."

"A taste? Interesting choice of words. Is the Shaktra feeding them something?"

"Drash does not know for sure. But if the Shaktra is, then it cannot stop." He added, "Or perhaps Drash should say, the dragons do not *want* it to stop."

Ali shook her head. "Now I'm really confused. Is the Shaktra feeding them an addictive substance?"

"Like opium?" Ra asked.

"Shh. Quit talking about your opium," Ali said.

Again, Drash was slow to answer, and his eventual reply was at best vague.

"Drash can see that the dragons have changed for the worse," he replied.

"I see," Ali muttered, before trying a different approach. "Can dragons blow out big streams of fire?"

"Of course," Drash said.

"And the kloudar are covered with ice?" she asked.

"Yes," Drash said.

Fire and ice, she thought.

Ali reflected on the damage to the woods she had seen that afternoon. "Are the dragons helping the Shaktra by burning off huge chunks of ice from the kloudar? And letting them crash-land?"

Drash nodded sadly. "The ice makes for a terrible weapon."

"The kloudar orbit far north of here," Ra asked. "We saw crushed trees south of here. How did that happen?"

"My father has commanded teams of dragons to pull several of the kloudar south. It is from those ones that the sheets of ice fell, and caused the damage you saw."

Ra turned to Ali. "That makes the kloudar into the equivalent of inertia weapons. I have seen programs about them on your TV. Scientists believe they are the weapons of the future, and fear them. All you have to do is get a few thousand tons of rock orbiting the Earth and you can toss them down when and where you want. The dragons are doing the same here. There's no way the other elementals could stand against such a weapon."

"The fairies, elves, dwarves, and leprechauns have all retreated into the east, trying to escape the hordes of scaliis and the falling ice," Drash said. "It's said the Shaktra has them trapped against the mountains. Their only escape is to surrender to the Shaktra and agree to enter the yellow world and live there."

"The Shaktra is trying to force the elementals to invade the Earth again," Ali said.

"It sounds like it," Ra agreed.

"The elementals just want to survive," Drash said.

Ali nodded. "I know that's true. I know they're not the real enemy."

Drash stared at her once more. "Can you help our world?"

Ali hesitated. "I'm here to help. But there is still much I don't understand. When I was born as a human, I lost the bulk of my fairy memories. That's why I keep asking you questions."

Drash looked disappointed. "Queen Geea spoke to my father many times before she left for the yellow world. Even then, with all her power, she could not persuade him from forming an alliance with the Shaktra."

"How many years ago was that?" Ali asked.

Drash considered. "I was young then. It must have been thirteen years ago."

"That is when Geea left?" she asked, although she knew the answer. It was no coincidence that she was thirteen years old.

"Yes," Drash said.

"Has Uleestar been overrun by the Shaktra?" Ali asked.

"Drash heard that it has been emptied."

"Emptied? Not occupied?" she asked.

"Drash has heard that there are no scaliis there."

"Why not?" she asked.

"Drash does not know why."

"You mentioned something called the ice maidens," Ali said. "What are those?"

Drash shook his head. "No one in this world understands the ice maidens. They live on the kloudar, and yet, they are not bound by them, for they can ride the kloudar to the other side of Anglar, and from there leave this world." Drash added, "It's said they're from the blue universe, but only come to this world to help with the dead."

Ali felt a chill. "How do they help with the dead?"

"They take care of them until they live again."

Ali did not understand his reply. "Where do they take care of the dead?"

"On the kloudar," Drash said.

"Do the dragons ever attack the kloudar when the ice maidens are there?"

Drash shook his head. "Drash's father would not be that foolish."

"Why don't the ice maidens help the elementals defeat the Shaktra?"

"They are ice maidens. They do not concern themselves with such things."

The others were showing signs of exhaustion, and Ali was feeling her own fatigue. It had been two days since she had slept. She decided to forgo the questions for the time being, which suited Farble and Paddy. They moved to the far side of the ledge, away from Drash, and laid down near each other, using stones for pillows. Maybe their rivalry was finally over, she thought, remembering how the troll had wept when Paddy had been attacked by the scab. The two fell asleep in minutes.

Ali prayed she could do likewise. Stretching out her sleeping bag, the pain in her hand seemed to get worse. Ra was sensitive, he noticed her discomfort. Again he pulled out his opium cigarettes.

"There's no shame in taking something for the pain," he said.

"I'm afraid to," she admitted.

"What are you afraid of? I know how much you should take. You will know it when you begin to smoke it. Take enough to dull your pain so that you can rest. From the sound of it, we're going to have a hard day tomorrow. You have to rest to be at full strength."

"I'm afraid to do anything that will dull my mind while I'm in this world."

"We're safe this high up, particularly with Drash standing guard," Ra said.

"It's not that. So much of what we will do next is dependent on me regaining my fairy memories. They come back slowly, as I walk around this place, and see the kloudar, and stare at the green sun. I'm hesitant to take the opium because I feel it will block that process."

Ra shook his head. "You're as much human as you are fairy. That burn on your hand must be killing you. I couldn't sleep through that kind of pain."

Ali took her remaining stardust out of her backpack. "This powder will help."

Ra frowned. "What is it?"

Ali hesitated. She noticed Drash looking over. "It's fairy stardust. It's made from gold, using a special process."

Drash moved a bit closer, peered at her stuff. "Drash was told that stardust was a dark blue, darker than even Anglar," he said.

"Who told you that?" Ali asked. Her stardust was a pale blue.

Drash shrugged. "It's a rumor Drash has heard since he was young."

Ali glanced up at Anglar, the blue moon, nodded. "I probably can't make the real thing in my world. But it still helps. I'll take a bunch, and I think I'll be able to sleep."

Ra was doubtful. "If you can't, you wake me."

Ali smiled. "So you can sit up and suffer with me?"

Ra nodded. "I would stay awake with you, Ali, to keep you company."

She liked when he said her name. "I know you would, Ra."

She wished him sweet dreams and Ra climbed into his sleeping bag and, like the elementals, he appeared to quickly fall asleep. She wasn't sure what Drash was up to. He retreated to the far corner of the ledge, and closed one eye, but the other remained open; it seemed to be scanning the area. For all she knew dragons never closed both eyes at once. His breathing, which was deep and slow to begin with, slowed down further, and soon he was inhaling and exhaling only once a minute.

Ali swallowed half her remaining stardust and crawled into her sleeping bag, using her rolled-up jacket as a pillow. Ra was on her right, only three feet away, and on her left was the edge of the cliff, and the vast nighttime view of the elemental world. For a long time she laid there, staring up at the floating kloudar and the immovable Anglar, gazing at the rivers, Elnar and Lestre. The beauty of the view was outweighed only by the sorrow she felt for the world. There was no two ways about it. She had to destroy the Shaktra, and bring peace back to the elementals.

At some point she must have closed her eyes. Faintly, she began to hear the music of inner space, the flutes and bells and stringed instruments, and the gentle sounds carried her on a soothing wave deep inside, until she felt as if she was floating in the center of her heart. Only the space was not constricted, like her physical heart, but vast and peaceful, a world unto itself. For a long time, it seemed, she drifted in that place, not awake, but not asleep, either. And it seemed, inside her heart, or perhaps it was inside her soul, that she saw and felt many things that she had long ago forgotten. . . .

Dangerous trials that changed kouls into dragons . . .

A river that flowed backwards, in the night . . .

A dark blue powder, that could kill or heal . . .

A crystal palace at the tip of an enchanted island . . .

And an ice cave, on the highest kloudar, where an ancient secret slept . . .

All these things she saw, not with her eyes or her mind, but with something else . . . something she could not have described with human words.

Ali awoke with a start, sitting up in her sleeping bag.

There was a strange noise, it could have been a moan, coming from nearby.

Ali scanned the area and saw that Drash was gone. Standing, she crept in the direction of the sound, around the corner of the ledge where the koul had earlier laid down. Unfortunately, the ledge came to an end, and she had to move forward carefully on the steep side of the rock wall with her fingers and her bare feet digging into whatever tiny crevasse they could find. Despite the danger, and the pain it caused her right hand, she kept going. The noise grew louder. It definitely sounded like Drash was in pain.

Ali found him a minute later, on another ledge, frantically twisting and turning his massive worm-shaped body, and banging his huge head against the stone as if trying to alleviate his agony. As she watched him it seemed that his very form was changing. Were those legs he was sprouting? Was his tail lengthening and sharpening? It was true: she could see the changes with her own eyes, and somehow she knew it was not a bad thing. On the contrary, something wonderful was happening to Drash.

"Are you in pain?" she asked gently.

"Yes!" he gasped, still squirming, but managing to look at her with his red eyes. They were both open and blazing with ten times as much light as before.

"Do you know what is happening to you?" she asked.

"I'm dying!" he yelled. It was interesting to hear him use the "I" pronoun.

Ali shook her head. "You're not dying, you're growing. You're taking the first step toward becoming a dragon."

It was his turn to shake his head, and there was bitterness in his face. "That is not possible. Drash has not passed the first test. Drash tried to pass it. Drash means . . . my father set it up for Drash to pass. But . . ." He added shamefully. "I am a coward."

Ali came closer, put her hand on his head, stroked him. "I went deep just now, and slipped into a trance, and it helped me remember many things, not just about fairies, but about dragons, as well. You were right, I was friends with them for many years, and I knew your father. Because of that I know the trials a koul must go through to change into a dragon. Now I don't know what happened the first time you tried to take the first test, and you don't need to talk about it, but I do know that in the first trial, a koul must risk his life to save another. Don't you see? You did that this evening when you rescued us from the scaliis! You passed the first test, and because of that your body is becoming more like a dragon." She added, "It'll change further when you take the next two tests."

Drash stopped thrashing, and listened, yet his doubts remained. He spoke in a troubled voice. "Drash did not enter that gully to save you from the scaliis. Drash went down there to die."

Ali was shocked. "Why?"

"Because Drash failed the first test! Because Drash is the

cowardly son of a cowardly father! Don't you understand? Drash is the only son of the only dragon king in all of history that has chosen to betray all the elementals simply to place himself and his friends above this world before it is their rightful time." Drash added, "It doesn't matter what Drash did this evening. His father is still a traitor. It changes nothing."

"That's not true. Already you are changing, and that is the first step on the road to repairing the damage your father has done. You lie to yourself when you say you were trying to commit suicide this evening. I know that is not true. Look, you saved us! And because you saved us you are being rewarded right now."

Panting in pain, Drash looked at her miserably. "This is a reward?"

Ali nodded. "This pain will not last, the change will soon be complete. Then you can travel with us tomorrow, to a secret place I have remembered, and you can take the second test."

Drash was puzzled. "Why are you so anxious to help Drash become a dragon?"

Ali pointed to the kloudar. "I had this waking dream right now, and I have had parts of it before. I had it back home in the third world even before I knew I was a fairy. And each time, in this vision, I flew up to the kloudar. Now I know I must go there, that my path lies that way."

"Drash still does not understand."

Ali had to laugh. "The kloudar are way up in the sky. Either I regain my fairy wings in the next few days, or else you're going to have to fly me up there!"

CHAPTER

16

M s. Smith answered the door, Nira by her side, and Steve and Cindy both did a huge double take. The woman had long blond hair, wore a black silk pant suit, and was clearly gorgeous. But it was her eyes that made them shudder. They were a bright green, emeralds harvested from the Earth's most blessed cave, and they could not have looked more like Ali's eyes. They even had the same penetrating light. Yet Steve could not have said if a warm heart shone behind them, although Sheri Smith grinned as she opened the door.

"So here are the famous Steve and Cindy. Welcome to my home," she said.

Steve nodded. "To us, you're the one who's famous. We're both big fans of your computer games."

"We especially love Omega Overlord," Cindy said.

Sheri Smith put a hand on top of Nira's head as the little girl stared directly at them without blinking. It was impossible to tell if she remembered them, but Steve liked to think she did. He was happy to see Nira there in either case, feeling Sheri Smith was less likely to gut them with a knife with her daughter in the house. They still had no idea if Sheri Smith was Ali's

Shaktra or not, but Steve was not likely to forget the e-mails he had uncovered.

"That was the game that made my fortune," Ms. Smith said.

"We were playing it this morning, before we came here," Steve said.

"True fans! I love it!" The woman gestured for them to enter, and they followed her toward the dining room. "I have a guest over right now, an employee, but he's just leaving," Ms. Smith said. "He's our lead system designer, Mike Havor. Have you heard of him?"

"Can't say we have," Steve replied. Ali had spoken to them about Mr. Havor, at the park where they had met Nira and Rose. She said he was a blind genius who was the brains behind many of Omega's most successful games.

"Mike is very nice, but I'm afraid I work him too hard," Ms. Smith said as they entered the kitchen. A very pale man, with slick black hair, sat hunched at the table. He wore thick sunglasses and a tan sports coat, white slacks, and no tie. He smiled in their direction, and Steve was struck by the gentleness in his expression.

"I heard that, and I must say it is not true," he said. "I never work longer than I want to."

Sheri Smith introduced them. "Mike, this is Steve and Cindy, from Breakwater. They have been helping Rose take care of Nira the last two days. I told you about them."

Mr. Havor nodded, a smile on his dry lips. "Pleased to meet you both. I heard you rescued Nira when she got lost in town?"

"We're not sure if she was really lost," Steve said, noticing that Ms. Smith knew they were from Breakwater, when they had told Rose they were from Bale. Clearly the woman had been researching them.

"And we didn't rescue her, we just offered her ice cream," Cindy said.

Mr. Havor stood. "Well, I'm happy I got to meet you in either case. But now I must apologize, for I have to get back to work."

Ms. Smith chuckled. "I told you kids, I work the poor man to death."

Mr. Havor nodded vaguely in their direction. "I do hope we are able to meet again. Steve, Cindy."

"That would be nice," Steve replied, and watched as the man expertly used his white cane to find his way to the front door, and then out of the house. Steve turned to Ms. Smith. "It is safe for him to walk around town?" he asked.

"He could find his way from here to my offices in his sleep," she said. "Mike has lived in this town for many years. He knows all the obstacles, and everyone knows him. I never worry when he's out on his own."

"It's amazing he can design games he can't see," Cindy said.

Ms. Smith stared in the direction Mr. Havor had disappeared, and an odd note entered her voice. "There are many amazing things about that man. He has been with me since the start of my company. I owe him a lot." Then she shook her head. "But let me serve you lunch, and then we can talk."

"Rose is not around?" Cindy asked.

"No. I gave her the day off."

Lunch was simpler than the day before—roast turkey, mashed potatoes, and green peas—but Steve found it just as satisfying. Ms. Smith served them efficiently, and it was not until she was filling his plate that he noticed she wore thin white gloves. He didn't know how he had missed them at first, but there they were.

Ms. Smith offered them their choice of soda, while she had a glass of red wine. Even though Nira sat at the table with them, her mother did not offer her any food, and the little girl did not seem to mind. She just sat and stared.

Steve asked Ms. Smith about the inspiration for Omega Overlord. The woman was quick to admit Mr. Havor had brought her the seed idea, but at the same time she tried to explain the deeper philosophy behind it.

"Overlord tries to strip the direction of humanity down to the basics," she said. "We are here, we are alive, and we want to survive. Now how are we going to do that? It points out that so far we've been lucky to progress as a species, stumbling around in the dark the way we have. But now that technology has reached a certain level, hard choices have to be made. The most obvious is probably the most important. Do we continue to allow people to breed indiscriminately? It is the point of view of the game that the answer must be no. Our genes are our wealth. If we squander it randomly, we will be left with nothing, and we will not survive as a race."

Steve realized the woman was not only expounding the game's point of view, but her own. "But who's to say which genes survive?" he asked.

"It doesn't matter, someone intelligent, someone powerful, possessed of vision. Overlord tries to make that point with the Kabrosh character. He's the first one to see that not only must our genes be controlled, but that the fusion of machines and humans is inevitable. That is Kabrosh's strength. He knows what is necessary, and he goes for it. He doesn't let primitive morality stand in his way."

"I always saw Kabrosh as a villain," Cindy said.

Ms. Smith sipped her wine. "Nonsense. He's the hero of the game."

"But it's possible to win the game by killing him," Steve said.

Ms. Smith stared at him with her green eyes. Physically, it was true, they were identical to Ali's, but the feeling that came off them bore no relationship to Ali's warmth. Ms. Smith was a smart woman with some pretty weird ideas floating around in her head.

"You think so, huh? You have only mastered one level of the game. If you keep playing and explore all its levels, you'll find Kabrosh returns and starts to take over the world. He actually returns in an altered form, as a cyborg, and he wields great power."

"It sounds like you admire him," Cindy said.

Ms. Smith chuckled. "I designed him, of course I have to admire him."

They ate for a while in silence before Steve asked how she knew they were from Breakwater. He thought the question bold, perhaps risky, but felt they had to take a few chances if they were to find out what Ali needed to know. Ms. Smith did not appear put off by the question. Nor did she answer it clearly.

"I'm always curious about those who are curious about my daughter," she said.

"We felt close to her is all," Cindy said. "When we first met her in town, we didn't know if she had family, or if she was an orphan. I mean, it's not that she was dressed like an orphan, she just seemed all alone."

"In a sense Nira is all alone. She can't communicate with the outside world."

"Are you sure about that?" Steve asked. "She seems to recognize us when she sees us, and we've seen her use simple hand gestures and a variety of expressions to try to communicate with us."

Ms. Smith shook her head. "She's my daughter and I can assure you that's just your imagination. I love Nira, I'll always take care of her, but there's no one inside her."

Cindy was aghast. "You think she's a vegetable?"

"Why act so surprised? She is what she is. It does not help to make her into something she is not."

"But you're her mother. Surely you must hope for her eventual improvement," Steve said.

"I don't," Ms Smith said flatly.

"That's not fair to her," Cindy complained, getting agitated.

Ms. Smith sharpened her tone. "I'll tell you what's not fair— to *not* accept her condition. You're right, I'm her mother, and it took me a long time to believe what I have just told you. Nira is a lovely child to look upon, but Nira does not exist, not the way you and I exist. That's the way it is and nothing is going to change it."

Her harsh remarks led to another long silence. Steve ate his turkey and his mashed potatoes. Yet Ms. Smith did not appear distressed by the topic, although she did suddenly change it—in a manner Steve found distressing.

"A red-haired girl about your age came into my offices two afternoons ago," Ms. Smith said casually. "She said her name was Lisa Morgan, and she spoke with Mike at some length. Do you know who I'm speaking of?"

"No," Steve said.

"Never heard of a Lisa Morgan before," Cindy added.

"I thought you might have known her, since she seems to have arrived in town at the same time as you two did."

"How do you know when we arrived?" Steve asked uneasily.

"Rose told me when you met her. It sounded like the same time this Lisa Morgan walked through my door." Ms. Smith added, "I found it odd, if you know what I mean?"

"I'm not sure what you mean," Steve replied, losing interest in his food.

Ms. Smith smiled briefly. "I'm sure it was just a coincidence. I regret that I did not get a chance to meet this girl. The way Mike described her, she sounded dynamic."

Steve and Cindy looked at each other, sat silent. Ms. Smith continued in a casual tone. "Rose told me you two have an interest in the tragedy that struck this town thirteen years ago. I'm talking about the power plant explosion. Rose said you drilled her about it."

"We just asked a few questions," Cindy said.

Ms. Smith grinned. It looked forced. "She told me you were curious about my *involvement* that night. Where I was exactly, and how I managed to survive the blast. You can ask me about it, I don't mind. Don't be shy, the subject no longer haunts me."

Steve took a moment to gather his thoughts. "We questioned Rose about that night because we were confused to hear you were there. According to the records we studied at the library, we didn't see your name mentioned anywhere."

Ms. Smith's grin did not waver. "Isn't it possible that I was there, but that I've since changed my name?"

Steve stared at her and, for an instant, he had trouble focusing on her. "Did you?" he asked.

Ms. Smith chuckled. "It's possible. You have to admit, Smith is such a boring last name, so many people have it. Why, just the other day I read that it's the most common last name in America. What do you think of that?"

"Were you there that night?" Cindy asked.

"Yes. I just told you I was there. Don't you believe me?"

"So you went to school around here?" Steve asked.

"Toule is my hometown. I was born and raised here. Didn't you know?"

"No," Steve said, remembering what Hector had told them. Clearly one of them was lying, and Hector had struck Steve as an honest man.

"What was your name in high school?" Cindy asked.

Ms. Smith shrugged. "What difference does it make? I moved away, started a new life, became hugely successful, returned home. Sounds like a soap opera, doesn't it?"

"We're not sure what you mean," Steve said quietly.

"That plant blew up thirteen years ago. All those people who died that night have been buried for thirteen years. It's all ancient history. What matters is the now, today, this moment." Ms. Smith paused, somehow caused the air to turn cold, then casually added, "Why are you *three* spying on me?"

"Excuse me?" Steve mumbled.

"You and your friend, Lisa Morgan. Or is her real name Ali Warner? Friends of mine in Breakwater say that's her name. Such a distinctive child, they say, with her long red hair and brilliant green eyes. She's not the sort of person people might confuse with someone else. Don't you think?"

Steve pulled back from the table, stood. "I think it's time we left."

Cindy also got to her feet. "We have another appointment we have to keep."

Ms. Smith stood with them, and this time her smile was not forced—it was pure gloat. "You really have to go? In the middle of lunch? That's kind of rude on your part. Yes, that's very rude—your parents should have raised you better. It's not the kind of behavior I would allow with my own daughter."

Steve glanced at Ms. Smith, then reached for Cindy's hand. "Let's go," he said.

Steve half expected Ms. Smith to grab a carving knife and bar their way, but the pretty blond woman did nothing, just continued to stand and grin as they hurried from the dining room. They made it as far as the front door, even opened it, before they realized that Ms. Smith had set her designs in motion long before they had decided to come for lunch. For there was someone standing on the front porch, holding a sharp switchblade. Someone they had been trying to find for a month.

"Hello guys," Karl Tanner said.

CHAPTER

17

It was afternoon before they reached the mighty river, Lestre. Along the way they ran into only two scaliis, although the second one had been created from a troll larger than Farble, and it took four of Ra's arrows to bring it down. Ra was beginning to run out of arrows, and he took the time to pull them out of both scaliis.

Of course, had she ordered Drash to attack, the creatures could have been dispensed with easily enough. But Ali was handling Drash carefully this day. He had just sprouted legs and a tail—much to the amazement of the others—and he appeared in a serious mood. It was possible he was contemplating the next test—the one she had promised him during the night. But he had not asked her about it.

Drash seemed hesitant when they reached the edge of the river. The water was a deep blue-green, topped with flashes of white foam, and roaring with the sound of distant thunder, a quarter of a mile across, and surrounded by thick trees and heavy brush. The others were confused what she wanted with it. She had already told them it was not her intention to try to cross the river.

"I'm searching for a harbor, it's around here," she said. She watched Drash hold back from the river shore—a narrow strip of yellow sand and loose gravel.

"How do you know it's here?" Ra asked.

"I remembered it, last night, while I was sleeping."

"Are you sure it wasn't a dream?"

"I am sure."

Ra shook his head. "What does this harbor have? Boats? You don't know if the dragons haven't already crushed them with their ice. I'd think the Shaktra would've seen a harbor as a prime target. And even if there are boats there, this river is running opposite the direction we're trying to go."

The way he said the last sentence, it was as if he was casting doubt on their course in general. Ali could not blame him. She had told him she was here to rescue her mother, but she had admitted she had no idea where her mom was and that she had only a sense that if she reached Uleestar, she would find out what she needed to know. It was time she gave him concrete information, so that he could have faith in their quest. Hanging over all their heads was the fear they would run into an army of scaliis that even Drash would be unable to fight off.

"I remember this harbor clearly," she said. "It was unlike anything we have on Earth, because a person could ride a boat all the way south to it from Uleestar, and then turn around and take another version of the river back north."

Ra frowned. "Another version?"

"Yes. Lestre has a parallel river directly underneath it, deep underground, that flows north, into the heart of Uleestar. The river is called Tiena, and it is less than half the width of Lestre. But the two rivers are connected—one feeds the other."

Ra considered. "How far is this harbor from here?"

"Two miles north of here."

"What if it has already been destroyed?"

Ali nodded. "The upper portion of the harbor could have been destroyed. But Tiena is deeply buried, I can't imagine that any falling ice, no matter how huge, could have penetrated to it."

"I have heard of Tiena," Paddy said suddenly.

Ra looked at him with disgust. "How come you never mentioned it before?"

The leprechaun shrugged his shoulders. "No one asked Paddy about it."

Ali laughed. "Get used to it, Ra. It is easier to pry a scab off a leprechaun than to get information out of one."

Paddy's face darkened, and he rubbed his left arm. "Let us not bring that up again, Missy."

They started north once again, hiking along the narrow shore, all of them except Drash, who obviously preferred to romp through the woods. Because the trees were tightly packed, and the koul was big, Drash made more noise than Ali would have liked. It did not matter how many times she begged him to join them on the shore of the river, he ignored her. Of course, from her memory of last night of the trials kouls went through to become dragons, she understood exactly what was going on.

Drash was terrified of water.

They reached the harbor less than an hour later, and Ali's heart immediately sunk. The place was in shambles, every single wooden boat had been reduced to splinters. Ra had been right—the Shaktra had chosen the harbor as a prime target for the dragons' ice. Even the surrounding forest had been crushed flat. What an insidious weapon the Shaktra had dreamed up, she realized. When the icebergs melted, they didn't even leave behind a sign of what had caused the damage.

Yet there were no bodies, and Ali was beginning to understand why.

The scaliis were the worst kind of scavengers. They ate whoever fell.

"You probably don't remember it this way," Ra said gently, standing behind her. Ali felt her eyes burn, but wiped at them quickly, not wanting to show weakness in front of the others.

"It doesn't matter," she said. "We are here for Tiena."

"Do you remember the way down?"

She pointed to an outcrop of broken stone on the far side of the harbor.

"There's a cave over there, and stone steps," she said.

Ra was doubtful. "It could take us a week to clear that mess out of the way."

"You forget we have a koul with us, who is changing into a dragon. He can do the work of a dozen trolls."

Drash was agreeable to clearing away the cave entrance. Simply by pressing the side of his massive body on the strewn trees and the cracked rock walls, he was able to clear enough space for them to enter the tunnel that led under the ground. Yet it was at that point Drash backed off, saying they would have to go on without him.

"It does not matter what type of boat you find underground," he said. "You will not find one large enough to hold Drash."

Ali spoke to him. "Let's make that decision when we reach Tiena."

He shook his head. "Drash cannot go with you."

Ali came closer. "So what is Drash going to do next? You're not going to join your father and fight alongside the Shaktra. You despise that monster, and they couldn't use you anyway. Remember, you're just a koul. Tell me, honestly, where can you go if you don't stay with us? This entire land has been overrun with war."

He pulled back. "Drash can take care of himself."

Ali nodded. "I'm sure you can keep alive in this place. You're plenty strong. But what do you have to look forward to?"

"Drash does not need anyone or anything."

Ali came close, leaned beside his ear, and whispered so that the others could not hear. "You have to come with us, my friend. We all need someone. I haven't forgotten what you said last night, about wanting to end your life. I still don't believe that is true, but I know you carry a lot of pain in your heart. I can help you with that, and you can help us. I told you last night that I need you to fly me to the kloudar."

Drash sighed. "Only a dragon can reach the kloudar."

"This time tomorrow, you will be a dragon."

"But Drash has two trials yet to pass. Where will they come from?"

Ali nodded to the tunnel opening. "One of them is down there."

His red eyes flashed. "How do you know?"

"I'm Geea, queen of the fairies. I know."

"But the river . . . the water . . . Drash does not want to go down there."

She put her left hand on his smooth rubbery hide. The pain in her burnt right hand continued to come in waves, like stinging ocean swells that contained long and huge sets. She tried not to think about it. What else could she do?

"Drash has to trust, to have faith," she told him. "That's how a koul becomes a dragon. There is no other way. You know what I say is true. You leave here, you leave us, and you will wander lost in the wild, with no goal, no friends, and no way to ever become what you were born to be."

Drash stared at her. "Drash is afraid."

Ali patted him and then took her hand back. "It would not be the second trial if you were not afraid," she said.

The descent down the spiraling stone stairway that led to Tiena was an exciting experience for Ali because for the first time she got a close look at fairy handicraft. The walls of the stairway were tiled with white rectangles, squares, and triangles—each etched with what could have been Egyptian hieroglyphics. She could not read the lettering, but it definitely looked familiar.

The way grew dark. Fortunately they had their flashlights, but Ali sought to save their batteries, and lit a handful of torches that were positioned along the way. The orange light of the flames cast lonely shadows throughout the tunnel, and their footsteps echoed before them like the feet of ghosts who had fought and died in a cruel battle. Even before they reached the river, Ali could sense the place had already been invaded, not just from the air, but by a force of scaliis. The air remained fresh but there was a deep tension to it. She felt it on her forehead, like the pressure of an invisible hand.

They reached the river, and it was as she had feared. The boats had been holed and sunk. They limped wearily in the dark water like cracked logs. Yet the area was silent, empty of any scaliis. Even the running water of Tiena was much calmer than its cousin up above. Here the river moved like a long black stage— or so it seemed to Ali, who could feel the rich history of the place without remembering the details. Again, she had to force herself not to shed a tear in front of the others. They were all looking to her to make the next decision, even Drash, although he was holding back from the water.

"We're not going to be able to fix any of these boats," Ra said.

Ali shook her head as she walked the shore of the river. "It doesn't matter, we don't need a boat," she said.

Ra was exasperated. "I thought that was your plan? That we would ride the river into Uleestar, and so come at it from below?"

"We're going to ride into Uleestar, and we're going to take

this river." Turning suddenly, she nodded in the koul's direction. "Drash is going to take us."

With her remark, the others looked dismayed, not the least of whom was Drash, who quickly retreated several paces up the winding stairway. The gang could see the koul was terrified at the prospect.

"I don't even think he can swim," Ra said.

"Aye. Paddy has never seen a swimming koul before," the leprechaun said.

"Bad idea," Farble mumbled, saying perhaps the most intricate sentence of his entire life.

"That's the point," Ali said. "I didn't have to be told that water was the scariest thing a koul could face. That's already obvious to all of us. But simply because it *is* the scariest thing, that makes it the key to a dragon's second trial." Ali raised her voice and addressed Drash. "To complete your path to adulthood, you must face your greatest fear. It was like that for me when I was regaining my fairy powers."

Drash cowered. "You expect Drash to carry you all the way to Uleestar?"

Ali gestured. "You can see all the boats have been sunk. To me that's a sign that you were meant to take us."

Drash moved farther up the stairway. "Drash will end up drowning you all!"

"That's not true," Ali said. "We're going to take this test with you. We're going to show our faith in you by climbing on your back right now. We're going to take the plunge at the same time you do."

Ra shook his head. "That's nuts! Let's at least see if he sinks first!"

"Aye. Kouls have nothing to paddle with. He'll sink like a stone," Paddy said.

"He has legs now," Ali said.

Paddy gave them a doubtful look. "Kind of scrawny, they are."

Ali spoke. "Trials like this are not based on reason, but on courage. I know this from what I went through. We have to help Drash find his courage by taking the risk with him. But I don't want any of you to be afraid. I know he is going to make it."

"Have you *seen* this?" Ra asked.

Ali hesitated. "Not exactly."

There was a long silence, and it must have seemed the longest to Drash. The koul had unwound his long dark body from the stairway, and crawled to where the bulk of the ruined boats lay floundering, but he was unable to force himself closer to the water. Ali walked up to his side.

"Your father is not here to know if you pass or fail this test," she said. "But if you do pass it, and the next one, I'm sure that one day soon you'll be able to face your father and confront him about the horrible things he's doing with the Shaktra. He might listen to you then, because you'll no longer be just a koul." Ali added, "You're tired of being one, aren't you?"

He nodded. "Drash is too old to remain in this type of body."

"Then let's climb on your back, and you slip into the water, and we will be on our way to Uleestar. When we get there, and you rest this night, you will change again, and in the morning you will be capable of breathing fire."

Drash stared at her in wonder. "But you admit you have not seen this in a vision?"

Ali shook her head. "Visions have their limits. They can't always save you when your back's to the wall, and our back is to the wall now. It's your heart and your courage that's going to allow us to continue on our quest."

Drash was curious. "What exactly do you seek, Geea?"

Ali hesitated. "Peace."

They climbed on Drash's back, even Farble, who seemed to understand they were in a desperate situation. Ali rode up front, near the koul's head, like the night before, but she did not give him any more time to think about what he had to do. When they were all settled, she told him to swim. Drash crawled to the edge of the gently flowing black river and carefully touched the water.

"But I don't know how to swim," he said.

"It's like riding a bicycle. No one knows how to do it until they do it."

Drash glanced up at her. "What is a bicycle?"

Ali laughed. "I don't think it's something a dragon would be interested in."

Drash appeared to believe her, in all ways. Turning toward the water, he slid off the shore and into the river, and it was only for a moment, a few heart-stopping seconds, that it seemed he would sink and they would all drown. But then he lifted up his head, a dozen feet above the water line, wiggled his long smooth body, and slipped into the flow of the current, and they were finally on their way to the heart of the fairy kingdom.

CHAPTER

18

They were led down a dark stairway, into a wide basement, and from there they took another stairway that was covered with dust and made of rusted metal, and which appeared much older. As they went deeper into the earth, Karl holding the switchblade at Steve's neck, Steve saw that they were entering a series of damaged caves that must have spread out like an ant farm beneath the old power plant. If he looked closely, he could see signs of the explosion: burnt gas tanks, twisted and darkened pipes, piles of ashes. How weird, he thought, that Ms. Smith had seen fit to build her mansion on the town's old scar. There was a cruelty in the woman that went way beyond reason.

Not that Karl was in a friendly mood. Whenever Steve stumbled, the jerk kicked him and pressed his blade deeper into his neck. For that matter, Karl had already cut him. Steve could feel the faint trickle of warm blood drying on the sweating skin of his throat.

Ms. Smith had a grip on Cindy, and wasn't treating her any better, although the woman appeared strong enough to not need a weapon. As if she were dragging a paper doll into her own private dungeon, Ms. Smith held Cindy by her hair and was happy to yank it when the mood struck her. Yet Steve was proud that Cindy did not cry out. Their courage was probably all they had left, and Steve was not sure how long that was going to last.

He just hoped Ali was able to rescue them soon.

In a poorly lit reddish cave that looked like it could have been carved out of a Martian mountain, they were chained to the hard walls with iron shackles that might have been a popular item back during the gold rush. Their arms were locked above their heads and out to their sides, in a vague crucifixion posture, although their feet remained planted on the ground. Karl was the one to lock them up, and when he was done he took a step back to admire his handiwork. What struck Steve was how little Karl had changed. With his blond hair and blue eyes, and substantial muscles, he looked like the same jock Steve had always despised at school. Karl even appeared to have on the same clothes he had worn when they had hiked up the mountain together a month ago.

Yet Karl was not the same, or else Steve was finally seeing him for the first time. He had the identical cold light in his eyes as Ms. Smith, and the way he clapped his hands and grinned at their discomfort, Steve knew he was dealing with a psychopath who was capable of anything. But hadn't Ali warned them? The guy had kidnapped her mother, after all. They'd had plenty of warnings from the start that they were getting in over their heads. Now look where they were. Steve could not get over the guilt he felt at dragging Cindy into this situation.

"How do you feel?" Ms. Smith asked sweetly, as Karl paced behind her.

"Lunch was good," Steve said. "Things have sort of gone downhill since then."

"Why are you doing this to us?" Cindy demanded.

"I told you, I don't like spies," Ms. Smith replied.

"We are not spies," Steve said.

Ms. Smith came closer, and once again, like upstairs, he had trouble focusing on her. He assumed it was the poor light—there was a kerosene lantern in the corner and that was it—or that there was something wrong with his eyes. But the more he stared at her face, the less real it seemed, and the more fluid it appeared.

He felt as if he was gazing at a TV screen.

"I think Ali sent you here," Ms. Smith said.

Steve considered carefully. He did not want to drag Ali into their mess—unless it was to fry this monster—but he needed some type of leverage.

"She knows we're here, but so do other people," he replied. "Cindy was telling the truth when she said we have another appointment in town. If we don't show, people will come looking for us, and those same people know we were supposed to have lunch with you this afternoon."

Ms. Smith smiled thinly. "Your friend has a gift. Perhaps she has told you about it, perhaps not. She might have been afraid to make you uncomfortable in her presence. That gift is the ability to hear when the truth is spoken. I have it myself, and I know you're lying to me. You've just told me that Ali suspects you're here, but that she's not sure. As far as other people knowing about your lunch date with me, that's another lie." Ms. Smith paused. "Am I right?"

Steve shrugged. "If you're so sure of your gift, why do you need to ask?"

Ms. Smith reached out and touched his chin with her gloved hand, and he flinched at the contact. It was as if she had used a sharp nail to cut him, but she had barely brushed him. Her pretty mouth showed amusement, her green eyes showed nothing.

"You're a smart young man, I can see that. I like that," she said. "But smart is not the same as being wise. You have been caught, you are in a precarious position. The wise thing for you to do right now would be to cooperate with me."

Steve met her gaze. "And if we don't?"

"You'll experience pain. Horrible pain." Ms. Smith added, "Do you know what that is like? No, you're young, of course you don't. But I can assure you that it does not matter how brave you are, how strong your will is. There is a limit to how much pain any human being can withstand. After that they crack—they all crack. You understand what I'm saying?"

Steve swallowed, nodded. "What do you want?"

"Information about your dear friend Ali. Give it to me and I'll let you go. I'll even let you finish your lunch. How does that sound?"

"Ali keeps her private business to herself," Steve said.

Ms. Smith chuckled, and looked at Karl. "This boy is much more interesting than you let on to me, Karl. He never answers a question directly."

Karl stopped pacing and glared at Steve. "Because he's a fat coward."

Ms. Smith shook her head. "I think there is more to him than meets the eye. I think the same about Cindy here. Honestly, I admire you young people, trying to help Ali save the world. But at the same time I do need to know certain things, and I want your answers to start flowing soon." Ms. Smith paused. "Where is Ali right now?"

Steve coughed. "Beats me."

Ms. Smith glanced at Cindy. "Where is Ali?"

Cindy snickered. "Go stuff yourself!"

Ms. Smith nodded slowly to herself. "Ali has entered the elemental kingdom, in search of her mother. I know this already."

"Then why did you ask?" Steve asked.

Ms. Smith was cheerful. "Think of it as a test, one you just failed. That is okay, the first test was not so important to me. But here comes the second one, and it is very important. If you fail it, you will start that horrible suffering I told you about. Ready?"

"Ali really does keep what is important to herself," Steve said quickly.

"How far do Ali's suspicions of me go?" Ms. Smith asked.

"I do not understand the question," Steve said.

"It is a pretty vague question," Cindy added.

Ms. Smith nodded. "In a way, it is an abstract question. Yet you two rode a bus to Toule with her, and you must have talked about me on the way. What did she have to say?"

"She said almost nothing," Steve said. "She had not met you at that time."

Ms. Smith shook her head. "What if I told you that was not true? That I met Ali before she even came here. But that once she was here, I carefully avoided contact with her."

Steve shrugged. "I wouldn't argue with you about it."

Ms. Smith grew hard. "Has she ever referred to me as the Shaktra?"

"What's that?" Steve asked.

Ms. Smith reached in her back pocket, took out a red Bic lighter. Holding it directly in front of his eyes, she flicked the flame into life, even as her cold voice came through the fire like fog through a broken windowpane.

"You have heard the word before," she said. "Ali has spoken it in your presence, and you lie to me when you deny it. But I told you, the time for lying is over. I'm going to ask one last time. Did Ali ever refer to me as the Shaktra?"

Steve trembled. "She was curious about you, that's all."

Ms. Smith smiled, nodded, and then let the flame drift slowly up toward his right hand. Steve felt the heat on his palm, at first just a pleasant warmth, although he was too afraid to look at what she was doing. But then he felt a sharp stab of pain, and heard an ugly sizzling noise. He tried to jerk his hand away but of course it was locked in place. A nauseating odor filled his nose. He knew what it was, he was smelling his own burnt flesh! Even though he tried, he could not stop himself from letting out a loud scream. Ms. Smith withdrew the lighter, put it out, lowered her head close to his.

"Now, please, tell me if Ali thought I might be the Shaktra?" she said.

Steve had tears in his eyes, agony in his palm. "I don't know," he mumbled.

Ms. Smith shook her head. "I'm afraid that's not good enough."

"Yeah, she thought you were the Shaktra, what's the big deal?" Cindy blurted out.

Ms. Smith looked over. "You find it hard to watch your friend suffer? That's a noble quality, also a weakness. But I'm glad you're in a mood to talk. I have questions for you as well, Cindy, and I have a different colored lighter in my pocket specifically for you. Amazing toys, aren't they? Spend three bucks in a drugstore and you get a whole packet of them. Yet they're capable of bringing the strongest man on Earth to his knees."

Cindy was bitter, but also terrified. "You will not get away with this," she said.

Ms. Smith put away the red lighter, took out a green one, and casually strolled to Cindy's side. "Tell me how Ali escaped Radrine's lair inside the mountain?" she asked.

Cindy stared at her. "I don't know."

Ms. Smith nodded. "The truth, good. Did Ali ever speak to you about Radrine?"

Cindy closed her mouth tight, but Steve felt compelled to speak.

"She told us that Radrine was the queen of the dark fairies, that's all," he said.

Ms. Smith stood between them. "Did Ali talk to you about the time distortion that she experienced on the other side of the red door?" she asked.

"She mentioned it," Steve said.

"That's all? She did not explain how she used it to get away from Radrine?"

"We told you, we know nothing about this Radrine except her name," Cindy said.

Ms. Smith stared at her. "You were on top of the mountain with Ali when the elemental army entered this world. According to Karl, you were close to Ali when she first picked up the Yanti, and then activated it for her own purposes and sent the elves and the dwarves back into their world. Now I'm going to ask you another question, and this one is more important to me than all the others combined. If you fail to answer it, I will get very angry, and that is not a sight either of you want to see. Do you understand?"

Cindy glared past her, at Karl. "Ali should have killed you when she had the chance."

Karl snickered. "Ali is too weak to kill someone like me."

"Shut up, Karl," Ms. Smith said, closing in on Cindy, her green lighter in her hand. "Tell me, Cindy, how did Ali activate the Yanti?" she asked.

"I don't know," Cindy said.

Ms. Smith paused, surprised. "But you were close to her. You must have heard her say something to the Yanti. A word? A chant?"

Cindy lowered her head. "I didn't hear her say anything."

Ms. Smith suddenly flicked the lighter to life, and Steve sucked in a terrified breath of air. Yet the woman made no move to attack either of them. She seemed to be thinking. It was clear that she sensed Cindy was telling the truth.

Nira suddenly appeared; she was like a flash of light in the darkness. Hurrying to her mother's side, she grabbed her hand and tugged on it, even as the witch stood in the center of the room contemplating what she should ask next, and whom she should burn. But then Ms. Smith shrugged, as if weary of the subject, and gave in to Nira's demand for attention. It made Steve sick to his stomach to see the woman reach down and brush the girl's short red hair. It was obvious to him right then that Ms. Smith must have the same bright red–colored hair as her daughter—that she had only dyed it to hide the fact.

Hide the fact that she was a fairy?

Who was Ms. Smith, he wondered?

"I'm afraid these questions will have to wait until later," Ms. Smith said. "My daughter is hungry and there are things I must attend to at the office."

"Do you want me to stay and torture them?" Karl asked hopefully.

"No. I want you to go sit in a room and cause no trouble." With Nira in hand, Ms. Smith walked back toward the way they had entered the cave. But she called over her shoulder. "Don't think you're getting off easy. Slow growing pain can be the most effective, and within an hour I'm afraid you'll find that the muscle spasms in your arms are close to unbearable. Honestly, Steve, Cindy, the next time we chat I think you'll be far more cooperative."

Steve called out before she disappeared. "What was your name when you went to high school here?" he asked.

Ms. Smith turned and blushed. It was almost as if she were shy to admit the truth.

"You mean, you haven't guessed?" she said.

"No," he said.

"I was Hector Wells's girlfriend."

Steve nodded grimly. "You are Lucy Pillar."

"Perhaps. Whoever I am, I'm not the person I used to be."

With that, Ms. Smith left them alone in the dark cave.

CHAPTER

19

The cavern above Tiena was dome-shaped, and made up of large gray stones, each set with black cement in an exquisite arc that spanned the exact width of the river. Once more Ali was sure she was staring at the handiwork of the fairies, and she wondered how many years it had taken her people to erect the lengthy tunnel around the subterranean river. For that matter, she wondered how old the elemental civilization itself was. Five thousand years? A million? She leaned toward the former, sensed its history probably paralleled humanity's. Then again, she thought, there were many scholars on Earth who felt there had been civilizations long before the Egyptians and the Sumerians.

Drash, what a crazy boat he made for them all. The odd thing was, the longer he swam, the more he seemed to enjoy it. He even began to tell her about his favorite foods. Apparently he loved what sounded like apples and bananas. For some reason, she was relieved to learn he was a vegetarian. But from the sound of it, so were fairies and elves, and that depressed her. She wasn't ready to give up her bacon and eggs in the morning!

The way was long but no one complained. They were all

happy that Drash was keeping them afloat—plus they were covering tremendous ground. Tiena flowed at only half the speed of Lestre, but in combination with Drash's swimming, they were probably going twenty miles an hour.

Ali did not have a watch, but estimated they had been on Drash's back for five hours when she spotted the torch up on their right. As they grew nearer, she saw a harbor similar to the one they had left behind at the south entrance to Tiena, yet this port was undamaged. There was a whole fleet of untouched wooden rowboats. The sight was reassuring, but not nearly as much as the two fairies waving the torch at them. It was clear to Ali that she and her pals were expected.

Drash swam them to the sandy shore, on the side of the wooden planks that made up part of the harbor, and Ali and her friends dismounted. Ra carried a torch, and was the only one to accompany Ali as she approached the two tall fairies—a man and a woman, both with long red hair, green eyes, white robes, and loving faces that seemed so familiar that she came close to weeping. These two had *not* been marked. Indeed, their faces shone with an enchanting green light that made her feel small next to them. Yet they bowed low as she came near.

"Geea," the man said in a soft melodious voice. "Welcome home."

Ali bowed as well, gave Ra a nudge to follow her example.

"I'm happy to be here, thank you," she said. "This is my friend, Ra."

They bowed in Ra's direction. "Welcome to Uleestar, Ra," the man said. "My name is Trae, I'm Geea's adviser of old. This is Amma . . . a friend of the royal family."

Amma spoke, and her voice was sweet as rain. "We have been waiting for you," she said. "But we were not sure when you would arrive."

"How did you know we were coming?" Ali asked.

"It was inevitable that you would return here, once you had the Yanti," Trae said. "And your capture of the Yanti from Lord Vak is well known in our world."

"I did not capture it so much as he let me have it," Ali said.

Trae nodded. "Forgive me, Geea, I have not had a chance to advise you in many years, and I think your estimation of your encounter with Lord Vak is more accurate. You see, we know a bit about your life in the yellow world, but there is much we don't know."

"But understand that we are here to help you in any way we can," Amma said.

Ali smiled. "Please, you speak to me like I'm your boss, when I'm just a visitor to this land. Let us talk as equals."

Trae smiled but shook his head. "You must forgive us, Geea. We remember you quite differently than you remember yourself. To us, you are the bright jewel of this land, and we owe you our lives and allegiance. Indulge us, and let us treat you as our ruler. It does not matter to us that you elected to be born in a human body. You are still our queen."

"Your queen is suffering from a severe case of amnesia, I'm afraid."

Amma came near, went down on her knees in front of Ali, peering up at her intently. As if to touch her hair, to caress her face perhaps, she raised her hand, but then thought better of it. A note of loss entered the fairy's rich voice.

"But a part of you remembers us, does it not?" Amma asked.

Ali felt a wave of emotion then, stronger than any she had experienced in her life. Yet the feeling was a brew of opposites: love and loss, joy and sorrow. Ali reached out and touched the woman's hair, let it run through her fingers, and it felt so nice . . .

"I don't remember you, I'm sorry. But I *know* you," Ali said.

That appeared to satisfy Amma, and she bowed her head and stood and took a step back. Trae spoke next in a respectful tone. "Geea, we don't know what you have learned about Uleestar in your travels in our world, but it has already been overrun by the Shaktra and its gruesome army. Fortunately, for reasons unknown to us, the enemy has chosen to leave our capital un-occupied. Amma and I, along with twenty other fairies, have managed to remain here by hiding in the Crystal Palace." He added, "Your home."

"There are no scaliis here?" Ali asked.

"None on the central island," Amma said. "But earlier this morning, Trae and I saw a group of dark fairies fly over the palace. They did not stop or land, but they have clearly been sent by the Shaktra to see that the palace is empty."

"These twenty fairies you speak of—they keep well hidden?" Ali asked.

"There are secret rooms in the palaces few could find even if they were given a map," Amma said.

Ali considered. "Do you know Radrine?" she asked.

Trae nodded. "We know a great deal about her."

"I had a run in with her the other day. I hurt her, she hurt me, but I think she is here in this world. Do you know if she was one of the dark fairies that flew by?"

"We did not see her, so we have no way of knowing for sure," Trae said. "But it is possible she is here, and in communication with the Shaktra."

Ali felt her heart pound. "So the Shaktra is definitely in this world?"

Trae turned to Amma, who hesitated. "Yes, it is here," she said. "But we believe it to be in the far east, in command of an army that is pressing the bulk of the elementals against a range of mountains we call the Morray."

"Is the fairy army there as well?" Ali asked.

"*All* the fairies are there," Trae said. "All that are left alive, or unchanged. The Shaktra attacked our land first, coming in force over the sea from the Isle of Greesh. The scaliis, the dragons, the crashing ice—they were an irresistible black wave. They came so fast, there was nothing we could do to fight back. We had to evacuate."

"General Tapor took command of your army, Geea," Amma said. "You may not remember him, but he's a great man—a brilliant tactician, a fearless solider. He fights with Lord Vak and Lord Balar as we speak."

"Even the leprechauns and the trolls fight with them, which has never happened before," Trae said. "But we have heard that their combined armies have been ravaged by the Shaktra's, and that they are being pressed to surrender—to eventually be exiled in the human kingdom."

Ali nodded. "The koul that travels with me told me some of this. Do you know if General Tapor, Lord Vak, and Lord Balar are considering surrender?"

Trae shook his head. "Our news is at best a week old. Much could have happened since then."

Ali glanced at Drash. "Do the dragons continue to fight alongside the Shaktra?"

"Yes. Along with other creatures I did not mention, the marked ones," Trae said.

"I know of them. We met several on the road," Ali said.

Amma shuddered. "Were they . . . our people?"

"Yes. I tied up one, and injured another, to stop them from reaching the desert . . . " Ali did not know how to finish.

Amma shook her head. "Nothing is sacred to our enemy."

"How are they marked?" Ali asked.

"It is said the Shaktra itself touches them," Trae said.

Ali frowned. "And their minds are just gone?"

"Or else imprisoned," Amma said.

Ali paused. "Do you know what the Shaktra is? Can you describe it to me?"

Trae and Amma exchanged a long look, and Ali saw a thousand words in it and yet could not read a single one. Nevertheless, she knew right then that even though they were her loyal servants and loved her dearly, there were things they did not want to tell her. It was Trae who finally spoke.

"Let us not speak of it in this dark place," he said.

The Crystal Palace. It took Ali several minutes above ground, in the fresh air and the green light, walking the vast rooms and the long halls of her old home, to realize that the palace had been carved out of a single giant clear quartz crystal. There were so many lovely wood carvings, and carpets, and big woven canopies, and laced curtains, that she did not understand that the basic structure was entirely made of stone. Amma had to explain how the place came to be.

"It is said that long ago the ice maidens brought this crystal to the ground, from the highest kloudar, to rest here at the tip of this island around which Lestre flows. Further, it is said that this crystal is forever tied to the kloudar, and to the ice maidens themselves." Amma added, "That might be the reason the Shaktra hesitates to destroy this place."

Ali had trouble listening, her eyes were too big as she strode from room to room. The only thing she could compare it to was the castle at Versailles, outside Paris. Her parents had taken her there when she was ten, and she had spent an afternoon lost in a dream. Yet the artwork of *her* palace surpassed the brilliance of the French. Here many of the walls *were* the paintings. Around every other corner she stumbled on a remote part of the elemental kingdom. So many scenes of beauty, so many tales told in pictures—Ali could not help but feel overwhelmed.

Yet the odd thing was that she felt comfortable in the palace.

Ali saw no other fairies as she explored.

"It's going to be hard to go home after this," Ra muttered.

"Aye. No leprechaun has ever walked these halls before," Paddy said, and for the first time she heard genuine awe in his voice. It made Ali stop and turn to Trae and Amma.

"Do you have gold here?" she asked.

Trae was puzzled. "Gold? Why yes, Geea, there is gold here."

"How much?" Ali asked.

Amma seemed to catch on, for she smiled. "As much as anyone could want."

Ali pointed at Paddy. "Give him a pot of gold. No, give him ten pots of gold."

Paddy's green eyes swelled the size of limes. "Missy!" he cried.

Then the leprechaun fainted dead away on the floor, and Ali laughed. She could not stop laughing, and the others joined her, even Farble, and it was a treat to hear a troll giggling, because he sounded like he was about to throw up. Ali regretted that Drash was not there to share the happy moment, but he was of course too big to fit in the palace. As far as she knew, he was still below, at the dock on the river.

Trae led the others away to eat, and Amma took Ali to her private quarters. Ali was surprised to find her waiting room had a small throne in it, upon which sat a jeweled crown. She put on the latter, but it was too big for her head, and besides she did not like it. Amma nodded at her reaction.

"You did not like to wear a crown when you lived among us," Amma said.

"I would have thought that I would have gotten used to it."

"You never did. It was not you, you used to say."

"I didn't enjoy being queen?" Ali asked.

"I would not put it that way. You had been queen a number of years before you chose to become human."

Ali was curious. "Did you help me with that decision? Did I talk to you about it?"

Amma hesitated. "A long time ago, yes."

She strolled into her bedroom, and was happy to find it simply furnished. There was a large bed, a chest of drawers with a mirror, an efficient wooden desk, a closet filled with clothes, mostly white and green robes, a shelf filled with books—hardly anything she would have failed to recognize on Earth. Yet one of the room's doors led onto a balcony that had a view few humans could have dreamed of.

Taking a step outside, Ali was amazed to see how much larger the flying kloudar appeared—even with the sun shining straight overhead—and how impressive Lestre was as it rushed around the twin sides of their island, Uleestar. Yet it troubled her to think that the barrier of running water had been of no avail against the Shaktra's forces. In the end, she had to ask herself, could anything stop the enemy?

Lestre was unable to erode away the island because of a barrier of gigantic white marble boulders that covered the north end of Uleestar. Ali was not sure if they were a natural formation or not, but could see that the rows of clear green pools and the intricate labyrinth of flowers this side of the stones had been purposely constructed. Her palace was at the very tip of the island, hence she saw no other dwellings.

But there was a magnificent mountain range that rose sharply a few miles north of Uleestar. Several of the highest snowy peaks seemed to brush the kloudar, although it might have been an optical illusion. Trying hard, she sought for a name for the mountains, and finally it came: the Youli. She could see that the Youli would make a natural stepping stone up to the kloudar.

"Best not to stay out too long," Amma said at her back.

Ali turned. "Sorry."

Amma smiled. "Please come in, Geea, I feel safer with you close."

Ali reentered her bedroom, closed the door at her back. She did not see any lights, yet the room was pleasantly lit. Then she noticed a dozen square crystals, a foot across, arranged in the corners, and the faint warm glows they emitted. She did not bother to ask Amma if they used electricity.

Ali sat on the edge of her old bed, opened the top drawer in the cedar table that stood near her pillows, found a small, oblong gold box, which she took out and set on top of her green sheets. Amma came quickly to her side as she opened it, almost as if in fear.

Inside was a flaky dark blue powder.

Stardust. The real thing. Ali recognized it immediately.

She went to dip her finger in it, to taste it. Amma grabbed her hand.

"No!" Amma cried.

Ali sat back, startled. "What's the matter? I know what it is."

Amma was anxious. "But do you know what it will do to a human body? Does anyone know?"

Ali shrugged. "I have made my own version of stardust in my world. And it has helped me integrate my powers into my body. I was just thinking a little of the real thing might allow me to regain my strength." She added, "Fighting Radrine took more out of me than I care to admit."

Amma gestured to her bandaged hand. "Does it cause you much pain?"

Ali hesitated. "The dark fairy burned all the skin off my palm."

Amma winced and jumped up. "I have something I can put on it. I'll be back in a moment." She added as she left the room, "Don't touch the stardust!"

The moment Amma left, Ali picked up the gold box again, and placed her injured palm above the flaky blue powder. Immediately she felt a pulsating magnetic current flow from the material into her hand. It was soothing, invigorating, but its power intimidated her, and she closed the box and put it back in the drawer before Amma could return.

"This gel is made from a special plant that grows only on the tallest peaks north of here, which perpetually lie in the shadow of the kloudar. It is very soothing," Amma said as she came back in the room and sat near Ali. Amma had in her hand a white dish that contained a red cream. Once again, she gestured to Ali's bandage. "May I see?"

Ali offered her injured hand, feeling safe with Amma. "I warn you, it is not a pleasant sight," she said.

Amma began to unwind the gauze. "Ra bandaged this for you," she said.

"How did you know?"

"He likes to take care of you, I see it."

"I only met him two days ago. He hardly knows me."

Amma smiled. "It is something to wonder about." She added, "Where did you meet him?"

"In Africa."

"You were in Africa?"

"For a few minutes." Ali added, "I used one of the portals in the mountain near my home, ran into him. You know about those?"

Amma hesitated. "Yes, I do."

"You must know about the different colored doors then?"

"All the high fairies know about the doors."

"I'm so curious about them. Where does the blue one lead?"

"To the blue universe."

Ali chuckled. "What is that? It sounds like a higher kingdom."

Amma nodded. "It is a much higher realm that the elemental one. You might say all the creatures who live here aspire to attain it, even if they are not consciously aware of the desire."

"But the ice maidens have attained it?" Ali asked.

"The koul must have told you about them. Yes, the ice maidens are free to come and go as they wish, to the stars even. But they do not interfere in our affairs."

"There's no way of talking them into helping fight the Shaktra?"

"That would be quite impossible. The ice maidens do not fight."

"But Drash said they take care of the dead, until they are ready to live again. How is that done?"

"When an elemental grows old here, and finally tires of life, and lays down to rest, the ice maidens come for that body, and shelter it in the ice caves of the kloudar, and help it heal, until it is ready to return to life."

"What if the elemental's body has been severely damaged? Say burned to a crisp by a dragon?"

"Then a new body must be grown for that one."

"Fairies have babies then?" Ali asked.

"An old elemental soul can be born as a tiny baby. But it is not the usual way for us. We prefer at the end of our lives to be taken by the ice maidens, and then returned to our land when our time comes."

Ali had to smile. "Sounds like you prefer to start life all grown up?"

"There are advantages," Amma said.

Amma grimaced when she finally undid the bandage, and Ali herself was not happy to see the bloody tissue. There was no sign of infection, but Ra had been right. The injury needed medical attention, and probably surgery. Healing had been going on but there was no skin left unburned with which to cover her muscles and tendons. Two days of recovery and it still looked like an open sore. No wonder it kept bleeding.

Gently, Amma began to apply the cream, and Ali was amazed but relieved to feel her pain level drop in half. The fairies knew a thing or two about medicine, after all. Ali asked if the cream could heal the wound and Amma told her it could, but that it would take time.

"You need to rest, and not channel your power through your arm."

Ali shook her head. "I don't think I'm going to get much rest until I accomplish what I came here for."

Amma gave her a look. "Do you know why you are here, Geea?"

Ali hesitated. "There are two main reasons. I'm trying to find my mother. She was taken hostage by Drugle over a year ago, and I'm positive he is hiding her in this realm."

"What's the other reason?"

"To help you fight the Shaktra."

"How do you propose to do that?"

Ali reached for the Yanti around her neck, brought it out so that Amma could see it. Her trust in the high fairy caught her by surprise—she seldom showed it to Steve or Cindy. There was just something about Amma that reassured her.

"I was hoping that by coming here I would learn more about the Yanti. But I have yet to meet anyone who knows about it." Ali paused. "Do you know how it works?"

Amma stared at the Yanti but did not touch it. "No."

"Do you know where it comes from at least?"

Amma spoke in a reverential tone. "It is said the Yanti came from behind the violet door."

"The sixth door?"

"Yes. But no one knows exactly how it entered this realm, or when."

"Was I the custodian of it? Before I left to become human?"

Amma hesitated. "Yes."

"There are questions you and Trae appear reluctant to answer. Why is that?"

"Neither of us is trying to hide anything from you. Yet there are answers you ask for that cannot be simply handed over."

"I don't understand."

Amma gestured to the bedroom. "Geea sat here many years trying to figure out how to defeat the Shaktra. Long before it attacked, she knew it was coming. But in all that time she never developed a strategy to confront it. Even with all her knowledge of the Yanti, she did not feel she could defeat the Shaktra by force."

"Are you saying the war is hopeless then?"

"Geea never gave into despair. Her mind was subtle, her plans went deep. She chose to become human when she did for a purpose."

"Do you know what that purpose was?" Ali asked.

Amma shook her head. "It is not something that can be explained with words. You must follow the path set before you, and you will come to an understanding of her mind that is much more profound than anything I can say to you right now."

"You are saying Geea kept her own counsel?" Ali asked.

Amma nodded. "Most of the time, you did."

Ali felt the shifting points of view disorienting.

"I appreciate what you say, and I will take on faith that you will tell me what you can. At the same time I need to know more details about the Shaktra. Paddy and Drash have told me it came from the Isle of Greesh. Is that true?"

"Yes."

"That was a stronghold of the fairies?"

"For centuries the fairies had controlled Greesh. Only in recent times was a layer of ancient ruins found there. Where they came from, no one knows. It is said that there the Shaktra discovered a great power, and was corrupted by it, and began to use it to build and consolidate its own kingdom, so as to destroy not only this world, but the yellow world as well."

"Did fairies help the Shaktra explore these ruins?"

"At first. Then it began to use the power it had discovered to *alter* them."

"It made the first scaliis?"

"Yes, and the scabs. Somehow it learned to mark every type of elemental, so that whoever was touched by it, was forced to obey its will."

"The marked ones I encountered were docile. Do they fight in battle?"

"When the Shaktra awakens them, they turn into fierce fighters. The ones you saw on the road had already been discarded by the enemy, and sent off to become scaliis."

Amma finished applying the red cream, and carefully wrapped the injury in a green silk bandage. When she was done, Ali stood and paced her old room.

"There is something that makes no sense to me," Ali said. "Before I left my world to come here, I ran into two people that had been marked. One was a teenage boy, who might have deliberately walked in front of a sports utility vehicle, and gotten himself killed. He had the identical mark on his forehead that the fairies I ran into on the road had."

"Who was the other one?" Amma asked.

"A little girl, Nira, and she lives in the same town as the guy I just described. Nira is about six, appears severely autistic. In that way she is like the marked ones I met. But there's something unique about her. When I stared into her eyes, I felt a vastness. It's hard to describe, but it was like she was a part of something that was bigger than humanity and the elementals combined. At the same time she is unable to take care of herself. I didn't know what to make of her. To top it off, her mother—a powerful businesswoman in that town—seems to be connected to my mother's kidnapping." Ali paused. "Do you know what any of this means?"

"They sound like they were both touched by the Shaktra," Amma said.

"But it is here. Trae said it was here."

"It is a mystery you must explore. Tell me, Geea, where do you expect to find your mother?"

Ali sat on the bed beside her. "I was hoping you could advise me."

Amma reached out, and this time she did touch her hair, and Ali was warmed by the comfort it brought her.

"You are already on your way, you have chosen a path. You tell me, where are you going?" Amma asked.

Ali sat back. "When I was on Earth, and I thought of my mother late at night, before going to sleep, I often had this dream where I was flying through the air beside a bunch of floating mountains. Now that I have seen the kloudar, I recognize them, and I feel they are the key to finding her. But I'm not sure if she is there. I have no reason to believe she is."

"Do you know what my queen used to say about reason?"

"What?" Ali asked.

"That it was overrated."

"If I do choose to go to the kloudar, will you come with me?"

Amma bowed her head. "I would be honored to accompany you."

CHAPTER

20

Ms. Smith might have done Steve and Cindy a favor by warning them that the static position of their arms over their heads would become unbearable. When the muscle spasms first started in their shoulders, they at least knew they were in for a rough ride. Yet Steve was shocked how soon the cramping drowned out the pain in his burned hand. His blistered palm became like a scratch.

Their corner of the cave was a box, a prison, its dimensions defined by the light and shadows the kerosene lantern emitted. Steve was surprised Ms. Smith had left them any light at all, but maybe she had wanted them to see each other's suffering. The air was warm and dry, the reddish walls were made of crusty iron dust and burnt-out memories. If Steve let his vision blur, it was easy to imagine he was in hell.

Cindy sighed, dirty sweat on her brow. "I would give anything to put my arms down for five minutes," she said.

"That's the point of all this. The Dragon Lady said it herself. When she returns, we'll be anxious to tell her everything she wants to know," Steve said.

"I think we already made it clear we don't know what she wants to know."

Steve nodded. "She is disappointed in us."

Cindy looked over. "Do you think she's going to kill us?"

"Do you want the optimistic version, or the truth?"

"The truth," Cindy said.

"She cannot let us go after treating us this way, and revealing so much about her past. Our only way out of this is to escape, or else for Ali to come to our rescue."

"Ali doesn't even know we're here."

"When she returns from the elemental world, and finds us gone, she'll come here."

Cindy shook her head. "She warned us to stay away from Ms. Smith. She told us the woman was dangerous. We should have listened to her."

"True. But we went on this hunt to help Ali."

"And to feel better about ourselves," Cindy added.

"You were interested in Ms. Smith because you were worried about Nira. You are suffering in a noble cause."

Cindy coughed. "It doesn't make it any easier."

"Are you scared?"

"Terrified. So are you. Because you're right about that woman. She is evil to the core. She is never going to let us live."

"What do you think about what Nira's mother said about her own daughter?"

"Lies. Nira's a special child, it's obvious. She's just autistic."

Steve frowned. "I wonder if she is even that. I wonder if her mother hasn't put some kind of spell on her."

"I thought the same thing. Ms. Smith is like a witch. Did you see the way she controls Karl?"

"She treated him like dog, and he didn't seem to mind," Steve said.

"He didn't look like he was about to turn on her any time soon," Cindy agreed.

"He always was a jerk."

"Why do you think she gave us that weird lecture at the dining table?"

Steve considered. "She was spouting *her* point of view on humanity, and which direction she thinks it should go. What surprised me was, that for such a smart woman, her arguments were so cliché. Practically every tyrant in recent history has said similar things. For someone who makes such exotic games, she seems uncreative."

"What did you think of her main programmer?" Cindy asked.

"He seemed like a nice guy, very innocent. It might be like Ali said, that he is the real brains behind the company."

"Odd how he is blind," Cindy said.

"Lots of people are blind."

"You know what I mean. He writes code to form graphic images, but he can't see what he's creating. How's that possible?"

"Didn't Ali say he works hand-in-hand with Ms. Smith?"

"Yes. Our lovely Ms. Smith. Who just happens to be psycho," Cindy muttered.

Steve fought with his upper shackles, which were attached to the wall with a thick steel bolt. The act was futile but he found himself doing it every fifteen minutes anyway.

"Her revelation as she left was pretty big," Steve said.

"She was just playing with you. She can't be Lucy Pillar. She's dead."

"It's not that simple. There's a mystery surrounding Lucy's death. We ran into it earlier. The authorities never did identify her body."

"You heard what Hector said. Lucy was burned in a car accident a year before the power plant explosion—on over eighty percent of her body. I might hate the woman but she doesn't have a mark on her. She's one of the most beautiful people I've ever seen."

Steve glanced over. "She looks almost too beautiful."

"What do you mean?"

"Did you ever feel, while looking at her, that you could not totally focus on her?"

"No. What are you talking about?" Cindy asked.

Steve frowned. "I'm not sure."

Time went by. With the pain in their shoulders and arms—which was steadily moving into their spines—they had nothing but slow moving time. Steve tried to think of other things to distract himself from the agony and it did not do one bit of good. His shirt was soaked with sweat, and he was so hot he felt as if he might melt. He would have given a lot for a glass of water. More than anything, he prayed Ali would come soon.

It might have been after sunset when Cindy started to whimper. Steve couldn't see his watch but it felt like hours had passed since they had been imprisoned. Cindy had closed her eyes and the sound she was making seemed to come from so deep inside her that it shook Steve to the core. He tried talking to her, soothing her, but she ignored him. She was not being a baby, and she was not trying to make him feel bad. She was in pain, and there was no way to stop it, and it kept getting worse. She couldn't help herself.

Steve wanted to weep, too, but he feared that if he started down that road, he would end up screaming and would not be able to stop. He felt if he lost it for even a second, Ms. Smith would get exactly what she wanted, and Ali would not be able to stop her from destroying the world. In the delirium of his pain, he began to see the woman as the Kabrosh character in the Overlord game. Kabrosh had burned to death on a radioactive battlefield and then—at least according to the witch—had come back to life.

Then he saw Nira. Little Nira, with her lonely lost eyes.

She was standing right in front of him, holding a lit candle.

Steve blinked and she did not go away. She was staring right at him.

"Cindy, Nira is here," Steve said.

Cindy stopped moaning and opened her eyes. "Nira!" she cried.

"Does your mother know you're here?" Steve asked Nira.

Nira just stared at him, the flame of the candle in her dark violet eyes.

"She knew enough to light a candle and find her way down here," Cindy said. "She can't be that mentally handicapped."

Steve nodded. "It's possible she knows these caves inside out. She might explore them when her mother is not around." He added, "How are you feeling?"

Cindy nodded. "A lot better than I was a minute ago. Do you think it's possible we could talk Nira into helping us escape?"

"I think she's here to help us. But God only knows what she understands." Steve shook his shackles. "Nira, do you know where the key is to these locks? Can you help us with these locks?"

"Keep it simple," Cindy advised, scanning the immediate area. "Maybe if she could give us a piece of pipe, or even a stick, we could use it as a lever on the bolt that holds the shackles in place."

Steve nodded to the far left, outside the circle of light cast by the lantern. "There is a metal bar lying on the ground over there."

Cindy got excited. "Let's try to get her to bring it to you."

Alas the plan, although simple, was too complex for Nira to follow. The girl stood there and stared at them. Even when she did look around, she did not seem to know what they meant by "metal bar." She never focused on what they were pointing to.

Just when they were beginning to think her visit had been useless, Nira suddenly put down her lit candle on a nearby oil drum and approached Steve. Reaching both arms up over her head, the little girl placed her hands on the center of Steve's chest. He felt an unbelievable warmth flow into him. It was as if he had been dropped into a hot tub, but without the water. As Nira continued to touch him, he felt himself growing stronger. To his utter amazement, the cramps in his arms and shoulders vanished. It was as if she were healing him.

The same way Ali could heal people.

Nira held him for perhaps two minutes, then moved on to Cindy, and the sigh of relief from his friend did Steve's heart good. Her face relaxed visibly, as did her posture, and she burst into tears, but they were good tears. When Nira released her all Cindy could do was whisper "thank you" over and over again. Steve thanked her as well, and tried to stop her from leaving when Nira picked up her candle and turned toward the direction she had entered. But the little girl left without another glance at him.

It was then Steve noticed the blisters on his palm had vanished. He told Cindy about it and she shook her head in awe.

"That girl has Ali's power," Cindy said.

"She might be even more powerful," Steve said. "When she was touching me, I felt as if it was nothing for her to heal me, not the slightest strain."

"I felt the same way. Like she was so big, and I was so small, it was easy for her to take away my pain."

Steve had to smile. "Too bad she didn't leave us a screwdriver."

Yet it was only a couple of minutes later that Steve noticed that the shackle behind his once burnt palm was loose. It was a miracle on par with the cessation of their cramps, because he knew he had yanked on the bolt only a few minutes before Nira's arrival. Yet now the bolt was three quarters of the way out from the wall. He told Cindy the good news and she got excited.

"She did it, I know she did it!" Cindy exclaimed.

Steve started twisting and pulling like crazy. Dust fell from the sides of the bolt, and it began to move. "I don't care who is responsible, as long as we get out of here," he said.

The bolt popped out of the wall five minutes later, and finally Steve was able to bring down his right arm and stretch it. Of course it was true he had only one free limb, but it was enough to give him leverage with the rest of the bolts. He worked on his left wrist next, and by constantly turning the bolt left and right, it slowly began to ease out of the wall. Cindy cheered him all the way, and within an hour of the little girl's visit, he had freed himself. Yet it was relative freedom. He could move, but he still *wore* the shackles, and they were both still at the bottom of a cave whose dimensions and design they did not understand.

Steve used the metal pipe to pry Cindy loose, and she hugged him as she broke free of the wall and gave him a quick kiss. It was nice, because it reminded him of the kiss Ali had given him on top of Pete's Peak after she had sent the elemental army back to their own realm. Cindy shook in his arms as he held her.

But he let her carry the lantern as they slowly made their way through the dark toward the metal ladder they had taken on their initial journey into this hellish place. He wanted to keep his hands free in case they were attacked. It was odd but Steve felt as if his sense of direction was off, as did Cindy. When they found a ladder, they spent five minutes discussing whether it was the right one. In the end they decided that as long as it was going up, they were taking it, and they did in fact climb up three levels before they entered another cave that did not look familiar. They didn't know whether to go right or left.

So they went right, and the cave began to twist and turn, and then they decided to backtrack, but they came to a fork in the road that they did not remember, and they went to the left. All the while their shackles jingled like pockets full of change, and the light of the lantern flickered like the rising and falling of their hopes.

Then they came to a sharp turn; they had to go right, no choice. Cindy held the lantern up high as they took the corner, but a flash of silver glistened in the dark, and the shadows abruptly wavered and then crashed into pitch black as Cindy let out a scream and the lantern disappeared.

A beam of white light exploded in their eyes.

Karl's flashlight. Karl himself, grinning like a white ghost from a black grave.

He held his switchblade in his right hand, and it was stained with blood.

Although she gripped the injury, red fluid flowed from Cindy's right wrist.

Without warning, Steve realized, he had cut her and she had dropped the lantern.

Reaching out, Karl pressed the tip of the blade close to Steve's heart.

"Going somewhere?" he asked in his fiendish voice.

CHAPTER

21

It was after dark when Ali went to visit Drash in the palace basement, in a storage area where sacks of grains and dried fruit were kept. From the look of the numerous torn burlap bags, it appeared he had helped himself to the fairies' food—something she didn't begrudge him in the slightest. Ali was both pleased and a little surprised that so many of the grains matched the ones on Earth. When Amma had fed her in her room, she had brought her a bowl of yogurt. Yet the berries buried in the yogurt had tasted like nothing she had ever put in her mouth before—sweeter than strawberries, more textured than blueberries, and possessing a soothing aftertaste that stayed with her long after she had emptied her bowl. Amma had called the berries jambis.

The hours had been long since she had seen Drash last, and he had already gone through his second change. His face had thinned out and lengthened, while his legs had grown and strengthened, and his tail was a wonder to behold—a long sharp sword that could decapitate a dozen scaliis with one stroke. However, it was in his eyes and nose that the biggest changes had occurred. Once again the red light had swelled in his pupils, and now a steady orange flame burned in his nostrils. Yet he acted unhappy with his complex transformation.

"Drash can hardly blow a flame," he said, tucked in the corner of the vast room.

"It will be there when you need it. These powers are like that."

"You know this? You have *seen* this?"

Ali smiled. "You are doing well, you have nothing to worry about."

Drash peered at her. "Have you found your mother yet?"

"No. We will have to go on, I warned you."

"Drash is happy to go with Geea."

"You like swimming now?"

"Still scares Drash, but exhilarating as well." He added, "Drash would never have got in the water without your help. Not even with my father's prodding."

"Yes, you would have, had you not lost respect for your father. So much of your self-doubt comes from him. Don't you see that?"

Drash nodded his dragon head. She could not even think of him as a koul now.

"Father mocked Drash when Drash failed the first test," he said.

Ali patted his side. "Do you want to talk about it?"

Drash lowered his head. "Best to forget."

"Have you had enough to eat?"

"Yes."

Ali sighed. "I must go visit with the fairies who have been hiding here. They want to see me with their own eyes, so that they know that I'm still alive. Trae insists on it."

"Why do you sigh?"

"I don't know what to say to them to give them hope."

"Is hope a good idea?" Drash asked.

The question stayed with Ali as she returned to the upper levels of the palace. But before she went to see the fairies, she stopped at an open window on the south side of the palace and stared out at the rest of Uleestar and got her first good look at Karolee itself—the fairy land surrounding the island. The soft blue light of the moon was enough to show that much of Uleestar was made up of simple white-walled structures that were arranged like vacation homes along the shore of a Greek island. In reality, Ali had never been to the Aegean Sea, but she had always wanted to go and had studied several travel books on the area.

Yet she felt Karolee was even more beautiful than the Greece in the brochures, for there was space between the homes, and gardens everywhere with colored flowers from every part of the rainbow, and flowing water, and grass, simple grass, that nevertheless grew six feet tall. . . .

How lovely, she thought. How much like home.

The contrast with Karolee only added to the beauty of the area, for the majority of the fairy kingdom appeared to be a redwood forest. With the aid of Anglar's enchanting rays, she could see the trees stretching for miles up and down valleys, around dozens of meadows. And these redwoods were not a thousand feet tall, but maybe three times that, and their branches, as they climbed toward the stars, were like wise welcoming arms.

Unfortunately, in more places than she could count, the trees had been crushed.

"The Shaktra attacked our land first, coming in force over the sea from the Isle of Greesh. The scaliis, the dragons, the crashing ice— they were an irresistible black wave."

Sighing, Ali went in search of her people.

Trae had gathered the fairies in a windowless inner room that was filled with sofas and rugs and some of the finest paintings in the palace. There was one of a sheltered blue-green lagoon surrounded with soft sand and haunting trees that made her chest ache for simpler times. Yet Trae said it was a painting of the far side of the Isle of Greesh, from whence the Shaktra had come.

The faces of the fairies shone as she entered and sat on a silk-draped seat at the front of the room. Candles burned in the corners, she smelled incense. So many green eyes, so much red hair, and the love—she could feel their devotion pouring over her like a wave. Unfortunately, she felt so unworthy. She could not even remember them. She was but a thirteen-year-old human girl, and times were desperate. She had brought nothing back from the yellow world to save them, except perhaps the Yanti, which she had so far failed to master.

They didn't care. They just wanted to look at her and thank her for the sacrifice she had made when she had decided to become human. That troubled her as well. She did not know that her being human helped anyone. The subtleties of Geea's plan eluded her, and she was Geea. Could anything be more maddening?

What was she to say? She told them about her life in Breakwater, and how she came to meet Paddy, and how the trolls almost killed her when they buried her with an avalanche of rock and gravel, and how she passed the first trial and the subsequent tests. She told them in detail about her friends, their adventure climbing the mountain, her battle with Radrine, and how she finally managed to turn back Lord Vak's army. The longer she spoke, the more comfortable she felt, and the fairies smiled and sighed at every turn in the tale, but mostly they just gazed at her with unblinking eyes, and let her voice travel deep inside them. Not once did they interrupt to question her. Not once did they look away.

At the end of the meeting she went around the room and hugged everyone, and the fairies were astounded. They had never touched their queen before. What hope she gave them, she was not sure, but the way they held on to her when she put her arms around them—she felt as if their faith in her would never waver. They *knew* that she *knew* what she was doing.

And here she hadn't a clue . . .

By this time her friends were asleep in rooms Trae had found for them, and so she returned to her own bedroom. She knew the next day would be long, and she wanted to get as much rest as possible. The cream Amma had applied to her palm continued to work its magic. She could honestly say the pain was less than a quarter of what it had been.

In her room she went through her things, hoping they would trigger old memories, but she was disappointed how little came back to her. Her hairbrush she remembered—it had only to be pulled through her hair once and all the knots and tangles disappeared. And there was a special drawer in her closet where she kept her jewels, but the diamond necklaces and the emerald bracelets held no attraction for her. She thought of giving the whole collection to Paddy. Trae had told her earlier that the leprechaun had insisted on sleeping with his ten pots of gold.

It was the stardust that drew her the most, and frightened her as well. Clearly she had left it in such an obvious place for a reason. Geea—the real Geea—had wanted her to find it. Yet Ali sensed truth in Amma's warning. The blue powder could bring back all of her old powers, or it could kill her.

How it tempted her!

Eventually, she laid down on her bed, under the blankets. The room was a fine temperature, and she had only to think that she wanted the light to lower, and the crystal cubes in the corners emitted less light. Her right hand continued to throb quietly, but she was able to ignore it. Yet with her eyes closed, in the dark, she saw vague but disturbing images of Cindy and Steve that were not so easy to push away.

They were in a cave, also in the dark, and they were in danger. Karl was near, as was Nira, and a third person—but this last individual she could not see at all. She only sensed their disturbing presence, as she might sense a perilous hole in the center of a nighttime path. Yet Ali did not know if the whole thing was just her imagination. How could Cindy and Steve be in a cave?

Yet she had not forgotten what she had glimpsed in Nira's eyes.

I was walking toward the bus, and I turned and saw something, inside her mind. . . .

Like a record of someone who was meant to die.

No, she told herself, no death was destined. Her friends were fine.

Ali eventually fell into an uneasy sleep.

And she dreamed a piece of the beginning, and a portion of the end.

Jira, son of Lord Vak, elven prince, and her lover, was excited to be on the Isle of Greesh to see the ancient ruins the others had spoken of, but for Geea, as they slowly descended the long shaft that led deep into the island's solid underbelly, she felt only dread. Jira knew of her intuition, and normally respected it, but today he brushed off her concerns as unimportant.

"This is the discovery of our time," he said, standing tall and strong in the center of the creaking elevator that the fairies above were slowly lowering into the heart of Greesh's only peak. Jira was handsome, a powerful warrior, and it was for neither of those reasons that she loved him. Jira had earned her love because he *was* love—he would do anything for her.

Geea pointed to the black walls of the shaft. "The ground is hard here because there is an exceptional amount of iron in it. Does that tell you something?"

"That this peak was once volcanic?" Jira said.

"No. Whatever volcano existed here, it was millions of years ago, when the island formed. This iron did not come out of the ground. It came from the sky."

He grinned. "Is this a joke?"

"No." She tapped the dark wall of the shaft. "A large meteor must have crashed here long ago. The hill at the center of this island is built on top of it."

"That's only a theory of yours." Jira added, "The meteor would have incinerated itself when it hit here."

She held his eye. "But it didn't. Nor did it incinerate what Doren has discovered. So maybe it did not crash-land here. Maybe it landed gently."

"Are you suggesting your sister's discovery is from . . . elsewhere?"

"Yes."

Jira chuckled. "You have an imagination, Geea, I grant you that."

She did not laugh. The shaft was warm but Geea shivered. "This place does not feel good. Many people lived here once, but when they died, it was not in a natural way."

"What do you mean?"

"This place is alive with pain, but it is the pain of the dead." Geea paused, feeling the cold going deeper inside. It did not come from the air, but the walls themselves, and it was not related strictly to temperature. She added, "Right here, long ago— I think many people killed themselves."

"That's impossible, no one would do that."

Geea shook her head. "Look at what is happening in the yellow world and tell me that is impossible."

They reached the bottom of the shaft. A narrow cave, lit by torches and dusted with black soot, waited for them. Jira went first—there was hardly room for one—and she followed closely. Their goal was a temple that had recently been uncovered in the last few weeks, and which they had heard was filled with magical artifacts their own civilization could not duplicate. So far, it was said, only a few fairies had been inside, and they spoke about it in hushed tones. Geea had no real idea what they were going to see.

They came to the massive stone door of the temple, and Geea saw the ropes and pulleys that had been set up to allow them to pull back the heavy gateway. But then she saw that the door had markings on it, a circular mandala with an unusual design. At first it reminded her of the Yanti, but it had six sides, not seven, and the inner triangle had been sliced down the middle with a splintered line. There was no central dot, no perfect place to hold the attention. To Geea, it was as if the temple's symbol had been designed using pieces of what was sacred to all elementals, but the pieces had been altered, if not corrupted. A troubling weakness entered her chest as she stared at the strange mandala. She pointed it out to Jira.

"A monster made this," she said.

Jira smiled. "There are no monsters, Geea."

She spoke in a soft voice, still staring at the mandala. "You haven't explored the seven doors—especially what lies beyond the red door." She added, "There are things there you could not imagine."

Jira lost his smile. "You have seen them with your own eyes?"

She did not want to answer his question because she did not

want to lie to him. Besides, it was not her place to speak of the dark fairies to any elf—even the one she loved. She nodded to the mandala. "The fairies who work and dig here did not tell us what's in this temple because they couldn't," she said.

"What are you talking about?"

Geea sighed. "This symbol has a power over the mind."

"I don't feel anything from it."

"But you're anxious to go inside?"

Jira shrugged. "That is why we came here."

Geea shifted her focus on the mandala, moved to Jira's side, put her palm on his powerful chest, and looked up into his eyes. The chill in her body had grown worse, and she felt as if she were flying near the highest kloudar, in the thin air even the birds could not breathe.

"Please, Jira, do not go inside this temple," she said.

"Why not?"

"There is evil inside."

He was doubtful. "But the other fairies said it is filled with amazing devices."

"But they described none of them to us. Why is that?"

"Because they said we had to see for ourselves."

Geea glanced once more at the door, the faint sketch in the crumbling stone.

"No. They lied to us because the temple affected their minds," she said.

He hesitated. "Doren said it was safe."

Geea frowned. "*She* could have lied like the rest."

"That's ridiculous, Geea. I have to go inside. I'm here at my father's command. I have to report back to him what has been discovered. You know this." He added, "I can go in alone if you are afraid."

Geea took his hand. "I am afraid."

He squeezed her fingers, then let go. "I will not be gone long," he promised.

"Jira, no," she pleaded, but his mind was made up. Using the pulleys, ropes, and levers that had been installed, he pulled back the ancient block of stone and took a torch and disappeared into the black opening. To her surprise the door closed at his back, without any movement of the pulleys, and she was left alone with her fears. The door was thick, she worried she would not be able to hear him if he cried out for help.

Yet she did hear him, a few minutes later, when he began to scream.

CHAPTER

22

li was in bed when the dark fairies attacked the palace. She had awakened several minutes before she heard any sound or movement, well before Amma came running into her bedroom with the news. The dark fairies were *not* shielded from her psychic senses—she had felt them coming miles away.

Yet she was not ready for their attack, she thought, not the way she should have been. The comfort of the palace after the rigors of the road had lulled her into a false sense of security. She was sitting on the edge of her bed actually *seeing* the dark fairies in her mind's eye as they landed in the palace courtyard, when Amma appeared. But she was not sure what course of action she should take. They could fight them or they could try to sneak away unnoticed. There were advantages to both plans—it all depended on how many dark fairies there were. She saw only a dozen in her head, but that gang might be merely a scouting party. Yet if there were only twelve, it would be better to kill them and let no news of what they had discovered get back to the Shaktra.

Amma looked worried but not scared. She quickly informed

Ali of the dark fairies and Ali nodded like she was learning about it for the first time. But she held up her hand when Amma tried to describe the enemy's position. Ali could *see* the dark fairies slowly probing the palace perimeter.

"What does Trae want to do?" Ali asked.

"He thinks we should all flee down to Tiena, and ride the river to a stronghold we have hidden in the Youli Mountains."

"How old is this stronghold?"

"Five years. Why?"

Ali stood in her green fairy pajamas. "The age might be important. Tell Trae to gather all the fairies in the room where I spoke to them last night. I want them to have some say in what we decide."

"They will not vote on the matter. They will look to you to decide their course."

Ali reached for her clothes. "Fine, gather them anyway, and go wake Ra and have Drash climb up to the game area you showed me yesterday, the one near the courtyard."

"Has the koul grown strong enough to help us?"

"I guess we're about to find out," Ali said.

It struck Ali then: She had no weapons in her room. She was going to have to use the fire stones again, risking more pain in her hand. Already, she had decided on killing the dark fairies, and then fleeing. She wondered if Radrine would be among them.

The long rest had softened the pain in her hand but not eliminated it. If there was to be fighting, she would have to be careful.

Ali dressed in two minutes, stashed her box of stardust in her pocket. Finding her way to the lush meeting room, she discovered most of the fairies already present. As Trae strode inside, she told them all to prepare to board boats on Tiena. Trae approved of her strategy, but was worried when she spoke of her, Ra, and Drash killing the dark fairies.

"If that is your decision, we can help you," he said. "Most of the fairies present here are excellent archers." He added, "A few are high fairies, they can fly."

Ali blinked. "Can you and Amma fly?"

"Yes."

"Where is she right now?"

"Not everyone in the palace has been told of the dark fairies. She's searching for those people right now."

Ali nodded. "Can you carry someone when you fly?"

"No."

"Why not?"

Trae seemed surprised by the question. "A fairy generates his or her own field in order to fly. It is unique to that person. Another cannot enter it, the person would fall to the ground."

Ali nodded. "That doesn't matter right now. My coming here brought the dark fairies. I don't want to risk anyone outside my group on them. Besides, I'm not worried; we can handle a dozen. What you can do for me is get everyone in the boats. Have them bring the bare essentials. Don't bother waiting for us, go straight to that stronghold in the mountains Amma told me about." She added, "Take Farble and Paddy with you. Let the leprechaun bring his gold, he will get upset without it. Bring red meat for the troll."

"We are all vegetarians here."

"Then give him a bunch of cookies, he has a big sweet tooth."

Trae paused. "Excuse me for questioning a direct order, but a few archers might be more helpful than you realize. I know I would feel more comfortable if you let a half dozen accompany you."

Ali had to remind herself not to get cocky when it came to

her powers, particularly when she was injured. Her hand throbbed as she spoke. "That's fine, I'll take six with me. But I want you and Amma to leave with the others."

Trae shook his head. "Either Amma or myself must stay with you if you are to find the stronghold. Its location is top secret, so to speak."

"Then have Amma stay behind," Ali said, although she had no plans to go to the stronghold. "But I want her to remain inside the palace until the dark fairies are dead."

"You do not remember our Amma. She will insist on fighting beside you."

Ali was firm. "That is an order, she is to obey me."

Ra was with Drash when she reached the game room, his bow and arrows ready. Ra nodded his approval when he saw the six archers Ali had brought along.

Taking out her fire stones, and reviewing with them where the dark fairies were heading, Ali hastily drew up a plan of attack. But Ra didn't like it; he thought they should split up, come at the dark fairies from two directions, with Drash on one side, the rest of them on the other. He especially wanted Drash outside, where he could unleash his flame.

"I've seen him. His fire is growing by the hour," Ra said.

"Is that true?" Ali asked.

The koul was uncertain. "Drash is a lot hotter in the face than last night."

"How many dark fairies can you kill at once?" Ali insisted.

Drash shrugged. "Depends on how close together they are."

"Can the blast of their fire stones pierce your hide?" Ali asked.

"Drash hopes not."

"He can kill all we need him to kill," Ra said confidently. "Have him exit the back side of the palace and crawl toward the front. We can follow him out the windows, and we'll know when he is in position. This way we get the hammer and anvil effect. Crush them from both sides." Ra added, "Ali, you know how dangerous it will be if even one of them escapes."

"I hate exposing Drash to their firepower," she said.

The koul shook his head and turned toward the rear exits. "Drash owes Geea. He wants to fight."

Ali called after him. "Protect your eyes! Don't light the palace on fire!"

Ra's plan was superior, Ali had to admit. They *were* able to follow Drash through the windows as he went out the back and then headed for the front. The dark fairies were spread along the edge of the palace, all on the west side, the direction the koul was going. As Drash closed on the first dark fairies, Ali and Ra and the other archers moved behind the monsters farthest away from the koul. Being able to look down on their enemy gave them a huge advantage, but Ali understood the dark fairies were staying out of the air so as to remain inconspicuous. They were evil but they were not stupid.

Ali saw no sign of Radrine.

The battle that ensued was no battle at all. When Drash bumped into the first of the dark fairies, he let loose with a blast of flame that was so ferocious it literally stretched out fifty yards, the length of an Olympic-sized pool. It was so wide, so hot, that the dark fairies standing in the center of it turned to crisp bacon. The other dark fairies came up to attack the koul, but he only had to suck in another breath, and then there was more dark fairy ash floating on the breeze. The archers shot two that tried to run away, and Ra and Ali did not even use their weapons. The skirmish was over in less than a minute.

Then Ali became aware of a dark fairy frantically flying away from the palace.

She did not see it, not out the window they were standing at, but she suddenly sensed it on the other side of the palace. Dragging Ra and the archers with her, she raced out the front porch and into the palace courtyard. The dark fairy was a quarter of a mile away, high up, flying fast in the glare of the green sun. Along with the archers, Ra tried shooting it down but it was out of their range.

Ali raised her fire stones and got off two good shots. One scored a direct hit, but to her surprise the creature did not drop. It was then Ali knew she was staring at Radrine. Only the evil queen could have taken such punishment and survived.

Amma came running out of the palace, carrying a long silver knife.

"I have to go after it, it will alert others that we are here!" she exclaimed, and Ali saw that she was about to rise into the air.

"Stay where you are! Let it go!" Ali snapped.

"Ali! If she can go after it, let her go!" Ra shouted.

Ali sensed a powerful field building around Amma, saw the woman gripping her knife tightly, her entire attention focused on the escaping dark fairy. Ali had to walk over and shake her.

"I'm your queen, you're to listen to me!" she said. "You're not going after it!"

Amma was dumbfound. "Surely you can see that it cannot be allowed to escape?"

"It is Radrine. You are no match for her," Ali said.

Amma met her intense gaze. "How do you know what I can do?"

"Let her try to kill it," Ra pleaded.

But Ali would not release Amma. For some reason, an intense urge to protect the fairy swept over her. "It doesn't matter, we are leaving anyway," Ali said.

"If Radrine was dead, maybe we wouldn't have to leave," Amma said.

Ali tried being gentle. "You said it yesterday, I have to follow the path I've begun. There is no point in staying here. Remember, you promised to come with me." She added, "You're not going to die on me before I get to know you."

A tear came into Amma's eye, but she didn't respond, just walked away.

They were in a wooden rowboat, the three of them: Ra, Amma, and Ali. As it turned out, they had killed the dark fairies so quickly they had reached the harbor before the others had left. Now, as a small fleet, they were floating north on the black waters of Tiena. Although she was not interested in the stronghold, Ali did not mind their direction for she felt it took her closer and closer to the kloudar.

They had oars but they were not using them, content to let the current push them forward. Swimming alongside their boats, Drash offered to tow them faster, but Ali told him to relax, to regain his strength after his successful battle. The other fairies had heard of Drash's ferocious flame, the whipping he had given the dark fairies, and had praised him for his help. This had done wonders for the koul's self-esteem.

Yet they had also heard that a dark fairy had escaped, and that was bad. Ali was not sure how firm their faith was in the stronghold they were headed for. She feared that when the Shaktra marked a fairy, it had access to its memories. She hoped that none who had been marked knew about the place.

Ali expressed her fears to Amma, who sat beside her in the rear of the boat.

"Few know the direction to the spot, and none have gone into battle where they could have been captured," Amma said. "It should be safe for the time being."

"I want Paddy and Farble to go there with the rest of the fairies." Her friends were in a nearby boat, and kept waving and smiling at her. Farble was helping Paddy count his coins, and the leprechaun appeared happy for the help.

Who said a troll could not count past two?

Amma merely nodded her head. "Whatever you wish, Geea."

"You think I was wrong to stop you back there?" Ali asked.

"You are my queen. I obey your word."

"My word," Ali whispered, mostly to herself. "What is the worth of my word when I cannot remember my name? You know, I had to be told it."

"Who told it to you?"

Ali regarded her in the dark, spoke softly. "Nemi. Do you know who that is?"

"I know what Nemi . . . I know of Nemi."

"Who is he? Where is he?"

Amma's face darkened. "I'm sorry, Geea, I can't tell you."

"Because you don't know? Or because you think I'm not ready?"

"Both."

"Maybe it's time you started to trust me more."

Amma was not offended. "Things will become clear when you reach the kloudar."

"There are so many up in the sky. How will I know which one to visit?"

"I will show you."

Ali felt her heart accelerate. At the same time, the ache in her palm increased. Thoughts of Ra's opium were tempting her more than ever.

"Do you know where my mother is?" Ali asked quietly.

Amma looked at the black water. "It is not the way you think."

"Then explain it to me!"

"I cannot. You have to . . . you have to understand yourself better."

Ali was confused. "What does that have to do with finding my mother?"

"Everything." Amma gestured to her bulging pocket. "You took the stardust."

"I might need it before all this is over."

"Take it now and it will kill you."

"You said in my room that you did not know that for sure."

"The stardust affects more than the body. It alters the mind. Right now—you have admitted it—you don't know your own mind. You can hardly remember Geea. How, then, can you swallow her most powerful potion?"

"She left it out for me to find."

"*You* left it out for you to find. See, you cannot even speak of her as identical with yourself."

"Try being human and you'll know why," Ali said, an edge in her voice.

"How do you know I have never been human?"

The question threw Ali off balance. "Have you?" she gasped.

Amma looked away again. "I cannot talk about it. Not now."

Ali was impatient. "Why not?"

Amma put a finger in the black water, stirred a small wave. "You ask me to trust you, and that is fine, you are my queen. I trust you with all my heart, Geea. But you have to trust me as well."

"It is hard when you keep speaking in riddles."

Amma stared at her. "Your life is one long riddle. Your questions are endless, but my words, my answers, they are not so important. Only you can solve the Geea riddle, the Ali riddle."

Ali considered. "Are they identical?"

Amma nodded. "You are making progress."

Perhaps because she was human, Ali was not ready to drop all her questions.

"When I was on Earth three days ago, I met a strange man in town—in our local barbershop. He looked like a wizard. He knew about the Yanti, and he demanded that I show it to him. It was like he cast a spell on me, and I almost gave it to him. Somehow I managed to hold on to it and then, when I tried to get a look at him in the mirror, there was an explosion of light and he vanished. I might have blacked out for a moment, I'm not sure." Ali paused. "Do you know who he was?"

Amma's face fell. "Did he wear gloves?"

"How did you know that? He had on white gloves."

"He wore the gloves because he did not want you to touch him."

"Why not?" Ali asked.

"Because one touch would have revealed who he was."

"I don't understand," Ali said.

"You will understand before this day is over."

"But do you know who he was?" Ali insisted.

"He was not a he," Amma replied.

Another riddle, Ali was sick of them. "At least tell me if I'll find my mother before this day is over," she said.

Amma turned away. "Perhaps."

As the watery miles slowly passed, Ali reflected back on the time she had spent with Mike Havor at Omega Overtures's headquarters in Toule. When he had taken her into the back offices, he had shown her the cover for their new game called Armageddon. Since it was a sequel to Omega Overlord, it was about the end of the world and the artwork reflected as much. It was dark and gray and depicted a battlefield where men and women and robots were locked in a fight to the death. Studying its dismal mood, Ali felt compelled to ask why he liked such disheartening themes. He sat down behind his modest desk and smiled at her question, his blind eyes hidden by his dark glasses.

"The superficial answer is because it sells," he said.

Ali sat across from him. "But you don't just do this for the money, I can tell. You do it because you like it."

He nodded. "You're a perceptive young woman, Lisa."

"But how can you enjoy so much death and destruction?"

"You play Overlord all the time? Why do you enjoy it?"

Ali reddened, glad he could not see the color in her cheeks. "Playing it for a few hours here and there is one thing. You spend years designing these games. Don't they depress you?"

"No. I'll tell you why. I think our games are educational."

"How so?"

"Because I think they show where we're heading as a race."

"You don't really think we're going to destroy ourselves, do you?"

"I think as a species we have to go down to rise up. The president of this country is talking about putting weapons in space to shoot down incoming missiles. This morning on the news I heard a scientist predict that within twenty years, over two dozen nations on Earth would have nuclear bombs. With all that going on, how do you think we're going to avoid World War Three?"

"I have faith in human nature. We'll never let it go that far."

"I hate to tell you this, but it has already gone past the point of no return."

"In your opinion."

Mike shrugged. "Everything I say is only my opinion."

Ali tried another approach. "But all this cyborg stuff you have

286

in your games—you don't believe that's going to happen, do you? I mean, no one is going to attach all that junk to their bodies. It won't happen in a million years."

"It will happen in the next twenty years. Let me give you an example, and play along with me for a few minutes and be completely honest—that is the most important thing. Say twenty years from now you are happily married and you have a wonderful ten-year-old daughter named Debbie. Now next door to you lives another happy family and they have a ten-year-old daughter named Sally. Debbie and Sally go to school together, but they're not really in the same classes because your Debbie is smarter than Sally. In fact, she has an IQ twenty points higher, which is a lot, trust me." Mike paused. "How does this sound?"

"So good so far," Ali said.

"But then one day Sally's parents hear about a new device that has the ability to boost their daughter's mental capabilities. It works by training the brain waves to stay in the alpha state. That's where your brain is relaxed, and most receptive to learning new things. The catch is this device has to be *implanted* in the brain to work most effectively. But once it's there, the person's IQ shoots up over thirty points. So when Sally gets it, she immediately begins to do better in school than your daughter."

"I get it. You're going to ask if I would buy it for my daughter so she could keep up with Sally?"

"Yes. But first I was going to add that all the kids at school end up getting it."

Ali shook her head. "I wouldn't let my daughter get the implant."

"Why not?"

"Because she's my daughter! I wouldn't let someone stick something foreign in her brain."

"I hear you. But what if as the years pass, Debbie begins to fall way behind all her friends, so that she has to be put in a special education class?"

"I can't imagine that would ever happen."

"Stretch your imagination further. Because in two decades there will be devices on the market that will boost the IQ by *over* thirty points. They will probably arrive sooner than that. They're already in the preliminary stages of development. The scenario I'm laying out for you is going to happen. If you deny your daughter the implant, she will fall so far behind in school that her entire self-image will be destroyed. And when she does get out in the real world, she probably won't be able to get a job anywhere."

"You exaggerate to make a point," Ali said.

"I tell it like it's going to be to make a point. Let me ask you again. Would you let Debbie get the implant?"

Ali hesitated. "Could it harm her brain?"

"No. It would just make it work more efficiently."

Ali considered. "I guess it's possible I might let her get it."

"Let's take it a step further. Have you heard about nanotechnology?"

"I've seen it in sci-fi movies. That's where they make molecular-size machines?"

"Yes. Have you seen how they inject them in people?" Mike asked.

"On *Star Trek*."

"Good. Say in our story that Debbie has finally got her implant, and she is doing much better at school, and keeping up with all her friends. The only problem is, she gets more than her fair share of flus and colds, and some of these turn into bronchitis, or even pneumonia. But then you read about this nanotechnology injection that she can get that will kill all the invading viruses and bacteria that enter her system so that she will not have to suffer from a cold or flu for the remainder of her life. Would you get it for her?"

"Probably."

Mike chuckled. "This time you don't hesitate. Why not?"

"Because it doesn't sound as scary as the brain implant."

"You are mistaken. The nanotechnology will bring about a deeper and more profound change to your daughter's body. She will not have one machine inside her, but millions, maybe billions."

"But just to keep her blood clean?"

"Exactly. Just to keep her blood clean." Mike paused. "You are bright enough to know where all this is headed."

"You're saying that the technological boosts will be too tempting to pass up. And that once we start down that road, we'll keep going."

Mike nodded. "Because it will be the easy thing to do. Because it will be the smart thing to do. Because we will be afraid to fall behind our peers. Because we will be afraid to grow old and die. Those are only a few of the reasons we will allow ourselves to merge with machines."

"That doesn't mean we'll all end up as cyborgs. That's just too wild an idea."

"The instant you add any machine to your body—whether to your brain or your bloodstream—you are by definition a cyborg. Even today, right now in society, we have millions walking around with artificial joints and insulin pumps attached to their bodies. It is all a question of degrees."

"Do you honestly believe that?"

"I am blind, and yet I can see this clearly. A hundred years from now we will be sitting at this same desk, you and I, and half our parts will be made of either plastic, polymers, or metal."

"Even our hearts?"

Mike smiled. "Those will be the first to go."

At one point, after hours in the boat, Ali felt the current increase. It was slight at first, and she did not pay it much heed, but then it accelerated drastically. Indeed, it grew as fast as Lestre above them, and they began to race along at a strong clip.

At least she assumed Lestre was still flowing above their heads. She asked Amma what was happening.

"The waters of Tiena are tied to the kloudar. That is how the river is able to flow uphill," Amma said.

"We are going uphill?" Ali asked.

"We have been climbing into the Youli Mountains since we left Uleestar. But now that the river closes on its source, it accelerates to join what you might call the antigravity of the kloudar."

"The kloudar exert pressure on the water?"

"Yes."

"They pull on the river?"

"Yes."

"How come they don't pull on us?"

"They do to some extent. When you stand directly beneath them, you feel lighter. But they have a special affinity for the waters of Tiena, which come from Lestre, and cycle around and around."

"But the bulk of Lestre flows into Elnar, and then into the ocean. I saw that when I came out of the cave on top of Tutor."

"True. But enough of Lestre remains to turn downward and feed Tiena."

"That happens far south of here. I don't understand how it works."

"It doesn't matter which end of the rope you pull on," Amma said.

Ali smiled at the example. "You should teach physics at my school."

What came next surprised her, scared her even, along with Farble, Paddy, and Ra. Ali suspected Amma deliberately didn't tell them what to expect so as to heighten the thrill of the ride. One minute they were cruising along at a decent clip, the next they were in the middle of roaring rapids. The most amazing thing was that the rapids were racing *steeply* uphill. It was almost like riding a waterfall in reverse. In the other boat, Farble and Paddy were panicking. All she could do was shout out for them to hold on. She was holding on for dear life herself.

"You knew this was coming!" she yelled at Amma over the roar of the water.

The fairy laughed. "This is the best part!"

The river banked sharply, flowing upward at a forty-five degree angle. A bright green glow appeared up ahead. Their speed increased further—it was as if the floating kloudar had grabbed ahold of the water and didn't want to lose it. Ali's long red hair flew behind her head, like it used to when she rode her bike down from her trips into the woods behind her house. A fine mist brushed her cheeks, and she had to admit the ride was a rush.

Then they suddenly burst outside, into the day, onto a vast blue-green lake.

Mountains towered around the water, so rocky and steep they looked like stone sentinels that stood only to guard the lake. The sun was high in the sky but eclipsed by a massive kloudar, the green light flaring around the floating iceberg like a beam shone out of an alien jungle. The air was cold and thin, dry on Ali's lips. The lake was as foaming as a seashore where they exited the

Tiena tunnel, but the water quickly settled as it was absorbed by the huge body of liquid. Yet several miles off to her right, she saw another river forming, this one heading down, and she asked Amma if that was the beginning of Lestre.

"Lake Mira is the beginning and the end of the two great fairy rivers," Amma said.

Ali tilted her head back and studied the kloudar. The effect on her body weight was noticeable, but she did not feel ready to fly yet. The blue moon Anglar was higher in the sky, no doubt because they were farther north and, as they swept around the moon in a great arc, the circular path of the kloudar was easier to trace.

"How long do the kloudar take to circle the moon?" Ali asked.

"Two of your Earth weeks," Amma replied.

"So for half that time they are in the atmosphere?"

"Yes. It is then the dragons, and the high fairies, are able to visit some of them."

"Not all?"

"No." Amma paused. "Or I should say it is rare that anyone— dragon or fairy—visits a kloudar where ice maidens reside."

"And the dead elementals?"

Amma nodded. "The ice maidens take care of them in hidden caves."

"But the dead are dead. How can they bring the elementals back to life?"

Amma challenged her. "Are the dead really dead?"

Ali hesitated. "I don't understand?"

"You left this world. Did you die?"

"I died as a fairy. I gained life as a girl."

Amma did not answer, but pointed to a kloudar that did not appear especially large, but which was clearly far away. "That's our destination."

Ali shivered as she stared at it. The kloudar was a hundred percent encased in ice. "How do you know that's the one?" she asked.

Amma spoke softly. "I was there two weeks ago."

"You were? Why?"

Amma did not answer, only looked away.

Finally, they used their oars. As a group they rowed toward the shore, away from the foaming return of Tiena and the steep exit of Lestre. The shore was narrow and stony, hard with plates of slick ice. As Ali stepped from her boat, her foot touched the edge of the lake, the water was bitterly cold. Indeed, she was surprised the lake was not frozen over.

"The kloudar do not let it freeze," Amma explained as they huddled on the shore. Trae and the other fairies had brought heavy woolen shawls, and Ali quickly donned one, along with Ra and Amma. Paddy was cold, too. She found a small blanket for him that he gladly embraced. Only Farble was unaffected by the cold, he appeared to like it.

Shivering, Drash crawled up onto the shore, beside the docked boats. His wide nostrils continued to flame, but it was a subdued red fire, no larger than a burning candle wick. Unfortunately, they had no blanket big enough to warm him.

"How were the dragons able to pull so many kloudar out of orbit?" Ali asked.

Amma gestured to the koul. "You should ask Drash. A grown dragon is very powerful, and the Shaktra commands hundreds. They were able to tow the kloudar at their leisure. Who was to stop them?"

"Drash said the Shaktra promised his father and the other dragons direct entry into the blue universe, if only they would follow it. Do you think that is true?" Ali asked.

"No doubt the promise was made, but nothing the Shaktra says is true."

The way Amma replied, it was as if she *knew* the monster. But when Ali tried to press her on the matter, she got nowhere. Yet Ali could see Amma was dropping more and more hints. It was as if she were preparing her for a major revelation. Or shock.

Trae wanted them to set out at once for the hidden stronghold, which he indicated was still another ten miles north of Lake Mira. He pointed to a division in the surrounding peaks on the northwest side of the water, explained that if they hiked without pause, they could reach the asylum before sunset. Ali had to break it to him—and all the fairies for that matter—that she had other plans.

"I'm going with Drash and Amma up to the kloudar," she said. "It's possible I can join you later."

"How are you going to get up there?" Trae asked, not surprised.

"Drash will take care of my transportation," Ali said, loud enough for the koul to hear. He raised his much more defined head and looked over. The fire in his nostrils briefly flared, but he did not speak. Trae glanced in his direction and shook his head.

"He is still a koul, he cannot fly," Trae said.

"Don't worry, he will be a dragon soon enough."

Trae was not wild about her plan; he turned to Amma for support. "Have you two discussed this?" he asked.

Amma nodded. "Our queen knows what she is doing."

Trae considered. "The terrain on any kloudar is dangerous if one does not have the ability to fly. For that reason, I must insist on accompanying the three of you."

"Hey, what about me? I'm going," Ra interrupted.

Ali spoke to him. "That might not be a good idea. It is doubtful you will be able to help up there and, like Trae said, the conditions on the kloudar are rough."

Ra was amused. "You never know when you will need me, Ali."

The surrounding fairies murmured unhappily at his use of her Earth name and his tone, but Ali had to agree with him. When she least expected it, Ra had turned out to be her greatest support.

"You and Trae can come if you want," she said.

That left Paddy and Farble, and Ali had to explain to them that they were to go with the other fairies to the stronghold. They were in no mood to say goodbye. Both got very agitated, and grabbed hold of her arms and legs, and she had to speak in soothing tones to get them to let go. They had tears in their eyes, and she had to fight not to show her own. They had been wonderful traveling companions, as well as loyal friends, yet she felt in her heart she would see them again, and told them as much.

"I'm not sure when I'll reach the stronghold, but I'll definitely come back for you."

"But Missy needs Paddy and Farble to help her," Paddy pleaded.

Ali smiled and patted his head. "Missy knows that is true. That is why Missy will return for you. But right now, where I'm going, it's not a safe place for leprechauns or trolls."

"Sad," Farble mumbled, trying to hold on to her with his hairy arms.

She patted his hard belly. "I'm sad, too. But I'm happy to know you're going to be safe. Trust me, the fairies will take good care of you guys. They love me and they know how much I love you."

Paddy wiped his eyes as he stared up at her. "Will they let me bring me gold to this place?"

Ali chuckled. "They will even help you carry it, Paddy."

The precipitous angle of the surrounding mountains did not intimidate Drash, and he was happy to let the four of them—Amma, Trae, Ra, and herself—climb on his back. He acted like he wanted the exercise to warm up. But Ali knew he was seeking to distract himself from what she had planned next . . . *his* third test.

Drash trusted her, she knew, but he obviously suspected the third and final trial would be the most difficult of all—a fact she would not have argued. It was going to be frightening for both of them. She pointed to the highest peak in the area, on the south side of the lake, a virtual white sword aimed at the green sky.

"We're going up there," she said.

"Why?" Drash asked as he moved to obey.

"Don't be afraid, you'll see," she said.

Amma muttered under her breath. "And you accuse me of being evasive."

Ali had to smile. "It works both ways."

However, she knew she was treating the koul properly. If he understood what was to come next, he would no doubt jump in the river and swim back to the place where they had found him.

With his last two days of growth, Drash had lost none of his ability to scale steep terrain. He was two-thirds a dragon—he went up the side of the peak at an easy twenty miles an hour, which meant they reached the summit in less than an hour, and were given no time to get used to the thin air. As they climbed off Drash's back into the snow, they stumbled about for several minutes, trying to catch their breath. Trae and Amma bore it the best—besides Drash—while Ra struggled the most. Ali was okay.

"This peak has got to be higher than Kilimanjaro," Ra gasped.

"Maybe you should go back down," Ali warned.

Ra shook his head, shivered. "I go where you go."

"Jira used to say that," Amma said.

They all stared at her. "Who is Jira?" Ra asked.

Amma smiled, shook her head. "We'll talk about it another time."

The view from the peak was staggering in all directions, up and down—although the former took some getting used to. Several kloudar floated so close to the summit that Ali had to close her eyes and remind herself that they were not going to ram the side of the mountain. Just five minutes after they reached the snowy peak, a relatively small kloudar drifted so near that the hair on her head rose and the ground beneath her feet trembled. For over a minute, the sky was blotted out and they huddled in the shadow of a total eclipse. Yet when the levitating island finally passed, the green sun seemed to shine brighter. Ra shook his head in amazement.

"No one at home is going to believe any of this," he said.

"No one at home should hear about any of this," Ali replied.

Ra nodded. "Understood."

"It is dangerous to approach the kloudar this way," Trae warned.

"Don't worry, I have a plan," Ali said, as she waded through the waist-high snow to Drash's side, coming close to his ear so that she could speak to him in private. "Are you ready to fly?" she asked seriously.

"Drash is ready but has no wings," he said.

"Do you know how a dragon gets his wings?"

"Drash is hoping that Geea knows."

"Geea does know. The third test is simple. I remember it clearly from my days as fairy queen. To fly . . . a dragon must fly."

"Drash does not understand."

Ali pointed to the edge of the cliff. Straight down, on the south side, away from the lake, she estimated the drop at one sheer mile. "You have to leap, with faith, and your wings will be there. You will fly, simple as that, and then you will be a dragon," she said.

Drash looked at her like she was crazy. "The wings will not be there. They could not possibly come that quick. Drash will die."

Ali shook her head. "You have to trust me, and trust what you are. You are no longer a koul, you *are* a dragon. The fact that you are here, right now, means you are a dragon. You just have to take the leap."

His red eyes smoldered as he stared at the edge of the cliff. "I am afraid."

Ali nodded. "I am afraid, too. But I have faith in you."

"Why is Geea afraid?"

"Because I am going to take this leap with you."

Drash shook his head. "The queen of the fairies must not die."

"The son of the king of the dragons will not fail the queen of the fairies."

Drash sighed. "The king of the dragons has already failed the fairies."

Ali pointed to his back. "Let me climb on your back one more time, and we will show your father who you really are, and how he has been deceived by the Shaktra."

Drash thought a moment, then suddenly raised his head high, and the red fire in his nostrils leapt out, and the light in his triangular eyes grew bright. He spoke in a clear deep voice.

"Let's do it," he said.

Before the others could understand what was happening, Ali climbed on his back to her favorite spot directly behind his head, and gripped the thick folds of his smooth oily hide, as Drash moved quickly toward the edge of the cliff. Behind her Ali heard the others cry out in dismay, but Drash needed no more encouraging words from her. This was his day, his moment, and he did not hesitate as they reached the last few feet of the cliff. He simply jumped, and then they were falling.

A cruel wind whipped around them as the distant ground raced toward them, yet Ali felt no fear, and suspected Drash felt none, either. They were way beyond committed. If a miracle did not happen in the next few seconds, they would both die, and that was a fact. Never had Ali felt so gripped by fate, and never had she felt so much faith in Geea's decision to take human birth. Everything she had decided since she had first spoken to Nemi in that wonderful tree deep in the woods had led to this moment, she thought. At the same time, she wondered if she had made any decisions at all, if everything that had happened to her so far had not been inevitable.

Still, she wanted to see those wings! Where were they?

The illusion was strong: They were not falling to the ground, it was rushing toward them. Ali felt as if she could see a thousand details directly below her: the green tinge of the ice, the softness of the snow, the sober gray of the gathered rocks. The wind seemed to turn to thunder, drowning out even her thoughts, and then it was as if they were struck by lightning. Yet there were no clouds, no storm, and this bolt from above could just as well have come from *inside* Drash. A red halo of light surrounded his body like a forest fire that had only air left to burn. Initially she did not see his expanding wings so much as she *felt* them, because as Drash first started to resist their insane plunge, his wings were not there, only the possibility of them existed. She had told him the truth without realizing how deep it was. To fly he had to fly.

Then she saw them, huge leather arms, wide as parachutes,

strong as tree trunks, fixed to his sides, and flapping with the strength of a thousand eagles locked together as one being. His wings were magical—she blinked and they were there. And even as he fought to gain altitude, she knew he had only to spread them and gravity would loosen its grip. At the last second he seemed to realize that and he relaxed, and they swooped over the ground like the space shuttle returning from space without power, without force, but in perfect control.

Ali vigorously patted Drash on the head. "You did it!" she screamed.

"*We* did it," he said. "Without you, it would never have happened."

"My friend, Drash, the dragon. I'm so happy to finally meet you."

He smiled at her joke. "Where to, Geea?"

Ali nodded. "Let's get the others. We have a kloudar that needs visiting."

CHAPTER

23

The distant white kloudar that Amma had pointed out turned out to be the largest of them all. It was its frightening elevation that made it appear small, at first glance. But as the four of them neared it, on the back of Drash, Ali saw it was at least two miles across, as large as her hometown. Plus it seemed to possess the greatest energy of all the kloudar. Drawing close, she felt as if the blood in her veins was turning into air. Almost, she believed that if she were to step off Drash's back, she would not fall, but drift forever alongside the kloudar on its eternal journey around Anglar.

They did not speak until they landed on the icy mountain, although Amma pointed out to Drash where he should set down. Ali did not like the spot—it was too near the top edge of the kloudar. She could see nothing around but ice and more ice.

The air was a nightmare; there was not enough of it. Ra staggered the second they landed, had to sit in the snow, his shawl wrapped around him, and fight for breath. Yet he assured her he was fine.

"This is good training for climbing Kilimanjaro," he muttered, his jaw trembling.

Ali turned to Trae. "He cannot stay up here long."

"He should not be here at all," Trae said.

Ali scanned the area, looked at Amma. "What is special about this spot?"

"This is where I was two weeks ago," Amma replied. She gestured around a white wall made of sharp icicles, and took a bold step forward. Ali did not feel safe to hike—the ice was too slick, the rim too near. Without Drash beneath her, it would be a long fall to the ground. However, she listened as Amma added, "There is a cave nearby. We can take shelter there."

The landscape altered as they trudged around the bend. Black rock appeared, as smooth as the frozen lava that lined the walls of the cave on Pete's Peak, and suddenly she saw a dark hole, a fresh cave to explore. Its sides were jagged, irregular—no human or fairy hand had taken the time to polish its ebony walls. Nevertheless, Ali turned to Amma with a question.

"Did the ice maidens dig this out?" she asked. The cold did nothing to decrease the heat in her palm. Indeed, since they had landed on the kloudar, her hand had begun to throb.

Amma replied, "The caves of the kloudar are natural formations. But since the ice maidens are a part of nature, the answer to your question might be yes."

"Will we meet ice maidens inside?"

"You might meet them, but that does not mean you will see them."

"They are invisible?"

"They are whatever they choose to be, at any particular moment. Come, let us get Ra and Trae inside. But then you and I . . . we must go on alone."

"Why?" Ali asked.

"That is the last time you want to ask that. In this cave, there are no whys."

Drash was unable to fit even partway inside the tunnel, but the conditions did not seem to bother him now that he was a full-fledged dragon. He waited outside in the snow, staring at the green sky, reveling in his glorious red wings and his fiery breath. Ali would have liked to use his hot nostrils to warm their bones, but Amma was anxious to press on. Ra was turning a worrisome shade of blue and Ali herself had a headache. She suspected that they were higher than any mountain on Earth.

The tunnel entrance provided some comfort. The temperature increased several degrees and the air grew slightly thicker. But the improvements were marginal, and Ra continued to suffer. Even Trae looked aged, his face paling the more he attended to Ra. Ali knew that the high fairy was feeding Ra life energy, and was grateful, for she had none of her own to spare. However, when she asked Amma to let Ra move deeper into the cave, Amma shook her head.

"It is not allowed," Amma said.

Ali almost asked why, but bit her tongue. She had to bite it to feel it.

Amma led them forward, and it was not long before they lost sight of the entrance. It grew dark, but not pitch black, as Ali would have expected. It seemed as if the tunnel walls emitted a faint blue phosphorescence, but she was unsure if she was seeing it with her eyes or with her mind.

If the ice maidens hovered nearby, they kept well hidden. For the life of her, she could not decide if she wanted to meet them or not. After all her questions to Drash and Amma, she still had no clue what they were. Only that they could bring the dead back to life . . .

"You know this tunnel?" Ali whispered as they walked.

"Yes," Amma replied.

"You were here two weeks ago?"

"Yes."

"I cannot ask why?"

"You need not, you know why."

Ali sucked in an icy breath. "You were dead?"

Amma paused, looked over at Ali, her luminous green eyes questionable comfort. For the fact that they shone with life meant they might all possess imperishable souls. Yet the same light in the high fairy's eyes opened doors in her that Ali was not sure she wanted to enter.

"Yes," Amma replied. "This body was dead."

"Why did you choose . . ." Ali stopped herself. *No whys.*

"I did not choose. The choice was made for me."

"By whom?"

Amma hesitated. "My daughter."

"Did I know her?"

Amma nodded, then unexpectedly shook her head. "None of us knew her."

"Amma . . ." Ali began. But the woman raised her hand, pointed down the tunnel.

"You have to go forward, alone. I will return to our friends."

Ali swallowed. "What will I find?"

Amma reached out and gently tugged Ali's ear, and the gesture felt so familiar.

"What Geea wanted you to find. The truth," Amma said.

Amma left, and Ali stood without moving for several minutes. She told herself she was trying to catch her breath, to gather her energy to face what she would meet next, but the truth was she was trying to make sure her heart kept beating. . . .

Here in this place where the dead slept.

Ali walked forward, and the blue glow grew strong enough that she could no longer dispute its reality. For a time she thought the ice maidens were watching her, that they were in front of her, then behind her. Then she decided that they were probably not interested in her at all.

The tunnel ended in a round room, a half sphere with roughly hewn ice walls and a crude stone floor. Inside, in a perfect row, were five glass cases. They looked more like quartz cocoons than normal beds. They might have been fashioned out of a rare form of elemental ice—an exotic mixture of water and crystal and cold that was not affected by time. Each case balanced atop a squat boulder that bore a vague resemblance to a granite pyramid.

Stepping inside, Ali felt as if she were violating a tomb.

She remembered her nightmare from two weeks ago.

She was standing in an icy chamber, with five glass coffins set on top of a row of low black boulders. The clear box on her left drew her attention, for a beautiful woman with long red hair lay sleeping in it. But as she approached, the case began to fill with bubbling red liquid. It might have been steaming blood, or worse, acid. As the red goo spread over the woman, she began to dissolve, like a wax doll in a boiling pot. In seconds there was nothing left but the sick liquid, with bits of hair and bone. It began to spill onto the floor, and splash her legs, and she let out a scream. . . .

Yet now the two on the left were empty, the three on the right were not.

There were women in them, beautiful fairies, their eyes closed, sleeping.

Or were they dead? Ali feared to approach.

Different colored lights hung over the fairies. The lights seemed to be coming from the fairies themselves, like auras, not from the cases. For that reason—and it may have been no reason at all—Ali did not fear the lights.

The clear coffins—she did not know how to think of them— were labeled in the same hieroglyphics she had seen in the southern harbor near Tiena. There was one word on the bottom edge of each case. Ali studied the fine blue letters, searching for a pattern, saw that three out of five of the words ended in the same letter. It looked like a capital "O" with a line through it.

Because of the labeling, Ali was confident the ice maidens had *not* built the glass cases. The fairies must have done so, as people on Earth erected private tombs for the whole family. Perhaps the elementals did so to aid the ice maidens in their reclamation of the dead.

Gathering her courage, she stepped to the first case on the left. There were white sheets inside, neatly folded, no lid, and one of the sheets was stained with a single drop of what looked like dried blood. Or *frozen* blood, the chamber was no warmer than the cave she had left behind.

She studied the second case. Again, there was no covering top, and she sensed an odor emanating from the sheets—of ash perhaps, something that had burned—and the smell disturbed her deeply, although she had no idea why.

Ali moved to the third glass case, saw a fairy inside. The woman was short and plump, with relatively plain features. Lying on her back, she had on a green robe, but she wore no jewelry of any kind, and did not appear to be breathing. A green light enveloped her from head to toe, although it was streaked with faint yellow rays.

Her heart pounding, Ali moved to the fourth case. Another fairy inside . . .

"*Who are you?*"

"*You.*"

"*Who am I?*"

It was the fairy she had seen the night she had completed her seven tests in the cave near the top of Pete's Peak, a month ago when the time frames had merged, and she had remembered who it was that had saved her from certain death a year before that.

Her double turned and their eyes met. Ali did not see her, however, nor did her double see her. They were suddenly both gripped by the same vision of the green being who had rescued them from the fire that dark night. They both remembered the creature's face. The magical light that flowed from her enchanting eyes. The hypnotic colors of the jewels in her golden crown. And most of all the love that radiated from her gentle heart. They both remembered who they were.

The woman was more beautiful than a goddess. Her long red hair burned, and her smooth skin was as cool as a blue moon. She wore no crown, but anklets and bracelets made of green vines, yellow petals, and silver and gold thread, and she had on a white silk robe. Her legs were long and shapely, as though sketched by an artist, and her face was a mystery. Even with closed eyes and silent ears, it was as if she saw and heard everything around her—in the chamber, on the far side of the green world, maybe on Anglar itself. Her kindness was a large portion of her beauty, for she did not need to speak for Ali to know the words she would say. Because her words would be about love . . .

Ali had only to stare at her still face to feel comforted.

She realized she was staring at Geea, queen of all the fairies, herself.

This was her *own* body, her elemental body.

Three colors shone from the fairy's forehead and heart, blending in soft bands of light like the colors of a rainbow created by a newborn sun: yellow, green, and blue. Ali wondered if the yellow was there because she was a human being, if the green was present because Geea was in fact an elemental. She did not understand the blue light, although it attracted her above all else. . . .

Her face, *her* body—it all belonged to her, and yet it was all so strange. She felt as if she were being commanded by fate to stare into a tall mirror, only this mirror was not made of glass, but of time, and Geea's memories had never felt so near. . . .

But she could not grab hold of the memories! She could not touch them!

Yet she reached down and touched her *own* hand. And it was warm.

"She's alive!" Ali gasped.

Yet Geea's eyes did not open, and she made no sound.

Happy, sad, Ali moved on to the fifth and final case.

This fairy was shorter than Geea, was not as stunningly beautiful, and had darker skin, and wore no covering sheets, only a plain white robe. Yet the various colored lights that emanated from her were far brighter than the ones that hovered near Geea, and there was a pulsating violet streak that permeated them all, which rose and fell like an unheard and unseen breath. It was apparent to Ali that this last fairy was the most powerful of all, and that it was also the most alive.

Careful, Ali reached for the fairy's hand . . . and got the shock of her life when it grabbed her! The fairy's eyes sprung open, and stared not at her but at the frozen ceiling. They were bright eyes, violet in color, and very much alive.

Oh God.

The fairy's lips moved, and Ali heard a voice she had heard before, not so long ago, in Toule. "Steve . . . Steve," the fairy whispered, and there was sorrow in her tone.

Then her eyes closed, her lips went still, and she let go of Ali.

Filled with foreboding, Ali retreated several steps, once more studied the names attached to each glass box. The first, fourth, and fifth were the ones that all ended in the same letter. But what was the letter? Mentally, she began to review the alphabet, trying to correlate it with people she knew. She did not have to go too far into the alphabet to find a pattern. . . .

The letter "A" . . .

Amma and *Geea* and *Nira* all ended in "A"!

Also, she saw that the first name, on the first case, began with the same letter.

Which probably meant Amma had been lying here two weeks ago!

In the first glass case, the one with the drop of blood!

Which meant . . . Ali was too terrified to imagine what that meant.

However, she had come to this spot to know the truth, and a large chunk of it detonated in her mind at once. Amma had been protective of her from the moment they had met. For that matter, they had been very careful with each other. Amma had known things about the woods behind her town—specifically the details of the cave on Pete's Peak. Most of all, Amma had seemed *very* familiar, as if they were the oldest of friends. . . .

Because that's precisely what they were.

Ali finally understood why Amma liked to pull on her ear.

Ali heard a sound, a distant roar, the crackling of fire, and a cry . . .

A terrible force struck the room.

The chamber shook as if caught in a major quake.

Instinctively, Ali retreated to the doorway, all the time fighting to remain on her feet. Then she realized the futility of cowering at the door. The kloudar itself was being attacked! She had to get outside and help her friends! Throwing one last look at the silent fairies, she raced for the tunnel and the outside.

She was halfway to the exit when she suddenly stopped.

There was *something* up ahead. A cloaked evil.

Slowly, Ali drew out the Yanti. She did not whisper "Alosha," but repeated it mentally, as she carefully placed the Yanti first on her forehead, her heart, and finally on the top of her head. The field that always surrounded her swelled in size and filled with light, and she knew the *thing* in front of her knew what she was doing, and was amused. Far off, it seemed, Ali heard female laughter, a mocking sound that told her it *welcomed* her efforts to dispel it. However, it was at that moment that the evil presence diminished, and appeared to depart.

Putting away the Yanti, Ali strode quickly forward.

At the entrance to the cave she found a nightmare.

Ra lay unconscious in the snow, barely breathing.

Trae also lay sprawled in the snow, his chest badly burnt, but alive.

Amma sat inside the cave, leaning back against a cold wall. There was a seared thumbprint on her forehead between her empty eyes.

Ali recoiled in horror. The Shaktra had come! The Shaktra had touched her!

Amma was now marked.

Ali knelt by her side, took her hand. "Amma. Amma!"

Amma's eyes did not blink, her head hung like a discarded marionette.

Weeping, Ali hugged her. "Mother!" she cried, and the word just burst out of her mouth, and it was true. The chamber was a *family* tomb, that's why Amma had led her to it. That's why Amma had only arisen two weeks ago, and returned to Uleestar, because her *human* counterpart had been murdered then. That was why there was blood on the sheets. Now that it was too late, Ali thought bitterly, it was all clear. Her nightmare two weeks ago had not been a premonition, it had been a recognition of what was happening right then.

Amma rocked in her arms like a lifeless doll.

All this time, Ali had been seeking what was right beside her.

Her heart heavy, Ali eventually let go of Amma and rose and knelt beside Trae. She was able to rouse the high fairy by stroking his forehead. Opening his green eyes, he stared up at her and his lower lip trembled.

"Sorry, Geea," he whispered.

"Tell me what happened."

He coughed. "A dragon came, a dark fairy, and something else, it was awful. We saw them in the distance, but the dragon was fast. It struck near here with its flame and a piece of the kloudar fell off. Drash rushed to meet it, in midair, to fight it, but it was four times his size . . ." Trae had to stop to catch his breath.

"Is Drash still alive?" she asked.

"Don't know. He fell close to where we landed. He was not moving."

"What happened next?"

"The dark fairy shot me in the chest. That's all I remember."

"You did not see the Shaktra?"

"No."

"It was here." Ali swallowed. "Amma has been marked."

"I know."

"She's my mother, isn't she?"

Trae nodded. "She could not tell you, you had to discover it for yourself."

"Why couldn't she tell me?"

"You had to *see* the truth with your own eyes to *know* the truth. You had to see *yourself*, so that you could know that there are two sides to the same coin—human life and elemental life."

Ali nodded. "We are all humans, and we are all elementals. At one time we're on Earth, at another time we're here. We cycle back and forth." She paused. "But I knew that already."

"Did you?"

"Well, not clearly. But I still don't understand how Amma could not tell me who she was. I mean, she was my mom, she *is* my mom, and all this time I've missed her so much, and I was with her, and . . ." Ali could not finish; a spring of fresh tears would not let her. Trae spoke gently.

"Perhaps you knew the truth with your head, but not your heart. That is key to understanding this great mystery. The elemental is the magical side of each individual, the heart, while the human being is the intellectual side, the head. One is not complete without the other and yet, so far, few humans—or elementals for that matter—realize that."

His words were profound, but did nothing to dispel her grief.

"Amma still should have told me," she whispered.

Trae stared at her with his own pain. "She did not expect it to end this way. She thought this moment, up here on this kloudar, would be the greatest moment of your life. That it would be magical." He added, "It was our hope that magic would enable you to regain your *complete* memory of Geea."

"She thought the shock of what I saw in there would trigger the memories?"

"Yes. That it would act as a catalyst." Trae paused, to cough, and the faint but explicit hope in his next remark could not be disguised. "Do you remember more now?"

Ali heard an unspoken level to his question, sensed the desperation in it, actually, buried beneath the words. "What are you asking?"

Trae hesitated. "Do you know how Geea planned to defeat the Shaktra?"

Ali hung her head. "No. I don't . . . nothing is there."

Trae took time to absorb the bad news. When he spoke next, his voice was very weak. "At least now you can see why it's hopeless for the elementals to invade the Earth. Neither side can win. They would just be killing themselves."

"Then why does the Shaktra want this war?" she asked.

Trae sighed, and closed his eyes. "It must be insane."

She went to ask another question, but Trae had blacked out. Worried about the cold, she pulled him farther inside the cave, beside Amma, and did the same with Ra. Her favorite warrior did not appear wounded, but her touch failed to wake him, and she could see that he would not live much longer at this altitude.

Ali went in search of Drash, found him lying so near the rim of the kloudar that a strong wind could have pushed him over the edge. His side was badly burned—many of his scales had been melted away—and his right wing lay shattered beneath him, his broken bones sticking through his torn skin and into the bloody snow. His blood was a dark red, as she had noted before, so much like a human's.

Yet he was alive, his red eyes opened as she put her hand on his side.

"How do you feel?" she asked.

He tried to smile. "Like a dragon," he said.

"Did you recognize the one you fought?"

"My uncle, Chashar." He added softly, "He did not hesitate to strike me."

"Did you see the Shaktra on its back?"

"There was something there . . . Drash did not get a clear look."

Ali examined his broken limb. "You're not going to get off this kloudar without two healthy wings," she said.

Weary, he closed his eyes. "None of us is going to get off this kloudar."

Ali shook her head, and sat in the snow by his side, so near the edge of the cold mountain that she could see practically the entire elemental kingdom in one glance. From her pocket she drew out the gold box of stardust, and poured the blue material onto her palm. For a long time she studied it—their salvation, or her death. Drash opened one eye and stared at her.

"What are you doing?" he asked.

"Playing our last card," she said, and with that she swallowed the lot.

CHAPTER
24

Karl had locked them back up against the wall in the cave, this time using long bolts that were hammered through their shackles into the crusty stone walls, and it had made them both think—for certain—that they were never going to see the light of day again. But then Karl had left them alone for the night, and to Steve's surprise, as well as Cindy's, the pain in their arms never returned to the previous level, although they were far from comfortable. It was as if Nira's healing had staying power. The blisters on Steve's palm never came back, and Cindy's cut had looked worse than it was. It had bled for only a few minutes.

During the night they both managed to doze, and when they were awake they mostly talked about inconsequential stuff: where they had gone on holidays, what movies and books they had liked, people at school. They scarcely mentioned Ms. Smith at all.

The dim cave disallowed any clear concept of time, but Steve figured at one point that the night had to be long over, and that it might even be late the following day. He was confused why Ms. Smith had not returned to question them further, but who knew what a witch like that got up to in her spare time? He hoped he got to see her once more before he died. He wanted to spit in her face.

Cindy felt the same way. They comforted themselves that they had not given Ms. Smith any useful information that could be used against Ali. That was one good thing. Their fairy friend had been wise not to share with them her deepest thoughts. They just prayed, even if they were doomed, that Ali was able to return and kill Ms. Smith. If the witch was not the Shaktra, she was still bad news. Most of all, they hoped Nira got away from her evil mother, if the woman was indeed her mother. They both loved the girl, they hardly knew why.

"Oh my gosh!" a voice cried out in horror while they were in the midst of one of their mutual dozing attempts. Opening their eyes, Steve and Cindy were thrilled to see Rose, with Nira in tow. The nanny rushed toward them, anguish on her face, and pulled on their chains. Of course she got nowhere, but that was not the point. Someone knew they were being held captive!

Steve smiled. "We are so happy to see you, you have no idea."

Rose was on the verge of tears. "Nira's been trying to drag me down here all day, I didn't know what had gotten into her. But I should have listened, you poor dears. How long have you been here?"

"If it's evening, it's been more than thirty hours," Cindy said.

Rose was a mass of nerves, she kept pulling on the chains. "We've got to get you out of here! We've got to get you out now!"

Steve sought to calm her. "Relax a second. Is Ms. Smith upstairs?"

"No. Is she the one who put you down here?"

"It wasn't the Easter Bunny," Cindy muttered.

"It was her, but let's worry about that later. Is Karl upstairs?" Steve asked.

Rose grimaced. "Who's Karl?"

"A kid our age, he carries a mean switchblade," Cindy said.

Rose shook her head. "The only people in the house are Nira and me. This is criminal! I have to get you out of here!"

"We're lucky the house is empty," Steve said. "These chains have been hammered into the wall. They're not coming off— they'll have to be cut. Do you know if Ms. Smith keeps a chain saw or heavy duty clippers in her garage?"

Rose nodded anxiously. "The gardener has these clippers that can cut through anything. I saw him use them on a fence when Ms. Smith expanded the backyard. The fence was down in minutes."

"That sounds perfect," Steve said. "Hurry and get them. You can leave Nira here."

Rose appeared dazed, touched the little girl's head. "Will she be safe down here?"

"We'll keep an eye on her," Cindy said.

Nira did not speak, or show any emotion, while Rose was gone. But Steve and Cindy sure did. They could not stop smiling, they could not stop blabbering. They were not going to die! They were going to be rescued!

"You saved us!" Cindy beamed at Nira.

The little girl did not return the smile, nor did her dark eyes brighten.

Rose returned in five minutes, and her clippers lived up to their promise. They were big for her to handle, but it was clear to Steve the blades were made of an alloy that was capable of cutting even stainless steel. He had to carefully guide Rose as to where to place the blades, but the second she clamped down on the wooden handles, the shackles snapped. In two minutes he was free, and he had Cindy loose seconds later. Cindy took Nira's hand as they limped upstairs behind Rose. The circulation in their limbs was poor, but at least Rose knew which ladders to take.

Once again, they were opening the front door when they ran into Karl.

He came off the porch like a madman, slamming the door at his back, pinning Rose to the wall, his blade at her neck, drawing a tiny drop of blood, which traced a thin red line down the nanny's neck. A wave of black despair descended over Steve. It was not easy, no it was really very hard, to go from ecstasy to terror in the space of two seconds.

Karl sneered. "Don't move an inch or I'll cut her throat!"

"Oh God, oh God!" Rose gasped, trembling in his hands.

Steve held up his palms. "Calm down. You don't have to cut her."

Karl was a maniac. "Don't tell me what to do!"

"What is your problem, anyway?" Cindy demanded.

"Please, please!" Rose cried.

"What do you want?" Steve asked.

Karl grinned, he appeared possessed. The pupils of his eyes were three sizes too big, and he could not speak without panting. Steve honestly believed that Ms. Smith had cast some sort of spell on him. For all his wickedness on top of the mountain, he had at least acted coherent. Now he was like a wild beast.

"Information!" he swore. "If you don't give it to me, I cut her throat! Right now, right in front of you!"

"Boy, you need to chill," Cindy said, but she was as white as Rose.

"Ask what you want. We'll try to answer," Steve said.

"How did Ali activate the Yanti?" he demanded.

"We don't know," Cindy replied. "We told your witch boss as much. I was near Ali and Lord Vak when she activated it, and I heard her whisper something into it. But I don't know what that something was. That's the truth."

"You're hurting me!" Rose moaned.

Karl shook her, turned back to them. "Not good enough! What did she whisper?"

Cindy gestured. "It was some kind of chant."

"Was it one word? Two words? Three words?"

Cindy shook her head. "It might have been one word, said over and over again. So much was going on right then, I couldn't hear it. Ali was careful, I doubt Lord Vak heard what she said."

"Tell me more!" Karl cried, the veins on his neck bulging.

"If she doesn't know, she doesn't know," Steve pleaded. "Let Rose go."

"Does Ali think Ms. Smith is the Shaktra?" Karl yelled.

"She suspects! The last time we saw her, she didn't know anything for sure!" Steve said. "We told Ms. Smith that! There's nothing more we can say!"

Karl glanced at Rose, then suddenly relaxed his grip on the nanny. The change in his demeanor was drastic—he went from a psychopath to an easygoing thirteen-year-old in a heartbeat. Rose, too, appeared to relax quickly. Wiping the line of blood from her neck, she went so far as to smile, and Steve began to get a sick feeling deep inside. Especially when Rose stood taller, and the air around her changed, and the room grew cold.

Her voice, when she spoke next, was not her own.

"That is most unfortunate, that you have nothing left to say," she said.

Steve stared, suddenly having trouble focusing on her face. "*Who* are you?"

In reply, Rose took a step closer, slowly removed her gloves, and yes, she wore black gloves, as Ms. Smith wore white ones—a coincidence he should have paid more attention to from the start. He studied her hand as she brought it near, and the skin was Caucasian, not typical of many Colombian nannies. The fingers were long and graceful, the nails were painted a lovely red. For a second he could have sworn he was looking at Ms. Smith's hand.

Then she touched him, brushed his chin, and her skin was like one hard scar.

Steve blinked. In between the instant his eyes closed, and opened, he saw it.

Her hand—a purple and red monstrosity. The disfigurement was total; the fingers looked as if they had been boiled in tar and bandaged with rags and left to heal in a desert. In that brief glimpse, he saw so much agony that he recoiled in the fear that it might enter his own body and drive him insane. That was the answer, of course, even though he was seeing only a piece of the puzzle. The burnt hand was insignificant. Her whole body had been roasted that night she and Hector had crashed into that tree.

He *was* looking at Lucy Pillar, Rose, Ms. Smith—they were all the same.

He could not stop looking at her. "You *are* the Shaktra," he said.

Her face transformed into that of Ms. Smith.

"And you are dead," she said sweetly.

CHAPTER

25

The inner sounds had gone away and left her behind on a barren plain. The sky above her was the same as the ground below—gray and featureless. But in the emptiness she heard a distant roar that seemed a compilation of all the music and words she had ever heard in her life. The roar seemed to encompass every *thought* she had ever had, every desire she had ever dreamed, and she moved toward it with the hope that it sprung from a place of love and light. Yet the truth was, she did not know where she was going—only that she was lost. Why, she could not even remember her own name . . .

The plain disappeared, the roar became her mind, and it howled like the wind, and crashed like the waves of the ocean. And yet there was a silence in the center of it that was so perfect, so complete, that she was willing to be with the roar for eternity as long as she could stay near the stillness. How she craved it! Not because it could teach her things, or show her visions, or grant her powers. All it did was comfort, and that was all she wanted right then . . .

She did not know how long she stayed in that glorified state, listening to the roar and seeking the silence, but as she once again became aware of time, she realized she had a body. It was in a cold place, where the air was thin, and there was misery all around—people hurt, elementals suffering. And oh how she hated to leave her newfound peace to attend to them, but it was as if the love she had discovered in the center, beyond the roar, told her to go back. Yes, Alosha, it is time to return and heal the pain of the worlds, and when you have, you can return. . . .

Ali opened her eyes atop the highest kloudar and looked out on the green world.

The sun would set in an hour, in both realms. She did not have much time.

Slowly, she climbed to her feet, taking stock of her body, her energy. There was no wound to her right hand—it had healed. Every cell in her body felt as if it were on fire, but it was a cool fire, one that could draw unlimited sustenance from the snow, and the air, and the stars, even from Anglar itself. Ali felt as if there was no power of Geea's she could not command. . . .

She was practically a fairy now. Queen of the fairies, with the strength to save her kingdom from the enemy. But did she have the wisdom to rescue them? The stardust had given her much, but Ali knew wisdom could not be gained by swallowing a powder. It was an issue she would have to worry about later.

Ali stepped to Drash, who still had one eye open, put her hands on his head, and let her field expand out to such a distance that she might have been able to heal an army of dragons. Then she focused on her friend, and the warm light that pulsed through her was as blue as it was green. There was yellow, too, bright as the sun above the Earth, and she felt a part of both worlds, and even a kinship with Anglar, where the ice maidens came and went as they pleased. To heal the dragon required only a fraction of her immense power, and yet she would have given her life for him. That was the deep secret of Geea's healing—her empathy.

Drash opened both eyes two minutes later, noticed his wing was restored. A tear slipped over his burning nostrils, before turning to steam. "You are the one," he said.

She patted him on the head. "You are the next king of the dragons."

Ali healed Ra and Trae in quick succession, and they sat up together and huddled in the cave beside Amma, and Drash was close when she kneeled beside her fairy mother and put a hand on her head and one on her heart and called upon the light and grace that flowed through her body. But even her tremendous power rebounded as it hit a thin halo of darkness that Ali could now see encased Amma's head. Crushed, she sat back on her knees, staring at Amma's dazed expression, and her tears were no different than the ones she had shed when she had found her mother marked. Her newfound power had changed many things, but not that.

"Keep trying," Ra said. "You can do it."

Shaking her head, Ali stood, stared down at Amma. "She is beyond my help . . . for now," she said.

Ra jumped up. "You don't know that for sure."

She looked at him. "I know."

Ra searched her eyes, worried. "What are you going to do?"

She spoke to Trae. "Drash will fly the three of you to the secret stronghold. Go there now, take care of Amma. I'll come when I can."

"You don't know where it is," Ra protested.

Ali nodded. "I remember."

Trae stood, spoke hesitantly. "Since Amma is marked, it might not be a good idea to take her there. The Shaktra might find us through her."

Ali shook her head. "You're not to abandon her."

"I was not suggesting that. But I must think of the others."

Ali studied her mother. "Even marked, she will not betray us to the Shaktra. Take her to the stronghold, that is an order." She added, reluctantly, "Blindfold her, put wax in her ears."

Trae bowed low. "As you wish, Geea."

Ali turned toward the snow, the sky. "I have to go now."

Ra grabbed her arm. "Where are you going?"

She tried to get past him. "My friends on Earth are in danger."

Ra would not let go of her. "You don't know how to fly!"

She reached out and hugged him, kissed his cheek. "I'll learn," she said.

Ali strode from the cave, patted Drash goodbye, and then ran toward the rim of the kloudar, the icy edge, and as the snow and ice and rock vanished from beneath her feet, she began to fall. However, her magnetic field quickly formed a bubble around her, without any doing on her part, and it was filled with green steam and red streaks of light. It warmed her limbs, and allowed her to see far off, and it lifted her up. She saw that she had merely to will the direction she wished to take and the bubble would obey. Tutor called to her, the southern mountain, and the seven doors, and just the thought of it was enough to send her racing toward the rocky peak.

Yet the bubble was not a hard shell. Air blew on her face, the wind was in her hair, and the sheer joy of flying through the Youli Mountains, over Uleestar, and along the long stretch of Lestre, was almost enough to make her forget her grief, at least for a time. Unfortunately, she knew that at the end of her first flight there was going to be violence. Either she was going to die, or *they* were going to die. There would be no mercy from her, not after what they had done to Amma. . . .

As she reached the cave opening, high on Tutor, she was ambushed by a dozen dark fairies who had hidden behind the boulders surrounding the entrance. But the attack was ineffective because she knew it was coming and had adjusted her field to repel their bolts of fire. With a smile on her face, floating fifty feet above the cave, she watched as the laser blasts bounced harmlessly off an invisible area in front of her chest.

She did not have her fire stones, she did not need them. Recalling an old Geea trick—that had been secret even when Geea had ruled the kingdom openly—Ali took a deep breath and blew forcibly on her palms. Then she smacked them together as hard as she could. The technique created a powerful sonic wave that her own field protected her from. It sent off a swell of highly compressed air, as an exploding bomb might, and when it hit the dark fairies, they were torn apart. In seconds their guts laid strewn over the side of Tutor.

Still floating in her protective bubble, Ali entered the cave. Radrine had not died with her servants just now, but Ali could sense her up ahead, racing toward the red door, and what the evil queen thought was safety. But Ali had locked that door with the Yanti.

It was not going to open for the dark fairy.

The trip down the length of the cave took only minutes. Her bubble automatically spared her from bumping the sides, and she was able to push her speed close to the level she had enjoyed in the green sky. The yellow door was open, as she had left it, and the red door was closed.

Ali could smell Radrine now as well as mentally follow her movements. The evil queen was now on the Earth plane—she had chosen to take the cave upward, toward the top of Pete's

Peak, the same route her friends had used a month ago. It was probable Radrine had heard the killing sonic wave and was running in fear. Ali went after her.

Yet she slowed as she passed the six caves that led to other parts of the world, reaching out with her subtle senses, and her nose, to see if Radrine had sought refuge in such places. But it seemed Radrine was flying in one direction as fast as she could. Ali pushed on ahead.

She discovered Radrine in the snow, in the shade, twenty feet outside the cave.

An orange sun burned on the horizon, the air was crisp and cool and clear, and the view of the woods, and for that matter all the surrounding towns, was unobstructed. Why, she could even see Toule.

Ali took a step toward Radrine, noticed how careful the dark fairy was not to step into the direct sunlight. It made her wonder if the evil queen could withstand it. The last time they had fought, beside the doors, Ali had assumed Radrine had flown back down to the cave entrance, and circled around to the top exit, and she still believed that. But just before she and her friends had entered the cave, heavy clouds had begun to blow in from over the ocean. They must have covered Pete's Peak.

But today there wasn't a cloud in the sky.

Radrine raised her fire stones and shot at her, a dozen times.

The laser blasts bounced off. Dejected, Radrine lowered her weapons.

No, she was much more than dejected. Her rotting wings shook and the nest of maggots-for-brains squirmed inside her translucent skull. She was so scared that she had no control over her long black tongue. It repeatedly licked her lips as her breath hissed between her yellow teeth. Ali enjoyed watching her cower.

"We can talk about this, Geea," Radrine said quickly.

Ali smiled, came closer. "What could *we* have to talk about?"

Radrine backed up a step. "I have information."

"What kind of information?"

"I was just in the east, near the Morray Mountains."

"You were just above the Youli Mountains. You're the one who shot my adviser, Trae. He's alive by the way, doing fine. He sends his regards."

"I know how the war goes in the east."

"Tell me."

"You must promise my life in exchange."

"I'll think about it."

"You must swear it, Geea!"

Ali chuckled. "What is the point of swearing to one such as you? A spawn of hell? You die here, Radrine, and I suspect you will return to behind the red door. You will be sent back bodiless, as a thrall, and you will burn in those fires I saw beneath your hive. Is that not so?"

Radrine retreated to within inches of where the sun shone on the white snow.

"My information is valuable to you!" she cried. "Say we have a deal!"

Ali shrugged. "Whatever. Speak."

"The elemental army is pinned against the Morray Mountains. Lord Vak is already seeking to negotiate a surrender with the Shaktra."

"What are the terms of the surrender?" Ali demanded.

"To be spared, the elementals must agree to march west toward Tutor starting in three days, and pass through the yellow door, and invade the Earth."

Ali considered. "I already knew most of that."

"You lie! Lord Vak just agreed to surrender!"

Ali walked casually toward her. "You do not ingratiate yourself to me, Radrine, by calling me a liar. Especially since your entire life has been a lie. It makes me think that *you* think we are alike."

Radrine glanced over her shoulder—no room left to maneuver. The dark fairy bowed her head. "We are not alike. You are a queen, I am your servant."

Ali suddenly leapt, grabbed her by her scaly throat. "You serve the Shaktra!"

Radrine shook in her arms, her filthy red eyes swelling. "We have a deal!"

"What deal? I would never deal with you! Tell me, where is the Shaktra now?"

"I don't know!"

Ali lifted her up so that the top of her egg-shaped skull brushed the last light of the day. Immediately the dark fairy's skin began to smoke, and Radrine let out a pitiful cry. Ali felt no pity.

"Is it in this world or the elemental world?" Ali demanded.

Radrine suddenly stopped trembling, looked at her in surprise.

"Why, it's in both worlds at the same time. Didn't you know?"

Ali took a moment to absorb the news. Then it made perfect sense.

"Thank you, Radrine, I didn't know that," she said.

Then Ali hoisted Radrine's head directly into the last of the sunlight, and the gentle orange rays, as they played over the dark fairy's hideous face, were like a spray of acid. Radrine went to speak, but her mouth filled with smoke as her tongue caught fire, and Ali saw her brains spasm inside her glassy skull. Then they too began to smolder, as the heat built inside, and the pressure . . .

The dark fairy's head cracked in two. A geyser of fire erupted from the top of her twitching body, and Ali threw her down on the ground in the white snow, and cursed her and her master. But in the end, Ali had to turn away.

She felt like she was going to be sick.

No time to grieve, no time to celebrate. Lately, she thought, since she had first spoken to Nemi and learned of her great destiny, her whole life had been that way. The sad thing was, she would have traded it all just to be able to return to that peace she had found with the help of the stardust.

Ali ran off the top of Pete's Peak and flew toward Toule like a meteorite close to burning up in the atmosphere. She knew her destination—sleeping Nira had provided her with enough clues. It was obvious anyway. Cindy and Steve had returned to Toule to try to gather information on Ms. Smith and had run smack into the Shaktra—in human form. Ali chided herself for having opened the door on that accursed town, before remembering it had been Steve who had made the connection. She just hoped they were both alive.

Flying through the air above the Earth was not the same as gliding over the forests and mountains of the fairies and the leprechauns. The Earth felt *heavier*—her bubble did not respond as well to her will. Swooping down on Toule, she was not out of control, but she had to concentrate to stay on course, mentally gripping the edges of her field to keep from plunging into the trees. She flew close to the latter, occasionally allowing a branch to brush against her bubble.

Ali landed in the woods between Omega's office buildings and Ms. Smith's house.

The sun had set, the trees were in shadows, and the air was

cooling quickly. How much drier it was here than in the green world! How many more smells the elementals got to enjoy! Ali wondered how long it would be before she returned to Uleestar. After all her travels, she could not honestly say where she felt most at home.

That worried her, that perhaps *home* no longer existed for her.

Through the branches, she could see the people of Toule walking up and down their main street. She realized that many of them must be just getting off work and that more than a few probably worked for Omega. How sad it was, she thought, that an entire town could be built around such a lie and not know it. Yet she passed no judgment on the town's inhabitants. On her last visit to Toule, she had suspected so little . . .

Ali turned her attention to the task at hand.

They were in the house. No, she sensed, they were *under* the house.

She strode up to the mansion, did not bother to knock on the door, even though it was locked. A quick twist from her hand and the knob broke and the door swung open.

Nira stood in the center of the living room, alone, staring at her.

Ali stepped inside, held out her arms, but the little girl did not come to her. Ali did not mind. Moving farther into the house, she knelt in front of Nira and hugged her, and it seemed, briefly, the girl hugged her back. As they separated, Ali saw tears in Nira's eyes, heard her sniffle, and then she spoke—perhaps her first clear words since her mother had marked her head and imprisoned her mind.

"Steve . . . Steve," she said, and her lips trembled.

Ali stood quickly, pain in her chest, and patted her on the head. "Stay here, Nira, do not leave this room. I will be back in a few minutes," she said.

Yet Nira took her hand and led her to the secret stairway that Ali sensed plunged many levels beneath the house. Nira did not make the descent with her, and Ali did not want her to, for the girl appeared afraid. Alone, her heart heavy, Ali found her way far under the mansion and into the complex maze of caves that must have existed even before the destruction of the power plant. For a time Ali was led by instinct, but suddenly she heard Karl snickering and Cindy crying. Then, consumed with fury, she *flew* down the rusty ladders and through the crumbling caves . . .

Until she came to them, and stopped cold.

One glance told her everything. Told her too much.

Cindy was pinned against a stone wall with handcuffs, her face streaked with tears and exhaustion. In front of her, Karl pranced and laughed, holding a switchblade that was as red as it was silver. He did not notice her arrival, and so Ali was subjected to several seconds of his torturous behavior. But then she spoke one word, and he froze.

"Stop," she said.

Karl looked over, his grin transforming into a grimace, and did not move.

Ali ignored Karl and Cindy, and strode to Steve, who lay facedown on the ground near a kerosene lamp. As Ali turned him over, she saw that his shirt was red with blood, and that his eyes were closed, and that he was not breathing. His heart had stopped—she could feel the lack of movement inside her own heart. But although her chest felt as silent as his, she felt it break anyway, in so many pieces, and they were like shards of glass inside her veins. They did not so much cut her physical body as they tore at her soul.

It was then she realized that no matter how much power she gained or how many dark fairies she slew, she was still human.

Her pain was a perfect example of how mortal she was—it was endless.

Leaning over, Ali kissed his lips, then stood and spoke to Cindy.

"Are you all right? Did he cut you?"

Cindy shook her head. "I'm all right."

Ali faced Karl. "So old friend, we meet again," she said.

He dropped his knife, backed off, his face pale. "What are you going to do?"

Ali walked slowly toward him. "Were you the one?" she asked.

"The one?"

"You know, two weeks ago. The one who killed my mother?"

He shook his head. "No."

Ali nodded. "You're lying. Fine, I expect you to lie. But this time, you have to tell me the truth. What did you do with her body?"

Karl swallowed. "We cremated her, spread her ashes in the ocean."

Truth. Ali took a moment to absorb it. "*We?*" she asked.

Karl backed up some more, hit a wall. "I did it. But Geea . . ."

"Shh," she said. He was going to say the Shaktra forced him to do it, and that would be the truth, to an extent. It was only then that Ali realized the reason she had been unable to psychically sense her mother's location after returning from her first adventure on Pete's Peak. The Shaktra must have been near her mother and emitting a powerful supersensory field that interfered with Ali's mental telescope. It was good to know for the future that the evil creature was capable of such a thing . . . should they meet face to face.

Of course they would meet, and probably very soon . . .

Ail came closer to Karl. "Where has Ms. Smith gone?"

"I don't know."

Truth. Of course, she wouldn't have told him. "Has she left the area?" she asked.

"I think so."

"She left you behind to dispose of Steve and Cindy?"

He hesitated. "Just Steve. She forced me to—"

"Quiet. Why did she leave her daughter behind?"

"I don't know. She hates the girl."

Partial truth. Ms. Smith had left Nira behind because she wanted to spy on them through the little girl. After all, Nira was marked, and Ms. Smith already knew how fond they were of her. The woman would assume—correctly—that Ali would keep her near.

Ali moved until she was only a foot from Karl. He recoiled at her nearness, but he did not try to lash out, nor did he run, and it occurred to her that he was hoping she would show him mercy, as she had before. Couldn't he see that she had neither hope nor mercy left? Steve was dead, her mother was dead, and her fairy mother was worse than dead. . . . No, she thought, he was making a mistake when it came to her. She was no longer one of the good guys.

Ali slowly reached out and gripped his neck. "I want you to tell me something."

Karl sucked in a shaky breath. "You're going to kill me!"

"I have this question. I want you to answer it."

He shook. "Geea . . ."

"*Who* is the Shaktra?"

Karl did not respond right away. But then a trace of his old cockiness returned.

He must have known he was doomed, for he suddenly laughed at her.

"You fool, she's your sister!" he said.

Ali froze for a moment. It could have been forever.

Doren.

"I thought so," she said, mostly to herself. Then she suddenly tightened her grip and, twisting his head *far* to the side, she heard every bone in his neck break. He died instantly. She let him fall to the ground.

Ali freed Cindy from her chains, hugged her and stroked her head, and gave her healing energy. But Steve was on the floor, in a pool of blood, and Ali finally had to let go of her and pick him up. And it was then Cindy broke down and cried and begged her to bring him back to life. But Ali shook her head.

"That I cannot do," she said.

Yet as she stared at Steve's peaceful face, far off she heard the roar that had come to her atop the kloudar, and the peace at the center of the thunder seemed to speak to her once more, and tell her that there was no end to life, as there was no reality to death. She thought she understood. She was an elemental and she was a human being, as were all the people and creatures in both worlds, and perhaps they were all growing toward something greater and more wonderful than they could imagine. She believed that, she really did.

Hugging Steve close to her heart, kissing him once more, she spoke to Cindy.

"Let's get out of here," she said.

Ali's Story Will Continue
in the Next Book in the Series,
The Yanti